CLEARING

LEGENDARY FARMER BOOK 1

This book is dedicated to my brother, Ethan, who supported me in every way possible throughout this process. Thank you to my mother, who sent me money, even though she hates reading digital works. Thank you to my husband, who lets me sit in front of my computer and produce nothing tangible, and thank you to my daughter, who reminds me every day to make my stories fun. Also thanks to all the readers on RoyalRoad, and especially Ethernet Storyhunter and Prysmcat.

Book One: Clearing

clear /ˈklir/ *verb*

gerund or present participle: clearing

1. free (land) for cultivation or building by removing vegetation or existing structures.

2. gradually go away or disappear.

Chapter One

Rouge

Rouge froze as she saw a flicker of movement at the end of the long hall. She squinted her eyes and a tag appeared above the head of the armored man pacing toward her. *Guard – Lv 27*. She flicked her eyes to the left of her interface and selected the party chat.

::There's a level 27 guard. I thought the place was supposed to be undefended tonight?::

Motte's deep voice was calm when he replied. ::The family is supposed to be at a party, and the Thieves Guild spy claimed they usually don't have anyone patrol inside while they're gone. Did he see you?::

::Of course not. But he's in front of the door to the trophy hall.::

There was a pause. ::Maybe they got some hint that there would be an attempt tonight. Do you want to pull out and try again another time?::

She shook her head, and said, ::No. It took almost two weeks to get this chance. I want to finish this quest. I'll try to sneak by, and if he catches me, I'll just have to try using my [Knockout] skill.::

::Are you sure? You only have a 50% chance of success on mobs higher than your level. The quest failure penalty is pretty hefty, too.:: Motte sounded concerned now.

::No. I need to get it tonight. I won't fail.::

Rouge firmed her jaw and triggered her [Sneak] skill in addition to the [Stealth] she was already using. The skill would improve her chances of avoiding detection by 2% per level, and she had 10 levels. It would only last 5 minutes, though, so she needed to hurry.

Silently, staying in the shadows to the side of the hall, she edged forward. She had to avoid the soft lights cast by small glowing stones set into deep sconces, or her [Stealth] would be broken. Twenty feet. Ten. She ducked into a convenient alcove, grateful for her slight stature. The guard turned his head away, yawning slightly. In the instant that his eyes were closed, she slipped through the open archway behind him. In the dimly lit room beyond, she could see a series of pedestals, and the walls were lined with paintings, scrolls, and the heads of rare beasts. She spun to the right, crouching behind the first pedestal, and kept her breathing as smooth and slow as she could.

The guard frowned, glancing around. He took a few steps into the room, looking left and right. He shook his head and stepped back out into the hall.

Rouge refused to sigh in relief. Her lips trembled holding it in, but she managed to control it. ::I'm in.::

Motte was clearly relieved. ::Good, now get the doll and get out of there!::

She looked around, her passive [Darkvision] making the dimness look like faded daylight. The doll was supposed to be on the third pedestal to the right. It wasn't a particularly expensive item, so hopefully there would be no alarms or traps on it. She duck-walked to the pedestal and peered on top, reading the information for the item there.

Doll of Contentment – a small handmade doll that brings happiness to whoever holds it. This one is well loved. Weight- 1 lb. Rarity – Very Rare.

::It's here! Right where they said it would be!:: She reached up to slide it from its pedestal.

::Did you check for traps?:: Motte's voice stopped her right before she touched the limp rag doll.

She scrunched up her nose, but did as he said, triggering her [Trap Detection] skill. She cursed softly.

::What did you say?:: Motte's voice was disapproving.

::Nothing, *Dad,*:: she muttered. ::There's a trap. It's just a pressure switch though.::

::Going to pull an Indy?::

She grinned. ::You know it.:: She pulled up the interface for her main Inventory and dug through her items. She, like many gamers, had a tendency to hang onto every piece of random loot that dropped. You just never knew when you were going to get a fetch quest for a hundred *Pieces of Chitin* or twenty *Duckbills*.

::Ah ha! Got it. One *Broken Deer Antler* coming up!:: Quickly, she pulled the antler from her inventory and held it over the pedestal by the doll. Her [Legerdemain] skill was nearly level 17, so hopefully it would boost her chances of succeeding. Smoothly, she took hold of the doll and lowered the doll while the antler came down. The instant she lifted the doll away, she knew she'd failed. Even though the two items both weighed one pound, the weight of the doll was spread all across the top of the pedestal, while the antler's weight rested on two points. Apparently, the weight distribution mattered, because a loud klaxon split the night a moment later.

::Dagnabit!:: She rolled to the side as a series of darts hidden in the base of the pedestal ejected into the surrounding area. One caught the edge of her gray and black mottled bodysuit. It sliced the soft fabric with its sharp point, revealing caramel skin beneath.

::Do you need help? I can be there in-::

::No! I'm going to run for it! You're too loud and slow, and everyone in the

3

area will know where we are. Just stay there!::

Rouge slipped back along the edge of the room and reached the area behind the first pedestal by the door just as the guard stepped inside the room. She saw his hand dip into a pouch at his waist and pull out a small glowstone. She gritted her teeth. She hated those things! The light they produced was nearly as bright as sunlight, and they were nearly as common as lights on devices in the real world. Whoever coded those really hated rogues.

Before the guard could activate the stone, she leapt, aiming the pommel of her knife at the base of his skull. She'd practiced this move a hundred times with Motte, but there was always a difference between doing it for real and doing it in practice. She triggered [Knockout], and prayed to Gina.

Gina has heard your prayer. Chance of a successful [Knockout] improved to 100%.

::Yes! I got it!:: The hilt of her blade smacked solidly against the guard's skull, and he dropped to the floor limply, the glowstone falling from his hand. She scooped it up, but couldn't pause to do more than that. If she was lucky, her passive [Pilfer] skill might still activate. Even at level 1, it had a .5% chance of stealing something from anyone unconscious or dead within 5 feet of her, so there was still a tiny chance of getting something from him.

She scampered down the hall to the large window on the east side of the building. Coming in, she'd climbed up the wall to a second floor balcony, but she didn't have time to go back out that way. She picked up a heavy porcelain jug from a small table nearby, and threw it at the window, following it up with the table for good measure, though she grunted at the weight of the solid wooden furniture.

The jug cracked the glass of the window, but bounced back to the floor, shattering with a loud *crunch*. The table hit the cracks and the window burst outward, table and glass shards raining down into the courtyard below.

Motte grunted, deep voice sounding annoyed. ::Ow. The table hurt.::

::Just practice. Incoming!:: Rouge leapt into the air, hearing the pounding of heavily armored feet coming toward her from both ends of the hall. She cast her level 12 spell, [Poof!], and a billowing cloud of smoke filled the hall, covering her escape. She vaulted through the window, twisting into a half-flip so she dropped through the air back first. She was caught in strong arms before she could hit the ground, and grinned up at the metal helmet of the heavily-armored man who held her.

::Let's go!:: Motte rumbled, slinging her small frame up onto his shoulder. Then, like a juggernaut, he began to run. What he lacked in speed, he more than made up for in sheer power, and his [Battering Ram] skill allowed him to barrel through the approaching guards before they could ready themselves to attack. A few knives were thrown after them, and she saw his health bar flicker, but she wasn't worried. Motte Bailey had a truly amazing ability to soak up damage.

The rogue and the tank were away from the estate of the wealthy lord before the city guards had a chance to respond to the yells. This was fortunate, because city guards could always see names, unless the players had much higher [Obfuscation] skills than Rouge's mere level 5. Motte's class, Guardian Wall, gave him no skills that concealed his identity at all. If the city guard had seen them, a warrant would have been issued for their arrest and things would have gotten hot in the city for a while.

The sixty second cooldown on [Poof!] was up, so Rouge used it again. The sounds of pursuit faded behind them. They reached their horses, hidden behind some bushes a few streets over, and swung up into their saddles.

::Did you get the doll?:: Motte asked as they rode away down winding roads, heading toward the docks, which would be busy even at this time of the night.

She flashed a peace sign. ::You know it! Now we just need to go deliver it.::

He shook his head. ::I don't know why you always take these random quests.::

Now that they were out of battle, Rouge put her hood into her inventory, and changed from her damaged cloth bodysuit into a blue leather jerkin and leggings with a simple thought. Beside her, Motte changed his gear from generic heavy armor to his usual all-black set. She ran her fingers through the black curls around her face, loosening them after their confinement in the hood. Her fingers caught on the long points of her ears, and she grimaced.

::I thought these ears were cool in the character design, but I didn't know how much they'd get in the way. Do you know how many times I've gotten them folded under when I put on the hood? Un-com-for-ta-ble. Anyway,:: she said, as she brought her horse around to head toward a street filled with small, quiet houses. ::I like these quests. I hate the repeatable ones. Everybody does those to grind XP or reputation, and they're boring. I swear even the NPCs look bored when they hand them out. These little quests nobody else bothers with are way more fun.::

Motte shook his head. ::Still, I wish you'd do more of the easy quests. I worry about you when I can't be on to back you up. If you were doing the same quests as everybody else, at least I'd know what you were getting up to.::

Rouge pulled her horse to a stop. ::This is it!:: She swung her leg around so she was facing her horse's rear, and then did a quick handstand into a half twist, sticking the landing. Her horse rolled its eyes back at her, then shook its mane, huffing.

Motte chuckled. ::Even your horse isn't impressed anymore.::

Rouge grinned. ::It's good practice. I still get a few percent toward my next [Acrobatics] level when I do that. Plus, it's fun.:: She raised her hand and knocked at the door of the small house. One knock. Pause. Three knocks. Pause. Three more knocks.

The door cracked open, and an eye peered out. It was even lower than Rouge's, and she was barely five feet tall.

A little voice asked, "Do you have it?"

"I do. Where's the reward?" Rouge held the doll up by her waist so the limbs flopped forward into the sliver of light that escaped around the edge of the door.

The door closed, and the pair could hear shuffling coming from inside. It reopened slightly wider, and a small child's hand emerged, clutching a bag. The sleeve of a nightgown was visible, and worn, soft lace fell around the chubby little wrist. "Ten coppers and a snake skin, just like I promised."

Rouge gently passed the doll into the little hand, carefully accepting the coppers and the precious treasure offered by the girl. The door opened more, revealing a brunette cherub clutching the worn toy. Her smile exposed two missing teeth and a dimpled cheek.

The rogue cleared her throat slightly. "You remember that you'll have to hide it now, right? They know it's missing, so they may come looking. They probably won't really think you could have gotten it back, but just in case, you should keep acting sad. They're more likely to think that another collector stole it, but I'd hate to see it taken away again just because it's rare."

Lower lip quivering, the little face scrunched up in heartbreaking sadness. "My poor dolly! Someone stole it! My daddy gave it to me before he went away to sea, and he promised it would help me be happy even when I missed him! I miss it so much!" The threatening storm of tears cleared away as quickly as it had come. "Like that?"

Rouge broke out into spontaneous applause. It was truly amazing to her how realistic the NPCs were in *Veritas Online*.

According to the advertising blurbs, the system actually allocated additional resources to characters with whom players interacted, but the little girl was still so realistic that it was amazing to think she wasn't actually dealing with another player.

Giggling, she said, "Exactly like that. Now go back to bed before your aunt notices you're missing." The child nodded and started to close the door. Rouge raised her voice for one more admonition, "And don't talk to strangers any more!" The door closed.

Motte chuckled. "You sound like me."

"Yeah, I guess being a killjoy rubs off on me, since I'm around you all the time." She rolled her eyes at him, but paused her banter as words popped into the air in front of her eyes.

Quest: "Well, Hello Dolly" complete.

You have returned the doll to Matilda, though not without some trouble.

Reward: 2000 Experience, 10 coppers, and a snakeskin.

Rouge blinked away the quest notification, and a golden glow surrounded her. She pumped her fist triumphantly. Switching back to party chat, she said, ::Level 20! Yes!::

Motte used an emote to throw confetti into the air. ::Congratulations! Now, it's time to log out and go to bed. We both have school tomorrow. Remember your promise, too. I have finals the rest of the week, so I won't be able to play with you. You need to stay nearby and do some 'boring' quests until I get back.::

Rolling her eyes again, Rouge sighed deeply. ::Fine. I'll log out in a minute. I want to assign my points.::

Motte nodded and patted her on the head. ::Good job tonight, kiddo. I'll have to go to work before you head to school in the morning, but I'll make some eggs for good brain food. Eat them. I don't make them so the dog can steal them off the table after you run for the bus.::

::Daaaaaaad. Come *on*. I know, already. Go to bed!::

He grinned and gave her a quick hug before his eyes went blank. Mechanically, the empty avatar of Motte Bailey turned and mounted his horse. Pulling the reins, his steed set out for the nearby Inn where they shared a room. Rouge knew the avatar, or the 'Zombie', as most players called it, would lay down in the bed there and rest until Motte logged back in and took over.

Rouge shook her head. Her dad was pretty awesome, but he was *such* a Dad. Quickly, she opened her character sheet and distributed her points, then looked it over.

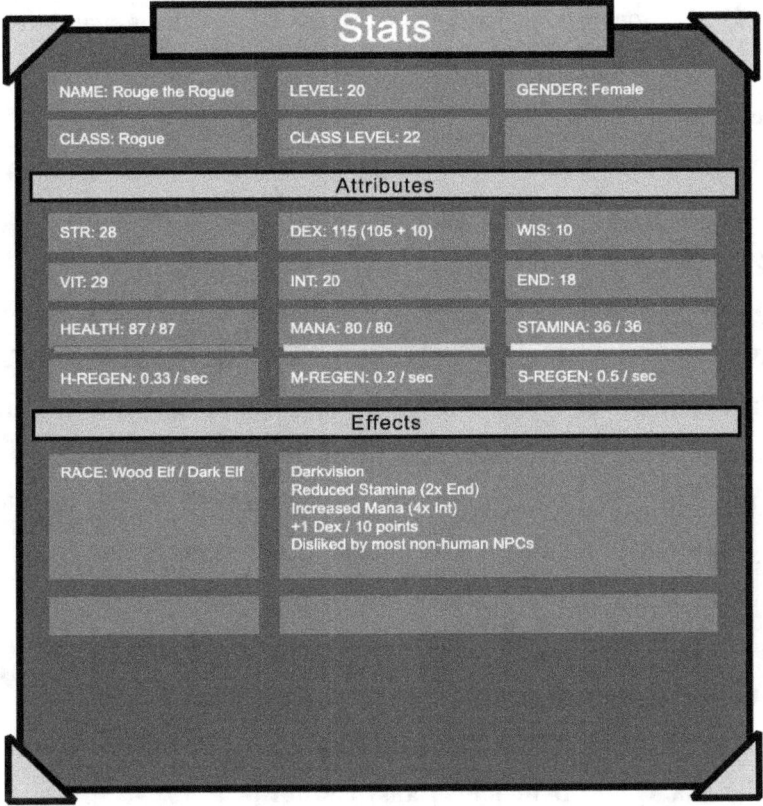

She pumped five points into Dexterity every level, so half her stat points were there. As half Wood elf, she gained an extra point of Dex for every 10 she put in, and she needed every one she could get so she could be as fast and sneaky as possible. She struggled with what to do with the rest of the points, however. Her dad told her that it was impossible to be an all-rounder in Veritas, but she really didn't want to be stupid, or squishy, or weak. It was fun to be able to do lots of skills, and someday she'd get more rogue spells.

From what she'd read in the forums, most rogues focused on Stamina and Dexterity so they could use lots of skills quickly. Possibly because of this, most of the rogue spells were silly, but Rouge really liked them. One of the great things about *Veritas* was that the spells and skill tree weren't fixed. Instead, they changed depending on how you played, and what skills - or spells - you used the most. Some people had even managed to create their own skill by just doing the same things over and over so many times that the game 'learned' the combination.

Smiling in satisfaction, she focused on the logout button and started to select it when a notification popped up in front of her.

SECRET Quest: "Come in From the Cold" begun.

This quest may not be refused. (This is a SECRET quest. If you tell anyone about it before it is complete, you will automatically fail it.) Gina, Goddess of Life, has heard your prayers. You are in a unique position to assist her with a little problem. Duke Penbrooke, the Lord of the North, needs to return to Bright. Dark forces are at work in the city, and only he can work Gina's will upon the instigators. Find Duke Penbrooke and convince him to return to Bright.

Success: 5 levels. 10000 Gold. +50 reputation points with Gina's faithful. +20 reputation points with Gina Herself.

Failure: -50 reputation points with Gina's faithful. -20 reputation points with Gina. Gina will no longer answer your prayers.

This is a chain quest.

Rouge stared, her mouth open. A secret quest? No one got those! Even the highest leveled players in the game might only get one *ever*. She'd read about them, of course, because she was fascinated by all the weird things that the creators of *Veritas* had hidden in the game. In interviews, Carl Landon, the owner of Veritas Corporation, which had created *Veritas Online*, had indicated that the game was actually capable of creating new quests, skills, spells, and everything else as players needed them, so every player's experience was a little different, depending on their own actions.

Secret quests were, as the name said, *secret*. Some of the first players to get one had logged out and immediately told everyone on the boards about it. Then, the next time they logged in, they discovered they had automatically failed the quest. A few people mentioned it in guild or party chat, and again, they failed the quest. One person claimed he told his best friend in person out of the game, and the quest continued, so he thought he'd bypassed the requirement. Then his buddy mentioned something in chat that he shouldn't have known, and the quest instantly failed.

One guy had even sued over the issue, claiming that the game was spying on him. Veritas Corp had quickly shut that down, showing that he'd chatted about it on a public forum, accessible by anyone, and that the EULA that every player signed clearly stated that Veritas could monitor public sites, as well as anything that happened in game. *Veritas* took secret quests very seriously.

However, her dad had *just told her* to stay close and do boring quests. This definitely didn't count as boring, and from what she'd heard about this kind of quest, they were always pretty epic, and required both time and travel.

Still. Five levels and ten thousand gold! Gold was fairly rare in *Veritas*, which primarily ran on the barter system. NPCs often gave items rather than coins as rewards for quests, and Rouge only had a few hundred gold in her pouch. What kind of gear could she buy with ten thousand gold?

Then there was reputation boost… or loss. *Veritas* had a huge pantheon, but Gina was one of the main goddesses. If she lost that much reputation with the goddess's followers, a majority of the regular NPCs in the city would 'Dislike' her. She'd also have to find another religion to join, because the reason players 'prayed' was because of the small chance that the deity might actually step in to help them. It was theorized that there was a hidden Faith stat, and she had a feeling she'd lose all her Faith, or maybe even fall negative if she let this quest go.

She shook her head. No matter what, she couldn't do anything about it right now. It was already accepted, so she was stuck with it. If she didn't at least try, she'd fail automatically. And that's what she'd tell her dad if he got mad at her later. Not her fault. Definitely.

She logged out.

❧ ❧ ❧

Zoey thought about the secret quest all day. She thought about it while she fed the eggs her dad made to the dog, Max. (Her dad was a pretty good cook, but scrambled eggs were slimy.) She thought about it while she ran for the bus, and while she rode to school. She thought about it when she was supposed to be studying for a quiz on *A Midsummer Night's Dream*. Bottom was her favorite character. Mainly because it made her laugh every time someone said 'Bottom'. Still, her dad was a Classics professor, and he'd been reading her Shakespeare and William Wells Brown since before she could walk.

At lunch, she thought about telling her only friend, Jace, while they sat behind the gym eating under an oak tree so that Mirna, a bully with more hair than brains, couldn't find them. Mirna had taken a dislike to both Jace and Zoey apparently on sight, and Zoey had learned a long time ago that it was easiest to just avoid people like that.

In the end, Zoey didn't tell Jace. It probably would have been safe because Jace didn't have a VR pod. He only used a headset and gloves to play *Veritas*, so he didn't play very often. The truth was, she had already decided to at least try the quest, and see how far she could get alone. It said it was a chain quest, so she might be able to do it in bits and her dad would think it was a bunch of little quests. Her quest rewards were too small to make much difference at his level, so they rarely shared quests anyway.

Once she'd made her decision, she didn't want to take a chance of telling anyone. Jace was the best friend she'd ever had, and he didn't talk to other people that much anyway, but she knew if he let anything slip, she'd be really mad. She didn't want to be mad at him for something she shouldn't have told him anyway.

On the bus ride home, she tried to decide what she needed to do first. She used her screen to look on the forums and official site for lore about this Duke Penbrooke, but came up empty-handed. As far as anyone knew, there was only one human Duke left.

Duke Geral of Bright was a war hero, the last great human general. During the first big game expansion, the forces of Lich Lord Akuji nearly wiped out the humans. Humanity had retreated further and further into the last human kingdom, Quarternell. The invading army, which consisted primarily of orcs, goblins, trolls, and various undead creatures, had massacred thousands of people, troops and civilians alike. The records indicated that Geral was the only commander who led consistently successful raids against the enemy.

The surviving nobility of Quarternell was very limited, and almost all of them were already in the capital city, Bright. There was King Chester, who rarely appeared in public or did much of anything. A few players claimed to have met him, but none of them could prove it. According to the lore, King Chester had never married, and didn't seem inclined to do so. *Veritas* had only launched a year ago - though that was two years in game, thanks to some kind of fancy time compression program that fell into the we-can't-tell-you-how-it-works-but-it's-totally-safe category.

Since all the other human cities were decimated in the Akuji event, Geral was the only Duke left. There were a few Earls, Barons, and various and sundry Lords and Ladies, but their lands had either been lost or reduced to ashes in the war.

Many people thought that Geral would become King if anything happened to King Chester, which was kind of a bummer, because Geral was well known to be arrogant and self-righteous, as well as hating anyone who wasn't entirely human. Since Zoey's character, Rouge, was half wood elf and half dark elf, she avoided the nobility, because they tended to follow Geral's lead, and had an automatic -20 Relationship points against anyone non-human.

All of which left good old Duke Penbrooke a mystery. Was he a noble who lost his position or lands when he fled Akuji's horde? Did he die, and she was meant to talk to a ghost? That wasn't entirely out of the question, and was probably the most entertaining option. The quest definitely said he was 'Lord of the North', though, so should she just take that at face value and head north?

She almost tripped getting off the bus, because she was still staring at her screen as she followed link after link looking for any mention of this guy. She walked the half block to her house, and keyed in the code for the lock without even looking up. When she walked in, the lights were already on, and she stopped in her tracks, blinking as she tried to figure out what was going on.

"Hey, Zoe!" her dad called. He poked his head out of the kitchen door down the hall. The creases around his eyes were a little deeper than usual, but he smiled broadly. "I caught a break and they moved one of my finals to tomorrow morning. Apparently, they double booked the lecture hall where it was supposed to be held."

She took a moment to process what he was saying. "Oh! I thought you already had a final scheduled for tomorrow, though."

"I do. Plus office hours. It'll be a really long day, so I figured I'd play hooky and spend some time with my favorite girl." He waved a wooden spoon at her, and it gleamed red in the hall lights. "Now get in here and grab an apron. I'm making lasagna."

Zoey grinned, stuffed her screen in her pocket, and headed to the kitchen. Lasagna was totally her favorite meal, and her dad's homemade lasagna was the best. Her voice was teasing when she replied, "I'm your *only* girl."

He waggled the spoon at her in a mock-threatening gesture, splattering sauce on the floor. Max slurped up the evidence happily and plopped down, big brown eyes following the spoon in anticipation. "That's only because when I tell the ladies I have a smart aleck fourteen-year-old at home, they all run for the hills."

She scoffed. "Dad, it's because you're a Classics professor. Cla-ssics. You're a huge nerd. They're afraid those sweater vests might be contagious."

Privately, she had to admit that her dad was pretty attractive. He was tall, with a nice square jaw, and a great deep voice. He was getting a little soft around the middle, but you really couldn't tell unless you caught him in his Dad-approved Shakespeare-quote pajamas. If he'd stop wearing those dorky glasses and get haircuts regularly so he didn't always have the beginnings of a scraggly

Afro, he'd probably get some dates. Which she would totally support. Probably. At least it would give him something else to obsess over besides her.

He tossed her an apron with a picture of Dante rowing down the river Styx on it. "Yeah, yeah. I'll send all my sweaters to the thrift shop tomorrow, and you can make me a Tinder profile."

"Ew, Dad!" She wrinkled her nose at him. "Dads do *not* get to be on Tinder. That's just gross. What if someone's finger slipped and they actually swiped right on you?" She tied the apron around her waist and grabbed the cottage cheese out of the fridge. They always made the white stuff in the lasagna with cottage cheese. She'd had it with ricotta at restaurants a few times, and it just wasn't as good.

He winked at her. "Hmm. I guess we'd get to find out how a beautiful lady would feel about a mouthy teenager, after all. What do you know about Tinder, anyway? You're not allowed to date until you're at least thirty." He stirred the meaty red sauce, and then tasted it. He shook his head and added some more garlic paste.

"Tinder is such a meme, Dad. Nobody actually uses it anymore, anyway. Plus, who wants to date? I'm going to stick to friends. If a friend is a jerk, you just tell them. Then they apologize, or you go make a new friend. If you're all *in looooove*, you're afraid to tell the truth, and then things blow up into a huge nasty mess." She added some parmesan cheese, egg, parsley, and pepper to the cottage cheese and stirred it vigorously, eyes locked on what she was doing so she didn;t have to look at her dad.

Her dad came over and wrapped an arm around her shoulder for a quick hug. His deep voice was a little sad when he said, "I'm sorry, Zoe. It doesn't have to be like that. I know things didn't work out with me and your mom, but that was about us, not love in general. Someday you'll meet somebody, and you better tell them the truth, no matter how much it hurts. It's all about *how* you tell them."

He hesitated, staring down at the gently simmering sauce. "You know, I give you a hard time, but you're in high school. If there was someone you liked… Maybe Jace?"

She bumped him with her shoulder. "Oh c'mon, Dad. You've told me that a million times, but the whole 'love' thing still seems like a lot more work than it's worth. Plus, high school kids are lame and immature. Jace is cool, but not, like, boyfriend cool. Plus, he totally has a crush on this guy in his math class."

Her dad's left eyebrow jumped up. "Already? I thought he was crushing on a girl in the swim club last month."

"Yeah, she told Jace she was dating Jeremy Tompkins, from the track team, so he gave up." She shrugged, and passed him the white goop to layer over the noodles.

He shook his head, smoothing gloopy goodness over the pasta. "At least this time there were no home-made stroopwafels and midnight serenades. I hope he can find someone who accepts him for who he is. At least he's not being bullied or anything." Her dad shot her a razor glance. "Right? He isn't being bullied, is he?"

She shrugged a little awkwardly, avoiding his eyes as she layered sliced mozzarella over the goop. "You know. Kids are mean. It's nothing we can't handle."

He reached over and gave her another one-armed side hug, briefly leaning his head on her curls. "You're a good friend, Charlie Brown. Let me know if you need help, though, okay? I feel kind of useless these days. I just make eggs for you to give to Max." He let her go and pointed at the slightly chunky chocolate lab, sitting happily by their feet as he waited for any more treats to drop to doggy level. "Oh, and I pay the mortgage. You don't even let me do your laundry anymore."

Zoey spooned steaming meat sauce onto the top of the lasagna, feeling her cheeks heat. "Jeez, Dad. Like I want you messing with my," *bras*, "clothes. You'd probably make them all blue again."

"*One* time! I forgot to wash a new pair of jeans separately *one* time!" He chuckled, slid the pan into the oven, and set the timer. "Tell me about *your* day. How'd you do on that Shakespeare test?"

And they were off. He always quizzed her on her day, dragging every moment of boring lectures and second-hand teenage angst out of her. They laughed together over the story of poor May Carter, who threw up all over her synthetic dissection frog in Biology. When the lasagna was done baking, they gorged themselves on lasagna and garlic toast while he told her about a student who fell asleep during his lecture and nearly drowned him out with his snores.

After dinner she worked on her homework. Her dad graded writing assignments, sometimes reading her some of the funny things his college students had written. She especially loved the student who wrote that he didn't know the answers to any of the questions, so he just made up his own questions about things he did know and answered those instead. That guy seriously made her question if she would actually be more interested in dating in college, or if she was better off just declaring celibacy now.

Then, after what seemed like *forever*, she finally turned off her screen. "There! I'm done!"

He glanced up. "Great. You're on dishwasher duty."

Zoey groaned. "Daaaaaad!"

Both eyebrows went up , and he peered at her over the top rim of his black-rimmed glasses. She wasn't getting out of it. "Fiiiiiiine." She did the dishes, then peeked into the living room at him. "Are you going to be on *Veritas* tonight?"

He shook his head, grimacing. "I need to focus on grading these papers. It's not exactly multiple choice, y'know. Why?"

She shrugged. "I just wondered. I figured I'd go to the square and talk to the NPCs, see if I can get another quest. I have a pretty high Reputation with the regular citizens of Bright now, so somebody will tell me something."

"I'm not surprised, with all those little quests you do. Don't get stuck running chicken noodle soup to a bunch of people for an old granny again, huh?" There was that eyebrow again, and she felt her own brow twitch with the urge to rise up in solidarity.

She grimaced instead. "That one was pretty boring. Though the recipe for chicken noodle soup I got for it has some nice stat boosts, and the ingredients are common. Once my cooking skill is high enough, I'm going to make so much soup."

He laughed, his deep, familiar voice filling the room with comforting warmth. "You do that. I'll eat your soup for you."

"No way!" Zoey shook her head. "Get your own soup, you mooch!"

"How sharper than a serpent's tooth it is to have a thankless child!" He mimed a stab to the heart, then shooed her away. "Go play in your expensive pod, paid for by your hard-working father, whilst I while away some of the few remaining hours of my life with these scintillating answers to basic questions."

She grinned unrepentantly. "Okay! Good night!" At last, *at last*, she ran off up the stairs. She used the bathroom, then stripped down and put on the high-tech, smart fabric, sweat-wicking bodysuit that went with the pod in her room. Quickly, she climbed in, pulling the hatch shut above her as she laid on the cushioned surface of the bed inside.

Chapter Two

Aspen

Aspen groaned and came to a halt as they left the shadow of the trees. Resting one hand against his aching lower back, he gingerly pushed his broad-brimmed hat back with the other hand, and took in the first full view of his new home. A derisive snort emerged from his rather beakish nose, which stood out proudly from his gaunt face.

Words popped up in the space before his eyes.

Quest: "There's No Place Like Home" begun.

Reach your new home - such as it is - before sunset.

Success: +1 point of Stamina, +1 point of Strength

Failure: Become *Unconscious* for 24 hours.

Aspen sighed. "Well, that's all I needed," he muttered. Sweeping his pale topaz eyes over the hovel resting in the field before him, he felt defeat pushing through the constant sense of detached melancholy that was his constant companion.

The 'building' was still a good quarter of a mile away, but even from here he could see that vines covered most of the rough stone walls. The windows that didn't gape open and empty were shuttered behind rotting boards, and there were black spots on the roof that he suspected were holes in the thatch.

A deep, rough snort came from his companion. <We can still go somewhere else, you know.> The ruminant's mental voice was irritable.

Aspen shook his head, sighing. He put a thin hand on the wide leather harness of the eight-foot tall goat drawing the large covered wagon next to him. "You know as well as I do that this is the safest place for us, my friend. It may not be much, but at least no one will murder us in our beds. Probably."

The goat huffed a sigh. <Well, I guess we'd better get on with it then.> He set one dinner plate-sized cloven hoof in front of the other, plodding toward the building which could only charitably be described as a house. After a few steps, he glanced back at Aspen, who was still standing with his hands bracing his throbbing back. <You should ride.>

Aspen shook his head and began to walk, though his steps were short and exhaustion showed in every line of his spare form. "I won't get stronger if I don't exercise. I have a lot of work to do, clearly, and I'm not going to be able to take it easy if we want to have some food and shelter before winter."

The Greater Goat nodded and spat a stream of green goo to the side. He lifted a lip to show square yellow teeth. <True enough. You'd better go faster then.> The goat picked up his pace, and soon left the man behind.

Aspen coughed and waved weakly at the resultant cloud of dust and glared after his friend. "Damned goat," he muttered, but there was no heat in his deep voice.

🐐 🐐 🐐

It was nearly sunset by the time the two road-weary travelers reached the house. Aspen was starting to think he should have accepted Khor's offer, but still retained just enough pride that he refused to say anything. Fortunately, the quest clearance notice popped up as they passed between the decaying remnants of an old wooden fence.

Quest: "There's No Place Like Home" complete.

You have reached your new home before sunset. Barely. Next time, just ride the goat.

Success: +1 point of Stamina, +1 point of Strength

The shimmering silver glow of stat gains surrounded him as he stared at the hovel in front of them. His direst predictions proved true, as the only part of the house that could be considered to be relatively intact were the worn stone walls themselves.

Moving slowly, every muscle in his frail body aching, Aspen unhitched Khor from the wagon. He let the tongue rest on a large tree stump near the house, and the wagon rocked slightly forward as its center of balance shifted. Khor groaned in pleasure as he shook his powerful body, fur and dust flying.

The two stared for several long moments before Khor spoke.

<That's a trash heap.>

"Yep," Aspen replied.

<We have to live here?> The goat asked plaintively.

"Yep," the man confirmed with a sigh.

<Well. Damn.>

Aspen smirked, though he patted the furry beast's shoulder comfortingly. Aspen looked like a hard wind might yet blow him down, but his squared shoulders and jaw revealed his determination. "Yep."

From inside the wagon came the small sleepy voice of a child, breaking into the males contemplation of the decaying shack. <Are we there yet?>

Khor groaned as only a goat can. <How many times have I heard *that* in the last two weeks?>

Aspen laughed, a rusty sound. He hadn't had much to laugh about lately. "Do you want to tell her, or should I?"

Khor's mental voice seemed to grow slightly louder. <Yes. We're here.>

The childish voice grew excited. <What? Really? Is it amazing? Is it wonderful? Is it...>

A tiny, fuzzy, large-eared head poked out of the gap beside the wagon's heavy canvas door. Large, round golden eyes grew even larger as they took in the remains of the building before them. <Is that… a coach house? Maybe an old stable?> The little voice grew hopeful. <Servant's quarters?>

"Try again, little one." Aspen's eyes twinkled in the shadow of his hat.

<That's… it? I don't even see any berry bushes or *anything*! What am I supposed to eat? I'm hungry!> The bat's squeaky little voice grew mournful, and her nose began to quiver.

Aspen reached out and scooped the little ball of fuzz into gentle hands. Softly, he stroked a spot right behind the wide, delicate ears. "It'll be all right, Silus. We knew there wouldn't be much here. We brought materials, and the map the Head Librarian gave us shows an orchard and creek nearby."

<Bugs?> The tiny voice was hopeful.

"Bugs," he said, firmly. At least, Aspen was fairly sure that there would be bugs. He had never particularly enjoyed being outside, and, in fact, had left the small town in which he'd been born as soon as he was old enough to do so. He'd never looked back, either. Not, he thought bitterly, that going back was an option any more. Lich Lord Akuji's armies had utterly annihilated Jumping Hollow, along with a hundred other similar human settlements.

He shook away the dark thoughts, struggling to return his focus to the present. The two weeks since they set out had been a steep learning curve interspersed with periodic chasms of ignorance. Nevertheless, bugs were fairly ubiquitous, especially around water, so he was fairly confident his small friend wouldn't starve.

"Are you ready to go explore?" His tone was as gentle as his fingers on the trembling bat's fluffy head.

<Yeees?> Silus sounded uncertain, but after a moment her voice grew firmer. <Yes! I will explore, and find all the bugs! And fruit!>

Aspen held his hands out, palms up and flat. "Go forth then, o mighty explorer, and return with news of the enemy!"

Silus paused with her little wings spread. <Enemy? You said there wouldn't be any more enemies!>

The lines in Aspen's pale face deepened with regret. "I'm sorry, Silus. I misspoke. This area was marked as safe on the map. The only enemies you should find will be dragonflies and owls. At least until we head out to explore the mines that are supposed to be a few hours east. The map indicates that the mine was abandoned because of some mysterious disappearances, so we need to be ready to fight some Carnivorous Lichen or Greater Voles."

Khor shook his great spiral horns, huffing deeply. <I'm already ready.>

Aspen clapped the goat on his shoulder, raising a cloud of dust. "I'm afraid you aren't likely to fit in a mine, even if you wanted to go, old goat."

The monstrous beast puffed up proudly, his broad chest nearly three feet wide. <True enough. I'm made for mountains and wide-open spaces, not narrow dark tunnels. Though I wouldn't mind killing a goblin or ten.>

"Ah ah, Khor." Aspen clicked his tongue, though he was more than half serious. He was tired of having enemies, no matter who they were. "Remember, the goblins are our allies now."

<I'll believe that when rainbows come from Atae's dark ar....>

<Khor!> The sharp feminine voice came from the wagon. <Watch your language around Silus, please. Refrain from blaspheming in my presence as well, if you will. Atae may not be our Lady any more, but there is no excuse for taking her name in vain.>

The final member of their group emerged from the enveloping canvas, eight sharp legs skittering into the fading remnants of light. Her two large front facing eyes gleamed over her sapphire fangs, while the other six smaller eyes glimmered amongst the bristles on her large head. <Silus, please go and scout the area. We need to know if there are any predators nearby before we decide on how we set the watch.>

She waved her pedipalps in the air decisively. <Aspen, brush down that goat, or none of us will get any sleep. He stinks. For that matter, so do you.

Silus, when you find water, come back and let us know where it is so these two can go bathe. Quickly now, and don't get distracted this time!> Her voice was firm but gentle, and the little bat squeaked an affirmative and launched herself from Aspen's hands, soaring away into the dimness.

Khor rolled his eyes. <I guess it was inevitable you'd come out eventually.> His voice grew a bit wistful. <I could use a good brushing though.>

Aspen slapped the goat's withers, coughing in the resultant cloud of grime. "Come on then, you great stench-making goliath. I'll get you cleaned up as best I can. I'm sure Sumi wants to check out the house."

Sumi's voice was slightly hungry, and her legs trembled with eagerness. <There are rodents in the house. I will clear them out and see what I can do about getting it ready to be some form of shelter for the night.>

Aspen smiled. "We'll depend on you, as always, Sumi. Come, goat. Let's clean up."

🦇 🦇 🦇

About an hour later, a plump and happy bat returned to the shell of a house. Sumi had woven webs to cover the windows and the holes in the roof, keeping any new insects or small rodents from entering, and fortunately it seemed likely to be a clear night. A small fire blazed in the fireplace, merrily burning the remnants of broken and rotted furniture. The chimney was filled with debris, but since the building was basically open to the stars, the smoke wound its way lazily up and away from the quartet of travelers. Khor stood with his bearded chin resting on the sill of the one window Sumi had left uncovered, and Silus landed in the tuft of wiry fur on top of his head with a small *oof.*

<There's a brook not far away. Some kind of animal has dammed it upstream, but I think if we clear the dam it'll be big enough for you to swim in. I found some fruit trees and berry bushes left to run wild to the west, and the moths are quite tasty, too.> The tiny bat laid on her back in her furry nest and burped.

Sumi turned toward the fuzzy creature and clicked her pedipalps disapprovingly. <Excuse you, Silus. Now, did you find any sign of large predators?>

Silus' mental voice was small and apologetic. <Sorry, Sumi. No predators. There's a badger who lives in a cave under a rotted log not far away, but it's just a regular badger, not a Greater creature. A family of brown bears has a den further downstream, but this time of year the cubs are large enough the mother won't be too worried about them. They're sleeping now, anyway. I did see signs of something large near a small pool between us and the beaver dam, but I couldn't tell what it was. I didn't see any sign of bones, though, so probably not dangerous?>

Khor huffed at the tiny bat. <If you're going to sit there, pick out some of the knots Aspen missed, would you? What kind of bat lies on her back, anyway?>

Silus giggled. <A very full one. If I tried to hang upside down right now, I might fall off.> She raised her head and peered into the house. <Is there anywhere for me to sleep, or am I going to have to stay in the wagon?>

Aspen pointed to a small cupboard tucked into the single back room of the house. "That thing was protected by what remains of the roof, and is relatively unscathed. It should stay warm and dark for you."

The little bat hiccupped. <'Scuse me.> She looked guiltily at the arachnid, who pretended not to have noticed, though Aspen knew nothing escaped her eight eyes. <Maybe this place won't be so bad. If we can get the house ready for winter, and get some food put away, won't it be all right? At least there are no goblins. Or orcs. Or zombies. Or....>

Sumi's soft voice interrupted Silus' list before the bat could get herself any more worked up. <Indeed. I think this place may be just what we need, given rather a lot of work. Aspen, if you're done with your dinner,> she looked at the thin man, who was holding a wooden bowl containing the remnants of a warm soup in trembling hands. <I think it best if you sleep as much as possible. Silus and I will keep watch, and Khor's presence should be more than enough to

discourage any 'guests' who might think about paying us a visit. You'll need your strength to get the wagon unpacked and begin preparing the fields tomorrow.>

Aspen nodded, his eyes hot and heavy. "That seems wise. We have a lot to do."

The three creatures watched as their frighteningly fragile friend set down his bowl, now wiped clean with some sweet grass, and made his way to a thick pile of the same grass laid out in the corner of two relatively intact inside walls. His warm, soft cloak was ready for him, and he fell asleep nearly as soon as his eyes closed. Only Aspen's deep, slightly labored breaths disturbed the silence until the three were certain the man was thoroughly asleep.

Silus' sweet little voice murmured; <He looks so weak. Will he really be all right?>

Sumi replied with uncharacteristic uncertainty. <I…don't know, little one. Gina said-> The arachnid broke off, tapping her clawed foot nervously on the table as if regretting her words. <We'll certainly do our best to make it so, but what he went through…. It's not something someone easily recovers from. I wish he'd been able to stay in Bright until spring.>

<May Gina help us keep him safe.> Khor said somberly.

All three bowed their heads.

🍂 🍂 🍂

It took four more days to finish unpacking the wagon and begin clearing the area between the house and the stream to create fields. While they hated to take the time necessary to clear the ground, it was unavoidable because they would need water for the crops. According to the books the Head Librarian had sent with them, if they hurried, they would have just enough time for a fast-growing crop to grow before the winter frosts hit.

It was decided that while Silus slept during the day and kept watch at night, Sumi would work on the house, and the much-larger males would go and clear the obstruction that was blocking the stream. Aspen agreed to ride Khor in order to conserve his limited energy, so it only took a little over an hour to reach the barrier. More accurately, Aspen napped on Khor's massive shoulders while Khor made steady progress, only occasionally muttering about ungrateful, lazy humans.

Khor whuffled as he crested a small hill and could finally see the mass of sticks, mud, and small trees that prevented the water from passing downstream. Aspen cracked an eye and groaned when his friend's hooves stamped lightly in the dirt.

"Are we there already?"

<Yes, you lazy human. Set your puny feet on the earth and do your job.> The Greater Goat's words were acerbic, but he bent his knees without prompting so Aspen could dismount more easily.

Aspen sighed and rolled off Khor's back, which was broad enough to count as a decent sized bed for the emaciated man. He grimaced when his feet hit the ground heavily and sent a lance of pain through his lower legs and hips. "Ow! Dammit!"

Khor's snort was unsympathetic. <If you were doing the exercises the healer set, you'd feel better. Also, you should take Sumi's medicine.>

Aspen's face turned a bit green. "It's spider milk, Khor. You don't drink it either."

<*I'm* not recovering from near death. Also, I have enough stamina for a thousand of you two-legged monkeys.> The Greater Goat's nostrils flared hugely as he tilted his head away proudly.

The human sighed. "Too bad the soul bond was severed when I was...injured. It'd be nice if you could send a little of that strength back to me."

Khor huffed softly. <I would, you know.>

Aspen smiled sadly and patted his friend on the shoulder. He left his hand there and allowed the huge ruminant to support him as they walked. "I know. Just as well, though. When I... I probably won't need it for long, anyway."

The goat ground his teeth. <Don't talk like that,> he said gruffly. <You'll

be well soon enough. Do you think we came all the way up here just to bury you?>

Aspen winced at Khor's bluntness, but offered a half-smile anyway. "I suppose not. All right then. Let's do this."

They walked down the hill together, and the Lesser Muskrats who were using the abandoned beaver dam as a home stared at the pair. It was clear the creatures had never seen a human or a giant, aggressive goat before, and had no idea how to react. When the two were only a few yards from the dam, the six creatures dove under the water, rising up in the safety of their home. Or so they thought. A moment later, huge hooves began beating in the side of the dam.

The large rodents stared, eyes wide. Cloven hooves quickly drove through the myriad trunks and branches, and sunlight poured in through large holes. The muskrats glanced at each other, and then, as one, leapt for the great beast. Biting furiously, their sharp teeth barely managed to pull clumps of fur from around the Greater Goat's hooves and belly, and did no damage to the skin below at all. The level difference was simply too large. Finally, the goat pulled one hoof out, a muskrat clinging tenaciously, and shook the animal off toward Aspen. *Here. This one is yours.*

Aspen clutched a heavy staff shod with steel on each end and nodded. His hands were shaking, but his topaz eyes were determined. With a grunt of effort, he struck out. The staff struck the animal solidly on the skull and it staggered. Aspen hit it again, and the animal's eyes closed as it fell limp.

The two repeated this process with all six of the three-foot long muskrats. By the time Khor pulled the last one from its hiding place with his huge teeth, Aspen was exhausted and barely able to grasp the staff. The rodent stared at them defiantly, baring its large orange teeth. Its long tail writhed behind it.

It seemed it would be a standoff until the muskrat whipped its tail around, throwing its whole body, rear end first, toward Aspen, using the tail like a whip. Aspen thrust out with the staff, but the rodent's agile tail simply knocked the weapon aside. As the body of the animal continued rotating, it opened its mouth for a bite.

Khor's hoof came down on the creature's head with a crunch. He tossed his head and rolled his eyes at Aspen in concern. <Are you all right? That was the last one. We should be out of combat in...>

A soft golden light emanated from Aspen's body, and he closed his eyes as an expression of sheer relief crossed his face. The lines of pain and weariness visibly lightened, and he took a deep breath as the glow faded. "Leveled," he said, grinning.

Khor snorted derisively. <From five Lesser Muskrats. Pathetic.>

Aspen glared at his friend. "It's a start. A few more levels and maybe I'll be able to get the roof fixed on the house. I *might* even manage to build a barn off of it before winter so certain oversized ruminants will have shelter."

<Fine.> The mental voice was acidic, but the goat was clearly relieved to see Aspen's condition improve, however slightly.

It took only a few minutes to gather the furs and meat from the defeated creatures. Aspen touched each one, and their usable items appeared beside him, while the remains returned to small mounds of *Fertile Soil*. Aspen closed his eyes in habitual reverence, knowing that Atae would guide their spirits to the Chaos Pool, from which the gods pulled the souls of the creatures they made.

All together, they gathered four pieces of *Rodent Meat,* three nearly intact *Small Furs*, six *Muskrat Claws*, and three *Sharp Teeth*. In the old, decaying dam, they also found one *Beaver Tail*, which could be used to create sturdy leather gear. Aspen loaded the items into the bags hanging from Khor's sides and wiped sweat from his forehead.

Together, they turned and looked at the remains of what must have once been a well-crafted dam. Water was flowing through it from the large lake that had accumulated above it. Larger and larger chunks of wood swirled away in the current as it broke down.

Aspen shook his head. "I'm glad we did this now. I'd hate to have planted the fields and then had to change everything when the water shifted. Plus, a few of those Muskrats were large enough they had to be nearly ready to evolve into Greater Beasts, and we aren't ready to deal with something like that."

Khor nodded grudgingly. <Sumi was wise to prioritize this task. Especially since it allowed you to level up at the same time.>

"I know the situation is difficult, old friend, but I do appreciate you-"

As the two were about to exchange warm words of gratitude and support, a furious sound came from downstream as the rapidly moving water reached a small pool and instantly transformed it from a tranquil place of rest into a mass of rapidly moving debris and quick currents.

"QQQQUUUUUUUAAAAAAAAAAACK!"

Quest: "Pacify the Duck" begun.

Yeah, the title pretty much says it all. Get to work!

Success: Variable.

Failure: Destruction of home.

Aspen stared, dumbfounded, at the words that floated in front of his eyes. "What in Atae's name...?"

Khor shook his head, long, curling horns swinging heavily through the air. <Dammit. Like we don't have enough to do.>

Blowing out a disgruntled breath, Aspen reached up and grabbed the harness resting on Khor's withers. Khor bent his leg so Aspen could mount laboriously, and the two turned to stare downstream. "Should we go home and talk to Sumi and Silus first, or just go check it out on our own?" Aspen asked, almost idly. He knew what Khor's answer would be, but wanted to be able to truthfully assure Sumi later that he had suggested it.

Khor huffed dismissively. <It's a duck. We can handle it. Sumi is busy, and the little one is no good in a fight anyway.>

Aspen raised an eyebrow at this. He knew very well that the little bat could handle more than the goat gave her credit for, but also knew it was in Khor's nature to take challenges head on and protect his friends. He rubbed the back of his neck tiredly. "Well, we can at least go look. That sounded like a very large, very unhappy duck, though."

Khor began to trot along the small river, agilely clinging to the sides of what had looked like a dry ditch, but they could now see was a ravine worn by water flowing for millennia before the neglected dam had blocked its path. <Unless it's a Greater Beast, you can likely handle it yourself. If it's a Greater Beast, *I'll* take care of it.>

Greater Beasts evolved from normal beasts by a simple method: gaining experience. Every creature in the world received quests from the Gods. Butterfly quests might be something like, "Drink nectar from ten flowers", while an owl might get "Eat five mice". By achieving the progressively more difficult quests, they leveled up. Once they reached some level, they would evolve into a Greater Beast.

What that level was depended on the type of animal, and, to some extent, the particular animal. A very slow and stupid rabbit might need to reach level 50 to evolve, while a fast and smart one might only need to reach level 40. Once they evolved, Greater Beasts gained significant advantages, and their offspring had a small chance of being born as a Greater Beast, or with some other bonus. Greater Beasts themselves varied widely in power. A Greater Mouse, for instance, could still be slain by a normal cat with high strength and stealth, though it would likely inflict significant damage during the battle.

Khor was one of the lucky few who had been born as a Greater Beast, while Sumi had evolved over time. While Silus was still a Lesser Fruitbat, thanks to Aspen bonding with her shortly after she was born, she was more intelligent than even a normal Greater Beast.

Thanks to Khor being born already evolved, the Greater Goat had never known the weakness of lesser animals, and so was somewhat inclined toward arrogance. He was certain that he could overcome a Greater Duck, and he was probably right. Still, Aspen thought it might have been best to go home and get Sumi and Silus.

As Khor covered the ground in a distance-eating stot, Aspen pondered the difference between his life and that of his animal companions. He had begun life as a very average human boy. He had experienced the struggles of an awkward child who was mostly ignored by adults, including his busy parents. He was often bullied by older, larger children, and had to level up through his own hard work. His parents only cared that he learned enough not to embarrass them, and once he chose his class, it was… Well, no trainers or books had been available to help him learn.

He had lost his levels when he nearly lost his life, and had all of his stats returned to nearly nothing. It had been a long and painful struggle since then to reach this point, and without his few friends, he doubted he would have bothered. Less than a year ago he was as weak as a newborn babe, and he had regained his first level from rolling over and crushing am insect in his sleep.

Unlike Khor, Aspen knew that you should never underestimate an opponent, especially one who was as upset as this duck sounded. Indeed, as they traveled further back toward the house, they heard more enraged quacking, and the sound of something large crashing through the underbrush. Finally, Aspen leaned forward and urged Khor to slow down.

Khor shook his head stubbornly, baring broad yellow teeth. <It's just a duck!>

Aspen patted Khor's shoulder and murmured into his large ear. "That's no normal duck, old goat, and neither of us is who we once were, either. Muskrats are one thing, but this is something else. Let's take it easy."

Khor reluctantly slowed, and finally stopped to let Aspen slide down. Aspen remembered to bend his knees and brace himself against Khor's furry side, so he didn't hurt himself this time. They pushed gingerly through the small bushes surrounding an expanding pond that was probably the one Silus had mentioned last night.

The pond was now more of a lake. The massive rush of water and small logs had swept through and covered everything nearby in nearly four feet of eddying water and swirling sticks. Standing to one side, near what seemed to be a large mound of small logs and soft white bird down, but had likely once been a tidy nest, stood an enraged Greater Duck. Her mottled brown and tan feathers were askew, and her eyes blazed red with fury. She stood nearly as tall as Khor, and her huge beak opened to emit the sound that had begun their quest.

"QQQQUUUUUUUAAAAAAAAAAAAAAAAAAACK!"

A small voice spoke into Aspen's mind, nearly making him topple from his awkward position crouched among the reeds. <Wow. She's *really* mad, huh?>

Aspen's head whipped around so quickly the world spun around him. Two large golden eyes and eight shiny black ones watched him from the shelter of a nearby tree. Silus was perched atop Sumi's head, where the spider sat in the lowest branches. "What are you two doing here?" he whispered as quietly as he could.

If a spider could look accusatory, Sumi managed it. <We got a quest. I assume you did as well. Why didn't you come get us?>

Khor interjected roughly, <We can handle a duck. You were busy, and Silus is supposed to be asleep.>

Silus' squeaky voice was sulky. <How could I sleep with that quest flashing at me? Besides, you're late. It's almost evening.>

Aspen was embarrassed. "I slept late. I'm sorry. Now can we handle the huge rampaging duck before it knocks down the hovel we'd like to make into our house?"

Growling, Khor began to step forward. <It's just a duck! I'll->

Sumi raised a front leg to halt the large ruminant. <Did you read the quest?> She clicked her chelicerae impatiently. <Of course you didn't. You never bothered to learn to read properly, so you still get pictograms. It says *pacify*, not kill. The reward is variable, as well. It would just be experience and duck parts if killing her was the only option. *I* believe it would be worthwhile to observe her for a bit longer before we make any rash decisions. For example, do you see what she's doing with her beak?>

"Quacking loudly?" Aspen winced as the infuriated sound echoed around them again.

<Yes, but watch,> the spider's tone was sharp. <In between the quacks.>

Man and goat stopped to watch. The gargantuan duck wasn't moving randomly. Instead, her irate waddling was leading her gradually downstream. Every now and then she would pause to poke her beak beneath a particularly large piece of flotsam and toss it aside.

Khor's brown eyes widened. <She's looking for something.>

<Indeed.> Sumi sounded like a schoolmistress pleased with the progress of a particularly slow student. <So, if we find whatever she's looking for before she reaches the house....>

Silus' squeaky little voice was excited. <Pacified! Pacification? Pacifetted?>

<Pacified, indeed, little one.> Sumi said with gentle amusement.

Aspen nodded. "Split up, but keep within sight of each other. Khor, go around and head downstream so she doesn't hear you. Sumi, look in the trees and brush. Silus, watch from above. I'll look in the water."

His companions scattered. Khor and Sumi might bicker, but they had long experience with working together in times of danger, and they had been working together to train Silus since she was orphaned. None of them needed further instructions, and even Khor could be surprisingly quiet when he needed to be.

Sumi vanished into the shadows among the dense foliage. Silus flew up into the sky, blinking against the sunlight, which had not yet begun to dim. Khor headed back upstream to find a place they had passed not long ago, where large stones would allow a sure-footed goat to cross easily. Aspen removed his clothes, setting them carefully in the tree Sumi and Silus had vacated. Then he slid forward until he reached the water, and slipped in as quietly as possible.

Aspen had spent his childhood in a land of lakes and ponds. Every child in Quarternell could swim almost before they could run. While he had spent more of his life in the city of Bright than in the pastoral land of his youth, he was still an excellent swimmer. Floating downstream in the roiling eddies of the newly widened river was only a challenge because of his low strength and endurance.

Taking a series of slow, deep breaths, he began to swim. The water was murky, and the dirt stirred up by the passage of the beaver dam's remnants and the release of the water from the stagnant lake upstream was just beginning to settle. Various confused aquatic creatures swirled this way and that, darting about in their changed environment. Aspen was quickly swept downstream, reaching out with all of his senses to find something that looked like it belonged to a duck.

The duck was still searching desperately, even as her bellowing quacks became more despairing and less infuriated. Aspen slipped by her beneath the water as she turned over a particularly large decaying branch resting in the reeds beside the river. They were getting perilously close to the house, and there was no sign of any duck-related artifacts.

Then, as Aspen surfaced downstream from the duck, he heard a curiously satisfied sounding *hiiiiiissssssss*.

He knew that sound. Eyes widening, he wiped water from his face with his knobby hand and looked around. His eyes met Sumi's large forward-facing ones, and he started involuntarily. The spider was resting in a crevice between rocks not far away. She had obviously heard the sound too. She waved a leg at him. <Snake,> she said, voice quiet even in his mind. She waved the appendage again to indicate he should follow her into the darkness.

Aspen nodded and risked whistling a short, low burst of song. The sound was nearly drowned out by the duck's near-constant sad quacks, but Silus heard and swooped down from above. Khor raised his great shaggy head and spiral horns so they were barely visible behind some bushes across the river.

Sumi spoke quickly. <I suspect I know the answer to our mystery. Silus, you and Aspen come with me. Aspen, you stay behind me. If I'm correct, you're not strong enough to handle this yet. Khor, you keep looking in case I'm wrong. Keep that duck from destroying our house, but *don't kill her*!>

The other three indicated agreement, and Silus returned to her perch on Sumi's head for a moment before darting deeper into the cave to see what they would face. Aspen pulled himself from the water, then grimaced as he realized that he had left all of his clothing behind except his underclothes. None of his companions cared, but he felt disturbingly vulnerable as a cool breeze tickled wet, bare skin.

Sumi skittered away into the darkness, and Aspen sighed. It was too late to second-guess himself now. He took a step into the blackness of the rough cave. The air inside was cool and still, and Aspen shivered as his skin began to dry. He smelled the seemingly universal musty, earthy scent of underground, and he felt his eyes dilate painfully.

Memories of being held captive in a similar cave began to rise in his mind, and he fought to keep his breathing even. He forced himself to let those memories go, banishing them into the furthest recesses of his mind. The monsters hiding there could be fought on another day, or better yet, not at all. Still, he struggled to make himself move deeper into the darkness.

A soft, furry head bumped against his cheek, startling him out of his reverie. <I found the snake,> Silus said, snuggling into the crook of his shoulder.

Aspen let out the breath he had been holding in a shuddering gasp. It was louder than it should have been, but in that moment, it was the best that he could do. "Where?" he murmured.

<There's a steep drop ahead. Most of the cave that way is underwater now, but there's a crevice to the right where the water drains away. If you cling to the edge, Sumi says you should be able to make it, though the ledge there is evolving.>

Aspen chuckled quietly and leaned his jaw gently against his tiny friend, taking comfort in the soft warmth of her body. "Eroding?"

Silus giggled slightly. <Oops. What does erode mean?>

"Wearing away. She means it may collapse if I wait too long."

<Oh. I hope that doesn't happen.>

He smiled wryly. "Me too, little one. Let's go."

Silus took wing once again, her barely audible squeaks guiding her way in the darkness. Aspen reached out to his right, feeling an uneven wall made up of dirt and roots as much as stone. He took careful steps, sliding each foot forward almost silently before transferring his weight from the back foot to the front. Sound was muffled, and echoed strangely, but he could hear a susurration of scales against stone somewhere ahead. Another satisfied hiss showed that the snake was yet unaware of their presence.

After what seemed an eternity, Aspen felt his questing toes reach a sharp lip of stone. There was no floor ahead of him. Sliding his foot to the left, he felt his toes squish into muddy water. To the right, he traced out the beginning of a narrow ledge formed by dirt and roots clinging to the rocky wall. He could feel that the dirt was wet, and he suppressed a curse as it crumbled a bit beneath his questing foot. He heard a distant plunk as the broken bits dropped into a pool below. His toes curled around the tenacious root that seemed to form the majority of the ledge, and he mentally sent a prayer to Gina as he continued in the darkness.

Several terrifying and precarious steps later, his extended hand touched a gap in the wall ahead. A few more moments revealed that the gap was an opening in the wall that was large enough for him to move his entire body into it. He quickly pulled himself around the corner and knelt, on solid stone at last. He gulped a few relieved breaths, then nearly yelped as he felt something hard and furry touch his back.

It was one of Sumi's long legs. <There's a chamber ahead, with a break in the ceiling above. That's probably how the snake gets in and out. I think the opening is too small for you, even if I could lift you up to it with my web, but we can get the eggs out that way. If there are any left by the time we finish this.>

Aspen blinked, and gratefully made out a dim glow ahead of him. His eyes, which had adjusted to complete blackness, watered slightly as the pupils struggled to contract again. Soon enough, though, he was able to use the faint light to edge forward and see into the surprisingly spacious cavern ahead.

The snake was huge, almost thirty feet long and as big around as a sixty-year-old oak. If it wasn't a Greater Snake, it was nearly there. Its dusky black scales rippled over four large lumps, and even as Aspen watched, another dirty white egg vanished into the creature's distended jaws.

Hovering text appeared in front of Aspen's eyes.

Quest: "Egg-scuse you" begun.

Rescue as many eggs as possible.

Success: Variable based on how many eggs are saved. Current total: 0/5

Failure: Rescue no eggs, and the mother duck will go on a rampage, destroying your house, and devastating the area nearby.

<It has no teeth, so it's not venomous.> Sumi murmured into his mind. <The danger will lie in the strength of its body, and the chance of being crushed against the stone wall. I believe I can handle it alone, however. I will simply need you to assist me in retrieving the remaining eggs once the reptile is defeated.>

Aspen clenched his fists in frustration. Once this would have been nothing to him. He could have destroyed this creature with little more than a thought. Now, though…he would have to accept the risk that his friend was offering to take for him. *I will become strong,* he swore internally. *Strong enough to keep them safe, so no one will ever die for me again.* His eyes touched Sumi's graceful dark shape in the dimness, and a more insidious thought followed the first. *Or strong enough to die for them instead.*

The memory of a rich, dark voice curled through him at the thought. His goddess had warned him, "If you choose to walk this path, the consequences will not be yours alone to bear." At the time, he had made the choice he thought was right, but he'd doubted himself a thousand times since. Now, seeing Sumi ready to risk her exoskeleton for him, he gritted his teeth and nodded.

Sumi waved a pedipalp at him briefly and skittered forward. The greedy snake was too busy gloating over the five remaining eggs to hear the faint scratch of her hairy feet as she leapt for its head. Her fangs sank deep into its vulnerable eye, pumping venom into it even as the serpent began to thrash. Thirty feet of corded muscle whipped around the cave. Cracks appeared in the walls, and dirt fell from the ceiling, glittering in the thin sunlight trickling in from above.

The snake's head reared dangerously close to the ceiling, and Aspen could see Sumi's abdomen flatten slightly as it was pressed into the hard stone. He was already taking a step forward when a tiny ball of fur and fragile wings flew out from where it had been hiding behind a root nearby.

<Give up, you baby eater!> Silus screeched as she flew into the other eye, biting down with her tiny teeth. She barely scratched the surface of the grapefruit-sized orb, but it was enough. The young bat's rarely used offensive capability took hold.

Sumi jumped away onto a now dangling root even as blood began to pour from the serpent's eyes, nostrils, and gaping mouth. Silus' [Pestilential Bite] skill inflicted a Bleed debuff, and between that and Sumi's venom, the snake slowly succumbed to unconsciousness, its body wracked with spasms until it finally shuddered and died.

Quest: "Egg-scuse you" complete.

Success: You managed to save all of the eggs. +1 level, +2 Strength, +2 Dexterity

Ignoring the giant corpse and the glints of stat and level increases surrounding him, Aspen rushed to his friends. Sumi's lovely black carapace was scratched, but there were no cracks or dents. She held one leg up, shivering, and pale blue ichor dripped slowly from the last joint. Silus laid beside Sumi, wings askew, and a golden glow glimmered around her small form. The bat visibly grew as she leveled up. Her wing span increased to nearly six inches, and hints of copper began to glimmer in the fur around her face and ears.

Aspen knelt beside them. Sumi's leg stopped oozing, but when she tested it on the ground, she immediately jerked it back up. Silus opened her golden eyes, blinked, and pulled herself up with her wing-thumbs. Aspen reached out and gently lifted the small creature into his hands, tenderly feeling for any injuries.

<I'm all right.> The bat sounded surprised, and Aspen let out a relieved little laugh. <Let's not do that again, though.>

Sumi waved a pedipalp wearily. <Indeed. That seems wise. For a moment I actually wished that old goat was here.>

As if on cue, a huge hoof was thrust through the earth above them. Chunks of dirt, stone, and roots rained down on the trio. Aspen leaned forward to protect the precious bundle in his hands. Sumi sighed mentally. <I take it back.>

Ruddy light fell through the opening above, limning the hooves, which were quickly pushed aside by an unexpected shape. An interrogative, "Quaaack?" echoed down into the cavern below.

The three below stared up in shock. Finally Aspen managed, "Khor? Did you... make a friend?"

The mental voice was indignant. <Once I explained that we were looking for her eggs, she calmed down. I'm very likable, you know.>

Aspen choked on his own spit, and beside him Sumi's pedipalps curled up as they did when she was trying not to laugh. Her scuffed carapace quivered.

In her innocent little voice, Silus piped up, <No, you aren't. Remember that one milkmaid who thought you were very handsome, and you pooped in her basket? And the saddler who was ready to make a saddle that would 'suit your perfection' until you farted on all the leather and gave it a permanent Stench debuff? And the female Greater Goat who->

<The girl kept touching me without permission, and is it my fault Aspen fed me fermented grain the night before the saddle fitting?> Khor demanded indignantly. <Anyway, it looks like *you* all barely managed to kill a mostly harmless Greater Egg-Eating Snake. Good job.> His voice practically dripped with sarcasm.

<It was still really, really big. And kind of mean!> Silus retorted.

A familiar snort echoed from above. <It doesn't even have teeth. You had

to use [Pestilential Bite], and now you're worthless for a week during the cooldown.>

Sumi broke in. <Khor, that was uncalled for. I erroneously assumed that since the snake wasn't venomous, it would lack resistance to poison. It had time to fight back, and Silus was afraid my exoskeleton would crack, and she came to my assistance. Just as *you* would have, if you were even able to fit down here, you great galumphing beast. Besides, she's worth far more than one skill, no matter how powerful. Now get out of the way so we can reunite these babies with their mother. She's worried!>

Indeed, the mother duck was attempting to wiggle her way in through the hole, causing chunks of dirt and debris to rain down around those below. Aspen quickly crossed the open space and lifted one of the large eggs from where they rested haphazardly on the dirt and stone floor. Grunting from the effort, he raised it so the mother duck could see that its hard white shell remained intact. The duck redoubled her efforts, until Khor edged between her and the cavern with surprisingly gentleness.

Aspen looked around for a way to get the eggs out, since he wasn't sure he could get back out the way they'd come in. He certainly couldn't do it with the eggs strapped to his body. "Sumi, can you spin some web to make a rope and sling? Khor can lift them up."

Sumi gingerly set her injured leg on the ground, testing her weight on it. After a moment, she raised it back up and waved it in agreement. <The leg will take another day or so to fully heal, but it's strong enough for spinning.> Quickly, she extruded some web and used her legs to manipulate it into a strong, smooth rope. Then she wove a net, into which Aspen gently placed all five remaining eggs.

The man hissed as he lifted the last egg. There was a small crack in the side, and blood had crusted around the opening. He showed it to Sumi.

She clicked her chelicerae in concern. <They must be nearly ready to hatch. The duckling inside is bleeding.> She touched the egg with her pedipalps while the mother duck quacked mournfully from above.

"Can you do anything?"

She sighed. <I'm not a healer like Birdie…was.> Aspen, Silus, and Sumi all visibly slumped at the name, but Sumi forged ahead. <I'll try my milk, and patch it with webbing. That's all I can do.> The others watched, helpless, as Sumi expressed some pale, milky fluid from her epigastric furrow. She soaked a small pad of web in the fluid, then pressed the patch to the crack. A few more bits of sticky webbing to tack it in place, and the repair was done. <I don't know that it'll hold up under the mother sitting on it.> The spider sounded worried.

Aspen gently laid the repaired egg in the web sling with the other four. "They've been through a lot already. If any of them survive, it'll be a miracle. We can only pray to Gina and let Mama Duck do her job." He threw the long end of the rope up to Khor, who swung his great horns beneath it. The loose end dropped back down to Aspen, who began to pull.

The net full of eggs rose quickly, much to the mother duck's great delight. When the eggs reached slightly above ground level, Khor carried them gently to a tussock of sweet grass, away from the opening to the underground cavern, and lowered the basket to the ground. It unfolded to reveal the eggs, and the mother duck settled onto them with no further ado. She gently prodded each with her beak, letting out tentative quacks, before sighing deeply and tucking her head under her wing, promptly falling asleep. Khor shook the rope from his horns and walked back to the hole.

Quest: "Pacify the Duck" complete.

5/10 eggs returned to the mother.

Reward: 1,250 XP, Friendship with the Greater Duck.

This time all four of them received the quest completion notice, judging by the way his companions suddenly froze, staring into space. A glow surrounded Aspen and Silus, brighter than before. Aspen stood a little straighter, and he drew in a deep breath, feeling like a heavy weight he had been carrying for months had grown slightly lighter. "At least two levels. Not bad!"

<She sat down right on top of the net,> Khor told the three below wryly. <Sumi'll have to make another rope if Aspen wants to get out this way.>

Aspen looked back at the narrow passage behind him. The darkness looked no more inviting this time, and he felt far less compelled to enter it. He had barely scraped through, and after gaining three levels, he was probably larger than he had been. He glanced at Sumi.

<I can do it. You know I've made far larger webs, and when I had much greater injuries.>

Aspen sighed, rubbing the back of his neck. His hair had dried into muddy spikes, and he grimaced as he realized he was going to have to take another cold bath before Sumi would let him back into the house. "You were…stronger, then. Anyway, I'dhoped those days were behind us. Farming shouldn't be dangerous."

Sumi clicked her fangs in her version of a laugh. <I think you should have talked to more farmers and read fewer books, Aspen.> She quickly spun another rope, which Aspen once again threw up to Khor, who caught it in his large square teeth.

Aspen grasped the rope, feeling the play of muscles under his skin. Just a few moments ago, he would have had to let the goat haul him up like a sack of potatoes, but now… He took a deep breath that seemed to reach parts of his lungs that hadn't fully inflated in nearly a year. He pulled hard, and lifted himself from the ground. His friends watched as he thrashed wildly, trying to wrap his feet around the rope to climb. Then he tried holding on with one hand while the other reached up above to pull his body higher. Finally, breathless and only a few inches from the cave floor, he looked up.

"A little help?"

Khor was laughing so hard he could barely move, muffled brays scraping past his clenched teeth, but finally he backed up until Aspen was able to reach the lip of the opening and pull himself out by grasping nearby dangling roots. Silus fluttered up after him, and Aspen threw the rope back down the hole for

Sumi, who skittered up it easily, even with her injured limb.

Khor collapsed on the ground, his great sides heaving, loud brays now emerging unimpeded. <That was amazing!> The goat was nearly beside himself with amusement. <You looked like a fish flopping around on a hook!>

Aspen sprawled on the ground not far from the large beast and glared. "*You* try climbing a rope when your strength and constitution are below average for a six-year-old child. I think I finally hit a threshold at least!"

<If you'd do your exercises-> Sumi tried.

Aspen turned his glare on Sumi. "I hate exercises. I'd rather chop wood or cut grass. What's the point of exercising without producing anything? Plus, you get diminishing returns the more you repeat the same action."

The three creatures were reminded that Aspen hadn't been particularly physically fit in his earlier career, either. Sumi and Silus glanced away simultaneously, and when Khor attempted to say something, Sumi stabbed him with a hooked foot.

"Fine," Aspen muttered, "I'll do my exercises. I can probably eke out a few more points in strength, and then we'll get to work. That should give Sumi time to recover, too." He pushed himself to his feet and turned toward the house. Full dark had fallen by now, but they weren't far from home, and he might as well walk.

Silus coughed a small embarrassed cough. <Um, Aspen? The house is the other way.>

Aspen sighed, turned around, and walked.

🐐 🐐 🐐

This was how they managed to spend three days unpacking the wagon. Sumi rested, other than telling Aspen where to put the few pieces of furniture and various kitchen implements they had brought with them. The long mahogany bed with the dense goose-down mattress was the single largest piece of furniture and took up most of the small back bedroom, so his few items of clothing had to go in a cabinet in the main living area.

Sumi had cleared all the rodents and small creatures living in the cellar on the first night, so the consumables went down there. Bags of seed and rootstock nestled amidst flour sacks and crates of eggs packed in salt. On the second day, Aspen set up a meat-drying rack outside in the bright summer sunshine, and built a small fire that they fed with logs and dry grass and leaves to smoke the muskrat and snake meat. Aspen and Khor had to go back to harvest the loot from the fallen snake, but as Sumi said with perhaps too much satisfaction, it was good exercise.

Besides several pieces of snake skin and meat, they also got two bony plates the snake apparently used to crush and swallow eggs, and some broken pieces of duck eggshell. Sumi said the shells would be good fertilizer, so they went down in the cellar as well.

Once everything was out of the wagon, they draped the heavy canvas over the top of the house as a stopgap roof. Not surprisingly, given the excessive size of the wagon and the rather unimpressive size of the house, the canvas covered the entire area, and Sumi could easily stick it down with her web. It wouldn't hold in heavy weather, but it helped keep the house cool during the hot days of late summer, and kept out small bugs and animals. Sumi and Silus, of course, could handle any pests that wandered in, but Aspen was glad not to have to deal with them while the two were sleeping.

Each day, in addition to unloading the wagon and his other chores, Aspen obediently did at least two full cycles of the exercises his doctor had prescribed. He ran as well, though he was barely able to run from the house to the river two small hills away.

On the second day, he was rewarded by the subtle silver shimmer of stat growth independent of a level up. Feeling slightly encouraged, he filled two buckets with water, draped a pole across his shoulders, and walked home, as smoothly and carefully as possible. He was drenched with sweat by the time he reached the house, and Sumi took one look at him and told him to go back to the river and bathe.

So he did.

By the fourth day, Aspen had grown remarkably. His chest had deepened until he no longer looked like a man in the final stages of a terrible disease. His cheeks had filled in, and his cheekbones now looked merely prominent, instead of having a knife-like sharpness. Even his eyes weren't so sunken and dull, but shone with intelligence and determination. The more home-like the stone hovel became, the more comfortable he grew, and he stopped jumping at every loud noise.

Finally, late in the evening on the fourth day, Aspen unwrapped something that had been resting in the center of the small dining table since they began. A reverent hush fell over them as smooth wooden shoulders were revealed, and the cloth fell away. It was a wooden statue of a woman, perhaps fourteen inches high, with smooth, burnished curves. Her flowing hair and clothes were so natural that they looked real. It was clear that whoever had made this was a master of their craft.

Aspen reached out and touched one small hand for a moment, marveling at the workmanship that detailed every crease in the fingers, and a look of deep sorrow momentarily burned away all the gains he had made since arriving, leaving him haggard and drawn once again. Then he shook his head and carefully pushed the statue over to one side of the table, as if she were going to join him for a meal. He and his three companions bowed their heads and prayed.

As soon as Aspen closed his eyes, the world felt like it was spinning. He was swept out of his body and into a place of warm spring sunshine and wide clover meadows. Cherry blossoms bloomed and bees buzzed dreamily. Songbirds gave their all to the chorus of joy.

A woman, a life-size version of the statue, burst through the slender saplings nearby. Trillium bloomed in her path as she nearly floated toward him, her faintly luminescent face filled with happiness. Brilliant red hair flew behind her as she threw herself into Aspen's arms.

"*There* you are! I waited and waited for you! Why did you take so long to call on me?!"

Aspen's arms hung at his sides awkwardly, but the woman clung to him, clearly unwilling to release him. Finally, he hugged her awkwardly, patted her back, and stepped away. She released him reluctantly, and a pout settled onto her full lips as she gazed up at him. He pulled off his hat, revealing short, sweat-spiked brown hair traced with silver and bleached gold, and clutched it uncomfortably in front of him, blocking another hug attack.

"Ah," he cleared his throat uncomfortably, "hello, your Holiness."

The woman frowned, and shook a finger at him. "Gee. Nuh. Gina! I'm your Goddess, not your high priestess! No one is judging you, so relax!"

Aspen rubbed the back of his neck, nervously beating some dust from his hat against his leg with the other hand. "Well, it just doesn't seem right to call you by name right to your face. Atae never-"

Gina waved her hand, and Aspen's voice locked up in his throat. "Ugh. Atae. Such a stick in the mud! Anyway, she gave you to me, and *I* want you to call me by my name. Pleeeease?"

The wheedling voice sounded so much like Silus when she had her eye on some shiny bauble or tasty treat that Aspen couldn't help but laugh, shoulders dropping from his stiff, upright posture. Gina smiled triumphantly, and waved her hand. "Now, try again."

Aspen smiled. His goddess was truly full of her aspect. It was entirely different from Atae's still, cool darkness and somber demeanor, and he relaxed a bit more. "Gina, then."

The voluptuous girl smiled and bounced, drawing his eyes to the low-cut bodice of her lustrous gown. As a proper goddess of abundance, birth, and life, her assets were generous and soft. He felt a distant twinge of dismay, and frowned a little. Before he could stop himself, he said, "Should you be wearing that? Someone might get the wrong idea."

Peals of musical laughter echoed around the meadow. The leaves on the trees tinkled as if they were a part of a forest of delicate windchimes. A season of fruit sprouted, grew, and ripened in an instant. Gina stepped forward and hugged him again, this time resting her cheek over his heart for a long moment. He patted her shoulder awkwardly.

She tilted her head back and smiled up at him, glowing eyes cycling through the colors of the rainbow before settling into a shining violet. "I'm so glad you're still you. I was worried after…." A shadow crossed her face, and it was as if clouds briefly covered the sun.

He gently grasped her arms and stepped back out of the lingering embrace. "I'm all right. I'm sorry." Silence laid between them, a thousand things unspoken but understood. "I'm sorry it took so long. We've been…busy." *Mostly fleeing for our lives,* he thought wryly. "Couldn't you check on me if you were concerned?"

She shook her head, glossy red curls bouncing. "Virac said I could only come when you sat down and prayed. He thinks I favor you too much, and don't pay enough attention to the rest of my followers."

Aspen's eyebrows lifted. Virac was the chief god of the pantheon. He was an aloof god, with few followers, and rarely intervened directly unless summoned by a member of his priesthood. The fact that the most powerful god in the world knew Aspen even existed was slightly worrisome. "Is he right?"

She tilted her freckled nose up and away, innocence personified. "I have a *lot* of priests and priestesses. They take care of that kind of thing. Plus, my head angel, Emilieu, makes sure I know if there's something I need to take care of personally. As long as plants grow and babies are spawned, my job is done."

Aspen couldn't help casting his goddess a chastising glance for her nonchalant attitude, but he only said, "Yes, well. I see what you mean. So, you didn't hear when we prayed to you?"

Gina clapped her hands and bounced on her toes. "Oh, did you?! I'll put a noti… um, let Emilieu know that I want to know whenever you pray from now on. Virac said I was to remain hands off until now. I still can't talk to you directly again until you harvest your first crops, but I'll definitely watch and listen. Oh, and you should take this."

She held out her hand and one of the cornucopia of ripe fruits lifted from a tree behind her and flew to her palm. "For getting your level to 10 and your stats up to human normal, I can give you a boon. You should eat this, but save the seed. Keep it on you. Don't put it away anywhere! Plant it in the spring and see what grows."

Aspen scratched his head and looked at the branches heavy with gleaming apples of all shapes and colors. "Apples?"

Gina grinned cheekily. "That would be telling! Just don't forget, and don't put it down. Now," she clapped her hands and looked sad. "We only have a short time before I have to send you back. You look like you're unconscious, and your friends are worried. Quickly, tell me what has happened since you arrived at your farm. What have you decided to name it, by the way?"

"Huh." Aspen looked up, thinking. "Hadn't even occurred to me that I should. I guess…Refuge? It seems right. I'm not terribly good at naming things."

Gina's full red lips quirked a bit. "Appropriate," she muttered. Then she cleared her throat and looked to her right, where a slim blond woman with an oddly emotionless face had silently appeared from thin air. "Just a minute, Emilieu! My time's not up yet."

Emilieu inclined her head respectfully, but didn't go away.

The goddess sighed. "Fine." Those shifting rainbow eyes flicked back to Aspen. "Now that I can hear you, please talk to me? You just have to say my name before you start talking. I won't be able to answer until the harvest, but I'll appreciate it." Her eyes glittered, and she blinked hard. "I miss hearing your voice. It's not quite the same as it was before, but…you're you, and I miss you."

Without thinking, Aspen reached out and ran a thumb beneath her eye, smearing away a thin film of tears. She laughed, a choked little sound, and laid her head on his chest again. They stood like that until the light faded, and when he blinked his eyes against the sudden darkness, it was to see the faces of his friends crowded around him.

<He's awake!> Sumi sounded relieved.

<We see that.> Khor muttered, pulling his head back from where he'd tried to thrust it in through a door too narrow for his wide horns. For a moment it seemed he'd be wedged there, but the door frame finally released him with a loud crack that made Aspen wince.

Aspen sighed. *It was rotten anyway*, he assured himself, *I would have had to replace it before we could hang a proper door.*

He felt movement on his chest and looked down. Silus was clinging to him with her tiny wing-thumbs, staring up with huge golden eyes. <What happened?> she squeaked.

"Ah, how to explain?" He looked at the wooden statue as though asking for guidance, then shook his head. "A certain air-headed goddess decided she wanted to talk to me. I'm sorry you were worried." He would have sworn the little statue stuck her tongue out at him, but when he looked more closely, the sweetly smiling face was the same as always.

His three friends just stared at him in shock. Then Khor shook his head and started to walk off. <Humans and their gods. Can't keep things simple, can they? No, they have to *talk* to them. In person.> His mental voice faded as he wandered toward the river, presumably to get a drink.

Silus wing-walked her way up his chest and leaned in for a snuggle. Her soft fur tickled his jaw, and he reached up to pet her. <I'm glad you're all right. I wish I could meet her ag-> The bat broke off, glancing at Sumi. <Um, is she a nice Goddess?>

Aspen debated questioning the bat, but was too tired to do more than make a mental note to ask about her slip later. He thought about the sweet smile, joyful laughter, and loving embrace. "Very nice."

<Good!> After one last snuggle, the little bat spread her wings and flew out the door. <I'm hungry!>

Sumi and Aspen were left alone. Sumi waited in silence, legs working gracefully as she wove something from webs.

Aspen finally sighed. "She's… different."

Silence.

"I like her. She's just not Atae. She reminds me of," his voice cracked, "Birdie."

One of the spider's legs reached out to stroke the little statue. <You humans look much the same to me, but I thought there was a similarity.>

"She makes me think of who Birdie might have been, if things were different. If there was no Akuji, no war, no…"

<She made her choice, knowing what the result could be. Well,> a hint of sorrow softened Sumi's voice. <not all of it, certainly, but she knew… that she might not come home.>

Aspen's voice was raw and choked. "I wish she'd chosen differently. I was ready to die. I did what I thought I had to do, and when I failed, I was willing to face the consequences. I never," tears began to stream down his hollow cheeks. "I never would have asked for that. I never would have allowed that."

Sumi reached out a gentle pedipalp and patted Aspen's knee. <She knew. She didn't ask. Even if she could have, she knew what your answer would be, and she wouldn't have listened. She could be stubborn.>

His laugh was short but heart-felt as he wiped at the tears still streaming freely down his face, "I know. She came by it honestly. Her parents were stubborn, too. I don't know where she got her generous heart though."

Sumi's eyes glittered in the soft light of the single wide candle that was now all that lit the small room. Night had fallen while Aspen was unconscious. <I *do* know,> she said meaningfully, and he shook his head in denial of the silent claim. <Now,> her voice grew more business-like. <What did your 'air-headed' goddess call you away for?>

Aspen chuckled, wiping at the tear tracks on his thin cheeks. "I think she mostly wanted a hug. Oh! She did give me this." He held out his hand, in which he held what looked like a very small, wrinkled, green apple. He frowned down at it. "It looked better before."

Sumi tsked and touched the ugly little fruit. <What did she say about it?>

He shrugged, unsuccessfully attempting to buff the apple back to some semblance of its former glory. "That I should eat the fruit, then keep the seed with me at all times until spring. Then I should plant it."

<Surprisingly clear instructions from a deity,> Sumi said dryly. <There was no rhyming, nothing like a riddle?>

"Nothing like that." Aspen looked at the apple dubiously. "I guess I should eat it then?"

<That does seem like the best course. Ignoring a god is generally unwise.> Sumi tapped a clawed foot on the apple, nudging it toward Aspen.

Obediently, Aspen bit into the fruit, expecting dry, leathery flesh. What he got instead was a chunk of liquid fire. He very nearly spat it out, but thought of Gina's affectionate words and sweet face, and forced the bite down. It continued to burn until it reached his stomach, where it sat like a coal. "Holy-"

A sharp motion from one of Sumi's legs cut him off before he finished the phrase.

"Sugar! Sugar is what I meant." He coughed, pounding on his chest, and looked around wildly for something to drink.

What he saw was a smirk on the face of the little Goddess statue and the rest of the fruit. Now that it had a bite removed, he could see the beginning of a faintly glowing emerald orb in the center of it, surrounded by several more bites of the vicious fruit. It had seemed small before, but now that he knew what torment it contained, it seemed larger than a watermelon. He looked at the statue, which once again had a serene smile on its small wooden face. "I have to eat all of it?" The serene smile didn't change, and he sighed in resignation and took another bite.

Fifteen excruciating minutes later, the rest of the fruit was burning merrily away in his gut, and he held a small green sphere in his hand. He looked over at Sumi and opened his mouth. "Oo I 'ill 'ave 'y 'eef?"

<I'm sorry, I didn't understand you.> The spider sounded suspiciously cheerful.

He closed his mouth and swallowed several times, forcing the fruit to stay where he'd put it, in spite of its disturbing tendency to want to erupt like a volcano. When he spoke, his voice was a hoarse rasp. "Do I still have my teeth?"

<As far as I can tell, you have as many now as you did when you began. It's not like I spend much time looking in that oozing orifice you call a mouth.> Sumi now sounded faintly disgusted.

Aspen paused, pondering all the responses he could make to this blatant insult, and finally decided it was better to take the high road. A soft silver shimmer lit his skin.

<Did you just gain a stat point? In what?> Sumi's voice was shocked.

The man's topaz eyes were wide. "Wisdom, I think. What in Gina's name?"

<Exactly.> Sumi sounded awed. <You just ate a stat boosting item.>

Quest: "Goddess' Boon" begun.

You have eaten the fruit given you by the Goddess Gina. You will gain stats at a tripled rate for the next week. After that, your stat gain will continue to be boosted by 10% as long as you have the item 'Goddess' Seed' on your person. If you remove or lose the seed, your stats will return to normal and you will fail the quest. Plant the seed after the last frost in the spring.

Success: Gain a permanent 10% increase to stat gain outside of levels. Whatever grows from the seed.

Failure: Lose all stats you have gained through the use of the item and 100 friendship points with Goddess Gina.

Aspen stared at the words floating in his vision, open-mouthed.

<What? Why do you have your mouth open again? I'm *not* going to count your teeth.>

He shook his head. "I just…I just got the best quest I've ever seen in my life. It actually makes the inferno burning in my belly worthwhile." Aspen reflexively rubbed his stomach, where it felt like the conflagration was slowly seeping out into the rest of his body. He explained the quest to Sumi.

Sumi was silent for a long moment. <Well. We'd better make sure that seed stays with you, then.> With rapid, efficient movements, she formed the web she'd been spinning into a small and held it out to him. Carefully, he placed the precious seed into the bag. Sumi sealed the bag closed where it sat on his palm. <Put it wherever you want to keep it. I suggest somewhere against your skin, so it can't get lost.>

Aspen realized what she was going to do and thought for a moment. Several options occurred to him, but he finally settled for the most obvious and rested the seed on his chest, near the expanding blaze inside him. With quick movements, Sumi used some of her adhesive webbing and stuck it firmly to him. <There. It should stay until spring unless you dramatically increase your rate of bathing, which I very much doubt with cooler weather coming. If you feel that it's loose at all, let me know and I'll seal it down again.>

He nodded. "I will." He pressed his hand to his burning abdomen. "Now, I need to get a drink of water."

Sumi chuckled.< I doubt it will help, but as you wish. It's time for me to begin my own hunt. Will you be all right alone? That old goat isn't back yet.>

He nodded. "I feel... good. Better than I have in a year, anyway. I'm just going to get a drink and go to sleep. I think I'll sleep well tonight."

Sumi waved a pedipalp in agreement. <Good. We need to take advantage of this first week. You'll be working hard tomorrow, so get your rest.>

Aspen sighed as the reality of his situation hit him. Sumi was a slave driver even when he didn't have a time-related boost. He wouldn't get a moment's peace until this week was over. He was exhausted already. "Yes, ma'am."

If he didn't know she couldn't, he would have sworn the spider smiled.

🕷 🕷 🕷

It was barely dawn, but Sumi was perched on the edge of the rickety wooden table, legs waving as she spoke. <Stat boosters are only known to boost the six

basic stats: Strength, Dexterity, Intelligence, Wisdom, Vitality, and Endurance. Some people theorize that there are three 'hidden' stats as well. These are Will, Faith, and Charisma.>

Khor interrupted Sumi's recitation with a derisive snort. <He doesn't need to worry about Charisma. Who is he going to impress out here? The duck?>

Sumi flicked a loop of web at the goat, neatly tying his muzzle shut. He let out an indignant muffled bray, and continued his mental rant. <Why did you do that? I'm speaking with my *mind*!>

Sumi rubbed her forelegs and pedipalps together, producing a startlingly loud hiss. <Because obviously your Wisdom stat is severely deficient. Now be silent!>

Khor grunted and looked away into the corner, sulking. Aspen noticed his ears were tilted back toward the conversation, however, and repressed a small smile.

Sumi tapped an impatient toe on the table. <As I was about to say; Will, Faith, and Charisma are theorized to exist, but give no sign when they increase. These abilities may in fact simply be the results of some combination of other stats. Regardless, while we will focus on the six primaries, do not forget about the others.>

She waved leg at the stacks of web-wrapped rocks on the table. <It is also known that repeating the same exercises in the same way produces diminishing returns. If you don't perform different activities, you eventually gain almost nothing for your efforts. Fortunately, for several stats, we are in the perfect position to provide Aspen with many different exercises.>

<Strength is the simplest. We have chopping wood, breaking up stones, hauling the stones from the fields, tilling, planting seeds, carrying water, and, of course, running, both forwards and backwards. As you get better at each tasks, we will add weights.> She motioned to the rock bundles again, and Aspen suppressed a groan. He'd had a bad feeling he knew what those were, and he'd been right.

<You and Khor should also practice with your staff. It may have been a while, but you were once, albeit briefly, a simple soldier, and you'll likely need those skills again. If it seems that those activities are less effective before time is up, we'll go to the mines.

<Dexterity is a bit trickier. We will place progressively heavier weights on you, changing the locations so that the balance of your body shifts often. You'll practice dancing with me in the evening, and all of us will attempt to attack you in different ways at random intervals, forcing you to react. You can also make some baskets using river reeds. Perhaps you could try a hat, as well. Your old one is somewhat reprehensible.>

At this unprovoked attack, Aspen clutched his well-worn and comfortable hat protectively. It had been one of his favorites since before they left Bright, and while it was now significantly more battered and stained, he doubted his ability to create something to rival it.

Sumi continued as if she hadn't just insulted his haberdashery. <Vitality and Endurance will naturally rise as you simply persist through all of your training. As for Intelligence, you will practice debating with me while we dance. You will also read *all* of the books and scrolls the Head Librarian sent with us, beginning with the books on farming, and continuing to carpentry, mining, and smithing. You'll have to gather materials and build a forge before you can start crafting anything, but gaining the skill and increasing Intelligence go hand in hand.

<Wisdom. Wisdom is found in listening to the better part of yourself. As you go through this trial, concentrate inside yourself. Find your mental voice, and listen to it. If it asks you questions, answer. Otherwise, remain silent. Unless you must speak, you are restricted from doing so from this moment until the boon ends.>

Sumi tapped her legs against the flimsy wooden table, causing it to creak ominously. <Do you have any questions?>

Aspen opened his mouth to reply, realized what she was doing, and shook his head. A soft glow shimmered around him. He fought the urge to bury his face in his hands.

<Off you go, then! Khor, don't help him. He must do it all himself, no matter how pathetic he looks.> The spider sounded severe, and Khor snorted.

<As if I would.> He scuffed his hoof on the ground outside the door like a petulant child. A rock came loose from the soil, and the goat deftly kicked it, sending it flying toward Aspen's head.

Aspen completely failed to duck, and the rock smacked him solidly in the middle of his forehead. He clapped his hand to the throbbing wound and glared at Khor.

<I was just doing what Sumi told me to! It's her fault!> The goat snickered, swishing his tail, and walked off nonchalantly.

Aspen switched his glare to Sumi.

<He's right. Now get to work, and next time, dodge.> The three-foot arachnid flung a line of webbing into the decayed rafters and began climbing.

Aspen sighed and picked up the axe leaning against the wall nearby.

For six days, Aspen did little but train. In deference to his weakened state, his friends allowed him regular food and water breaks, but he never knew when one of them would hide a rock in his food, or an angry wasp in his mug. He was also allowed six solid hours of sleep every night, but his dreams were so filled with thoughts of his efforts that he gained two points in Wisdom and one in Intelligence while he slept.

By the end of the first day, he had even accumulated several quests.

Quest: "Diggin' It" begun.

Dig ten stumps from your field area. Stumps must be a minimum of 5 inches in diameter.

Success: Experience, 1 point Strength, 1 point Endurance.

Failure: Field will produce 15% less produce.

Quest: "You Call That A Row?" begun.

Plow three straight furrows 50 feet long and 6 inches deep within 3 days, with no assistance.

Success: Experience, 1 point Strength, 1 point Endurance, 1 point Dexterity.

Failure: Anyone who sees your field will feel compelled to mock you. Produce may randomly move from one row to another after planting.

Quest: "Basket Case" begun.

Create a basket capable of holding seeds within three days.

Success: Experience, 1 point Dexterity, 1 point Wisdom.

Failure: Your friends will mock you (especially the goat).

Quest: "Don't Take De-bate" begun.

Beat Sumi in a debate.

Success: Experience, Variable increase in Intelligence and Wisdom.

Failure: Live your life knowing a spider is smarter than you.

He sighed each time one of the quests popped up in front of him. Never before had the notices been so specific or snarky. He had a feeling Gina was keeping her promise to watch over him.

Aspen dug out stumps, built drainage ditches, broke up rocks, and stacked one pile of lumber for firewood and another pile of straighter pieces to use for building. His axe strokes gradually became more certain, and eventually every stroke left a perfectly split log. He neatly piled stones to be used to build a garden wall, a shelter for Khor, and add a room onto the small house.

He also cut sod from the area where they planned to plant the fields, and began the extremely laborious process of laying in a sod roof. Fortunately, learning the process from one of his books gained him three Intelligence points. During all of this, Khor stood to the side, observing and occasionally adding a pithy comment or another object flung with unnecessary force.

His baskets, sadly, left rather more to be desired. He only had one book that briefly mentioned this process, so simply figuring out how to prepare the reeds for weaving took significant trial and error. After getting his reeds too dry and then too wet, after which they quickly grew mold, he gave up on crafting that style of container.

Instead, he used the small knowledge of rope-making he'd gained during his brief stint as a trainee in Quarternell's army to twist together long grasses into thin ropes. With Sumi's guidance, he sewed the coils into baskets, using a flexible stick to create a circular base.

His first semi-successful basket would never hold anything smaller than a plum, but by the tenth one, he thought it might be useful for seeds, depending on what kind of seed it was. Even his best one was slightly lop-sided, but he was still proud of how far he had come.

Hour by hour, day by day, the shimmer of stat gains glimmered around him. He also received and completed a few additional minor quests for things like tilling, watering, and creating the sod roof. He lost track of his stats as one stat gain ran into another, and he gained three levels as well. Frankly, it was ridiculous. His stats were certainly nowhere near where they had once been, but they were already well above those needed by the farmer he planned to become.

By the end of the fifth day, the stat glow was an occasional thing instead of nearly constant. He certainly still had plenty to do, but he had built a ramshackle harrow and used it to break up the soil in their first field. He pulled the plow himself, since Khor refused to help, and while his first furrows were shallow and meandering, the last ones were straight and deep, allowing him to complete the associated quest.

He even managed a very simple irrigation system by digging long channels from the river to the field, making them progressively deeper as he went from the high bank of the river to the lower field. He would need to dig a well eventually, but he wasn't sure how to find an underground water source yet.

One of his books discussed dowsing, and he would likely need to attempt it soon enough.

He stood, hands on his sore lower back, grubby hat shoved away from his dirty face, as he stared out over the field. He had been too ill to help with packing the wagon, but his companions and the Head Librarian had managed to gather quite a wide range of seeds. Sumi claimed that because of the mountains to the east, this area should be sheltered from early frost. He hoped she was right, because if she weren't, his first winter here might be his last.

This thought brought a melancholy smile to his lips. On the journey north, he had half hoped that this winter *would* be his last, but now he wanted to see the spring come. He looked forward to seeing the fragile green shoots burst to life in his fields. He picked up a bag of seeds marked spinach and began to plant. As he went, he focused on each tiny germ of life that he placed into the ground. In his mind, he prayed to Gina for a bountiful crop.

After planting two rows of spinach, which was already more spinach than he thought he'd have the stomach for, he continued with carrots, peas, and beans. A row of cabbage and another two of broccoli finished up the small field. Then he stopped and looked out over the mostly tidy rows of dirt.

What the hell am I doing? He wondered. *I'm no farmer. I don't even* like *vegetables!*

At that moment, he felt a motion behind him, and spun to pluck a fist-sized rock from the air. Without hesitation, he sent it back the way it had come, raising a puff of dust from the ground near Khor.

<Not exactly a stellar performance,> Khor said dryly, <but at least you won't be nursing a lump the size of mother duck's eggs this time.>

Aspen paused. He had almost forgotten about the duck! If Sumi was right, and the eggs were nearly ready to hatch when they'd found them, did the mother duck have a duckling or two by now? Had any of the eggs hatched? The offspring of Greater Creatures were usually larger and sturdier than those of their Lesser brethren, but they were likely still just normal beasts.

Once or twice over the past few days, he had slipped up and spoken when it wasn't time for debate with Sumi. The first time, he had woken to find himself webbed to his bed, and it had taken nearly an hour to escape. The second time... He shuddered and tilted his head, then made a motion in front of his mouth as if he were opening a duck beak. Then he shrugged his shoulders questioningly.

<Do you have fleas? I haven't noticed many parasites around here, but if they're here, I'm sure they'll find you.> Khor sounded suspiciously amused, and Aspen glared, but made the beak motion again, this time adding a little duck waddle for clarification.

<Are your pants too tight? That's why we goats don't bother with such things.> The goat snickered.

Aspen wriggled a little at this, resisting the urge to tug at the seat of his trousers. His pants were indeed a little tight. All of the clothes that his friends had packed were loose-fitting, no doubt in hopes that he would be able to gain some weight, but by now his nether regions felt like they were in sausage casings when he got dressed in the morning.

He was uncomfortably aware that if he gained much more strength, he might split his pants, and then what would he do? There was an upper limit to how much stat changes should affect the body, or all warriors would be muscular behemoths, and scholars have bulging craniums, so he was fairly certain his personal expansion was the result of some secret amusement of his goddess.

<Khor, stop picking on him! You know Sumi will have him walking around with a stack of books on his head answering questions about the ratio of materials in bronze and steel again. He wants to know about the ducklings!> Silus' piping little voice was welcome, and her weight settled lightly onto his shoulder. Almost too late, he twisted his head away as her tiny sharp teeth scraped his earlobe, and the shimmer of a stat gain settled over his skin. He turned to glare at her, barely dodging a wing-thumb aimed for his nostril.

<I'm really sorry,> the little bat said, sounding genuinely apologetic. <Sumi says it's for your own good. I missed this time! Good job!>

Aspen reached up and rubbed the nearly healed puncture marks on the other ear while he tried not to be angry at Silus. It was Sumi's fault. No, it was the fault of that red-headed goddess! *He* would have been fine gaining stats at a normal pace! Khor would have plowed the field, helped break up rocks, pulled stumps... Aspen had planned to depend on the goat's ridiculous strength for all of that. It was due to this situation that he had to do it all alone. He was a farmer! Why did he need to split out of his pants?

Silus rubbed her little head against his cheek. He flinched away at first, but for once she offered no attack, so he just enjoyed the soft nuzzle. <There are three ducklings. Two are doing well. The third one is,> she hesitated, <different. It hatched from that cracked egg, and there's something wrong with it. It doesn't move like the other two. I don't know what the mother will do. They'll have to fly south in a few months, and the odd one may not be able to go. I think our friend the mother duck left it nearly too late to have her brood as it is, and this duckling...>

Aspen drew his brows together and shrugged questioningly.

<I don't think there's anything we can do. The mother duck is still a wild creature, though she tolerates us nearby. She won't let us help.> Silus' childish little voice was sad.

Aspen nodded understanding. He patted his little friend and smiled in gratitude. Then he hefted his dibbler - a small wooden tool for making holes for seed - and headed toward the house. It was time for his dancing and debate lessons. Also, he hoped Sumi would move the weights strapped to his thighs and upper arms. He felt like he was waddling. At least he had finally completed all of his quests. Well, all except the debate quest. He had a feeling that one could be there for a very long time.

Behind him, from the shadows, an eight-legged form silently emerged from the low shrubs still surrounding the fields. Carefully, Sumi touched one of the rows of seeds. A minute sprout, just a hint of green, showed above the surface of the fertile soil. A spot check of the other rows revealed the same thing. She rubbed her pedipalps together thoughtfully, then sank back into the darkness, rapidly outpacing Aspen's slow trudge toward home, though only Silus noticed her pass.

They would need to set guard on the fields. These plants, already growing when they should still be resting, would be tempting to the local wildlife. Perhaps a stone fence would be needed sooner than she'd anticipated.

Chapter Three

Rouge

Zoey wiggled into a comfortable position, pulled on her headset, and spoke out loud. "Emily, start *Veritas*." The bed molded itself to her body, wrapping around her limbs until she felt like she was muffled in a bulky snowsuit. The pod began sending signals to the nanofibers of the suit, which loosened and tightened. It was always slightly uncomfortable at first, but quickly settled until the bodysuit felt like a second skin. When the pod completed the startup process, the light in front of her eyes flashed, and the familiar sensation of falling swept her away.

When she felt her heavy cloak settle around her shoulders, she blinked her eyes open, and the road in front of Matilda's house appeared. "Darn it," she muttered, "I forgot to set my Away instructions again. What a waste!"

Veritas Online had a unique game mechanic, simply called Away. People on the boards often called it "Zombification", because your avatar remained behind in the game while you were out in the real world. Commands could be pre-programmed for the avatar to obey, ranging from something simple like,

'Return to the nearest Traveler's Guild and sleep' to 'Craft as many *Simple Copper Rings* as possible, then sell them for 5 Gold each'.

The 'Zombie' couldn't participate in combat, and any item it crafted would be identical, with no chance to get a lucky item of higher quality or with a stat boost or buff. Most people just opted to have their Zombies 'sleep', since the Well-Rested buff was actually pretty good, and included a minor XP boost for the next sixteen hours in-game.

Time in *Veritas* ran twice as fast as real time, thanks to the revolutionary ability of the hardware to interface with a player's brainwaves and boost their processing speed. Rouge liked to use every minute of that extra time leveling, since she was only allowed to play for a few hours at most on school days. As a result, she usually set Zombie Rouge to gather items or complete non-combat fetch quests while she was away. The Zombie couldn't actually accept or turn in quests, but it could do the boring running around, and Rouge took full advantage of that fact.

Unfortunately, that meant that she had to set her Away instructions individually every time, though she usually had a 'Go to bed' default set up. She'd set the default to inactive since she was running a relatively lengthy quest with Motte, and might have to log out for a minute to use the restroom or something. In her excitement over her Secret Quest, she'd obviously forgotten to reset it.

It had been 20 hours real time since Zoey logged out. Rouge had been standing there in the street for 40 hours. Zoey wasn't sure what the NPCs thought about this, or if they actually even processed the strange behavior of the PCs. In any case, Zoey should have had Rouge ride back to the inn room she shared with Motte and sleep or practice a skill. Even a few percentage points toward the next level would be better than nothing. At least Bright's streets were designated Non-Combat, so no one could steal from or murder her Zombie.

That said... Rouge looked down at her feet. Yep, it never failed. Every time she forgot and left her avatar on the street, something bizarre or disgusting happened to her. If she was outside a tavern, someone would throw up on her, causing a Stench debuff that lasted until she took a bath. If she was near a butcher shop, someone might throw a bucket of offal on her that would cause a low-grade Disease debuff. This time it was poop, or 'Animal Byproducts', as the game called it.

Her horse, Blackie, was standing next to her, right where she had left him. She *should* have returned him to a stable to be cared for, but instead he'd been standing in the street with her Zombie for almost two days.

She popped open his status screen and winced.

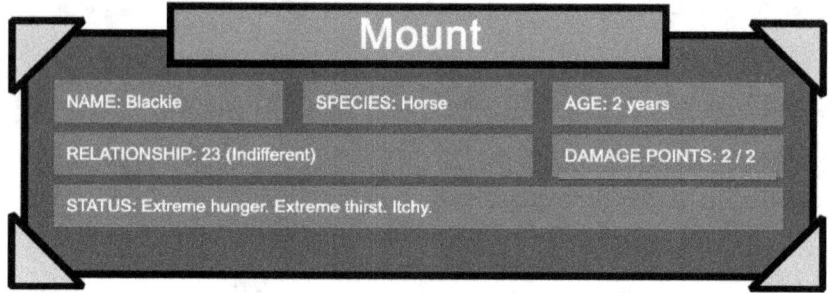

Ugh! When she left, his relationship was at 63! That was a huge drop, and definitely accounted for the extremely large pile of filth on and around her boots. She flicked her eyes up at the debuff icons at the edge of her vision, and they expanded so she could read the descriptions.

Filthy. You are dirty, and you smell bad. Relationship -30 to any sentient close enough to smell you. Relationships will not drop below 0 from this debuff, but passersby will avoid you.

Disgusting: You are covered in something those around you find offensive. You may lose up to 5 Relationship points permanently from anyone with a Relationship lower than 40 (Cordial).

Double ugh! Quickly, she reached into her Ring of Holding and pulled out five carrots and an apple and fed them to her horse. This raised his relationship with her to 30, which was Cautiously Friendly. That was the minimum required to be able to ride him, so she was glad she'd picked up some veggies last time she wandered through the market. Shaking off her feet, she mounted up and cantered through the streets to the inn.

❦❦❦

An hour later, clean and clear of debuffs, she headed for the library. It wasn't far, so she decided to walk. It was pretty easy to gain affection from common horse mounts, which every player got as part of a quest at around level ten, but Blackie needed some pampering after being left unattended for a few days.

The library was the repository of lore for the city of Bright. Since Quarternell was the human nation, and Bright its capital city, that meant it held the accumulated knowledge of the human race in general. It had occurred to her that this Duke Penbrooke might not even be human, but it was a human title, and a human sounding name, so she was going to see what the Head Librarian knew about the guy first.

When the human race had been ascendant, and Quarternell only one of several human countries (as recounted in lore, since humanity was already on the decline when the game launched), the library of Bright had been famous all over the continent. People had supposedly traveled here from all over to read the rare and unique books found within its walls.

However, the library, much like Bright itself, had fallen on hard times. The original building had been a white marble edifice, covered in gargoyles, with great echoing halls and a hierarchy of librarians that would have made any organized religion envious. When the Lich Lord's army began advancing through Quarternell, that building had been turned into a palace, then a hospital, then housing for displaced refugees. The gargoyles had been broken off and sold, or possibly flown away, depending who you asked. The contents of the library had been winnowed down to a single copy of each book, scroll, or tablet, and carried away to an old school.

The children of Quarternell were now educated at home by relatives or hired tutors. Public education had all but vanished, so in a country that had once boasted a literacy rate of 86%, now not even half of the population could read more than a few words. As people traveled to avoid war and famine, schools closed, and teachers were conscripted, died, or retired, and were not replaced. The old Lady Bandy's School for Young Ladies was only one such casualty.

It was a gothic monstrosity. The walls loomed over the surrounding buildings, with more arches, high vaults, and large windows than seemed possible in one structure. It seemed as if the walls were so laden with flying buttresses and intricate stonework that they should fall down under their own weight. Most of the stained glass windows had been broken and replaced with clear glass or wooden shutters, but a few remained. From these windows young girls in starched gowns buttoned from neck to toes trailed along behind upright teachers like goslings with particularly imposing mother geese.

Meanwhile, the interior was in chaos. Books, some on shelves, but many not, laid about in heaps and stacks. Scrolls were stuffed into cubbies lining the walls. Tablets were stashed willy-nilly in closets and under benches. Three librarians, overworked and underpaid, worked in shifts to categorize and organize the knowledge that remained, in case someday someone decided they needed the tablet containing the 'Memoirs of Grimtooth the Horse-Thief' for something other than an awkwardly large paperweight.

As Rouge entered, a middle-aged woman with two long, blonde braids looked up and smiled. "Rouge! How lovely to see you! It's been ages! Have you come to help the Head Librarian again?"

Rouge grinned back, shrugging a little. "Hi, Lisette! Not unless he has something I can do quickly. I need to find out about someone, and I figured this was the best place to come. I swear you guys know everything."

Lisette looked pleased, and a notification popped up in front of Rouge.

+1 Relationship with: *Lisette, Second Librarian*

Rouge sighed a little and popped open her settings, putting 'Relationship Improvement' notices back on Ignore. There had probably been some kind of patch to the slightly wonky Relationship system that had changed her settings back to the default, but Rouge preferred a more immersive experience, and constant notifications was definitely not conducive to that.

She pointed off down the hall. "Is his office still in the same place?"

Lisette made a face and waved a scroll in the same general direction. "I think he's still in the same chair. You'll probably need to oil him before he can move. We hired a new girl with the extra funds we have now that we're not constantly paying you Travelers to kill rats, and she thought he was a statue and tried dusting him. It didn't help." She rolled her big blue eyes. "You know the way."

"Thanks, Lisette!" The rogue waved as she walked down the hall. Books lined the walls and littered the floor, though she was pretty sure they looked more organized than the last time she was here. Now that the rat problem was solved, maybe they could actually get ahead of the chaos!

Rouge had taken a quest at the library when she was only a level 3 newbie. It was a starter quest that every player who spawned in Bright took as part of the tutorial. It was so cliche that it made most experienced gamers groan.

Quest: "Hide and Squeak".

This is part of the tutorial and cannot be refused. Enter the basement of the library and kill rats. Bring five _Rat Tails_ to the Head Librarian as proof of your mighty deeds.

Success: +10 Gold, +10 Reputation with all Library personnel

Failure: Try again. This quest must be completed as part of the tutorial.

Once they finished finding their five rat tails, most players left the library and never looked back. Rouge, of course, hung around. She noticed that the Head Librarian still looked rather harried after he paid her for the tails, so she asked her favorite question: "Is there anything I can do to help you?"

As it turned out, there was. She had done everything from filing books, to dusting, to killing massive spiders (which were below snakes, but above rats in her personal Ick list). After more than two in-game weeks of doing small quests and raising her reputation with the librarians, she finally got the last quest in the chain.

Quest: "A Tale of Two Tails" available.

Two mother rats have occupied the basement of the library. They eat the books and use scrolls for nesting material. The librarians constantly battle to control the population of their offspring. Kill the mother rats, recover the written material they've been snacking on, and stop the rodent plague.

Success: +100 Gold, Maximum reputation with all library personnel

Failure: None

Accept: Yes/No?

She had accepted, asked for Motte Bailey's help after the rats killed her a few times, and the rest was history. In *Veritas,* actions had lasting consequences, so what a player did, whether they were online or Away, could be hugely important. If someone killed good ol' King Chester, he would really be dead in the game, no matter what server you were on. There were no respawns for named NPCs. The political scene would shake up and eventually someone else would become the ruler of Quarternell, but Chester would be gone for good.

Fortunately, this rule didn't work for common mobs, so you could go kill a village of orcs, and within a week of game time, the village would respawn. The chief NPC, however, would be different, with a new name, skills, and back story. The same went for little Matilda. Now that she was a named quest NPC, if something happened to her, the game might spawn another little girl to give similar quests to other players, but that NPC wouldn't be Matilda.

Similarly, any changes to important buildings or landmarks would stick. If someone, player or NPC, blew up the palace in Bright, it would stay blown up. The city would have to build a new palace, or designate a different building as the home of the royal family from then on.

You could cut down a tree in the forest, however, and a new one would grow to adulthood within a game month *unless* you built something else in its place. Cut down a forest and build a village, and when you were done, you would have a village with limited wood resources.

In the case of the Hide and Squeak quest, it suddenly vanished from the tutorial, and a different low-level fetch quest took its place. Hundreds of bloggers had to change their tutorial walkthroughs, and Rouge's Reputation with the librarians maxed out at 100. There were still quests available for players who visited the library, but they were much less exciting.

It had been a few months in game since then, and Rouge's Reputation at the library had dropped a few points, but it was still in the upper 90s, and should be more than high enough to get answers about her mystery noble if they were available.

Rouge grinned at the memory of the furor on the boards at the 'sudden' change. She hadn't claimed responsibility, mainly because some of those people seemed genuinely upset, even though that was the nature of the game. Still, it was cool to see her actions affect the game in such a small but profound way, and she had been searching for ways to repeat the experience ever since.

She was so focused on her memories that she tripped over a pile of dusty tapestries. Fortunately, her [Acrobatics] skill kicked in and she did a quick one-handed vault over the top, flipping and stumbling, but not (quite) falling.

Shaking her head, she continued on, carefully avoiding several more similar obstructions. She passed two halls on the left, one on the right, and took the narrow winding stairs up into one of the ridiculous spindly towers. At the top of the stairs, she rapped on the solid wooden door. Unsurprisingly, there was no answer, so she cautiously opened the door and poked her head in.

"Head Librarian?" she called. As far as she knew, the Head Librarian's first name was Head, and his last was Librarian. He had obviously been born (or spawned) for his job. Sure enough, sitting at a desk piled high with papers and the detritus of literature, she saw him. He was very close to her own five feet in height, and his head was barely visible above the top of the desk. His position at the desk could be determined thanks in no small part to a rather large, dusty, red hat.

At the sound of her voice, the hat shifted, and a creaky, disused voice replied, "Eh? What? Rouge? Is that you?"

She entered the rest of the way, carefully shoving a pile of scrolls out of the way aside with her foot. "It sure is, Your Librarianness! I came to say hi, and see if I could ask you a question."

Wrinkled hands separated the piles on the desk enough that she could see a brown face, gnarled like a walnut, blue eyes twinkling brightly under the ridiculous hat. "Why, of course, my dear! Sit down and have some tea, and we'll have a chat! Lisette just brought me some fresh tea a little while ago..." He looked around, obviously disoriented, until he spotted a distinctly dusty pot mostly buried beneath pages of words written in a language Rouge didn't recognize. "Ah, well, perhaps it was a day or so ago. I do get caught up in my work. In any case, how may I help you?"

She laughed at his antics, and said, "I need to find out about someone named Duke Penbroo..."

Before she could finish, the little codger was out of his chair and across the room. One surprisingly calloused hand was covering her mouth, and with his other hand he shoved the door closed with a *thunk*.

After three months of playing Veritas, Rouge's reactions were pretty well honed. Her hand twitched toward her knives. But she remembered how grateful the Head Librarian had been after she finished the chain quest, and her eyes flicked up, squinting slightly. A stat bar flickered into sight above his head, and she saw the green icon for NPCs with a Relationship level above Friendly. Instead of drawing or summoning a weapon, she froze, eyes wide above the gnarled brown hand clamped over her mouth.

"Where did you hear that name?" he nearly hissed, pulling her deeper into the room.

Argh! It was a secret quest! She couldn't tell anyone, not even an NPC, or she would fail it! She shook her face free of his hand, and thought fast. "I was at the Great Temple, praying to Gina, and overheard someone mention him. I thought Geral was the only Duke left, so I was just, um, curious. I figured you guys know everything, and I haven't been by in a while, so…"

The Head Librarian's eyes were calculating beneath his bushy gray brows. "Gina's temple? Well, that's possible. No one there should be talking, though." His gaze pierced her. "Did you see who it was? What did they look like?"

She shook her head. "N… Nothing. I didn't see anything. I was praying before a mission, and, uh, I heard someone talking behind me. When I looked, they were gone."

The old man pulled at his long gray beard, muttering. "Idiots. They could ruin everything. I'll have to talk to Priestess Penelope. Loose lips burn books…" Finally, he looked back at her. "Have you mentioned this to anyone else?"

Rouge shook her head vehemently. "Nobody." *Is now when he stabs me to shut me up? What is going* on *here?* She never in a million years would have expected the absent-minded old man to act like this!

The Head Librarian blew out a long, shaken breath, sinking back into his chair behind the desk. He stared at her for a long moment, eyes disturbingly assessing. "Well, perhaps it's for the best. Really, there's no one else I trust who could do it…"

Swallowing, Rouge pushed out those seven little words. "Is there something I can help with?" Instantly, a quest prompt appeared in front of her.

Quest: "Follow the Red Brick Road" available.

The Head Librarian needs you to take a package to an old friend. You must deliver it, unopened, within one week.

Success: 5000 Experience. Another clue in your search for Duke Penbrooke. Maximum Relationship with the Head Librarian which will only be reduced if you betray his trust.

Failure: -50 Relationship points with the Head Librarian.

Accept: Yes/No?

Rouge bit her lip. What was she supposed to do? The quest didn't specify where this friend was, but the quest name implied it was somewhere outside the city. All the roads in Quarternell were made of large, flat red bricks except those inside towns and cities with more than a hundred residents. Not only did it tell you exactly where the town limits were, but if you were in a public area, standing on bluish stone, you were in a Non-Combat Zone. If the bricks were red, you could be robbed and attacked.

Was there another way to find out about Duke Penbrooke, without leaving Bright? The implication was clear that there were other people looking for him, too, and if she went around asking about him, she might run afoul of them herself. Maybe part of the reason *she* even got the quest, and not someone else, was because she had such a high relationship with the Head Librarian, so she would be more likely to go and talk to him, and he'd be more likely to give her this quest.

She sighed, frustrated and intrigued. This was exactly the sort of puzzle that made her love *Veritas Online*. You just never knew what would happen, and the game designers always seemed to be a step ahead of you. Before she could think better of it, she made her choice.

The old man continued as if nothing had happened. "I have a friend who recently moved up north. He left some things behind, and he'll need them before winter. The passes usually close due to snow any time after the next week, and few people head that way this time of year. Could you take him the package? I'm afraid it's rather personal, so even though I know you, I need to specify that it must remain unopened."

She nodded vigorously. "Of course! What village does he live in?" She and Motte had traveled to several of the nearby villages in the last few months; doing quests and earning experience. She could fast travel to any village she'd been to before, though it would cost her some gold. She could get there fairly easily even if this 'friend' lived outside of town (though few people lived outside population centers, and the protection offered by the bluestones).

Then she processed his words. "Wait, the *passes*? How far north are we talking?"

Now that the matter was settled, the geezer was relaxing into his usual absent-minded affability. He stepped back out of her personal space and began distractedly shuffling books and papers. "Oh, it's about five days past the Vargo outpost. I know you Travelers have some special methods of *travel*ing," he chuckled at his own wit, "faster than the rest of us mere mortals. I trust you can get there in time."

Rouge stared at him. "Five days north of Vargo? Vargo itself is twelve days from here, and the closest I've been is North Goose!"

The Head Librarian slapped a grubby cloth against his leg and began attempting to clean the small patches of wood that indicated there was a desk beneath the debris. "Ah, North Goose! What is it like nowadays? There's a lovely fishing hole with a waterfall there."

"It's a pig sty," she said, bluntly. "There's only five hundred people living there, and they're all about as smart as slime mold. If you rubbed two of them together, you couldn't make a spark. Motte and I went up there to catch some fish that supposedly only lives in that pond. I hate fishing, and that was the highlight of the trip. I've refused four quests that would have sent me back there because it took three days for the Stench debuff from sleeping at the inn to wear off." She took a calming breath to get her escalating voice under control. "You want me to travel a distance that takes at least two weeks in just one? Do you know how expensive that will be?!"

The gaffer grinned, thrilled. "So you do know how to do it! Wonderful! I knew you were the right choice. Now," he turned around and dug through a mountain of papers behind him, sending pages from the top of the heap fluttering down, and causing nearby outcroppings to sway precariously. Triumphantly, he pulled a good-sized box from the stack, and the things that had been set atop it *whumped* down, and then, miraculously, settled back into place, looking slightly tidier than before.

He handed her the box, and she accepted it, bemused. She felt her arms strain beneath the weight, and raised her eyebrows. Her 30 points of Strength weren't much compared to other, higher-leveled players, but for a regular NPC, most of whom hovered around the human norm in all their stats, it was akin to a candidate for Mr. Universe. If the Head Librarian's stats were that far outside the norm, it was a good indication that he really was a special or even unique NPC.

The Head Librarian nodded toward the door. "My friend's name is Aspen. He works a farm up there. Only human habitation north of the mountains, so if you follow the road, you can't miss it. Now you'd best head out, while there's still some time to pack for a long trip. Off with you, young Rouge." He waved his hand and his bushy eyebrows with equal enthusiasm.

And don't let the door hit you on the way out, she thought, wryly, as she put the box into her inventory and opened the door. By the time she crossed the threshold, the Head Librarian was buried behind his desk again, and all she could see was the slight waggling of his hat.

It took a few minutes of shell-shocked wandering to find her way back downstairs. Lisette was gone from the entry area, replaced by a harried looking young girl with cobwebs in her hair and dust on her nose. She barely acknowledged Rouge's existence, merely flapping a limp hand at the other girl as they passed each other. Rouge laughed a little, remembering being that girl herself.

Outside, the bright sunshine made her blink. It was around lunchtime, and she could smell the delicious aromas of roasted meat and grilled vegetables coming from somewhere nearby. She followed her nose to the stall of a large man selling skewers of mixed grill a block west. From there, she continued west, meat and vegetable juice dripping from her chin as she ate. One of her favorite things about Veritas was the ability to eat all you wanted of anything you could afford. There were no allergies in this world, and you couldn't gain excess weight beyond what you chose to include when you generated your avatar.

Wiping her face with her sleeve, she listened to the calls of the market as she drew nearer. This area was one of her favorites. There were several similar markets scattered throughout the city, and though each one had its own unique stalls and NPCs, the wares they sold were often indistinguishable. Every part of the city, though, did have something it did particularly well, and the stalls in the markets there would be skewed to favor those items.

This part of the city was run by the weaver's guild. Most of the shops making and selling textiles were located in the area, though a few rogue elements popped up all over. So, while the market here had its fair share of food, armor, weapons, jewelry, spices, and anything else you could wish for, a noticeable majority of the vendors sold cloth.

The city of Bright, not surprisingly, liked bright colors. So did Zoey. Rouge, being a rogue, tended toward more subtle color combinations, and had a definite inclination toward black, browns, and grays. Zoey, inside her avatar of Rouge, loved wandering through this market. Bold patterns and jewel-like colors surrounded her. Silks rippled, rainbows flew in shades from pastel to brilliant, and fabrics drifted like gauze and hung in heavy, metallic self-importance.

Rouge always felt a bit like she was crossing the Bifrost Bridge when she ventured into the Textile Market. Much like that mythological overpass, she went from being surrounded by primarily beige houses and workspaces, to the enthusiastic vitality of shop-keepers and stores. Calls of "Silk for sale!", "Finest rat on a stick in town!", and "Get your high-quality swords here!" surrounded her. Everyone vied for the attention of the passers-by, and she picked up her step as if the energy was contagious.

As usual when she entered the market, she was inundated with a flood of quests:

Quest: "Come One, Come All" available.

Visit ten shops and talk to the shopkeepers to find out what they have for sale today.

Success: 100 Experience, 5% reduction in the cost of any items you purchase within four hours after quest completion. +5 Reputation with

each shopkeeper you talk to.

Failure: None.

Accept: Yes/No?

Quest: "In for a Penny, In for a Pound" available.

Steal at least a pound of goods without getting caught.

Success: 250 Experience. +5 Reputation Increase with members of the Thieves Guild.

Failure: Jail time or fine, depending on what you were attempting to steal. -1 Reputation with all Upstanding Citizens.

Accept: Yes/No?

Quest: "If I Only Had a Heart" available.

Listen to the story of Young Jenny the Chambermaid, and carry a letter to her beloved John. Return John's response to Jenny.

Success: 175 Experience. +10 Reputation with Young Jenny the Chambermaid, 10 Gold.

Failure: -10 Reputation with Young Jenny the Chambermaid. -10 Reputation with John.

Accept: Yes/No?

These were the kinds of quests every player started with, and Rouge still did them sometimes, because they led to other much more interesting and lucrative quests surprisingly often. Today, though, she had a goal, and dismissed all the offered quests with an impatient wave.

She plowed through the crowd to a large wooden stall near the center. It was manned by a bored looking player who stood guard over the cash box and the bulletin board. Rouge grinned. "Got you again, did they, Fred? I thought you said you weren't going to take the Desk Job quest anymore?"

The player, whose tag read 'Fred the Dead', gave her a disgusted glance. "I failed the Rank Up exam again and lost rep with the guild. This sucks, but it's the fastest way to gain Guild Reputation. Next time, I'm going to go in the sewers and farm rats until I get at least two more levels. I'll pass for sure, then."

Rouge's eyebrows lifted. "Maybe you should try doing something more interesting. There's a lot to do in the game besides Guild quests and Sewer dives, you know."

He laughed scornfully. "Yeah? Off to get cats out of trees again, are you?"

She shook her head reminiscently. "That was a fun one. It was a baby gryphon, not a cat, and I got a gryphon feather out of it. Fortunately, I had a banana in my inventory left over from a quest to make a banana split, and gryphons love bananas. Easy peasy." She glanced over at the quest board. "Anybody doing Zombie runs up north?"

If you wanted your Zombie to go somewhere, you had to have either been to the place you sent it, or follow someone else there. Only an idiot would send their Zombie anywhere that wasn't designated Non-Combat without a guide. Your empty avatar wouldn't attack or defend itself, so you had to trust the person you followed to protect your Zombie until you returned. For this reason, there was quite a good market for explorers who would lead trains of Zombies to other towns or dungeons, while the Player whose avatar was being transported lived their life in the real world.

Fred the Dead shook his head, the long orange plume of his ridiculous floppy hat falling into his eye. He puffed it away before answering. "I think everybody's out right now. Doom Bloom is probably up in Bloodhaven. She loves that place." He made a disgusted face. "PvPers are crazy."

Rouge had to agree with that, to some extent. One of the advancement options of her own class, Rogue, was Assassin. A *lot* of people who preferred Player vs Player combat took Assassin, thanks to its boosts in both [Stealth] and attack.

She was hoping to find a unique class option by playing differently than those guys did. According to the game manual, there were still a lot of Classes no one had unlocked yet, and Rouge wanted one so badly it hurt. As a result, she had never fought a single duel or engaged in PvP. It just wasn't fun to hurt people or be hurt. She was going to stick with character quests and farming respawn mobs, and find out what class lay at the end of her own path.

She sighed. "I was hoping to find someone starting from North Goose, since that's the furthest I've been. I guess I'll have to fast travel up there, hike to Bloodhaven, and then see if I can hire someone. Do you have any quests from Goose to Bloodhaven so I can make a little money while I'm at it? I'm kinda low on funds."

His eyes shifted up and he absent-mindedly blew the feather away again. "Got a fetch quest for 20 Umber Rabbit Teeth, but you'd want to be at least level 30 for that. You're still Copper Rank, right? You can't take that one anyway, then. Hmm." His eyes flickered as he scrolled through the quests available. "Here we go! Right up your alley, too, with the weird quests you like." He flicked a wrist at her, and a parchment unrolled in her vision.

Quest: "Solomon's Temple" available.

Solomon the Salesman died in North Goose after an ill-fated incident involving a meat cleaver and a party trick. Solomon's body was returned to his son in Bloodhaven, but unfortunately his head was misplaced when the other parts were packed. Take Solomon's head to Bloodhaven so that he can have an open casket funeral. *Timed quest: Must be completed before 5 tomorrow night.*

Success: 500 Experience, 100 Gold. +10 Reputation with Solomon's family. A Body Bag.

Failure: -30 Reputation with Solomon's family.

Accept: Yes/No?

"What's a Body Bag?" She squinted at the item name.

Fred the Dead shrugged. "Dunno. Juvie-Record was thinking about taking the quest, but when he looked the bag up, it didn't appear on any of the item lists. It's a pretty lame quest, otherwise, so no one's willing to take it for an unknown item. No way it's going to be worthwhile."

Rouge rubbed her chin. "I dunno. I could use the money, and I'm going that way anyway. Might as well. I'll take it." She selected Yes with a twitch of her finger, and it was added to her list of current quests.

The other player grinned. "Hey, thanks. Selling that one got me another Reputation point. I only need five more before I can go level."

She threw him a thumb's-up. "No problem, man. Now, can you hook me up with a Fast Travel to North Goose? Might as well get this show on the road."

He nodded and pointed to the ring of standing stones behind him. "That'll be two hundred gold."

She nearly choked. "It was fifty last time!"

"Oooo. Did you break level twenty?"

She nodded, puzzled.

"You're not a newbie anymore. After level twenty, you're supposed to have the dosh or be able to fight your way to where you're going. Be glad it's not Bloodhaven. Costs five hundred to go there." His voice was unsympathetic.

Rouge ground her teeth and initiated a trade with the till. That was the big downside to her way of playing; getting stolen dolls back for little girls generally didn't pay well. Fortunately, Motte had a fair amount of money, and he'd given her some in case she needed something. Gold wasn't super easy to get in Veritas, but a focused player could grind out a thousand a week starting at a fairly low level.

Fred completed the trade, and the stones began to swirl with color behind him. "Have a good trip!" His voice was annoyingly cheerful, and she grimaced as she headed through the portal.

Time to go get a head.

🦆 🦆 🦆

Acquiring the head was surprisingly simple. When she appeared in the Stone Circle in North Goose, the Guild representative there (an NPC hired by the guild because no player was willing to hang out in a muddy field surrounded by the Aroma of North Goose) handed her a bag with the head in it. Apparently, it was just waiting for whatever idiot had accepted the quest. Judging by the stench coming from the bag, no effort had been made to preserve poor Solomon, so the chances of that open casket funeral weren't smelling good.

There was no point hanging out in Goose, so she whistled for Blackie, and…

Oh. No.

No Blackie. She'd left him behind to recover from his traumatic abandonment, and she'd been so excited to get going that she'd completely forgotten she'd need him. Now what? She glanced over at the Guild rep, her fingers still in her mouth from the sharp whistle the game used to call mounts. They would come from anywhere to find their masters…as long as they had a high enough Relationship. Which Blackie most definitely did not.

The Guild representative was staring at her with his mouth hanging open. This was actually fairly normal for a basic NPC, because no matter how awesome *Veritas'* software and hardware was, there was a limit to the amount of processing power available. When players weren't around, timers ticked down, but nobody was 'home'. When a player did show up, the system then retconned anything that was needed for the current situation. Since Rouge wasn't talking to the guy, and he was just an extra, he probably had about as much processing power as the average planaria.

Still, the drool was taking it a bit too far, and she could tell from here that he was missing more teeth than he had left. She coughed, and leaned hard on a real-life skill learned by every kid ever in the history of the universe: [I Meant to Do That]. Withdrawing her fingers from her mouth, Rouge caught a few stray curls in her damp grasp and smoothed them down. She smiled disarmingly. "Uh, do you have any mounts for sale or rent in town?"

The man dug his pinky into his filthy ear as if he couldn't believe he'd heard her right. "Ah, nope. Not any as you'd care for, anywho." He stuck the finger in his mouth, and she shuddered.

Rouge served up a smile so fake it trembled. "No, really. I'm not that picky. My horse, um, got sick. I can't ride him, and I need to get to Bloodhaven." She thought longingly of the 20% speed increase she'd had on Blackie when he had 63 Relationship points. She swore (not for the first time, but definitely for the last) that she would Never Again log out without setting her Away instructions.

When she saw his muddy eyes flicker, she continued, cajoling, "Really. I'd ride a pig, if it would take me to Bloodhaven." The moment she said it, she knew it was a mistake. This was a pig farming town. They probably really had riding pigs here. If she showed up at Bloodhaven on a pig, she'd never live it down!

The scrawny man seemed to choke, then spat a stream of viscous goo onto the ground. "Terrible thing to do ter a pig, that'd be. Pigs is fer eatin', not ridin'." His voice was cold.

"Oh!" She laughed, ignoring the hysterical edge to it. "I was just joking, of course! No pig riding, no sirree! I meant, I would ride a…" she cast about wildly for an idea. Elephant? Donkey? "Ostrich! I would ride an ostrich!"

Quest: "Ostrich-sized" available.

A few years ago a young farmer in North Goose decided to try spreading his wings and try something new. He acquired several ostrich eggs from a traveling salesman, and hatched his own flock. The other farmers around him didn't appreciate his attempt to diversify, and ostracized him. The father of the young woman he was planning to marry told him that he'd never give her away to a glorified chicken rancher. The young farmer swore to sell the ostriches and buy a stake in his father-in-law's piggery with the funds, but he has been unable to sell the last remaining male. In a last-ditch attempt, he trained the creature to be a mount, but no one wanted to ride a cock. Go and buy the ostrich so that the farmer can finally marry his sweetheart.

Success: 500 Experience. A new mount. +30 Relationship with Struthio. +30 Relationship with Millie. -20 Relationship with Millie's Pa.

Failure: Walk to Bloodhaven.

Accept: Yes/No?

Rouge was already selecting Yes before she could even finish reading. This was exactly the sort of quest she loved. Who came up with this stuff? How did they know? Was there really some algorithm that just knew someone would someday need an ostrich in North Goose, or was the whole thing spawned in an instant just for her? She could barely stop herself from snickering.

The man scratched at his greasy brown hair. "Well, there's young Struthio down the road a bit. He's out on the edge a town, so I reckon you'll go right past 'im anyway. Might could be he'd have an ostrich left. Just look fer the big sign with a pitcher of a bird on't."

"Yes! Okay, thanks, bye!" Rouge waved and flashed the brightest smile she could manage with the stench of the pig sties surrounding her seeping into her sinuses. Turning, she ran away as quickly as her feet would carry her.

It was good that she'd been in North Goose with Motte not too long ago, because one pig farm looks pretty much like another. Fortunately, she recognized a lightning blasted tree stump that led her to the inn. From there, she could make her way along the road out of town. With the grunts of the pigs and the squeals of the townsfolk (or was it the other way around?) behind her, she made quick time toward the ostrich farm.

It took about twenty minutes to find the crudely painted sign of an ostrich. Struthio really had been relegated to the very outskirts of town. The farmer had even made an attempt at rudimentary writing. "Ostrik fr sal. Chep." Cheap was good. The Zombie run north was going to cost her pretty much everything she had left, so she needed to convince this Struthio to sell her the animal for next to nothing.

She took a deep breath, promptly regretted it, and walked past the sign.

"Hello? Struthio?" She tried to keep her voice as light and friendly as possible.

From the small, dingy barn came a disconsolate voice. "A-yup. That's me."

Rouge strained her eyes against the shadows. Her [Darkvision] worked best when she herself was in darkness, so she could barely make out a round form camouflaged against the weathered wood.

"Um." She suddenly realized she hadn't bothered to get the hired Guild rep's name. "Someone told me you might have a mount for sale-"

Struthio was big. Huge. He had to be at least as tall and wide as Motte, but most of it was fat. He jiggled when he walked. He bounced with each step, as though a wave machine had set off a motion in a tidal pool. He held a cinnamon roll in one hand, and a muffin in the other. His mouth was full, and his eyes were nearly lost in folds of flesh.

"Ah oo!" Crumbs sprayed from his mouth in his enthusiasm. He gulped down his mouthful. "I do! Got an ostrich! Trained 'im real good until, well," he motioned to himself, causing another seismic movement. "Guess mebbe I got a little too big for 'im."

Rouge winced at the thought of this man attempting to ride anything smaller than an elephant, and she had a suspicion the elephant wouldn't be too pleased with the situation either.

"Could I see him? How much are you asking?" She fought to keep her eyes on the area of his face where his must be. He grew larger and larger the nearer he drew to herm and she noticed a strange thing. The scent of pig, and pig byproducts, was gone. It was replaced by the mouth-watering smell of cinnamon and yeasty bread.

The door of the little house nearby creaked open, and a shining blonde female head popped out. "Who is't, Struthio?" A tall, powerful woman, arms bulging with muscle, stepped out into the sunshine. The cinnamon smell intensified. Rouge could see that the woman was wiping her hands on a clean dish towel, and flour was coating the front of her apron. The lovely Amazon looked at Rouge with a wary expression.

Struthio's face creased as he looked at her. It was hard to tell, but the expression seemed to be one of sheer adoration. "Millie, this girl wants ter buy Codswallop!"

Millie's face instantly relaxed into a broad smile. "Yer do? Yer one o' them

Traveler's, ent ya? Guess ya don't care 'bout what kinda creature ya ride, eh? Yer jest a wee slip of a thing though, eh? Can ya afford 'im?"

A chill ran down Rouge's back. "Uh, yes? Probably? How much is he?"

The two adults exchanged looks, and Millie's face fell. "Well, that's a'right. Mebbe someone else'll come buy 'im. I know Pa said he'd marry me to Rubico if'n you couldn't buy 'im out soon, but…"

Struthio shoved the rest of the roll and half the muffin into his mouth, and tears trickled silently out of the slits of his eyes. Millie rushed over to him and patted at his cheeks with her dish towel. The woman looked over her shoulder at Rouge and stage whispered, "'E's a bit o' a stress eater."

Rouge could only nod in understanding as the man continued to eat, and the brawny blonde continued to soothe him. Finally, all the food was gone, and Struthio was sobbing pitifully into Millie's broad shoulder as she patted his back.

"Um," Rouge ventured. "How much is," she gulped, "Codswallop?"

"It's all right, lass." Millie smiled sadly, "Twenty gold is far too much for the overgrown chicken, but it's what we need t' buy out m'Pa so we can wed. A' this point, we'd give the bird t'ya fer free, but…"

Rouge reached into her pouch and took out twenty gold. She held out the coins.

Both adults froze. Then, slowly, Struthio reached out his massive sausage-like fingers and accepted the coins.

Quest: "Ostrich-sized" complete.

Success: 500 Experience. A new mount. +30 Relationship with Struthio. +30 Relationship with Millie. -20 Relationship with Millie's Pa.

It took only a few more minutes to complete the details of the transaction. Then Struthio whistled sharply, and a large bird raced in from a field nearby. Codswallop was a handsome fellow, with dense black and white feathers and intelligent eyes in his large-beaked face. He scratched at the ground with his two-toed foot when Struthio hugged him, but seemed only curious when ownership was officially transferred.

Rouge checked the big bird's stat sheet:

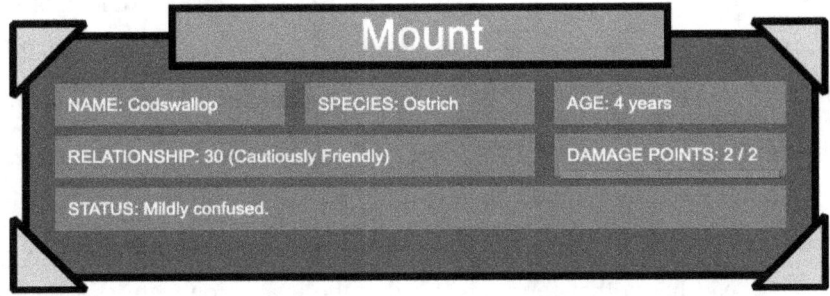

Mount

NAME: Codswallop	SPECIES: Ostrich	AGE: 4 years
RELATIONSHIP: 30 (Cautiously Friendly)		DAMAGE POINTS: 2 / 2
STATUS: Mildly confused.		

Millie insisted on giving Rouge Codswallop's small racing saddle at no extra charge, and the girl was grateful, because she hadn't even thought about how she was supposed to ride a giant bird. Then the newly engaged couple threw in a dozen fluffy cinnamon rolls that were still warm from the oven and smelled delectable. Rouge's mouth was watering so much by the time she took her leave of the happy couple that she could barely speak.

Struthio was ripping down the "Ostrik fr sal" sign as she left, leading the surprisingly calm bird by a small harness attached to his neck. Codswallop seemed far more interested in the cinnamon roll she held than in the fact that he was leaving the only home he had ever known. As for Rouge, she was concentrating on the stones beneath her feet and keeping the bird's beak away from her bready treasure.

It was only a short way past Struthio's farm that the bluish stones of the road ended, marking the official edge of North Goose. Once she stepped onto the red bricks beyond, she could be attacked, robbed, or even killed with no warning and, honestly, little chance to defend herself. Nonetheless, this was still a relatively easy area, and the creatures nearby should be fairly low level, and not very aggressive. As long as she was careful and stayed on the road it was unlikely she'd have too much trouble, especially with the 15% reduction in aggro she gained from riding. No, she was far more concerned about larger predators: humans.

Bloodhaven was a 'free trade' city. No taxes were levied by the crown for goods exchanged there, though they were taxed crossing all other political boundaries in Quarternell. As a result, the crown had declared that it wouldn't pay for the niceties that could be found in Bright, such as well-maintained public spaces and law enforcement.

What this boiled down to was that the government didn't interfere within Bloodhaven's walls. Legal, properly declared goods were taxed going in or out, but Rouge had heard that for a small bribe, the inspection stations would let almost anything slide, so almost anything could be found in the Free City. If someone had a problem, disputes were handled by those concerned either personally or using a hired third party. Bloodhaven was the only city anyone knew of that had no bluestones.

For players, this meant that Bloodhaven was the only place where they could engage in PvP within city limits. Most players who only wanted to play by their own rules played in and around Bloodhaven, and there were often more players than NPCs there, especially since no one blinked when murder was committed unless the victim had business partners or family who sought vengeance.

Motte had told Rouge that she wasn't to go there. Technically (very technically) she wasn't going to break her promise. The Guild board was just *outside* the southern gate. She didn't need to set foot inside, so long as she could turn in Solomon's Head and post her Zombie Escort quest. The area around the board was relatively safe, since the Non-Combat Zone around all Player's Guild locations was still in effect.

The large safe zone around the Guild was there to prevent spawn camping. Spawn camping was when PvP players lurked near an area where new or recently resurrected characters appeared, specifically so they could kill and rob them. As long as Rouge could make it there, she would be safe until she could find an escort.

All of which left one large stumbling block to her cunning plan: getting to

Bloodhaven without being robbed or murdered. Because Pkers and other less savory sorts loved Bloodhaven, they stalked the area surrounding the city. If you couldn't pay them, you'd better be able to beat them. It would be better if she could [Sneak] all the way there, but at her level, she had to walk and stay in shadows, and that could take days. It would be best if she could ride straight there without even seeing anyone else, but the odds of that happening were miniscule.

Absently, she ate a cinnamon roll as she pondered her options. Her eyes shot wide as she finished the last bite.

You have eaten a *Cinnamon Roll* created with Excellent ingredients by a Master Chef! You have gained +10 to all stats for the next 30 minutes. You feel invigorated!Your Stamina recovery has doubled for 30 minutes! Your speed has doubled for 30 minutes!

She stared at the sticky sugar glaze left on her fingers. Oh yes. Yes, this could work.

After licking her fingers clean, she vaulted into Codswallop's tiny saddle. Removing a cinnamon roll from her inventory, she held it out.

"Here you go, Wally. Let's see how fast you can run."

It turned out that an ostrich on cinnamon buns could run really, really fast.

🐦 🐦 🐦

Rouge burned through another six cinnamon rolls over the next three hours. She found out that she could, indeed, take damage from the Blistered debuff caused by the saddle and the not-rider-friendly way an ostrich runs. She also discovered that ostriches could jump very high.

The first attack came over an hour after they left North Goose. It was very sudden, with three players leaping out in front of Rouge as she and Codswallop raced along the road. Without breaking stride or receiving any input from Rouge, Codswallop simply leapt over their heads. As they nearly flew over the two men and one woman, Rouge took a video capture of the gobsmacked look on their faces and let out a triumphant whoop. That was when she got the quest.

Quest: "Jumping to Conclusions" available.

Reach Bloodhaven. You must stay on the road. You cannot stop. You must jump over any obstacle in your path.

Success: Codswallop's [Jump] Skill will become 10% more effective.

Failure: None.

Accept: Yes/No?

She accepted the quest without a second thought, grinning like a loon. Best. Quest. Ever.

Fortunately, Player Killers rarely played well with others, so the next three attacks were by single players. She captured images of their faces, too, as she and her Mighty Riding Ostrich sailed over their heads. The third attacker was an Archer class of some kind, but he couldn't have been much higher level than her, because Codswallop zigged, zagged, and leapt, and only one arrow clipped her thigh. She lost 17 hitpoints to that one, but they were past and running faster than anyone not hopped up on sugar and carbs could go.

They dodged, leapt, and hurdled a total of seven attacks; five by players, and two by large, aggressive mobs. Other than the one arrow, nothing else posed any real danger. Her cinnamon roll count was down to four by the time the looming southern gate of Bloodhaven came into view. The clock was ticking down on whether or not she'd have to feed another one to Codswallop to renew the buff, and she whooped with joy when she saw the stone circle with the familiar bulletin board and desk nearby.

Then, as she crested a small hill, she saw the line. Of course there was a line. People had to declare their goods before going into the city, and pay whatever bribes the guards decided to levy. It took time for all those wagons, mounts, and carriages to be searched. The road was completely blocked for a good quarter mile before the gate.

The quest said she couldn't stop. She couldn't go around. She had to *stay on the road*. So there was really only one option. She reached back, and with a muttered apology, plucked a single feather from Codswallop's fluffy black and white tail. The bird opened his beak and squawked with righteous indignation before putting on a burst of speed and leaping with all his might, desperate to escape whatever had caused so much pain to his rump.

His first foot came down on the head of a blonde woman on a white horse. She screeched. The second foot pushed off of the top of a covered wagon. Then a heavily laden pack, the back of a cart filled with barrels, the rear of an armored steed… On and on they went. They were followed by curses, bellowed threats, and thrown stones (among less pleasant things).

All she could do was shout, "It's a queeeeeest!"

At last, with a final push from the bustle of a dour matron's dress, Codswallop vaulted forward, ran three feet straight up the wall above the gate, and flipped over in midair. Rouge, who was barely clinging to the saddle at this point, felt herself slip away completely, and only [Acrobatics] allowed her to use the bird's momentum to change her own trajectory.

Codswallop landed on the ground, swayed, turned in a circle, and fell down, his long neck lying straight out in the dust. The rogue came down beside him, legs bent, one hand reaching down to stabilize her landing.

Quest: "Jumping to Conclusions" complete.

Mount *Codswallop's* [Jump] Skill is 10% more effective.

Immediately after the notification came another one:

Your [Acrobatics] Skill has increased by one. It is now level 15.

There was a moment of silence, which was then broken by catcalls and spatters of applause (mostly from those who hadn't been stepped on), and Rouge felt her face burn red. She wasn't really the type that was comfortable as the center of attention. Nonetheless, she stood and made a sweeping bow, only slightly unsteady on her feet.

Turning, she knelt by her exhausted mount. Stroking his head, she murmured to him until one billiard-ball-sized eye blinked open and he peered up at her. A surprisingly cute interrogatory chirruping noise came from his beak, and she patted his neck. "I'm really sorry, Wally. Are you okay?"

The ostrich ululated feebly, and struggled to his feet, his bedraggled little wings hanging tiredly at his sides. He shook his whole body, fluffing as dust and feather fronds drifted away in the wind.

A voice came from behind her. "Where'd you get an ostrich? That's so cool!"

Rouge spun, her hand falling to the hilt of her knife. Codswallop hissed, his neck snaking out over her shoulder. As a riding mount, he couldn't actually participate in battle, but he certainly looked fierce.

The player stepped back, holding up his hands. An ingratiating smile stretched his lips, but didn't touch his eyes. "Hey, no trouble here! I've just never seen any kind of bird mount before. Almost everybody has some kind of horse, and I was wondering if there was some quest chain or something that got you an ostrich. I'll pay for the info." He mimed reaching toward the small money pouch hanging from his belt.

She narrowed her eyes, examining him. The tag above his head read 'Lamer65: Level 38'. He wore basic boiled leather armor and a longsword. His hair was dirty blonde, his eyes hazel, and he looked like he wasn't much older than she was, though he was quite a bit taller.

She shrugged and gave him back a smile as insincere as the one he'd offered her. She wasn't in the Guild enclosure yet, and she wasn't going to trust anyone. If she died now, she'd have to come all the way back here from Bright, and she desperately needed every gold she had to pay her escort. "It was a unique quest. I had to say just the right thing, and there was only one ostrich left. There may be more somewhere though, because they mentioned a traveling salesman with ostrich eggs."

She took a step back and to the side. One step closer to safety.

Lamer65's mouth twisted. "C'mon. It's no big deal. Is he a legit mount? Where did you get him? He's really fast!"

Another step. The boy's eyes flickered behind her, and she heard a warning hiss from Codswallop just in time to drop and roll beneath a sword that flashed through the space recently occupied by her neck. She threw a knife at Lamer, who really was lame, and he grunted as it sank into his arm.

You have dealt 41 points of damage to Player *Lamer65*.

The tall boy yanked the knife from his arm and it vanished into his inventory. He didn't even wince, so his pain threshold was set pretty low (probably at the minimum required for minors, like Rouge's). He also didn't bleed much or stagger, which was a bad sign. He was seventeen levels higher than Rouge, and had obviously pumped a lot of points into Endurance.

She cast [Poof!] and the heavy cloud billowed around her. Even as the players attacking her began to swing wildly and cough from the Smoke Inhalation debuff (to which she was thankfully immune) she grabbed Codswallop's bridle and tugged him toward the Stone Circle. Unfortunately, her attackers knew she had to go that way, and even though they couldn't see, their swings began to close in on her when she was only a few feet from her goal.

Her passive racial [Darkvision] kicked in as she dodged through the heavy gloom of the smoke, and she ducked a sword blow that probably would have incapacitated her. She briefly debated using [Stealth], but again, she only had one way to go, and she had to take Wally with her. She was already committed, so she moved quickly, knowing the smoke cloud would begin dissipating at any moment.

At the last possible moment, she caught a hint of movement ahead of her. A sword was swinging away from her, and the player's back was toward her. She had almost run straight into him in the darkness. Without hesitation, she pulled a second knife from her inventory and used Codswallop's strong back as a springboard to launch herself onto the PKer's shoulders. She grabbed his hair with one hand and swung the blade with the other, triggering [Backstab]. It was only level 2, but she was behind him, he was disoriented, and they were in darkness.

CRITICAL! You have dealt 212 points of damage to Player *Dorkness*

Rising. You have slain player *Dorkness Rising*.

You are now level 21.

You have gained one level of [Backstab]. It is now level 3.

Catapulting from the shoulders of her victim, she rolled out of the fading cloud and into the safe zone around the Guild desk. As the last wisps of [Poof!] vanished, she saw a crumpled form on the ground. Lamer65 kicked his partner's corpse in the ribs, hissing through his teeth. "You suck, Dork."

He looked over at Rouge and bared his teeth. "Hey, can't blame a guy for trying. I don't know what a level 20 is doing here, but you're dead as soon as you come out of there. You're like a little raw steak wandering around mooing for someone to eat you." He sheathed his sword and shrugged. "Won't be me, though. I have better things to do than wait for you. So long, itty bitty snack." He waved a hand at her and returned to his place in line.

Rouge looked at the body on the ground. *Veritas* was very realistic, and she couldn't deny she felt a little bit queasy. This was the first player she'd ever killed. Still, she knew she should go and loot the corpse. He was unlikely to drop anything but gold, since items currently worn by the player and anything inside their primary inventory couldn't be lost, but it was possible he was carrying something in his pack, if his inventory was full. Besides, he'd almost definitely drop some money, and she could certainly use it. She knew, though, that for all she couldn't see Lamer65 anymore, he or someone else was just waiting for her to step foot outside the safe circle around the Player's Guild.

Finally, she heaved a sigh and closed her eyes, turning her face up toward the sun. It just wasn't worth it. He'd have to lie there until his corpse faded in 24 hours. At least she'd gotten a level! She pulled up her character sheet and distributed the points.

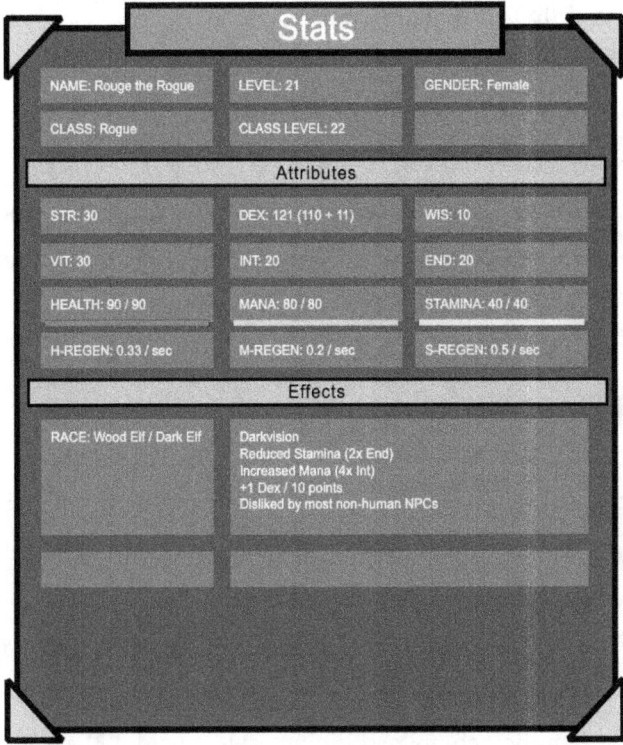

She looked at all the round numbers in satisfaction. She knew Motte would tease her about it, but honestly, until she knew what her advanced class was going to be, there was no way to know how she should distribute her stats. She didn't want to be a Thief, Assassin, or Burglar, which were the most common classes taken by Rogues. A few players had been offered a Pirate class, but that required a ship, and she would never be able to keep a straight face if she had to tell someone to walk the plank.

She flicked away the sheet, and looked up. A few people were standing around, but none of them were paying any attention to her. Apparently, the fight and her ostrich weren't enough to hold the interest of these battle-hardened players. All for the best, because she really didn't have time to talk to anybody.

Quickly, she walked over to the desk, Codswallop trailing after her like a puppy. There were several people already standing near the desk, but she opened a trade with the till and dropped the bag with Solomon's head into the trade list. As soon as she selected "Offer Complete" and locked in the trade, text popped up in front of her.

Quest: "Solomon's Temple" complete.

Solomon's head has been returned in time for the funeral. Unfortunately, it's a little too far gone for an open casket, but his family is glad to have a complete set of parts nonetheless.

Success: 500 Experience, 100 Gold. +10 Reputation with Solomon's family. A Body Bag.

The Body Bag and 100 Gold appeared in the till's side of the trade box, and Rouge accepted the trade. She opened up her inventory and looked at the item.

Body Bag – **This item can hold any number of bodies and body parts. It will only take up one slot in your inventory.**

She whistled silently. That was a pretty good item! Each player got a personal Inventory (affectionately nicknamed 'Bag of Holding' by old people like her dad) when they completed the tutorial. It held 200 stacks of up to 99 identical items, and items inside could not be stolen or dropped. That seemed like a lot, until you realized that you could *only* carry two hundred different things.

You could easily get more than 99 of some low-level item during a dungeon or farming run, and end up filling your whole Bag with Sticks and Tattered Fur. Then, when you got something cool like a unique weapon or some high-quality cinnamon rolls, you had to do major inventory management to keep them safe. You could always buy other containers, such as a belt pouch or backpack, but any items outside of your primary Inventory could be lost, whether through carelessness or nefarious intent.

Almost every player carried an extra bag or two to keep the not-quite-junk items they planned to sell, or that they hoped might be needed for a quest or crafting eventually. After a while of not dying, though, players got cocky and tired of the constant inventory management. Anyone who didn't 'plan' to die probably kept some good things on their person. That plus the fact that up to 10% of any gold they carried could drop upon death kept the PvPers going strong.

Of course, the smart thing to do was to keep everything you didn't need in the bank, but only Bright and Bloodhaven even had banks. Few players could be bothered to go to the bank until they were overloaded with items. Plus, the basic bank account only held 100 stacks of up to 99, and a lot of the things you liked enough to squirrel away were rare, and didn't stack. That meant you only had a little over a hundred items in the bank. You could buy more bank space, but it was expensive.

Which was where the Body Bag came in. It would only take one slot in her Inventory, and it would hold any amount of body parts. Kind of gross, but... She dug through her inventory, quickly dumping Frog Eyeballs, Fly Wings, Tattered Fur, Pig Trotters, and twenty-three other random items into the bag. Then she put the Body Bag into her Bag of Holding and, voila! She now had almost thirty more slots of empty space!

Grinning, she turned to the bulletin board. Now to hope she'd get lucky and find a Zombie Run. She started scanning through the notices, but quickly realized that this board was even busier than the one in Bright. Even as she watched, notices went up and down before she could read them. She pulled up the search feature and typed in "Zombie".

It turned out there were a few Runs headed out in the next day or so, but there were none going north. It made sense. The only decent-sized settlement to the north was Vargo, and as a military outpost, they mostly only worked with military vendors and official sources. Only players opting for a military class would have any reason to go there. She kicked the dirt in frustration, and Codswallop laid his head on her shoulder in commiseration. She scrootched his soft feathers and felt a little better.

Taking a deep breath, she searched for 'Corpse'. It was a longshot. When the game first started, some people called the guiding of Away players 'Corpse

Runs'. Apparently, that was gamer speak from when people played some hard-core games where when you died you dropped everything, and then you had to go back and retrieve it. It sounded sucky to her, and she was glad games weren't like that anymore. Anyway, it confused people, and newer players liked the term 'Zombie Run' instead. But there were always a few die-hards who refused to change their ways…

"Ah ha!" Two players nearby cast her annoyed glances, and she flushed. She shrugged apologetically, turning back to the board.

Corpse Run: I'm headed to Vargo for a quest. I can take two Corpses with me. I'm leaving at 6pm local tonight. You pay 2,500 Gold. One way only. Meet me at the Dead Tent. Doom Bloom

She glanced at the in-game clock. It was just after five. Perfect! Now she just had to fortify herself for the inevitable disdain she was going to face soon. She slapped her cheeks bracingly. With an almost imperceptible gesture, she tagged the notice as accepted, and paid her 2,500 Gold. That left her with just little more than a hundred Gold to her name. Thank goodness for Solomon's untimely demise!

The Dead Tent was where most players spent their Away time, especially in a dangerous area like this one. You could always try hiding in a tree, under a bush, or in a cave, or you could use one of several items that let you set up a safe camp for a set amount of time. If mobs or players found you outside of a camp item or a Non-Combat Zone, they could kill you.

Stumbling over a sleeping Zombie wouldn't aggro a passive creature, but an aggressive mob could take down even a high-level player through sheer persistence. Zombies didn't dodge, defend, or use any combat skills, even passive ones. Once injured, they wouldn't recover damage received while the player was Away. They couldn't enter dungeons or instances, and would be ejected if the player logged out while they were inside. They were essentially completely helpless.

A Zombie escort would defend the avatar of a logged-out player, and if the avatar was damaged, they could use special heal skills or items on them. A Tent protected them from attack by mobs or players. A Sleeping Bag concealed them from mobs, but not players. A Non-Combat Zone like that around the Guild, including the Dead Tent, kept avatars safe from all attacks by anyone.

If you were too far from an NCZ, had no Tent or Sleeping Bag, and couldn't afford an escort, you either took your chances in a tree or you found the nearest Guild Circle and the Dead Tent. The Tent provided a unique instance for every player or group of players that went inside. For a nominal fee, your Zombie would stay there until you logged back in, and it was pretty comfortable, with a large bed and soft blankets, so you even got your Well-Rested buff. Players in and near Bloodhaven, which was the only large settlement that was not an NCZ, stayed in the Dead Tent more often than not.

Rouge was getting pretty tired. She'd had a very long day at school and at home, and had now spent almost three hours of real time in the game. That was a long six-hour shift of running from one place to another just in order to get here. Only another half hour or so and she could log out and go to bed.

Codswallop settled down in the dust nearby. He fluffed his feathers and scratched in the dirt a little bit, creating a dust bowl for his soft body. After a moment, Rouge sat down beside him. She leaned against his side, sheltered beneath his wing, and closed her eyes.

About twenty minutes later, she felt a toe nudge her side.

"Hey." The voice was feminine, and the tone was neutral.

She cracked open her eyes and looked up into the bright blue eyes staring down at her. A pale face set in a noncommittal expression was surrounded by a halo of golden hair, backlit by the sun. "Oh, hey, 'sis'. Guess who needs an escort."

Doom Bloom glowered down at Rouge, looking like someone who just found half a worm in their apple. "I couldn't believe it when I saw that stupid nickname on my group list." She looked around suspiciously. "Where's your dad?"

Rouge shrugged. "I'm on my own this time. Dad's busy grading tests. I was surprised to see your post, actually. I figured you'd be taking finals, too."

The older girl shrugged. "Different college. Our finals are in two weeks."

Nodding, Rouge smoothly jumped to her feet and brushed off her rear. "So... How's Mom?"

"Now you care?" Doom's voice was ice cold.

Rouge sighed and tugged at a curl of hair. Glancing to the side, she said softly, "Yeah. I've always cared. I'm not the one who decided to move to the other side of the country."

"No, but you *are* the one who decided to stay full time with your dad instead of going with us. You haven't even visited in years."

Rouge looked up and met the judgemental blue eyes. She smiled ruefully. "And you were glad I did, right, Lily? You didn't exactly like sharing. You thought you were going to get a mom who was completely devoted to you, and I was supposed to be a cute part-time little sister who'd let you tie bows in her hair. I wasn't really part of your happy little family, was I? All I did was 'ruin everything!'" Rouge looked straight into Doom's eyes, daring her to deny the accusation.

Doom's gaze fell first. "Whatever. Think what you want," she muttered. "So how are we doing this?"

Rouge ticked a shoulder up. "The same way you always do it, I guess. I'll set my Zombie to follow you, and then you escort me up to Vargo and leave me at the Dead Tent or in a Non-Combat Zone. I'll set my Away to take care of Wally here after that." She hitched a thumb at the ostrich, who loomed tall and disapproving behind her shoulder. The bird's brown eyes were fixed suspiciously on Doom Bloom.

Doom Bloom nodded. "Fine. Put on your heaviest gear, so you have better defense if we get attacked. I'll take you half-way before bed tonight, set up a Tent, then finish the other half tomorrow before my afternoon class. You'll be up there by tomorrow night, real time. Set a notification. I have my own quest to do, so I'm not going to hang out and wait for you to log in."

The pretty blonde looked away, cheeks pinkening slightly. "You'll be okay, right? I mean, you have a plan? That area isn't for newbies. Don't set your respawn up there and get stuck. You better have a quest in the outpost, or you should wait for Motte."

Rouge's eyebrows shot up. She had honestly expected her step-sister to be more than glad to abandon her and go on her way. That's if she didn't 'accidentally' drop Rouge's avatar right outside the NCZ. Her own voice was a little uncertain when she answered. "Yeah. I'll be fine. I'm just going to talk to an NPC." *An NPC who lives a minimum of three days to the north, but yeah.*

Doom coughed slightly, hand covering her mouth until her face returned to the neutral expression she usually adopted in game. Doom Bloom was level 121, a veteran player, and she was well-known enough to have a reputation for being tough and steady under fire. "Good. Now, we just need to wait for our other Corpse, and we're ready to go. They only have five minutes left to get here, or we leave without them. Get your travel gear on and set your Away Instructions."

Rouge nodded silent understanding. She squinted her eyes untilher interface snapped into focus, and pulled up the Away Instructions screen with a flick of her fingers.

- **Follow Player *Doom Bloom* until arrival in Vargo/Vargo's Dead Tent.**
- **Secure a stall and food for Mount *Codswallop*.**
- **Return to Vargo Dead Tent.**
- **Rent Vargo Dead Tent until log-in.**
- **Send notification <u>Tasks Done</u> to @RougeTheRogue**

When she completed the commands, the game sent a request to Doom Bloom to allow Rouge the Rogue to follow her. Doom selected yes, and a green check mark appeared next to the first command.

Rouge then dug into her inventory, looking for the equipment with the highest Defense. Usually she went for light to medium armor, mostly cloth, since that allowed her the best movement speed. She did have a few pieces of heavier armor that she'd stolen and hadn't sold or offered to Motte yet. She pulled up a stylized image of her avatar and slotted a heavy pot helm on her head, chain mail on her torso, heavy greaves on her thighs, and knee-high boiled leather boots on the feet. Her gloves were just her usual leather ones, but she did strap on a small shield to give her midsection a little more protection.

When she was done, she looked like some kind of armored hermit crab. None of her pieces matched in either quality or style, but at least they increased her Defense by 23 points. She looked over at Codswallop and wished she had some armored gear for him, but really his best defense was his ability to jump and dodge. The weight of her armor would slow him down enough.

Doom Bloom looked over at Rouge, and her eyes widened. Rouge almost thought she heard her stoic step-sister snicker, but if there was a twitch at the corner of the full pink lips, it didn't last long. Rouge glared, daring the other girl to comment.

Doom just shrugged. "Better than nothing." Her blue eyes flicked to their right, going distant for a moment as she read a notification Rouge couldn't see. "He's here. Get ready."

Rouge turned around just in time to see a very short, very wide player come bustling up. He was bristling with weapons: there was an axe strapped across his back, a bandolier of knives across his chest, and a small crossbow attached to his belt, along with a quarrel of short bolts. When she squinted, the tag above his head read "Weapon Shortage: Level 87".

The Dwarf stuck out a massive hand. "Sorry for being late. Had to finish up a trade. I'm a weapons dealer. Go by Wep. Don't call me Shorty unless you have a respawn point nearby." He mock-glared, but the genial twinkle in his eye said he wasn't too serious about it.

Doom Bloom ignored the hand, but Rouge shook it, feeling the thick calluses, especially across the palm and fingers of his hand. Definitely a crafter or fighter, as well as a merchant. It was really neat how *Veritas* picked up on that kind of thing. Every avatar was truly unique and customized, intentionally or otherwise. "Nice to meet you. I'm Rouge."

Warm brown eyes glanced above her head, and he whistled quietly, the heavy curtain of his mustache moving in the breeze he produced. "What're you doing up here? You should be back in Bright, kiddo." Those eyes took her in, lingering on the pointed tips of her ears poking through her glossy curls. "Or maybe up in Elfhame. I thought that's where all the elven players spawned."

Rouge shook her head. "Not if they're a half-breed. They don't like my kind any more up there than the humans do down here. Less, probably. Not that I'd know for sure, since I've never met a High Elf." She shrugged.

Doom Bloom cleared her throat meaningfully, glaring at them. "We're late. Wep, set your Away to follow me, and both of you mount up. I have better things to do than listen to you chat."

Wep rolled his eyes, but nodded and put two broad fingers in his mouth. He whistled sharply, and the largest pig Rouge had ever seen barrelled around the corner of the Dead Tent.

The beast was easily 800 pounds, and probably more. He had huge white tusks that jutted from under his curled lip, and his black bristles looked thick and sharp enough to inflict an injury without even trying.

From behind her, Rouge heard a strange sound, and spun, hand on the pommel of her dagger. What she saw made her start giggling uncontrollably. Codswallop, a giant ostrich from a town *full* of pigs, was clearly terrified. He had his head buried in the dust, and his knees were quaking. The strange sound was dirt shivering away from his trembling body.

"Poor baby!" Rouge threw her arms around Codswallop's neck, trying to sound sympathetic while choking back laughter. "It's all right, Wally," she soothed. "That old boar's not going to hurt you. He's a mount, too!"

Poor Wep was looking befuddled, while Doom's mouth was pinched in either annoyance or an attempt to hold in her own laughter. Her voice was as cool as ever, though, when she asked, "Is this going to be a problem?"

"Oh. Uh, no. No!" Rouge finally succeeded in coaxing the bird's head out of the dust, though he was still swaying in place and looking rather wild eyed. "It's just some chick-hood trauma."

🐓 🐓 🐓

Five minutes later, Zoey pressed open the lid of her pod and pulled the headset off. She rubbed her eyes with her fists, and glanced at the clock. After 10 pm. Not good. Any second now-

A firm knock came at the door. "Zoe? You up?"

Quickly, she fluffed her curls and vaulted out of the embrace of her gaming pod. The years of gymnastics lessons her mom had sent her to paid off in more than the game. "Yeah, Dad. I was just getting ready for bed. Don't come in!"

His voice was chastising. "You weren't still in *Veritas*, right? You know bedtime is 10."

She sighed and rolled her eyes. He knew perfectly well she was in the game. Since she was a minor, her parent or guardian had access to all her game logs. Her dad trusted her, but she knew he did keep track of how much time she spent online. Still, it was nice of him to let her keep what remained of her dignity.

"Yeah, Dad. Sorry. I just had to set my Away Instructions. I forgot last night, and Blackie pooped on my boots. It was gross." Zoey plopped her bodysuit into the cleaning bin and pushed the button. Blue fluid filled the small chamber, and the bodysuit whirled lazily in the solution.

He chuckled, and his deep voice was filled with affection when he replied. "That's rough. Okay. Watch the time, though, kid. I don't want to have to set an auto logout for you. You need to be off by ten on school nights and get to bed."

Win by amusement value, huh? She'd take it. "Okay, I know. I'll set an alarm to remind me. G'night, Dad. Love you."

She could hear his hand come to rest on the closed door between them, and wished for a moment that she was still comfortable wandering around in front of him in her pajamas. This growing up and developing boobs thing sucked sometimes.

His voice was soft when he answered. "Good night, Zoe. I love you too." She heard a step, and then he paused. "Hey, Zoe? Eat your eggs in the morning."

She grimaced as she pulled the soft cotton of her nightgown over her head. "Yeah, Dad. I'll eat my eggs."

After a moment, she heard his feet going down the hall, back toward the stairs. She knew he'd be up grading papers for at least a few more hours. Being a teacher was rough. He was never able to just leave his day behind when he came home. He always had lesson plans, emails, calls, homework, or tests to deal with.

Her pod beeped as the bodysuit stilled in its special disinfectant bin, and she glanced at the dim timer above it. It would soak in the soup under UV lights for another thirty minutes, and then drain and switch to the dry cycle. She checked the level of the cleanser and saw that her dad must have filled it recently, since it was nearly full. Reassured that everything would be ready for her after school tomorrow, she tugged a satin sleep cap over her curls, and laid down.

"Lights off, Emily." The lights turned off, and she remembered thinking it was funny when she renamed her smart house interface with the same name as the Veritas UI (or User Interface) bot. Now that she had a Secret Quest, and with all the conspiracy theories that Veritas had ways to monitor you outside the game, it actually seemed a little creepy. Maybe she'd change it tomorrow.

Zoey yawned and glanced at her screen, which rested on its charging station on the little table beside her bed. The message icon was flashing gently, so she unlocked the screen with a touch of her finger. It was from Jace.

@JaceCo: What was the history assignment? I didn't write it down.

@RedZ: Read chapters 12-13. Write a 500 word essay on one of the most important battles of WWII. Due Monday.

@JaceCo: Ugh. Thanks.

@RedZ: No problem!

She grinned. One of the reasons she was friends with Jace was because he used complete words and sentences online. They'd met in fifth grade when Jace had moved into the area with his family. He had rescued Zoey from the Incident That Shall Not Be Discussed (there was a snake), and then they had an English project with another kid. They'd had to work on it outside of class time, and the other kid had used so much txtspk she wanted to punch him. Jace had started out using some, but quickly picked up on the fact that she hated it, and they had bonded over their mutual dislike of the poseurs who could only text if they didn't have to use vowels.

Her screen blinked in the darkness. Another message.

@JaceCo: I was thinking of logging on Friday night. You have anything fun you're working on?

@RedZ: 😬 Sorry, I'll be away for a while. Probably not back in Bright for a week or so. What level are you now?

@JaceCo: Still 17. Hoping to get 18 on Friday.

@RedZ: You'll finally be legal. 😄

@JaceCo: Yeah, laugh it up. You've been playing way more, and you're only, what, 20?

@RedZ: Just made 21!

@JaceCo: Congrats! All grown up!

@RedZ: 😎You know it!

@JaceCo: See you tomorrow, Zoe.

@RedZ: Night!

Zoey smiled, setting her screen back into its cradle. She might have told her dad she wasn't interested in Jace, but that was only about seventy-five percent true. He was cute, in a geeky kind of way, and he was definitely the nicest guy she knew. She was pretty sure his interest in her as anything other than a friend had solidly bottomed out when he'd tried kissing her in sixth grade and she kneed him in the nads, just like her dad taught her. Honestly, the boy went through crushes like a kid whose favorite ice-cream flavor changed constantly, so she probably wouldn't accept even if he decided that she was his latest (and greatest!) flavor of the week.

She didn't really want a serious relationship anyway, and she honestly wasn't interested *at all* in anybody except Jace. She didn't really even want to date him. Odds were, they'd go to different colleges in a few years, and that was a heartbreak she didn't want to invest in. Better to keep a life-long friend than make a future ex-boyfriend.

Sleepily, she burrowed into the heavy purple satin blanket that covered her bed. She felt a lump near her knee and reached down to pull out Mr. Bun. The well-worn, much loved, brown and white rabbit had been with her since she was four years old. She'd gotten him as a Christmas present the year her parents got divorced. She'd asked for a rabbit or a sister, but her mom was allergic to animals, and sisters took time to produce.

By the next Christmas, Zoey had had a new step-sister, but she'd been an angry, miserable, confused five-year-old by then. Any chance she'd had at forming a positive relationship with Lily vanished when Zoey took her mom's fabric shears to all of Lily's Christmas presents after her mom and Ken, Lily's dad, went to bed. Lily, all of 9 years old, and filled with early tween angst, was furious, even though all the presents were replaced by the next day. That was the first time Zoey was sent back to her dad before her scheduled time with her mom was over, but certainly not the last.

Zoey sighed, and buried her face in Mr. Bun's soft, worn fur. It was too late now. Her mom lived near Seattle with Ken and Lily. Zoey talked to her sometimes on the screen, and they sent polite emails back and forth, but they hadn't met in person for almost two years. A tear trickled down her nose and into the plush, lost with a thousand others the toy had absorbed over the years. As the last tear dried, Zoey fell asleep.

Chapter Four

Aspen
"Hi Ho, Hi Ho"

The next day was the last day of the boon. Aspen could barely feel the fire in his belly anymore, and he'd gotten used to it enough that now he felt a little chilled without it. He pulled a heavier shirt over his usual thin linen one, picked up the large pack by the door, and headed out into the chill of predawn.

Silus murmured a sleepy good morning from the small, hand-woven basket tied securely to the pack. The basket was inverted, so the bottom was open and she could fly out anytime she needed to. Sumi stood in the deepest shadow near the eastern side of the house, which now looked much more cheerful and home-like with its cheerful green sod roof, lacy web curtains, and stonework patched and cleaned of ivy and mud.

<Be careful. Remember this is just an exploratory mission. Simply find the mine and only venture far enough inside to be certain if it will need

reinforcement before we can use it, and if any creatures or monsters have taken up residence.> Sumi's business-like voice had a trace of concern she couldn't hide.

In order for Aspen to level, he needed to gain more quests and complete them alone. Silus would scout in the mine and keep watch at night on the way back. In case things went badly, she could also fly back quickly to get help from Sumi and Khor.

<I still don't see why I can't go,> the massive goat said resentfully. <I won't help him.>

Sumi threw up her forelegs in exasperation, and Aspen had a strong suspicion that if she could have rolled her eyes, she would have. <He has to walk and carry the pack himself. I'm sure he'll get a quest once he starts. If you're with him, the party level will be higher, and it might prevent the simpler quests from appearing. You're too big to go into the mine, and you hate enclosed spaces anyway. You'd be worthless there. We need you here to take care of the plants and keep predators away during the day.>

<We don't know if I would be able to go into the mine, and small spaces *don't* bother me.> Khor said petulantly.

Aspen and Sumi studiously avoided looking at each other, but they both knew they were thinking of the turnip-frog incident. It would never be spoken of again.

Aspen reached out and patted his large friend's head reassuringly. Aware of Sumi's continued proscription on vocalizations, he kept his mouth shut, but he knew the goat understood.

<Fine,> the goat muttered rebelliously. <I'm going next time, though.>

Aspen nodded enthusiastically. Being able to pile supplies onto Khor, nap on the way, and cut 3 hours travel time would definitely be worth putting up with the acerbic beast. Plus, when Khor forgot his dignity, he was actually quite a good traveling companion.

Waving goodbye, Aspen took off down the barely visible path. Silus had scouted out the way over the last few nights, and she had said that as long as he stayed near the river, he should enter the low foothills in about six hours. Which, frankly, was rubbish, and Aspen wished he was riding on Khor's broad back instead. Adjusting his pack so it rode more comfortably on his shoulders, he settled into a steady pace.

ểểể

Quest: "Beat Feet" complete.

Travel by foot from Refuge Farm to the Small Goat Hills in less than six hours.

Success: +1500 experience, +1 point of Strength, +2 points of Endurance, +1 point of Dexterity

Due to the unexpected boost he got while running away from a hungry Lesser Bear, it only took about five and a half hours to make the trek. Silus slept securely in her basket the entire time, and thanks to Aspen's recent Endurance boosts, he was only out of breath for a while after he left the bear in his dust.

His feet hurt, his shoulders hurt, his back ached, his lungs burned, and his stomach growled loudly by the time he felt the steady rise beneath his feet that meant he'd arrived in the foothills. He glanced up at the sun high overhead and judged that it wasn't yet noon, but he was ready to stop for some lunch. Besides, he needed to look at the Head Librarian's map again now that he was surrounded by the landmarks on it.

Grunting quietly, he sat down on a log. Seeing several ants crawl across the bark nearby, he got back up and moved to a different log. Even remembering the aftermath of sleeping in a tent built on an anthill was enough to send him into a cold sweat. Perhaps because of the fact that Sumi looked as much like an ant as she did a spider, he treated the innocuous-looking insects with wary respect.

He slid the pack off his shoulders and set it down between his legs. Carefully opening the top, he pulled out a small packet wrapped in oilcloth. Inside were two boiled eggs and two thick slices of rather dense, flat brown bread that was still significantly more edible than his first several attempts. The bread quest had been rather disheartening, since it simply called for him to make something a blindfolded person wouldn't confuse with a dog treat. Apparently, Gina didn't have much faith in his future as a master chef.

Chewing with grim determination, he choked down the dry bread and followed it up with the much tastier salted eggs. After brushing the crumbs from his shirt, he tucked the oilcloth away, and took out his map. It wasn't a particularly detailed or high-quality map. The house was marked with a rectangle the map's brief legend simply listed as 'A building'.

A few other rectangles were scattered quite a distance away, but those were almost certainly ruins by now. Still, something else to add to his long to-do list. Perhaps he would check them out in the spring. If he was still alive. He sighed wearily, and shook away such pessimistic thoughts.

His new abode had been the home of the previous watchkeeper, a man whose sole job was to watch for any sign of invaders headed toward Bright and send a carrier pigeon if he saw anything. The man had been recalled over five years ago as Quarternell, the last bastion of the human race, fought a losing battle against the forces of the non-human races and Lich Lord Akuji. After humanity's 'miraculous victory' just over a year ago, sending someone back out here to watch over land that no one wanted was no doubt the lowest priority on King Chester's list, falling right after assigning a junior pot boy to the castle kitchens.

Now here Aspen was, staring at a hastily drawn and already smudged piece of parchment. He shook his head at the vagaries of fate and traced his finger along the path of the river from his house's small rectangle to the curving lines indicating the foothills in which he sat. Raising his head, he looked around for a landmark. To his left, just out of sight through the trees, he could hear the merry burble of the river. Off to the right…. Ah ha! There was a very large tree growing up from where it had taken root in a crack in a large boulder. He tapped the circle topped by a multi-limbed Y marked on the map. Given the distance between the river and the stone-tree on the map, and the small and very encouraging skull that marked the mine, it should be…southeast another ten or fifteen minutes on foot.

He took a long draw on his waterskin, which he had filled right before veering away from the river to start heading inland a short time ago. The cool water soothed his dry throat, and he closed his eyes, enjoying the sounds of nature, the sun on his face, and the refreshing feeling of the water assuaging the fire that lingered in his belly. Then he carefully folded the map and put it away, and attached the waterskin to his belt again. Shrugging the pack back onto his shoulders carefully so as to avoid disturbing his small passenger, he set off deeper into the woods.

After only a few minutes, a narrow track started to become visible in the underbrush. Chunks of flatter stone appeared, and finally the remains of a rutted, fragmented road became clear. Aspen followed it until he came to the broad wooden beams that marked the entrance to the mine. An abandoned ore cart sat on rusted tracks just inside the dark opening, and something small and squeaky scurried away as he approached.

He stopped at the entrance and reached over his shoulder to tap softly on the woven basket. There was no response. He tapped louder. <Aspen?> came the sleepy little voice.

Glancing around as though Sumi would jump out and start quizzing him on smelting methods, he cleared his throat and murmured teasingly, "Who else would it be, little one? Would you sleep on if I had been killed by bandits and your basket stolen? Or perhaps I might be a particularly persistent piculet?"

<A persnickety person with a partially plump persimmon?> The little bat giggled as she poked her head out of the bottom of the basket and peered around. <I wouldn't mind a persimmon, you know.> Her voice was dreamy as she dropped down and with a few beats of her wings lifted herself back up to her favorite place nestled in the crook between his neck and his shoulder.

Aspen reached into his pocket and pulled out a few slightly bruised apples with a flourish. He pulled a small paring knife from its sheath at his waist and sliced a thin sliver from one of the fruits. Apples could be a little difficult for the small bat to eat on her own, but with a little help, they were a tasty treat. "Your wish is my command, milady. Not a persimmon, but all I saw that I could carry without crushing it."

The little bat hungrily devoured the fruit, and Aspen barely snatched his fingers from a sharp nip at the end. An unrepentant little voice said, <Blame Sumi. More?>

Aspen thought all three of his friends were taking the opportunity to commit sneak attacks against him with a little too much enthusiasm, but carved off another slice of fruit nonetheless. He had a suspicion that Gina had struck again, and given his companions secret quests to harass him. Secret quests would fail automatically if anyone discovered them, so he kept his conjectures to himself.

Once Silus' appetite was sated, the two of them prepared to go into the mine. Silus would go first, looking for areas that might be dangerous for Aspen to attempt, whether because of aggressive beasts or unstable support beams. Aspen would follow after, using a glowstone. Glowstones were rechargeable items which lit up a ten-foot radius around themselves with a clear light for up to twelve hours.

Unfortunately, none of the four of them had the ability to cast spells, even one as simple as the recharging spell, and they only had fifty of the egg-sized rocks. While that was more than enough in Bright, where it cost a few silvers to have an apprentice mage recharge a basket of them for a household, out here they became precious single use items. Still, they had decided that it would be safer for Aspen to use one than risk a torch going out or, worse, igniting a gas pocket with an open flame.

Aspen set his pack behind the old mining cart, where the shadows and its odd bulky shape combined to make it appear to be just another pile of rocks. He took up his staff, a full waterskin, a long rope woven by Sumi from her strongest webbing, and a pouch containing two oilcloth-wrapped meals and some more apples. Silus darted into the darkness, quickly vanishing, and Aspen flicked the glowstone sharply with his fingernail four times.

It was a risk to make noise, but if something aggressive had taken up residence in the mine, he'd rather face it in the open than in tunnels it knew far better than he did. After a long, breathless moment in which nothing happened except the glowstone adding its soft illumination to the ambient light, he relaxed his fingers on his staff and squared his shoulders.

It was time to explore.

The damp cave smell grew stronger as Aspen headed down the passage. A soft drip of water came from somewhere ahead, and the whisper of the slight breeze faded until there was no air movement to dry the sudden chill of sweat on his skin.

Aspen hated caves. He hated the dank smell, the misleading echoes, the sudden drops, sharp stalactites, and pallid cave creatures. He especially hated the memory of the time he had spent in one such cave, imprisoned, alone, dying, with only the faintest distant hope that he would be able to slay his enemy before his own inevitable fall. His escape had cost the life of the person he cherished most, and he considered it a poor bargain: his life for hers.

But in order to live his life, the life Birdie had bought for him at such a terrible price, he had to move on. That meant following Silus into the big, scary mine and whacking at whatever he found there. He hoped it was iron. He could really use some iron to make better tools. The ones he had brought had to be as small and portable as possible, and they simply weren't going to last long term.

Quest: "What Happened Here?" begun.

This mine was marked on the map found in the Great Library. No information was appended, and the mine is marked with a skull. This is unlikely to mean good things for you. Why was this mine abandoned? What was mined here? Find the answers to these questions.

Success: Experience. Unknown ore.

Failure: Variable. Loss of the opportunity to mine in this area.

Aspen read the notification and rubbed his face wearily. "Here we go again."

The first long passage was wide and, other than some debris left from animals that had resided here at various times since the mine was abandoned, in good condition. Honestly, he half-expected to find a miner around one of the corners, sitting down as he ate his lunch before continuing his work. The near-total silence was oppressive, and Aspen found himself listening for the quiet susurration of wings indicating that Silus was returning.

After several minutes of walking, during which he felt himself progressively descending, and the air growing cooler around him, he finally came to a split in the path. The track of the minecarts continued straight ahead, but a branch of the tunnel took a sharp turn to the left. He frowned a little as he looked at it.

The tunnel he was in looked much like he would have expected, if anyone had asked him what a mine might look like inside. The walls were rough stone, with visible marks from pickaxes. Heavy wooden beams had been squared against the walls periodically, with cross beams between to support them in case of a cave-in. The ceilings were around seven feet high, probably the highest the miners could get a good enough angle to dig.

The corridor itself was wide enough for the small minecart and the tracks, with just enough extra space for a particularly slim miner to cling to the walls as the cart passed. It wasn't straight, but the curve was subtle enough that the area revealed by the light of his glowstone appeared to have no bends.

The round opening beside him was an anomaly, very different from the rectangular tunnel before. The walls were smoother, with an odd pattern of rings, no pickaxe marks, and no support beams. The ceiling was lower, perhaps only five feet, and he would have to crouch to travel through it. The diameter was probably around five feet as well, and curved top and bottom to create a slightly ovoid space, with a narrowed top and a broader base. All in all it was a very odd shaft, and generally, 'odd' equalled 'bad' in Aspen's experience.

Aspen stared into the darkness. On the one hand, if this opening led to something dangerous, he didn't want to go past it and leave an enemy behind him. On the other hand, if this opening *did* lead to something dangerous, he didn't want to face it alone. It felt strangely organic, and it was possible that some large creature had made it. So, the question was, should he go down this strange tunnel, or walk on by?

Unable to decide, he sat down and took the apples from his pouch. For nearly half an hour, he practiced tossing the apples from one hand to the other. His Dexterity was high enough now that he could slowly juggle two apples, so he did. He got a quest to add a small rock to the mix, and he did that. A linked quest appeared, and he added another rock. Finally, after three shimmering increases in his Dexterity, he took out his paring knife and began tossing it back and forth as well.

He was sucking a cut on his finger when Silus returned, flying in from the broad path ahead. She flapped over to his shoulder and looked at the oozing digit curiously. <What happened? Were you attacked?>

Aspen tilted the knife toward the oblong opening beside them. "I didn't know which path you took, and there is no way I'm going in there and being eaten by a Rock Worm or a Fell Snake. I figured you'd be back soon, and we could decide what to do together." A flash of light twinkled around him for a moment. Wisdom, probably.

Silus tilted her head. <How did that lead to bleeding? And what do you mean, which path? There's only one path.>

Aspen stood abruptly, causing Silus to clutch him with toes and wing-thumbs and squeak indignantly. "That's it," he said, turning and briskly walking back toward the entrance. "We're going back to the house and waiting until Sumi comes too. There's no way I'm going down a tunnel you can't even see. That means magic, and we are *not* ready for magic."

Silus giggled. <No, I can totally see it. I just thought it was funny.>

Aspen buried his face in his palm, forgetting about the knife in his hand and nearly putting out an eye. "Of course. Hilarious."

<I already went down there. It ends about fifty feet further on, in a small

alcove. There's a big stone table-thing, but that's it. I don't know why the tunnel is different, but there are a couple more of them further on. They're all short, and all end in the little rooms. Someplace for the miners to rest? I don't know. Nothing dangerous, anyway.> She peered over his shoulder at the smaller tunnel. <Did you really just sit here waiting for me? How long?>

Aspen cleared his throat and focused on cautiously returning his short blade to its sheath at his belt. "Doesn't matter. Just a few minutes. Did you find anything at the end of the tracks?"

Leaning her fluffy little head against his cheek, Silus nodded. <A big cavern with a circle of track in it. A few more mine carts, some nearly full of ore. A switch to change the path of the cart. Eight much narrower tunnels that aren't nearly as finished-looking as this one. Maybe those tunnels were newer? Also, a skeleton.>

"A skeleton?"

The soft ears tickled his cheek as she gave her version of a shrug. <Humanoid. The bones are thick, and it seems short. Could be a dwarf or a human, or something else I don't know about. The skull is missing.>

Aspen scratched his head, missing his hat, which he had left behind with his pack. "How did he die? Could you tell?"

Silus shifted slightly. She sounded troubled. <I didn't see any significant marks or breaks on the bones. No obvious clues. All the rest of the bones are together. Just... The head is gone.>

He huffed a breath and tucked away his knife and the two apples, tossing the stones back where he found them. "I guess we should go check it out. Did you go down any of the smaller passages?"

<No.> Silus' voice was small and embarrassed. <I wanted to get back to you once I found the skeleton.>

Aspen nuzzled the small head gently. "Good job. Let's go see. Do you want to come with me, or fly ahead?"

She flapped off his shoulder with a beat of her wings and took off. Her little voice faded as she got further away. <I'll go ahead. If there's anything to see, I'd rather sneak up on it than wait for it to find you and your very bright light.>

Gripping his staff and his 'very bright light', Aspen followed after his friend, his footsteps seeming suddenly terribly loud.

It was nearly another mile of sloping tunnels before he reached the larger cavern Silus had described. He saw two more of the strange ovoid side passages, but just walked past after making sure nothing was lurking within range of his light. They seemed to be placed at regular intervals, so perhaps Silus was right, and they were some kind of rest area. It seemed strange, but he really didn't know that much about mining.

He found the cavern when the darkness around him seemed to suddenly grow deeper. Instead of seeing rough-hewn walls, ceiling, and floor lit by his glowstone, suddenly there was only gloom in front of him. He felt his eyes widen in a vain attempt to let in more light.

"Silus?" he whispered into the murk.

The bat's nervous little voice came clearly into his mind, so she was nearby. <Follow the cart tracks. It'll split in a few paces. Take the left path to the second full cart. The skeleton is on the far side of it.>

As silently as possible, he followed her instructions. The scuff of his shoes on the stone floor and the never-ending drip of water seemed to echo inside his skull.

"Did you find the source of the water?" he murmured as he reached the ore cart and leaned around it so he could see the bones resting on the floor, right where Silus had said it would be

<I can smell it coming from a few of the small passages ahead. They must have dug deep enough to find it. It was probably a relief not to have to bring in all their water from outside.>

The skeleton was indeed short and dense. The bones lay together, only slightly tumbled from the tendons and ligaments dissolving and letting them fall away from each other. To his eye, it seemed that they hadn't even been cleaned by insects, but rather the flesh had simply rotted and turned to dust. Oddly, there were no cloth or leather remnants, though there was a solid-looking pickaxe near the right hand.

<How long do you think he's been here?> Silus' voice was small but determined. Unlike the others, she had never experienced a battle worse than the one against the Greater Egg Eating Snake, having been too young at the time the war ended. Other than the loss of her mother and Birdie, both of which occurred far from her sight, death was still only an acquaintance to her.

He shook his head, gently prodding a femur. He frowned as it resisted the movement. Old bones were generally dry and brittle, and this felt incredibly solid. "No telling. We know this mine was last in use around thirty-five years ago, when Chester's father was in his early expansionist phase."

Aspen's mouth twisted sourly at the mention of King Chester's father, Chadwick. It was Chadwick's constant pushes into any land he could conceivably claim that had first resulted in bringing Quarternell to Akuji's attention. The Lich Lord would have come for them soon enough, but humanity might have had another short lifetime of peace if Chadwick hadn't poked a bear best left sleeping.

Of course, King Chadwick the Ill-Advised had died at the young age of fifty after attempting to send Akuji's Greater Ghoul harbinger back to its master without its head. When the predictable result happened, then-Prince Chester had been abruptly thrust onto the throne at the tender age of twelve. It was a position that he was constitutionally unsuited for, but because of the divine right of primogeniture, he had less choice in his future than Aspen, who was at that time a fifteen-year-old recruit in Chadwick's poorly-trained army.

Aspen brought himself back to the present and picked up the femur, testing it between his hands. "I can tell you one thing, though," he grunted slightly as he snapped the bone, and it flashed into motes of glittering dust. "These aren't real bones, and whoever put this here likely did it more recently than thirty years ago."

A small sharp pain pricked the back of his neck, just beside his spine. He instantly froze.

A female voice heavy with an unfamiliar, musical accent, voice hissed into his ear. "I work hard on that. You take hint and leave!"

Quest: "I'm a Believer" begun.

There's someone here with you. Find out who it is, and why she's here.

Success: Experience, +1 Intelligence, +3 Wisdom. A pickaxe.

Failure: Variable, but probably death. What happens after that is the variable bit.

The sharp prickle at the back of his neck lasted only a moment before a nearly-inaudible screech sounded. This was followed by wing flapping and a yelp as the person behind him began swinging wildly in an attempt to get the enraged bat to stop dive-bombing her. Aspen dropped and rolled away, coming up against the old ore-cart with an awkward thump. It was still better than where he was, since he was uninjured and could now see his assailant.

Silus was clinging to the long, matted hair of a short, scrawny, green woman. Her large yellow eyes were squinted against the light of the glowstone as she flailed away with what looked like a long kitchen knife. Her body was nearly as emaciated as his had been a week ago, and one long ear swept up through the tangled mess of her hair in a graceful arch. The other ear ended in a ragged grayish stump that looked painfully inflamed and dripped something unpleasant.

"Silus! Come back!" Aspen swept his staff out, grateful this attack occurred in the larger cavern space instead of the narrower tunnel. He smacked at the thin green hand holding the knife, and the goblin female dropped the blade with a yelp, then fell to her knees, scrabbling after it.

Silus flew up away from the woman, winging back up into the darkness above. <I can bite her, Aspen! I saved you, and I can bite her!>

"Yes, you did, little one. No biting for now, though. We need to talk to her. I got a quest." Aspen's voice was rough, and his heart beat as though it would thump out of his chest. The last time he had seen a goblin… Well, the last time was when his friends dragged him, nearly dead himself, through the abattoir of the last battlefield of a thirty-year war. The time before that, though, four goblins were holding him down while…

He shook his head sharply. That was an image from another life. In *this* life, goblins and humans had made peace. Or so he'd heard from the Head Librarian as he was smuggled from Bright in the deepest part of the night. 'Peace', yet here was a goblin, clearly in fear for her life, deep in human lands. He maintained his grip on his staff, but held out the other hand to show that it was empty.

"Hold, female. I mean no harm to you." The thin woman, who he could now tell was a sickly gray beneath her natural olive-green hue, scrabbled backwards. She clutched her blade before her in hands that shook, and her shining yellow eyes were lit with both suspicion and fever.

"Why are you here?" Aspen continued, struggling to keep his tone gentle as an almost visceral urge to attack made his hand clench on his heavy staff. "The nearest goblins should be back in Bright. I hear they have their own borough now. Do you need help to reach them?" He kept his words slow and clear. Few people now spoke the goblin's native tongue, but at one time the language humans now spoke had been nearly universal, and most members of the sapient races still spoke at least a little of it. He had heard her speak in human language earlier, so she should understand him.

The goblin backed to the edge of his light and hissed at him through sharp, triangular teeth. "Not goblins nor humans are friends me. I no friends, and neither are you such." Her accent was lisping, and her phrasing slightly broken and archaic, but he understood her well enough.

"I'm not your enemy, either. I have no reason to wish you ill." He gestured toward her ear, which had to be intensely painful. "I see you're injured, and you look half-starved. I have a potion." *Well, Spider Milk, but it'll work on goblins, too. Probably.* "And some food. They're back by the entrance. Will you let me help you?"

The goblin's yellow eyes gleamed suspiciously, but the atrophied muscles of her arm were sagging under the weight of the knife. Now that she was holding still, he could see that she was nearly at her limit. She tilted her head so the putrid remnants of her ear were more clearly visible. She spoke slowly and carefully, making sure her meaning was clear. "I goblin'te and *verschladt.* You should kill me on sight. Why yet you help one who has slain many of your people?"

Aspen sighed and cocked his head to the side. He forced his hand to loosen its grip on his weapon, though he remained ready to move. "Have you? Killed many of my people? I've certainly killed many of yours. Wasn't that our only path to existence, not that long ago? Yet here we are, in this strange new time, and all I see is one of me, one of you, and you're hurt." He flicked his eyes back toward the entrance to the cavern, and nearly missed the warning shuffle of her feet as she lunged toward him, blade straight out.

He agilely side-stepped, silently thanking Sumi for her bloody-minded determination that he recover as quickly as possible. He snapped his staff down on her wrist, which was awkwardly overextended, and caught the knife as it tumbled from her nerveless fingers. She yelped and dropped to her knees, curling up around her belly as she tried to roll away.

"No! No!" His light glimmered from moisture in those big eyes. "Spare me yet, human! I leave this place, and you never will see me again! Let me go! I beg you!" Clawing at the dirt, she tried to get away, and as she did, he saw the loose rags that made up her clothes stretch taut over her thin body. His eyes widened and he felt as if he'd taken a punch to the gut..

"Great Gina!" He barely kept himself from dropping the staff. "Are you…with child? What-"

At his words, she stopped mid-crawl, her faintly luminescent saffron orbs flashing to his face. "Gi-na? You know Gi-na?" There was a hitch between the two syllables of the name, but it was clearly that of his goddess.

He held out an empty hand. His voice was hoarse when he replied. "I am here by the grace of the goddess Gina. I am as much hers now as I am anyone's, I suppose."

"You… worship Gi-na?" Her voice was faint, and the subtly melodic accent grew stronger with every word.

Smiling ruefully, Aspen shrugged. "I don't know that we mean the same being. You say her name a little differently. Mine is a goddess." He held his hand to his shoulder. "About this tall. Red hair. Eyes that change colors. Does all kinds of fun things with growing plants and, um, reproduction?" His eyes shot to the distended belly, clearly visible now that he knew to look for it.

The goblin woman started to reach out toward him, then stopped. Her eyes were even larger than before, and tears spilled from the corners, cutting tracks through the brown filth caked onto her skin. "She spoke to me. In my dreams." She closed her eyes, and more tears poured down her cheeks. "I thought I crazy maybe, but I was looking…for you. Oh, Gi-na!" Her voice cut off abruptly, and her eyes rolled back in her head. She slumped down, unconscious.

Before he could think, Aspen lunged forward and scooped the cold, limp body into his arms. If she woke, or if she was pretending, and she had another weapon, he was wide open to an attack. Nonetheless, he had seen too much death in his life. He had a feeling that he would see more of it if he hesitated even a moment, and he didn't want to dig a grave today. Not even one so pathetically small as it would take to bury this small woman and her unborn babe.

Quest: "Run For Your Life" begun.

Seriously. Run! You have 10 minutes. Get yourself and your companions out of the mine.

Success: Experience. +5 Endurance, +2 Strength, +1 Dexterity

Partial Success: (Get only yourself and one other out of the mine in time). Experience. +2 Endurance. The death of a companion.

Failure: Death

Death? Why would they *all* die? He clutched the goblin against his chest, dropped his staff to the ground, and started running. Questions later. Run now.

"Silus! Lead the way!" With that, he raced back down the corridor as quickly as his much-increased Strength, Endurance, and Dexterity could take him. Silus flew past him down the tunnel, staying just ahead of the bubble of light cast by his glowstone. They had traveled at least a mile and a half down a sloping tunnel. While the angle had been barely noticeable going down, going back up quickly made his legs and lungs begin to burn. He barely noticed the gleam of stat increases as he raced onward, but he certainly did notice how his travel became slightly easier each time he gained a point.

"Why…didn't…I…bring…the potion…in?" he roared as he finally made his way into the late afternoon sunlight. Dust motes spun gracefully away from him as he fell to his knees beside the backpack. He gently laid down his burden, then dug frantically through the items packed tightly into the pack.

Quest: "Run For Your Life" complete.

Success: +500 Experience. +5 Endurance, +2 Strength, +1 Dexterity

Silus flew down to rest beside him, shifting from foot to foot uncomfortably. She was too small to help, but he could see her tension in the way she leaned forward, blinking at each item as he removed it and then shoved it aside.

"Who keeps the healing potions in the bottom of the pack, hmm? Who doesn't bring the potions *in* when he explores a mine marked with a damned *skull?* Idiot!" His fingers finally closed over the small metal container, and he pulled it out, nearly fumbling it. He flicked the stopper open and poured the viscous liquid into the goblin's open mouth, gently massaging her throat until she gulped once. He wiped the remains of the potion on the mangled end of her ear with trembling fingers, grimacing as foul fluids coated his hand.

"Gina… Damn it, Gina… I don't want to see anyone else die. Especially not a mother. Not even a *goblin* mother. Please, Gina…" Aspen didn't even realize he was praying as he felt the warmth of the infected flesh beneath his hand. It was burning hot in comparison with the too-cool skin of the rest of her body.

He could clearly see the blackish veins threading away from the wound.

As he gently pressed on the wound, hoping to expel some of the corruption while the poor woman was still unconscious, a glow began beneath his fingers. He thought briefly that it must be another stat increase. Dexterity perhaps? But it grew until there was a brilliant flash, far brighter than any level or stat gain. He jerked his hand away, but leaned protectively over the fragile body lying so silently in the dust. Instinctively, he reached out to cover Silus with his clean hand, as though protecting them both from an unknown attack with his own body.

<Aspen?> Silus' voice was shaky. He blinked open his eyes, fighting a sudden inexplicable exhaustion. He could see that she had her wings drawn in around her body, and her adorably fuzzy face held an expression he'd never seen there before. She reached out and gently touched his hand with her wing-thumbs. <I'm okay. But look at the goblin.>

Aspen turned his eyes toward the goblin, and met shocked yellow eyes. Her face was pale and dirty, skin a sickly green like dry lichen, where most goblins he'd seen before ranged from dark olive to the color of spring grass. Her face was all shadows and angles, her chin and cheekbones equally pointed and protruding. Her ears were inhumanly large, and swept back through the filthy tangles of her hair.

Wait. Ears? *Two* tapered ears? Both delicate, long, and *whole*. The wound and the poisonous black lines were entirely gone.

The goblin took a shuddering breath. Her face relaxed into a smile of utter relief, and he realized that she had been under tremendous strain since the moment they'd met. Even when she was unconscious, her knife-edged features had been twisted in pain. She reached up stick-like fingers and touched her ear, tentatively at first, and then with more vigor, until she was tugging on it as if it might come off under her hand.

"It gone!" she cried, tears welling up again. He wondered for a moment if she had gone mad, because the ear was back, not gone. She forced herself into a sitting position, though he could see that it was difficult.

"*Vershla* is gone! Impossible! What you do? How…?" Thick tears poured down her cheeks, traveling through the dark runnels created by the previous deluge. She swept her hands down her body, pulling out of his hand as she did so.

Aspen suddenly realized he was still looming over her, and rocked abruptly back onto his rear in an attempt to give her space and privacy. She didn't even notice as she pulled her ragged tunic up to reveal the almost grotesquely distended curve of her belly. The flesh was pale, with only the faintest hint of green tinting it, and she ran her hands over it as though amazed. A lump pushed against her hands from the inside, and she traced it with one trembling finger, tears trickling from her cheeks to track down over her exposed abdomen.

Finally she looked up at him, tears still flowing freely. "I *verschladt*," she whispered. At his look of confusion, her eyes shifted as she searched for the right words. "Poison from within? I given the *verschla*'s kiss." She reached up and touched her restored ear. "It is poison. Bad, bad poison. No recovery. They cut ear, here." She traced the graceful tip of the leaf-shaped appendage.

"They want me to die slowly. I watching baby grow, only to perish. Day before day before, I saw the black blood reach here." She pressed a shaking hand to her sternum. "I knew…it end soon. I try to find courage to end life. End it before baby died in *dihaj*, but I could not do it."

The goblin bared her sharp teeth in a grimace of self-loathing. "Gi-na forbid self-murder. I wish to join my Jeremy when I go to A-tae place." She stroked her stomach again, and as if on cue a tiny foot kicked, pressing out to reassure its mother that it was still there and strong. "I hope that maybe I meet child after death. We go together to death. I hold her just once, maybe, after we die…" She trembled, her words shifting to the lisping clicks of the goblin tongue. The only word he could pick out was 'Gi-na'.

Aspen leaned his head back and smiled up at the sky. It was an exhausted, painful smile, but no less heart-felt. Far from making a horrible mistake in a moment of insanity, he had somehow managed to fulfill some small part of whatever Gina wanted from him.

Then he frowned, puzzled. So what had the quest meant about *him* dying, and then something variable? While the near-dead female goblin had certainly had the will to kill him to defend herself and his child, he doubted that her weakened body could have done the job, even when the blade was against his neck. After that short period, he had never really been in danger.

Even as he realized that he must be missing something, the earth shuddered beneath him. Rumbling came from the tunnel leading into the mine, and a billow of dust and small stones whooshed out of the dark opening. The debris stung as it impacted his skin, and he instinctively reached up to cover Silus with his hand.

He stared, wide-eyed, at the mine shaft, which was now mostly blocked by several large stones and fallen timbers. "The mine collapsed?" He tried to think of an area of weakness, any sign that the mine was unstable, but couldn't remember anything. There had been no warning except for the mysterious quest. If he hadn't raced out with the dying goblin when he had, he would have been inside when the shaft collapsed.

The goblin beside him blanched. "I do it," she whispered. "There was," she paused struggling for a word, then mimed an explosion with her clawed hands. "Big boom gas down tunnel. I smell from great distance. Goblin'te have been miners from time before time. I knew to avoid, but when I saw you come," she shook her head, thin lips pinching over sharp teeth. "I thought you would kill me. I no want to die without vengeance, so I left fire branch on the edge of pit. When it burn down enough, it fall in, and set off the gas. I think you die in the cave-in, or be trapped until *urushi'mi*, vampires, found you."

Aspen felt himself pale. "Vampires?"

She nodded. "They sleeping now, or sleeping past? Three *urush'mi*. I know smell from Great Lord Akuji army. They sleep in room after round tunnel. Myself, I not enough to wake them, but I leave as soon as the baby born, if able am I. Now, this place safe for *verschladt* goblin. No monster come near this place because of stinky vampire." She wrinkled her long nose in disgust.

Silus wriggled in embarrassment. <I'm sorry,> the little bat whispered. <I smelled it, but I just thought something had died in those rooms. I should have told you.> The goblin was still speaking, so Aspen just stroked the bat's big ears comfortingly, and she pressed her head against his hand.

The woman's voice grew small. "I...sorry. I not know-," She broke off, waving her hand to indicate her ear, her belly, the potion bottle in his hand, and the dusty haze still hanging in the air. "We must go now, fast fast. Vampires not be killed by just this. Unless tunnel is blocked, they wake and hungry. They come. Hunt."

Aspen held out his hand as he scrambled to his feet. "What's done is done. Let's hurry and get as far from here as possible before dark." He leaned down, holding out a hand.

Cautiously, the little goblin placed her scrawny hand in his. He pulled her gently to her feet. He marveled at how thin and fragile she seemed, now that she was in full light. How could he ever have seen her as a threat? As lightly as he could, he pressed her hand between his two much larger ones and spoke formally. "However it may have come about, I'm pleased to meet you. I am called Aspen. May I know your name?"

She smiled tentatively. "I name Sarave." He liked the soft hiss of her name. Sah RAH vay. He bowed over her hand, and her smile broadened, revealing the tips of many pointed teeth. Together, they gathered the hastily discarded contents of his pack and refilled it.

Aspen used a branch to sweep away the signs of their feet and bodies on the ground. It would be best to leave as little sign as possible that anyone had been here. Vamps, being undead, had poor physical senses, except for their innate ability to smell blood and sense body heat from several yards away. If Aspen, Silus, and Sarave were very, very lucky, perhaps the vampires would believe that the explosion had occurred naturally.

It was less than four minutes before they were ready to leave. Aspen secured his pack on his shoulders, and the goblin woman led the way back down the broken, stony path. He dusted away their prints as they went. As he worked, he glanced over at Silus, who was perched on his shoulder, unusually silent.

"Are you all right, little one?"

The bat pulled her wings up around her shoulders. <I put you in danger.> Her voice was even smaller than usual.

He shook his head, chasing a particularly stubborn boot mark with his makeshift broom. "You didn't know. Your mother once convinced me a large rock was a troll, lying in wait."

<Mom did?> Silus perked up, as she always did at any mention of her mother, Miya. <At least she told you something was dangerous when it wasn't,> Silus muttered. <I missed vampires. *Three* of them!>

He tilted his head to rub his cheek against her soft body. "And next time you won't." He stepped down into soft green grass, leaving the dusty path behind.

Quest: "I'm a Believer" complete.

Success: One point Intelligence. Three points Wisdom. A pickaxe. Wait, you didn't grab the pickaxe? Do I have to do everything for you?

A sudden weight tugged at the pack on his back. He knew without looking that it was the promised digging implement. He wasn't sure what he was going to do with it now that the mine was likely destroyed, and definitely infested with vampires, but that was a question for another day.

By the time they reached the end of the foothills, Aspen was all but carrying Sarave. Finally, she collapsed at his feet, and her hands clutching her belly told a story of a fear to which she didn't want to admit. Aspen knelt beside her and offered her water, one of his eggs, and a chunk of chewy bread. She accepted it all, and ate daintily, in spite of her half-starved condition. After wiping her hands on her rags rather ineffectively, she smiled at him, lips trembling. Twilight was falling, and her eyes once again glowed an eerie yellow.

"I sorry, Aspen. I wish I go more, but even with Gi-na aid I not make it." Sarave's hands shook as she pushed her tangled and dirty hair back from her face. Her thin face was hopeless and unhappy.

"You go now. If vampires come-"

Aspen held up a staying hand. "No one is leaving. We'll rest here tonight, and continue in the morning. We're close to the river. The sound and smell of the water and the animals that live nearby should help cover up any sign of our presence. It's still warm enough that we'll be fine without a fire, and we've already eaten. Silus and I will split the watch, and you can rest."

<Should I go on to the house and tell Khor and Sumi to come?> Silus interjected worriedly.

Aspen shook his head at her. "By the time you get there and they come back, even as quickly as you all can go, whatever is likely to happen will be over. We need you here as a sentry far more. *If* vampires come,well," his lean face grew grim, "they won't be the first vamps I've had to send to their long-delayed final rest."

Sarave, who could only hear his side of the conversation, looked back and forth between them, but was too tired to comment. She probably had experience with someone who had a Pet Class. The bond between Aspen and his friends was much closer than that, but it was too difficult to explain, so it was easiest to let others think that was their relationship.

Aspen turned back to the goblin with what he hoped was a reassuring smile. "I have a cloak in my pack. We knew we might have to spend the night outdoors, so I packed for that eventuality. You can bundle up in it, and I'll make a bed of grass for myself. That will help keep me from sleeping too soundly." He smiled wryly, and Sarave ventured a wan smile in return.

The goblin woman's voice was plaintive when she asked, "Why you do this for strange goblin? Human and Goblin'te enemies since time before time."

He shrugged, and when he answered his voice was as tired as he felt. "I'm done. Done fighting, done hating, just…done. That's why I'm all the way out here." *That and the fact that it seemed like half of humanity wanted me dead.* He sighed heavily. "Besides, you haven't met my other friends yet. They like to pick on me, and you seem nice. It'll be good to have someone around who doesn't think it's funny to bite my, uh, bottom."

Sarave placed a small hand over her mouth, and a rusty giggle came from behind it. "I try not to bite you certain, then." They smiled at each other, and then Aspen got busy building a small camp.

As the sun set behind the trees, Aspen tucked a corner of his cloak up under Sarave's pointed chin. She had fallen asleep nearly as soon as she curled up in the heavy fabric, looking very small wrapped in a garment meant for a man nearly twice her height.

Aspen and Silus had agreed that he would take the first watch. If anything was going to happen, it would be more likely to be in the latter half of the night, and she was far better at night watch than he. She had been awake much of the day, and was tired and hungry. She had flown off to hunt just a few minutes ago, and would be back to rest for a few hours as soon as she had eaten her fill.

He stared out into the darkness, listening more than actually looking at anything, and pondered the day. It had been a wild ride, from the early wake up, to the long hike, to the utterly unexpected contents of the mine. Who was Sarave? She was certainly the strangest goblin he'd ever met, though he had to admit that most of them had at least tried to butcher him at some point.

Still, her way of speaking, her polished manners, and most especially the fact that she was a worshipper of Gina, and not one of the darker gods... Well, it all made for a very intriguing package. In spite of the way Sumi had been pushing him, or perhaps because of it, he needed some distraction, and this mysterious goblin was certainly distracting. Plus, he was certain that he and his companions could protect themselves from one sickly goblin, so it wasn't like he was really risking anything. He glanced around the campsite and his gaze caught on the pickaxe lying beside his pack. He remembered the first quest he'd received as he entered the tunnels. He concentrated as he tried to remember the exact wording. Fortunately, he had long experience with this, and the words sprang easily to mind.

Quest: "What Happened Here?" begun.

This mine was marked on the map found in the Great Library. No information was appended, and the mine is marked with a skull. This is unlikely to mean good things for you. Why was this mine abandoned? What was mined here? Find the answers to these questions.

Success: Experience. Unknown ore.

Failure: Variable. Loss of the opportunity to mine in this area.

He was supposed to find out why the mine was abandoned? Well, he'd certainly done that. Presumably the second question was what was keeping the quest from completion. He wished he'd taken some of the ore in one of the carts, but on the way in, he had been more concerned about being weighed down with rocks if he needed to fight than gathering a sample. He'd assumed it would be easy enough to stash a few rocks when he passed back through.

Perhaps Sarave knew what kind of mine it was? He could ask her in the morning. He could certainly use the experience gained by completing the quest, and maybe he'd even level up. That would be good with the possibility of vampires lurking nearby.

His eyes unfocused a bit more as he contemplated their schedule for tomorrow, and how he'd explain coming home with a pregnant goblin to his war-weary friends. Khor especially would not be fond of the idea of living under the same roof as one of his green-skinned foes. Aspen's head was filled with what-ifs and if-thens, and the exhaustion engendered by the events of the day carried him away to sleep.

He woke to the sensation of something tugging at his chest. His mind instantly filled with images of slavering, hungry vampire faces. Massive canines reached for his jugular, and he flung himself backward with a hoarse yell, violently pushing whatever had been on him away even as his other hand tugged his shirt closed. He felt no pain, but there was a loose flap of… Web? It was the webbing Sumi had used to attach the Goddess' Seed to his skin! He fumbled at the dangling seed, feeling himself pale at how close he had come to losing the precious seed, and the many stats he had gained with its help!

He could barely see in the darkness, but the light of the moons above was enough to show him two pale, almost luminescent forms on the ground before him. One was sprawled awkwardly where it had landed after he pushed it, and the other was cowering next to the first, frightened but refusing to move.

What were they? Definitely not vampires. Some kind of animal. They were fluffy, with long fur dangling down to cover their eyes and… hooves? "Goats?" he muttered out loud, wondering. They were vaguely Khor-shaped, though much, much smaller. "Young mountain goats?"

He clambered to his knees as the two juvenile ruminants stared at him with accusing eyes that peered out through tufts of fur. Their pupils were huge and round, not rectangular like Khor's, but they obviously weren;t the same species as the war goat. The animal on the ground tried to get up, but one leg buckled under its weight. The other one pressed close to the first, unwilling to leave its side.

Quest: "Yep, Definitely Goats" begun.

These two sisters lost their family to predators two days ago. Since then, they've been lunch waiting to happen for some carnivore. Apparently, they thought the Goddess' Seed smelled tasty and tried to eat it. Fortunately, you woke before they could get it. (Maybe stay awake when you're supposed to be on watch next time?) But now you've injured one, and they're helpless. Take them home. You have a farm, and they grow wool. Seems like a win-win.

Success: Experience. Two wool-producing animals.

Failure: You're a big meanie for abandoning them.

Aspen let his head fall back and he stared up at the sky. "I know what you're doing," he hissed at his goddess. A lilac-scented breeze tugged at his hair, and he could practically see her giggling.

<What happened? Who are they?> Silus' voice spoke into his mind as he considered what to do. The little bat fluttered down to land on his shoulder,

staring at the goats. She must have just returned from her hunt.

He shook his head, then crossed over to his pack. Reaching in, he took out a precious item. The one thing the only goat he knew absolutely couldn't resist. Cheese. Carefully, he crumbled the cheese in his hand, then tossed a small piece toward the two animals. Nostrils flaring, the uninjured one lunged toward the cheesy crumbles. In an instant, the food had been inhaled, and the young goat looked guiltily back at her sister.

Aspen crumbled more cheese, took a step closer, and gently tossed some again. He repeated this several times, each time sidling slightly nearer to the two young creatures. They were nervous, tossing their heads and trying to edge away, but with the one injured, there was only so far they could go. Soon enough he had a hand resting on the healthy one's withers as he fed them both cheese.

"What I do?" It was a soft voice, and he glanced back at Sarave, who had probably woken with his first yell. The goblin was wise enough to remain still and quiet until she could assess the situation. He had only known she was awake when she cautiously emerged from the cloak after he pulled the cheese from his bag.

"There's a rope in the pack. Can you bring it to me?" He spoke in as soothing a tone as he could, and the little animal under his hand barely quivered at his voice. He wondered if they had been part of some goatherd's flock, and they and their parents had wandered away. He didn't think there were any settlements near enough for them to have wandered away from, but they seemed very trusting for truly wild animals.

Sarave searched the pack, her sensitive eyes no doubt allowing her to see far better than he in the dimness. She pulled the rope out and brought it to him, walking as slowly and carefully as she could with her ungainly belly throwing off her center of balance. She held it out in one hand, and as soon as he took it, she fell back into the shadows so the small creatures didn't feel threatened.

Slowly, Aspen made a loop and passed it over the standing goat's head. He could now see that she was slightly larger than her wounded sister, and a single lock of darker fur dangled over one wide eye. He held his breath as the light weight of the spider silk rope fell around her shoulders, but she didn't move, just shifted her weight from one hoof to another.

Once the loop was gently tightened, he released his breath. "I got a quest to take them home with us," he murmured to his companions, and Sarave nodded in understanding.

"I sleep again, then, Aspen? All is well?" Sarave's voice was drained now that the excitement was over. She had probably gotten less than an hour of sleep.

Aspen nodded, continuing to feed the two animals small pieces of cheese. He heard the goblin female moving behind him, and a soft rustling of cloth as she crawled back into the cloak. From the limp weight resting between his shirt collar and his neck, he suspected Silus had fallen asleep as soon as she was sure Aspen was safe.

Aspen sat in the quiet darkness, feeding two random goats some cheese, until both furry little heads came to rest on his leg, and the kids, too, slept. He let his hand rest on their silky shoulders, feeling their ribs rise and fall. This time, he stayed awake until the moon was high overhead. When he felt Silus stir, he prodded her gently and passed the watch. Then he, too, fell asleep, one hand clutching the Goddess' Seed tightly through his shirt.

Chapter Five

Rouge

T he eggs were cold and slimy by the time Zoey ran into the kitchen the next morning. She wrinkled her nose, but dutifully microwaved them until they were warm and slimy. Put them on some buttered toast, and they were barely edible. Max watched as she shoveled each bite into her mouth, his big brown eyes glistening with deeply pathetic longing.

She put her plate into the sink, ran a splash of water over it to rinse the crumbs before they set, and patted the dog on the head. His tail thumped twice, sadly. "Sorry, boy. Blame Dad. I don't know what his objection is to a bowl of cereal." Max whined, and she sighed. "Yeah, yeah. Carbs." She patted her flat tummy. "Carbs are goooooood." Max woofed in agreement, and she laughed.

"All right, fella. See you tonight!" With that, she grabbed her jacket and her backpack and ran for the bus. She was followed by Max's melancholy howls.

The hours crawled. She had World History first period, and sat next to Jace. She took notes without really listening, and nearly ran to her second period. She checked her messages in the hall between classes. Nothing. They read an act of *King Lear* in English, and she scribbled down the homework before dashing off again. Check messages; nothing. Third period, PE. It was practically a meme that this was the class she shared with Mirna.

Mirna was tall, a little heavy, but pretty, with rich brown wavy hair and big brown eyes. She usually wore her hair up in a side pony with a different colored braided extension in it every day. Her mouth was curled in a perpetual sneer, or maybe that was just how it seemed to Zoey, because Mirna made that expression every time they met. That hour, at least, flew by, because it was filled with avoiding badminton birdies that sought out Zoey's face like heat-seeking missiles.

At the end of that hour, Zoey pulled her regular clothes on over her sweaty gym clothes and ran out of the locker room. She'd quickly learned that trying to take a shower even after hot days of running around the school for an hour would only lead to humiliation. More than once, her clothes had vanished, leaving her to wear her gym clothes the rest of the day, and Mr. Theese had almost written her up for it. The last straw was when she'd found a liquid that smelled suspiciously like pee in her shoes, which was just *nasty*. Since then, she just figured her last three classes would have to deal with her smelling a little ripe.

It was lunchtime at last, and she quickly made her way to the spot behind the gym that she and Jace had staked out for lunch this week. The only good thing about having the class right before lunch with Mirna was that she knew she'd left the other girl behind, still changing, so there was little chance for the bully to catch them on their way to their out-of-the-way nook.

Jace showed up a few minutes after she did, his round face slightly pink. He never seemed to tan, but only burned, so they sat under an oak tree while they ate their lunches. Jace's hair, pale blonde and a little too long for the shape of his face, blew in the breeze, and he tucked it behind his ear impatiently.

They traded sandwiches, her bologna and cheese for his peanut butter and jelly, and ate in companionable silence for a moment. As he polished off his sandwich, Jace spoke through a mouthful of pseudo-meat and cheese.

"What're you up to that took you out of Bright? I thought your dad wanted you to stay in the city unless he was with you?" The slight southern twang he still had left over from his childhood in Georgia made his "R"s soft, and his "oo" sound more like a long "uh". She loved it.

Zoey shrugged and swallowed the bite she was chewing. "It's not a big deal. I have a quest to talk to an NPC." The story had worked on Lily, so why not Jace?

Jace's pale blue eyes narrowed. "What aren't you telling me? You only say something's not a big deal when it's a big deal."

She nearly groaned. Oh, yeah, that was why. Lily was her estranged step-sister, and Jace was her best friend. He actually *knew* her. She thought desperately about what excuse he might believe, and finally decided on a part of the truth. "I can't really tell you about it, but it's timed." Her hazel eyes pleaded with him to take the hint.

"What d'you mean, you can't…" He paused, eyes narrowing further behind the round lenses of his glasses. He almost looked like he was squinting, and if she hadn't been so worried, she would have laughed. "Wait, you mean you *can't*?"

She nodded vigorously. *C'mon, Jace, get it!*

"Seriously? I thought that was an urban myth! You've been tracking down stuff like that since-"

She cut him off, speaking very deliberately. "Jace. I. Can't. Tell. You."

He groaned in frustration. "Yeah, okay, I get it." Pointing at Zoey, he continued, sounding stern. "When it's all done, though, you better tell me *everything*."

Zoey grinned. "Uh, yeah, of course!"

They returned to eating, and barely managed to finish before the bell rang for fourth period.

Biology. Break. Check her screen. Nothing. French. Break. Check the screen. Nothing. Sixth period. Geometry. Break. Her screen buzzed in her pocket as she picked up her pace toward her locker. She pressed her thumb to the biometric lock, and shoved her stack of books into the small space. Why did some teachers still insist on physical media instead of digital?

The instant her hands were free, Zoey dug the screen out of her pocket and read the message.

Veritas Notification System: Automatic notification. Tasks Done.

It was all she could do not to shout in victory. Now she just had to get home, eat, finish her homework, and log in. Zombie Rouge was resting in the Dead Tent, so she'd even get a Well-Rested Buff! Then her screen buzzed again.

@Lily: *I gave you back some of your transport fee. You might need it, since your dad's not around. Pay me back later!*

She stared at the message, shocked. Since when did Lily care about what Zoey needed? Lily had barely even talked to her the last time they'd seen each other, and it seemed like she actively avoided being around when their mom called. Well, whatever. Zoey couldn't worry about it now, and she really did need the gold.

🍎 🍎 🍎

Zoey was one of the lucky ones who were dropped off early in the bus route. It only took twenty minutes for her to get home, but some of the kids rode for over an hour. By the time she scarfed down her dinner and got a few assignments done, they'd just be getting off the bus. She shook her head as she nearly tripped down the tall steps and faceplanted onto the curb. Once she got a car, she was never taking the bus again.

She jogged half a block, to the little house with the broad porch and white picket fence where she lived with her dad, and thumbed the lock. She was half expecting her dad to be home early again, but the house was quiet, except for Max, who sat and waited for her to pet him, because he was a Good Boy.

Dropping her backpack on the floor by the door, she went out back to play with Max. The chocolate lab had his own dog door, which was keyed to his subdermal microchip, but all he did when his humans weren't home was some obligatory barking. She tried to make sure to play fetch with him a couple times a day, even if she couldn't take him for a walk around the neighborhood.

When she'd gotten Max to the panting and 'are you really going to make me chase that again?' stage, she headed to the kitchen and snagged a plate of cold lasagna. While it warmed up to somewhere hopefully short of lava in the microwave, she put dry kibble in Max's bowl and checked the filter in his water, which sometimes got clogged with mysterious Max-fuzz. The big brown dog gave her a reproachful look as he sniffed the lasagna-scented air, but finally heaved a dejected sigh and ate his food.

Zoey patted his shining brown side. "Sorry, Max. Dad says you've gone past trim and slim, possibly because of all the eggs you've been eating. Gotta cut back for a little while." The dog whined, but followed her into the dining room and sat by her feet with his head on his paws as she ate.

Dinner devoured, Zoey pulled out her laptop and started on her homework. It wasn't nearly as much fun without her dad there, but it was faster. It seemed like forever, but she was done, dishes rinsed and in the dishwasher, and headed upstairs by 4:30. She would be able to get in her maximum four hours of play today. Yes!

After going to the bathroom, she wiggled into her bodysuit, which smelled faintly of chemicals. She was in the pod and starting up Veritas only a moment later. A sensation of dizziness, falling, and then…

Rouge blinked her eyes open in a small, cloth-sided room nearly filled with a single twin-sized bed. It was lit by a single glowstone, dimmed behind thick orange glass in a lantern. She sat up in bed and pulled up her interface, for once appreciating the clear and steady light. A few thoughts and finger-twitches later, and she was in a fresh set of leathers. These were mottled brown, tan, and green, since she'd be traveling through the woods. She settled the matching cloak around her shoulders, and stood up.

Then she remembered she was within range of the Traveler's Guild, and could still access her mail. Sure enough, there was a gift from Doom Bloom. No message, just 1500 Gold...and two tents! Tents were 250 Gold each to make at an NPC shop, and required materials including 6 Canvas, 10 Sticks, Rope, and a Sleeping Bag, which was another 150 Gold by itself. Counting the cost of the Tent Doom Bloom had used getting them up here, she'd barely broken even on transporting Rouge. Something was definitely weird there.

Rouge shook her head. No time for that. Whatever was going on with her step-sister could wait. She had some shopping to do!

She pulled up the super basic map of Vargo that her avatar had received when she came into town. She'd checked it out on the boards, but it was good to review. Rouge wasn't really great at directions, and could pretty much get lost anyplace she hadn't been at least twenty times. She flipped the map up into the upper right corner of her interface and walked out of the Dead Tent.

It was late night, heading toward dawn, and Vargo was quiet. Since it was a military outpost, some soldiers were on duty at all times, so there was an open pub for the enlisted soldiers, and an inn for the officers. Brawling was frowned upon at either establishment, so she could probably go and get rations at either place, and the pub was likely to be cheaper. Eyes on the mini map, she made her way through town, nodding at the guards she saw, who didn't nod back, but dismissed her with a flick of their eyes.

The pub was called 'The Hairy Lemon', and the sign that hung above the door showed a faded yellow lemon with a head of moldy greenish hair. Gross. She shook her head and pushed through the door, looking around. Rouge was a people-watcher, and she quickly sorted the patrons into two groups in her mind. The early risers could be identified by their cups of small beer and plates filled with eggs and sausage links, while the night-shift guards had large mugs of grog and bowl of stew.

No one really looked around as she came in. They were used to Travelers coming through at all hours, so once the soldiers' assessing eyes sized her (and her level) up, they passed her over as being of no particular interest, except for a few who curled their lips in response to the sight of an elf in their settlement.

She did see one familiar face, however. It was Weapons Shortage, the dwarven player who had come north on Doom Bloom's Zombie run. He was staring disconsolately down into a mug of something green, and a plate of delicious-looking fried bread and bacon sat next to him. She hesitated a moment, but the last time she'd seen someone looking that depressed, it was an NPC rat-catcher after some player spawned a bunch of stray cats and put him out of a job. Wep was a player, but she sat down next to him and asked the same question she'd asked the rat-catcher.

"Anything I can do to help?"

The dwarf laughed and shook his scruffy head. "I look that bad, do I?"

Rouge just grinned back at him and stole a piece of bacon. [Legerdemain] was good for more than just picking pockets, after all. Any skill that got you bacon was a good skill to have.

The short, wide man sighed disconsolately, picking at a piece of bacon. He didn't seem to notice the gap on his plate, so she nibbled at her ill-gotten treat without even trying to hide it. Wep just started talking, still looking glum.

"I came up here for a quest. I knew it was a long-shot, but I had to try. I got a trading quest back in Bloodhaven, and the reward was a letter of recommendation addressed to Vargo's commanding officer. The catch was, I had to find or craft an item of Very Rare or better quality and try to sell it to him. If I succeeded, I'd get a military contract and be set to sell all the weapons and armor I could get my hands on. At premium prices, no less."

He shrugged, stabbing at a perfectly cooked egg with his fork. "I failed. I guess my relationship with the military was too low. I probably should have farmed some reputation quests before heading in, but the Bloodhaven quest made it sound like it was practically a done deal."

He set down the fork with a gummy click, lifted his mug of green goo to his whiskered face and, she assumed, took a gulp. A moment later, two green sparks shot out of his nose, separated, and traveled to the ends of his mustache, which stood stiff and quivering for a moment before falling back into their usual jumbled mess.

Rouge blinked in amazement. "Whoa. What is *that*?"

He raised the mug to her in a salute, his eyes crinkling in genuine amusement beneath his bushy brows. "Haven't seen that before, eh? It's Dwarven Kombucha. The item description says it's mushrooms fermented in a barrel with a dead rat. Downright deadly poison if you're not a Dwarf. To me, it tastes a lot like," he rolled his eyes thoughtfully, "Cherry Coke, Mountain Dew, vanilla ice cream, and just a hint of battery acid. Takes a little getting used to, but it's pretty good once you do."

Rouge just stared at him, mouth open. "Why... Why would you drink that?"

"Eh." He shrugged again. "When you spawn in a Dwarven city, you get a quest to drink the stuff as part of the tutorial. Once you try it, you just kind of keep going."

She looked around, and he followed her gaze automatically. She grinned, lifting another piece of bacon. "They sell that stuff here?"

He shook his head. "Nah. I always carry some with me. As a trader, you never know when you'll meet another dwarf and need to make friends. Or," his mustache lifted in a grin, "when you'll meet someone you don't like and need a strong poison."

She narrowed her eyes. Poisons were one thing she'd never really gotten into. That was more of an assassin thing, and she didn't kill people, even NPCs. Well, not until Dorkness Rising, and she felt no guilt over that. Unlike the NPCs, he'd revive in just a few hours, only short a little experience. Plus, he totally deserved it.

Now, however, she was heading into high level wilderness with no support but a surprisingly-amiable ostrich. A little insurance wouldn't go amiss. Her hazel eyes narrowed thoughtfully. "Is it a good stabby poison too?"

The man choked out a laugh, spewing virulent green goop over the plate of food. She eyed it and decided against practicing her skills on it any more. Even bacon wasn't worth that.

"Stabby poison? You mean will it work if you put it on a blade and stab someone with it?" He nodded, his gaze sharpening. "You looking to buy something like that?"

Whoops. She may have overplayed her hand. She could practically see his merchant senses tingling. "Well, I have a quest nearby too. I'll have to head out into the wilderness, and a DoT would probably be good. It's okay, though. I'll be fine without it." She couldn't quite hide the quiver in her voice at the end.

The Dwarf cocked his head. "I'm not sure what your angle is, Miss Rouge, but I tell you what. I'll sell you some of my Kombucha for a good price if you'll also buy this weapon I was supposed to sell to the Major." He reached into his inventory and took out a long, oddly-shaped blade in a sheath and set it on the table between them. It almost looked like someone had welded an extra blade onto the back of a shallowly curved mini-scythe, but while it should have been awkward, it just looked vicious instead.

She reached out, then looked over at him. "May I?" He nodded, and she examined the knife.

Starter Mambele of Return **– An iron blade with a curved back section and rearward spike. In battle, it can be used as a hatchet or thrown. This one has a spell on it so it will return to the wielder after being thrown. Good for training. Wielder must have level 10 [Thrown Weapons] Skill and be under level 30. Weight – 2 lbs. Rarity – Very Rare.**

Her little thief's heart lit with an avariciousness she hadn't felt since she saw the huge sapphire that served as an engagement ring for Lord Portswine's third wife. The poor girl, only a few years older than Rouge herself, could barely lift her hand with that rock on it. It had taken a week and a half of scoping out the Lord's surprisingly small estate before she was able to sneak in.

The heartbreak she felt when she discovered the rock was little more than colored glass was nothing compared to the pain she suffered as she pushed the wicked weapon away from her.

She shook her head. "No way I can afford that."

Wep snorted and then sighed. "As a merchant, I should agree with you, but the fact is that up here, the darned thing is nearly worthless. Honestly, even in Bright it'd be little better. I got it myself as part of a job lot from an auction-house clearing sale. The [Return] spell is worth a lot, but the level 30 cap is just…" He shook his head, "No one who has leveled [Thrown Weapons] up to level 10 is also going to be below level 30, or if they are, they won't stay that way long enough to be worth buying it. The Major just laughed at me when I showed it to him. I thought since it was Very Rare, it wouldn't matter what it actually was. I was wrong. He told me none of his soldiers were under level 50, and to take my trash to the midden where it belongs."

He looked at Rouge, eyes slightly unfocused. He hiccupped, and iridescent green bubbles flew out of his mouth, landing on the table and popping with an acidic little hiss. "If I want this trip to be worthwhile at all, I need to sell this thing. You're a level 21 Rogue, but you're up here among the 50+ mobs. You must have some high-level skills. Can't you use it?"

Rouge gulped.

🐛 🐛 🐛

The sun was coming up by the time Rouge walked out of the pub. Her purse was lighter by most of the gold she'd gotten from Doom Bloom, but her inventory was heavier by five days of water and rations for her and Codswallop, several comically large jugs of Dwarven Kombucha, and the Starter Mambele of Return.

She consulted her mini-map and headed for the stable where Codswallop's icon blinked a contented green. It was a few blocks away, near the soldiers' barracks, and she could hear men and women talking and moving around, interspersed with authoritarian bellows such as "Move it!" and "I want that stable so clean you could eat your mama's apple pie off the ground!"

Codswallop was so excited to see her that the bird nearly choked on his breakfast. She laughed and patted his fuzzy head, which he insisted on shoving into her hair. Fortunately, her Zombie had paid for his care last night, so once he finished eating, she just saddled him and walked him out into the hazy morning sunshine.

She looked around her, taking in the bustle beginning to overtake the outpost. Uniformed men and women walked to and fro confidently, looking ready for action. She, on the other hand, was a massively outclassed Rogue with no delusions that she wasn't about to die.

She pulled up the quest.

Quest: "Follow the Red Brick Road".

The Head Librarian needs you to take a package to an old friend. You must deliver it, unopened, within one week.

Success: 5000 Experience. Another clue in your search for Duke Penbrooke. Maximum Relationship with the Head Librarian which will only be reduced if you betray his trust.

Failure: -50 Relationship points with the Head Librarian. Fail the "Come in from the Cold" Quest.

Time Remaining: Four days, 17 hours, 12 minutes.

She blew a curl away from her eye with an impatient puff. This was going to be close, but if she followed the road, used her remaining four cinnamon rolls wisely, and had Codswallop leap anything he could, there was a chance. Like Weapons Shortage, she was willing to take the risk for the sake of the grand prize.

There was only one more decision to make. Where did she set her respawn point? A player could spawn at any Traveler's Guild, the center of any town, or, if their Reputation with the followers of a certain God or Goddess was high enough, any official shrine or temple of that deity. Her save point was currently the center of Bright, and her options now were Vargo's town center or Vargo's Dead Tent.

She pondered it for a long moment before shaking her head. The honest truth was, if she died, there wouldn't be time to try again. Leaving her respawn in Bright was undoubtedly the fastest and cheapest way to get back. That would leave Codswallop wherever she died, if he didn't die too, but the game would send him to her at his best pace, so he'd find her in Bright in a week or two. If he did die, she could resummon him at the spawn point after one in-game day.

Decision made, she vaulted into Codswallop's small saddle, tucked her legs under his warm, fluffy wings, and took off at an ostrich-trot.

The road was wide and solid as it wound up into the mountains. It was obviously made to be able to handle a caravan, though no trade wagons had passed through these mountains in years, as far as she knew. The military outpost maintained the road, though, since digging ditches and maintaining infrastructure was a great use of manpower in times of peace.

The road began to narrow as she entered the first pass. It was more of a hill pass than a mountain pass, but the wall rose steeply on one side of her as the ground dropped away on the other side. Codswallop maintained a steady, ground-eating stride, however, and they were on the other side, with broad tracts of brown grass and stunted trees in every direction, before she even thought to be worried about falling.

This close to the outpost, it seemed that the mobs had been thinned pretty thoroughly by the soldiers, and the few monsters she did see kept a respectful distance. She did see a *Lesser Capybara – Level 52*, and a *Chinchilla – Level 46*, but they were both too involved with their own activities to pay much attention to her.

Her first challenge came when she was halfway through the first true mountain pass. It was cold, and she had pulled on a heavy cloak. The thick, loose cloth of the cloak saved her life. She and Codswallop were precariously making their way across a narrow shelf barely five feet across. A much wider path had branched to the left over an hour before, but she could tell from her map that that would be a slower, albeit easier, road.

She was walking alongside her ostrich. She figured that way, if one of them slipped, the other could try to save them. She flipped her Mambele from hand to hand, getting used to its balance and weight. Occasionally, she would throw it toward a nearby object - mostly scrubby bushes and twisted little trees - and mentally call it back to her hand. She had been doing this since they left Vargo, and her [Thrown Weapons] skill was already nearly level 13, which was almost two levels higher than when she'd started. The Mambele was a challenging weapon, and just not stabbing herself with it was worth a little experience.

As Rouge threw the weapon toward a defenseless overhanging branch in front of them, she heard a hiss. She glanced up, just in time to see a large mountain cat leaping toward her. She let out the girliest shriek that had escaped her lips in several years, and threw her arms up, completely forgetting everything about fighting she had learned since joining Veritas. Her cloak flew up above her head, and tangled around the big cat's paws, throwing it off just enough that it only dealt her a painful but non-serious blow to her left arm, instead of fatally gouging her throat.

The *Lesser Puma* deals you a glancing blow. You take 15 points of damage.

The clasp of the cloak gave way under the furious pulling of the predator, and Rouge gasped as it was yanked from her throat. She rolled away, toward the cliff wall, where she bounced to her feet and pressed her back to the reassuring solidity of the stone. She whipped out her hand, summoning her weapon, and felt the hilt slap into her palm.

She squinted as she looked at the angry animal in front of her. The tag above it read: *Lesser Puma – Level 43*. Not as bad as it could be, given that mobs around here ranged in level from 40-60, but no mob was a good mob when she was twenty levels too low for the area.

The Puma circled as best it could on the narrow stone shelf. It was in between her and Codswallop, and it tried to keep a wary yellow eye on both of them at once. It was evidently trying to decide which of them to attack, now that its initial ambush had failed. Making up its mind, its tawny haunches bunched as it readied for another leap.

Rouge cursed herself for not yet applying the Dwarf's poison to her weapon. She hadn't wanted to take the risk, since there was a very real possibility of cutting and poisoning herself while she was practicing. A player couldn't commit suicide in *Veritas Online* (even accidentally), but if she managed to take herself down to 10% health, the game could think she was trying to kill herself.

Players usually did this to get out of a sticky situation they didn't want to deal with, but some people just used it as a relatively easy way to get 'home' quickly. To prevent that, *VO* had the Suicide Debuff, which would reduce her stamina recovery to 0 for an hour for each attempt, set XP gain to 0 for 24 hours, and double the respawn time and XP loss for death. No bueno.

Rouge threw her Mambele as hard as she could, aiming for the far-too-close head of the beast. The puma dodged, but at this distance, it couldn't escape uninjured. The Mambele lodged in the large muscle of its shoulder, buried deep enough that the second shorter blade on its back side dug into the meat of the animal's side.

CRITICAL! You have dealt 47 points of damage to the *Lesser Puma*.

A crit, and it had only done 47 hitpoints of damage? She was seriously outclassed. She summoned the weapon back to her hand, and it ripped out of the lion's muscle and fur as it flipped back to land in her palm. She was greeted by another message.

You have dealt 12 points of secondary damage to the *Lesser Puma*. The *Lesser Puma* is Bleeding.

***Lesser Puma* takes 10 points of damage from Bleed.**

Yes! It was a general rule of thumb that basic respawn mobs of any physical attack type would likely have around five hp per level. That meant this creature was likely to have around 200-250 hp. It should be down around 20% of its health, and the Bleed debuff, which would continue doing damage over time, could well be what allowed Rouge to survive the creature's attack.

On the other hand, her first hit had been a critical, and it was very unlikely she'd get another. The puma had backed off, eyeing her warily. His hissing yowl indicated that he was extremely unhappy with the discovery that his lunch could fight back.

Just then, Codswallop hissed like a teakettle about to explode, drawing the big cat's gaze back to him. Codswallop's feathers were puffed up, and he danced from foot to foot, his powerful legs looking ready to deploy the long talons at the end of all four toes. He couldn't actually attack the puma, but if she didn't know that, she would have believed he could, and obviously no one had told the big cat that mounts had no attack capability.

The moment the mountain lion's attention shifted to the large bird, Rouge used the shadow cast by the overhang above them to shift into [Stealth]. She crouched down, edging away from where the cat had last seen her. When he flicked his eyes back to her position, she was lost in the shadows, and his ears pressed flat to his head as he realized he'd lost track of his prey.

Codswallop hissed again, sounding more like an infuriated teapot than an enormous flightless bird, and the puma crouched to leap. In the moment before it could jump, Rouge threw herself onto its back, triggering [Backstab].

[Backstab] failed. Normal attack deals 23 points of damage to the *Lesser Puma.*

Rouge hung on for dear life. Beneath her, there was a writhing, yowling mass of claws, teeth, and muscle. She swung her Mambele over and over, ignoring the slew of notifications that minimized to the side of her vision. The long, curved edge of the weapon bit into the beast over and over, but it continued to thrash and roar. Twice the blade was pulled from her hand, and she had to call it back to her.

When the beast tried to scrape her off against the cliff face again, she muttered a curse through bleeding and swollen lips. Her knife was torn from her hand a third time, but she hung on, desperately trying to avoid being pulled from the lion's back, as that would be an instant death sentence. She spat to clear her mouth, and shouted, "Come on, Gina! I'm on *your* quest! Can't you give a girl a chance?!"

Suddenly, the cat choked, and Rouge looked up from where she was clinging to its shoulders. Codswallop was pulling one clawed foot back from the lion's throat, and preparing the other for an attack.

Rouge gaped. That was impossible! Mounts in *Veritas* were just that; mounts. The only classes that could have a combat mount were Knights, and a rare pet class, the Beastmaster. For all that Codswallop had looked threatening a minute before, Rouge had been all too aware that it was simply posturing. Now, though... Now the game had changed. Literally.

She grinned wildly and summoned her blade back to her hand. Raising her arm, she swung it down at the momentarily stunned cat beneath her, stabbing deep into the side of its skull. She felt something give, finally, and warm blood ran over her fingers. Vomit filled her mouth, but she pressed on, cutting into the beast until it finally fell limp.

You have defeated *Lesser Puma*.

You have gained one level in [Stealth].

You have gained one level in [Thrown Weapons].

You have gained three levels in [Knife Wielding].

You are now level 22.

You are now level 23.

For several long moments, Rouge lay on the rocky ledge beside the corpse of the puma, eyes closed, gasping for air as her Stamina and hit points regenerated. The big cat had dealt her 79 points of damage in total, and she had used all but the last dregs of her Stamina. Now that she was out of battle, her wounds were able to heal, and she quickly felt better, at least physically.

The first twenty levels of her *Veritas* career hadn't prepared her for this. The vast majority of her experience had come from doing reputation quests. While some of those quests had involved battle, it had rarely been mobs higher than her own level, and when it was, Motte had been there to tank, so she rarely took more than a few points of damage. Also, mobs of level 20 and lower were much less *terrifying* than a huge, hyper-realistic mountain lion.

When she finally managed to bring her heart rate down to a reasonable level, she pulled up the battle log, flipping past all the notices of damage dealt and taken. She was looking for... There!

The Goddess Gina has heard your prayer! The Goddess Gina grants you a miracle! Your mount will be able to attack for 30 seconds. Give thanks to Gina!

She wiped dirt and crusty blood from her face and muttered, "Thank you, Gina." She half-expected some kind of response, but all she heard was the sound of the wind whistling through the pass and Codswallop's concerned warble. She chuckled at her own whimsy as she pulled herself to her feet.

She took a moment to loot the corpse, gathering one Tattered Puma Skin, one piece of Gamey Meat, and four Puma Claws. When she was done, she pulled a waterskin from her bag and poured Codswallop a bowl of water before she drank herself. She also fed him some generic mount feed, though she wished that she could have afforded something better. Finally, she pulled up her character sheet and allotted the points from her two levels:

Stats

NAME: Rouge the Rogue	LEVEL: 23	GENDER: Female
CLASS: Rogue	CLASS LEVEL: 22	

Attributes

STR: 34	DEX: 132 (120 + 12)	WIS: 10
VIT: 32	INT: 20	END: 24
HEALTH: 71 / 96	MANA: 80 / 80	STAMINA: 29 / 48
H-REGEN: 0.33 / sec	M-REGEN: 0.2 / sec	S-REGEN: 0.5 / sec

Effects

RACE: Wood Elf / Dark Elf	Darkvision Reduced Stamina (2x End) Increased Mana (4x Int) +1 Dex / 10 points Disliked by most non-human NPCs

Leveling complete, she was back on the road, somewhat the worse for wear, and certainly much more cautious. They finished crossing the narrow path in just over an hour, and Rouge gratefully climbed back aboard Codswallop. No fancy flips now. She needed to keep her eyes open for predators.

About an hour later, they saw a *Black Bear – Level 50*. The bear was busy fishing enormous trout from a rocky stream, and had no time for a large bird and a smallish girl. Rouge and Codswallop respectfully made their way around the animal, keeping as far away as they could without going off the road.

There were a few more sightings, including a *Roc – Level 58*, and a *Greater Mule Deer – Level 42*. The Roc dipped a wing down toward them, examining them with a great black eye. Its shadow covered them, the road, and a good part of the dry, hard ground nearby. Rouge quickly turned her bird toward a heavy copse of prickly pine trees. They sheltered there and ate a small meal until the immense bird got bored and flew off to find easier prey.

By the time Rouge ran out of playtime for the day, they were high in the mountains, and they could see their breath as they puffed in the noticeably thinner air. Rouge had acquired a Winded debuff that reduced her Stamina recovery to .3/second. She sent up constant prayers to Gina that they could continue unmolested, because if she had to use any skills, things could get rough.

The good news was that despite reducing her use due to the slowed stamina regen, her [Thrown Weapons] skill was nearly level 15. At level 20, she would be able to throw two knives at once, though not well. The bad news was that Skill training tended to have reduced returns when you repeated the same activity, and it soon wouldn't be worth it to practice by attacking trees as they passed.

Just before ten pm in the real world, Rouge checked her quest timer.

Time Remaining: Four days, 19 hours, 22 minutes.

According to her calculations, it would be at least twenty hours before she could play again. Tomorrow was Friday, but she still had a full day of school, dinner, homework (though her dad wasn't as picky about getting it all done Friday night), and her dad's Daily Interrogation. Twenty hours in real time was forty hours in *Veritas*. Which would only leave her three days and three hours. Ish.

She and Codswallop could travel far faster than a regular NPC. In fact, she was fairly certain that the bird moved faster than a basic horse mount, like Blackie. Her improved relationship with the bird gave him an even greater boost to his speed, so they were actually making really good time. She also still had four cinnamon rolls, though if she were honest, she wanted to eat them herself, not feed them to an overgrown chicken, however awesome he might be.

She might make it.

She might not.

It would, frankly, be far too close, and depend a lot on how quickly she could get back online on Saturday. Sometimes after finals her dad was super tired and slept in, so she could play. If he hadn't finished grading, or was worried about getting grades in by the deadline, he'd be up bright and early and expect her to eat with him. If she was *really* lucky, he might have to go back to the university for Saturday office hours. She hated to wish that her dad would stay away longer, but, well…

Rouge sighed, and leaned back in the saddle, tugging her valiant steed to a halt beside a stream just off the road. There was a small clearing with a cliff rising up on one side, and she reached into her bag to pull out one of the precious tents Doom Bloom had given her. She glanced at the item description.

Tent – A simple canvas tent, suitable for up to four people. While the tent is active, everything inside it and all mounts within ten feet will be undetectable by all players, NPCs, and monsters (except Boss monsters.) Weatherproof. Can only be deployed when out of combat and no enemies are within twenty yards. Tent will last for up to 48 game hours. Cannot be reused. Weight - 15 lbs. Rarity – Common. Activate – Yes/No?

Rouge selected Yes with a twitch of her finger, and the tent fuzzed into view in front of her. It was a good size, and looked like it could actually hold four people. An instant campfire burned merrily in front of it, and a hitching post stood at each corner. The back of the tent snugged up to the cliff face, so theoretically nothing could sneak up on them from that direction, if she somehow didn't make it back before the 48 hours ran out. Remembering the puma, she cast a suspicious eye up the sheer cliff, but the tent wouldn't have activated if there were any mobs nearby.

Carefully, she tied Codswallop's lead to the closest hitching post. Pulling off the small saddle, she brushed the bird down as best she could. Clouds of dust and bits of fluff filled the air. As soon as she was done, the bird shook his feathers, puffed up, and began preening his feathers with his beak.

She patted him on one soft black wing. "You're a good bird, Wally. You saved my bacon today, and you're going to let me complete this quest, too. When all this is done, we're going to go back to North Goose, find Millie, and buy you all the cinnamon rolls you can eat." She grinned. "And me, too. I might even give my dad one. If he doesn't kill me first. Actually, maybe I should hang onto a cinnamon roll and bribe him with it before he finds out. Everybody feels less murderous with a bellyful of pastry."

Quest: "Let Them Eat Pastry!" available.

You should always follow through on your promises. Next time you're near North Goose, find Millie and acquire at least six *Cinnamon Rolls* for Mount Codswallop.

Success: A belly full of joy. Improved Relationship with Mount *Codswallop*. Improved Relationship with Millie.

Failure: Nothing.

Accept: Yes/No?

Laughing, Rouge selected yes. Codswallop chirruped agreeably, and she patted his soft feathers again before opening the tent and stepping inside. It was lit by a small glowstone, and a pile of furs in each corner were ready to receive a player. It wasn't exactly luxurious, but it would be more than enough to grant her the Well-Rested buff when she logged back in.

Sighing, she climbed into the comfiest looking pile and closed her eyes. With a thought, she pulled up her interface, and logged out.

Chapter Six

Aspen

Once the fluffy young goats finished off his cheese, they seemed to have decided that Aspen represented safety, and rarely strayed more than a few yards from his side. This was fortunate, because Aspen had no energy to spare chasing down toddler goats, so, quest or no, he likely would have had to leave them behind if they'd run off or lagged too far behind. Fortunately, Kayli's leg seemed to have healed overnight, and she was none the worse for wear.

Still, it was the next evening when Aspen, Silus, Sarave, and two kids, who he'd decided to name Kayli and Kayti, finally got near enough to see the tiny stone house that would become their home. Silus was asleep in her travel basket strapped to the pack, Sarave trudged beside them with exhausted determination, and Kayti and Kayli pranced near them with the eternal energy of youth.

Sarave, who had spent more time watching her feet than anything else, looked up and saw the house. She gasped, though Aspen couldn't quite read the complex emotions that crossed her inhuman face. "Is that it?"

He coughed, slightly embarrassed. "It is. I know it's not much. We'll build some rooms off it, and an animal barn too. There's only one bed, but I can sleep on the floor or in the wagon. I think we can make it work, at least until the baby is born and you decide what you want to do next. You don't have to-"

Tears began to trickle from the goblin's large yellow eyes. "It is *house*. It has walls, and a roof. My people-" She looked away, clearly struggling to find the right words. "Goblin live underground, and in mines, for year and year. We sleep on stone floor. Maybe blanket, maybe not. Human not...respect for *goblin'te*. But you offer me house, room, and bed. Only my husband wish to offer me this, and he was," her voice choked, "killed soon. Too soon." Shaking her head, the small woman was no longer able to speak, but she began to walk faster, as though gaining energy from the sight of her new home.

Before Aspen could respond, he saw a dust cloud rising from the house. It grew larger and closer, and he could hear the thunder of huge hooves coming from inside it. Khor's mental voice injected itself into his head. <Where *were* you? You were supposed to be home by lunchtime! We were trying to decide if we should->

Aspen knew the moment the huge goat realized what – who – was traveling with his friend. A ferocious bleat tore the air, and Khor reared back, flashing his sharp cloven hooves. <Is that a goblin? Did it take you prisoner? Get down! I'll kill it!>

In a heartbeat, Aspen was standing in between Khor and Sarave, arms spread wide. "Khor!" he shouted. "Stop!"

For a frozen moment, Khor's hooves hovered in the air only inches from Aspen's face. With a desperate effort, the massive goat managed to twist aside. He landed on his side with a thundering crash, grunting in pain. Thrashing wildly, he heaved himself to his feet, shaking long strands of grass from his horns. <What in Atae's tiny t->

Sumi's sharp voice cut in. <Khor! There are children listening! That poor woman is clearly no threat to anyone. Use whatever it is that functions as your

brain and calm yourself!> The spider's ant-like body appeared in the path beaten through the grass by Khor's hasty approach. Her large central eyes took in the travel-weary party before her, and she spoke crisply. <Khor, let Aspen and the goblin woman ride. They're exhausted, and the female is gravid. She needs to sit down before she falls down.>

Khor's huge brown eyes rolled wildly in his head, showing the whites all the way around. <Let a goblin ride me? I'd rather lick Duke Geral's h… and.> He stuttered at the sharp click of Sumi's deadly fangs. Hanging his head, the goat's spiral horns nearly dragged in the dust, and he sounded more than a little petulant when he continued. <Do I have to? Aspen can ride, but the goblin looks fine. Entirely too healthy, in fact.> He bared his large square teeth at the goblin, who glared back with fierce yellow eyes, hands protectively crossed over her abdomen.

Sumi just stared, black eyes glittering in the sun.

Khor scuffed his hoof on the ground. <*Fine,*> he muttered.

Only when he capitulated did Aspen take his eyes from the angry ruminant. He released the breath he'd been holding, grateful that Sumi had followed so closely on the goat's hooves. Aspen could have talked Khor down, but the gat knew better than to push Sumi. She had left him bound in webs overnight more than once for lesser infractions.

Aspen glanced at his new companions, only then realizing that the kids were pressed up against his legs as if he was the only shelter in a storm. He crouched down and pressed a reassuring hand on each small goat's shoulder. Then he met Sarave's accusatory gaze.

He bowed his head a little, embarrassed. "I'm sorry. I did try to warn you."

Her voice was sharp, sharper than it had been since they'd left the cave. "You said friend be little upset!" She waved her hand toward the dejected goat, speaking carefully to make her displeasure clear. "That is more than upset!"

Aspen rubbed the back of his neck, feeling stiff, sweaty hair beneath the brim of his ragged straw hat. "I was hoping Silus could fly ahead before they noticed us, and let them know what to expect. I'm very sorry."

<I just woke up,> came the little bat's voice. <What happened? Why does Khor look like he ate a cartload of rotten papaya again?>

Khor shook his head angrily. <That wasn't my fault! I didn't know what it was supposed to taste like!>

Sumi waved her foreleg again. <Then *perhaps* you should have exercised some prudence and not eaten it all. Now hush. Let's get back to the house, and we can discuss the situation like civilized people. I take it, Aspen, that we will be having company for dinner?>

Aspen nodded and pointed to Sumi. "Pardon my rudeness. Sarave, this is Sumi. Sumi, Sarave. The big lunkhead over there is Khor. Khor, this is Sarave. She'll be our guest for the foreseeable future."

Little teeth pulled at his shirt. Kayti was taking advantage of his crouched position to try eating the Goddess' Seed again. He gently pushed away the velvety muzzle, barely visible under the long fringe of silky black and white fur, and stood up.

Kayli poked her little head from around Aspen's legs and looked up at the goat, who must seem like a veritable giant to her. After a long moment of silent contemplation, she let out a high pitched "Maa-aa!" Running beneath Khor's barrel chest, the little animal stood looking up at him, nearly quaking with joy. "Maa-aa!" she bleated again.

Aspen waved his hand. "These trouble-makers are Kayti," he pointed at the slightly larger one with the black streak of fur who still hid behind him, "and Kayli." He indicated the smaller all-white kid.

<They're-> Khor seemed to choke, staring at the young animals.

Aspen shrugged. "I know. You don't really like Lesser Goats, but I got a quest saying their parents were killed a few days ago, and telling me to take them home. I couldn't leave them behind anyway. They're barely more than babies. Plus, I can shear them when they get bigger. That fur of theirs doesn't get dirty at all, and even thorns and twigs just fall out instead of getting tangled.

It must have some amazing properties, and I bet anything made from it would be at least resistant to dirt."

Khor still seemed unable to respond, so Aspen plowed on. "They'll have to live in the barn with you for the first year. We don't have time or materials to make more than one building, but I don't think they'll get all that big. Plus, Kayli seems to like you! I'm sure Kayti will warm up to you, too."

The eight-foot tall goat just shook his head, brown eyes locked on the little animals, whose clean white fur practically glowed in the dim evening light. <What... kind of goats did you say they were?>

Aspen scratched his head. He was going to need a very long bath after this latest adventure. "Some kind of mildly-magical mountain goat, I guess. They shouldn't be much trouble, and they're really cute." He tried for a disarming smile and felt the dust on his face crack.

Khor bent his head to nose at the little goat happily snuggling against one of his tree-trunk legs. He was surprisingly gentle, and Aspen began to hope he wouldn't have to listen to too many snarky comments about how annoying the little animals were. <Mountain goats. Well.> He looked back up at Aspen, sounding bemused. <You got a quest?>

"It just says to take them home, and something about how they have wool, so it'll be good for the farm. So," he cleared his throat, "you're okay with it?"

Khor tilted his head at Kayti. <There, there, little one,> he said, his voice a gentle rasp Aspen had never heard before. <It's all right. You'll come to no harm here.> To Aspen he added, <We'll need to get a building up for them quickly. Predators will be attracted to them. They should sleep in the house or with me until that's done.>

Aspen stared, tired mind unable to deal with this unexpected twist. "Sleep *with* you? I was sure you'd want them fenced as far away from you as possible."

Kayti edged out from behind Aspen's legs, her nose stretched out curiously toward Khor. When her nose touched his, she jumped up and back in the sudden bounce he had already learned to interpret as excitement. Quickly, she joined

Kayli beneath Khor, though she wasn't quite ready to snuggle with him yet.

<They're fine.> Khor's voice was brusque, but he shifted his hooves gingerly, as though afraid to squash one of the little beings taking shelter beneath him.

"Ooooo-kay." Aspen was too tired to question it any further. He was just glad this had gone better than when Khor had met Lesser Goats in the past. Having been born as a Greater Creature, Khor disdained most lesser creatures as little more intelligent - or important - than the rocks beneath his hooves. A ubiquitous necessity, but not something to be invited in for tea.

Meanwhile, Sumi, Sarave, and Silus had been getting to know each other. Sumi had quickly spun a web cloak, and gently placed it around Sarave's thin shoulders. Aspen had given the goblin his heavier overshirt, which covered her from neck to ankles, but she still shivered a bit in the evening chill. The little bat was chattering away about the mine, the skeleton, meeting Sarave, and running away from the vampires.

Sumi shook her pedipalps at the mention of the undead. <Vampires! I thought all of them were killed at the Battle of Bright!>

Aspen began to walk slowly toward the house. Khor seemed to have forgotten all about carrying him or Sarave, but Aspen felt renewed energy after the brief break. The walk would be a good chance for everyone to get comfortable with each other before being confined in a very small space together. The others followed after, with Khor by far the slowest as he tried to dodge the kids prancing carelessly between his hooves.

Aspen listened to Silus and Sumi's silent chatter, and looked down at Sarave, frustrated. "I wish you could hear them. We'll have to figure out a way for you to communicate. Sumi is wondering why these vamps weren't destroyed at Bright."

Sarave shook her head. "I think vampires been there long before Bright. *Hozinte*, what humans call Dark Races, were small part of *hu'we* Akuji's army. Goblin'te told little, just follow orders, but *hu'we* Akuji call all undead to fight.

Why these three not called, I not know. Vampires without food for long, sleep many years until food come. I just glad that vampire smell was enough to keep away other dangerous thing."

<So there is a chance that the coffins were empty, or the vampires dead?> Sumi's voice was hopeful. Aspen repeated the question to Sarave, who shook her head.

"Old ones dust when die. Not much stink. Young ones are still meat. These very old, I think, but smell was still strong. If young dead, smell like stinky meat. If old dead, just dust. They sleep, but no more." Her weary voice lifted slightly. "Maybe they die if the coffins were crushed, or trapped until starving? I hope." One knobby green hand caressed the bulge of her belly through Aspen's oversized shirt.

A grim silence fell over the group until they finally reached the old stone house. There was still no door, and the door frame had buckled slightly where Khor's horns had gotten stuck, but Sumi had woven a heavy curtain to cover the entry. The clean gray stones of the wall and the fresh green sod of the roof were bright and welcoming in the fading light.

Aspen moved the curtain aside and motioned for Sarave to enter. He tried to force some cheer into his voice, though he was afraid he wasn't terribly successful. "Welcome to our humble abode, Sarave. I hope you won't be too disappointed."

The human, goblin, spider, and bat entered the house, and Khor stuck his muzzle in through the window by the door. The two kids took long drinks out of the rough-hewn trough next to their new guardian, and then promptly flopped down in the soft grass between his hooves and fell asleep. A notice flashed in Aspen's vision.

Quest: "Yep, Definitely Goats" complete.

Reward: 2000 experience and two wool-producing animals.

Bonus: They're so cute!

Aspen smiled at the notice. He'd hoped the experience might be enough to give him a level, but apparently, he was high enough now that this much wasn't enough anymore. It was actually a good sign, indicating that he was now well on his way to recovery.

Sarave looked around, her luminous eyes glimmering in the dim interior. Sumi had started a small fire in the fireplace, and a pot was sitting on the hearth nearby, keeping warm. The spider had learned to make a hearty stew with some roots, mushrooms, and herbs Aspen had gathered from the riverside. He had already been growing tired of it before he left on his short journey, but now the familiar earthy scent made his stomach rumble.

Aspen sniffed appreciatively. As a spider, Sumi's food was often much different than something he would have made himself, since it was put together based on years of observing how humans combined and prepared food, rather than any innate understanding. Nonetheless, her meals were simple and edible, and sometimes even good. Tonight, the simple stew smelled like the grandest feast a chef might set before a king.

Sarave hovered for a moment, and then, forgoing the careful decorum she usually displayed, she sat in the chair at the table. Pressing her hands over her belly, and smoothed and massaged it as if to convey reassurance to the babe within. As she did, her eye caught the statue of Gina sitting on the table across from her. She gasped.

"Gi-na!" Then she frowned a little. "But human, not goblin'te?"

"Ha!" Aspen said triumphantly. "I wondered! I thought it unlikely that goblins would be worshiping a human goddess. So she appears to you as a... goblin'te?"

The small female nodded. "Gi-na and sister A-tae oldest gods. More goblin worship A-tae, but some still follow rules of time before time."

Aspen huffed. "Atae has more aspects than just death. She's the goddess of change, and she guards the Chaos Pool so that the dead can rest in peace until the gods call them to return to the cycle of life. She can be a very peaceful Goddess, unlike Gina, who seems far more excitable."

Sarave just blinked as she stared at Aspen. "You know well."

Aspen looked up, rubbing the back of his neck. "Not well exactly. I've spoken to them once or twice. It's...complicated."

Yellow eyes shining, Sarave reached out a shaking hand to him. "I never think I meet chosen of Gi-na. Like old song."

He felt heat rise in his cheeks, and waved his hand dismissively. "No songs, if you please. I'm just a farmer. A farmer with a two-room house, one field, and a menagerie without a barn."

Clearing his throat, Aspen looked at the pot from which the mouthwatering smells were rising. "Now, let's eat, shall we? Tonight, you can sleep in the bed, and I'll sleep on the mat over there." He pointed to the remains of the sweet straw bed he'd slept on until he'd set up the real bed in the back room, and then reached into a small cabinet for some bowls. He began ladling the gently steaming stew into two wooden bowls with a generous hand.

Sarave accepted her bowl and the roughly carved spoon that went with it. "I see door," she said tentatively, tilting her head to indicate the trap door that led to the storage space under the house. "I like house, bed, all, but feel safe below ground. Is maybe cellar?" She began to devour the stew with bites that were somehow both large and dainty. Flashes of sharp teeth showed between her thin lips as she ate.

Aspen nodded, digging into his own meal. He swallowed hard, feeling the warmth of the stew as it traveled down to his empty stomach. "There's a good-sized cellar, actually. Nearly as large as the house, not that that's saying much. We have some goods and food stored down there, but there's certainly enough room for a small bed. If you're certain that's what you want?"

She nodded firmly. "Stone walls above, and earth below. Good."

They ate in silence for a while longer, and then both set their bowls aside with a mutual sigh of satisfaction. They smiled at each other, feeling the sense of camaraderie brought on by sharing a good meal. A deep snore disturbed the moment, and they both looked to the side, startled. Khor's chin was resting on the windowsill, and the goat had fallen asleep standing there. A small string of drool dripped from his mouth as another large snore erupted from him.

Aspen grimaced. "Sleeping in the cellar is probably a good idea. Sound will be muffled down there."

Sarave covered her mouth with her hand and giggled.

Chapter Seven

Rouge

Friday somehow managed to be even longer than Thursday. Zoey felt like she was the Zombie, and Rouge, waiting in the game, was real. She suffered through her classes, barely listening to the teachers, and even Jace's company couldn't make the day go any faster. He seemed to be able to tell that she was preoccupied, so at lunch he just said, "Hey. Still working on the thing?" At her nod, he ate his lunch in silence and left her to her thoughts.

The school bus traveled its usual leisurely route, and she wanted to yell at the driver that she could have walked home faster. She didn't, mainly because it wasn't quite true, but she really wanted to.

When she opened the front door, Max barked a greeting and her dad called to her from the dining room. "Zoey? There's pizza in the kitchen! Help yourself!" and the day got a million times better. She snagged two slices of her favorite double cheese, chicken, and mushroom, and took her plate in to sit at the big, rectangular table.

Her dad looked super tired, with circles forming under his eyes, and a crease between his brows. He looked up with a smile when she came in, though, and she gave him a quick hug before sitting at the end of the table that wasn't covered in papers and his large work screen.

"Hey, kid," he rumbled. "How've you been? I missed you yesterday. I was going to call, but I saw you were playing *Veritas*, so I held off."

She rolled her eyes and pointed to her mouth, indicating that she was still chewing. Why did people always ask questions when they knew you couldn't answer? Swallowing, she said, "School was okay. I missed you, too. Two finals and office hours on one day is rough, huh?"

He rubbed his eyes and chewed on the end of his stylus, a nervous habit that he only gave into when he was really stressed. "Yeah. Dr. Frasier called in sick today, too, and it happened to fall right between my two, so I was volunteered to be a proctor. Then the school intranet went down. Tech support finally had to reset the servers to a backup from this morning. They think some students hacked it to cover up missing their deadlines. It was a *mess*."

"Oh my gosh, Dad. Did you lose anything?" Zoey's eyes were huge, and she actually stopped shoveling in pizza for a minute.

He shook his head wearily. "I'm one of the lucky ones. My finals yesterday were papers the students e-mailed in, but the ones today were in class using the Blue Book app. Those go directly to the local admin via wifi, bypassing email." He waved his pen at the stacks of papers around him. "A bunch of yesterday's students got paranoid after the outage, and actually printed out their papers and brought them in. I had to reassure each one that their work hadn't been affected, and I'm not sure half of them believed me." He chuckled. "Honestly, I prefer it. I'm a red pencil kind of guy."

She rolled her eyes. "Tell me about it." Her dad had been taking that red pencil to her homework since she was a kid. She always got good grades on the papers he helped with, but she also got *really* tired of that red pencil.

He laughed, momentarily easing the lines of tension on his face. Then he shook his head. "Anyway, kiddo, I'm afraid it'll be a late night for me, and then an early morning. I'll have to head back to school first thing. Things are still being lost in the shuffle, and, as James Baldwin said, 'confusion is a luxury which only the very, very young can possibly afford.'"

Zoey nodded, desperately trying to cover the grin that threatened to spread across her face. This meant she could just suck down a bowl of cereal in the morning, instead of lingering over eggs and conversation! She shoved half a slice of pizza in her mouth and nodded understanding. After a few more minutes of questions, during which she saw his eyes flick toward the screen more than once, he finally gave in when she asked to be excused. Usually, he would have had her work on her homework for at least an hour before he let her go, but he just wasn't on top of his dad-game tonight.

She practically ran up the stairs, taking them two at a time. She stripped down and put on her clean bodysuit, then climbed into the pod. Log in!

Rouge opened her eyes in the dimness of the tent. She pulled up her quest timer, and shook her head to get rid of the usual disorientation.

Time Remaining: Two days, 19 hours, 4 minutes.

She could play ten hours worth of game time tonight. That would leave two days and nine hours. She could log on as soon as her dad left in the morning, which would put her about another eighteen hours or so in, leaving fifteen hours to beat the quest. She could make it, and still stay just under the real-time maximum she was allowed to play on Saturday.

"Yes! Let's do this!" She bounced into a rising handspring (a move she'd never mastered in real life, but that the game made easy for someone with as much Dex as she had.) Parting the tent flap, she stepped outside, and...

"It's snowing."

Codswallop, covered in wet feathers and icicles, hooted miserably at the sound of her voice, pulling his head up from where it was buried under a snow drift. She immediately began to brush him clean. "Poor Wally! How long has it been snowing? It looked fine when I went to sleep!" She rubbed him dry as best she could with a blanket she pulled from her inventory, then laid a fresh one over him to keep him warm. Once that was done, she gave him some generic *Mount Feed*, and let him drink from a bowl.

That done, she looked around at the gray and white expanse. The cliff behind them had sheltered them somewhat, but the frozen white crystals were piled at least six inches deep everywhere else. The world was silent in that strange muffled way it gets when it's covered in snow. The only sounds she heard were the soft sigh of the wind and a few desultory chirps from birds sheltering nearby.

"Gah! At least it's not a white-out blizzard! We'd never make it." She shook her head. "Just when you think things are finally going your way, right, Wally?"

The ostrich warbled a sad reply, tucking his head beneath her arm.

Rouge took a deep breath of the freezing air and nearly coughed. She patted the ostrich's strong neck comfortingly. "There you go, you big chicken. It's not like mounts in this game can actually freeze or get sick. You'll be fine. Here." Reaching into her inventory, she pulled out a brilliant orange piece of warm wool fabric that she'd been unable to resist buying a few weeks ago. Using her Mambele, she cut it into strips, then wound the strips around the ostrich's long neck. When she was done, it looked like he had ten scarves stacked on top of each other, but he chirped happily.

She cut one more strip and wrapped it around her own neck and face. She had several face coverings to conceal her identity while she performed her more, uh, *sensitive* quests, but they were all designed to be lightweight and cool. She felt better immediately as her own warm exhalations melted the ice crystals forming on her face.

Cold Resistance increased by 1%.

"Huh. That's something at least," she muttered. Looking up at her bird, Rouge patted him reassuringly on the shoulder. "Well, Wally, we can't hang around here." She took Codswallop's saddle from her inventory and set it on his back, activating it. "This is going to suck, but we can still make it."

Two hours later, she wasn't so sure. The road was still climbing, and while they had brief respites from the snow when they passed through ravines, they also had terrifying periods when the road narrowed, leaving them clinging to the side of the icy mountain. Flurries piled up on them, and ice stuck to Codswallop's legs and feathers. She had to climb off and scrape him clean several times, and the snow was up to her knees now. Today was not a good day to be short.

The good news was that all the monsters seemed to be staying in their nests and dens. None of them were desperate for food yet, so they had no reason to venture out into this first snowstorm of the season.

It was just over another hour before they reached the top of a particularly narrow pass and looked down. Their breath plumed in the still air, and the only sound was the crunch of snow settling beneath their feet. She fed Codswallop another *Mount Feed* and patted him absently as she stared down the steep road ahead.

Finally, Rouge shook her head. "Nope. One big nope with lots of little nopes hitching a ride. We'll never make it down without falling on our butts and breaking our legs, or our necks. I don't have any of those nail thingies you see mountain climbers use, and while I do have some rope, it's definitely not long enough for this."

Morosely, she pulled up her inventory and started flipping through it. Her eyes went wide, then narrowed in calculation. She looked from Codswallop to the nearly vertical slope ahead of them, and a slightly maniacal grin plastered itself across her face. "But maybe falling on our butts wouldn't be so bad. Wally, buddy, I have a cunning plan."

It took way longer than she expected to make a toboggan. Her first attempt, which was really just a large tanned hide, quickly folded up under them from the friction of the snow. Codswallop gave her a disgusted look from where he ended up on his back, feet waving in the air, stubby wings and long neck thrashing gracelessly as he tried to right himself.

Next, she tried using wood from her inventory to attach something like sled runners onto a large shield. She tried that one out by herself, and while she went a bit further, she quickly learned that the wood really had to be completely straight and smooth, and her [Crafting] skill wasn't up to snuff.

Digging through her inventory, she finally found something that might work. One of her very earliest quests was a dive into the Sewer, the only real dungeon in Bright. Well, technically they were *beneath* Bright, but they were attached, which was close enough.

In any case, she had to enter the Sewer and kill some of the overgrown pets that were wreaking havoc in the tunnels there. Apparently flushing animals people didn't want anymore wasn't limited to just fish and alligators in Veritas. During her time in the Sewers, Rouge fought a Greater Hamster, more rats than she wanted to think about, and finally a Greater Box Turtle.

In the grand scheme of things, it could have been much worse. A snapping turtle would have been far beyond her abilities. That part of the tutorial was trying to teach newbies to work as part of a group, especially a pick-up group, or PUG. She, of course, had Motte Bailey. Motte tanked the turtle while she snuck up behind it (that was before she had the [Stealth] or [Sneak] skills) and she picked at it until she was finally able to bring it down. The loot it dropped wasn't much, though the *Turtle Soup* she made during the follow-up quest was gross but tasty.

"Ah ha!" She pulled a giant turtle shell from her inventory and dropped it into the snow beside her.

Giant Box Turtle Shell **– A simple turtle shell. Nearly impenetrable. If you take it to a blacksmith, they'll make it into armor for you. Weight – 50 lbs. Rarity – Common.**

The turtle was a respawn boss that everyone had to fight, and the armor that came from the shell was serviceable but heavy. It was an attempt by the tutorial to teach her how the Blacksmith shops worked, and she had ignored it, since Motte had already told her all that. Also, she already knew she wanted to be sneaky, and rattling turtle armor was not. So, she'd shoved it in her inventory and gone to learn how to make soup.

The shell was large. Not *quite* large enough for her and Codswallop to fit comfortably, but if they crammed inside its domed walls, they could make it work. The only problem was that there was no way to steer. Once they got started, they wouldn't stop until something got in the way or they hit an uphill steep enough to kill their momentum. She just hoped it didn't kill them first.

She bowed grandly to the ostrich. "After you, Wally."

The bird's big brown eyes went to the shell, and then back to her. He took one long, slow step back.

Rouge tugged at him. "Come on, Wall," she wheedled. "It'll be fine. I'm going to get in too, and then we're going to zip down out of these mountains before you can say cluck. or chirp. Or whatever."

Codswallop just blinked, his frost-covered eyelashes looking ridiculously long.

She tried to pull him, and he dug in his powerful claws. She tried to push him, and he jumped up and *backwards*, landing behind her. She growled. "Okay. That was a good trick. We'll have to practice that one. But right now, we have to go. I have six more hours of play time, and if we keep going the way we have, I might as well have stayed in Bright, because there's no way we're going to make it."

A slow eyeblink was her only answer.

Rouge sighed and pulled up her inventory. "All right, Wally, buddy. I didn't want to do this, but…"

She pulled out a fresh, warm cinnamon roll. The smell of it hit her frozen nose and her mouth filled with saliva. She swiped at the corner of her lips. Codswallop stepped forward, eyes locked on the bready delicacy. "Come on, buddy. You know you want it."

Quickly, she tore a small piece off the cinnamon roll and tossed it into the shell. Codswallop glanced that way, but remained focused on the larger chunk still in her hand. "Seriously? You want the whole thing? Come on! If we're going to blow one, I want some too."

The bird tilted his head to the side and flicked his gaze from her hand to the shell.

"This one is coming out of your pay, Wally. When we go hit Millie up for rolls someday, you owe me one," she threatened.

The ostrich chirruped agreeably and waited.

"Fine!" Rouge tossed the whole cinnamon roll into the shell, and Codswallop jumped in a fraction of a second later. The girl caught the edge of the shell and pulled herself in after, licking her fingers the moment she landed. She would have cried if she could.

She felt the shell teeter under their combined weight. The greedy bird was gobbling his treat, head bobbing. She leaned, and…

"Wheeeeeeeeeeeee…..!"

Chapter Eight

Aspen

The group quickly fell into a routine. Sarave helped Sumi in the house, while Khor and Aspen returned to working the fields and clearing the area around the house. At the end of each day, Aspen and Sarave dropped quickly to sleep once they were in their beds. Silus flew off to hunt and scout, leaving Khor, Kayti, and Kayli snoring just outside. Sumi was the only one awake and aware enough to hear the sound of racing feet heading toward the house.

The thick web curtain covering the door was thrust aside without fanfare, and a pretty young wood elf stuck her head in. A large bird head popped in beside it. The girl saw Sumi and did what so many of the humanoid races did; she shrieked.

This, of course, awakened everyone. Khor snorted, raising his head and slamming his horns into the top of the window frame, which creaked in protest. Outside, the little goats bleated in disapproval at the rude awakening. Aspen rolled out of bed, fully clothed, his hand on the staff he'd left near his bed. He had spent too many nights on the battlefield to sleep unprepared when an unknown enemy lurked.

The elven girl, a child no older than her early teens, at least in human years, pointed at him when she saw him. Unfortunately, her hand still clutched a strange, fanged dagger, making the gesture more threatening than she seemed to intend. "You! Are you Aspen?"

He nodded, bemused, since no threat seemed forthcoming.

"Woo*hoo*!" She did a little dance there in the doorway, and the dagger vanished, instantly replaced by a small crate. Aspen's eyes widened as she tossed the box across the room. He caught it reflexively, and her eyes flicked up, staring into apparently empty air. A broad grin stretched over her face. "I *made it*! Four minutes to go, and I made it! Take that, impossible quest giver!"

Her eyes focused back on him as the golden glow of a level up suffused her. "Oh, by the way, there's a vampire about ten minutes behind me." Her hazel eyes looked apologetic, and she tugged on a black spiral curl. "I didn't even know there were any of those left."

Khor let out a bellow that had the girl leaping into the house with all the grace of a startled cat. <A vampire!? I'll stomp it! I'll kill it! I'll->

Aspen kept a wary eye on the strange el, who was now prowling around the small house, picking things up and examining them as if no one would object to such behavior. "You'll do no such thing. We don't know what level it is-"

"Oh, it's level 97," the girl said absently. She reached toward the statue of Gina, and Sumi skittered between it and her hand. The elf recoiled, and her knife reappeared, though she didn't actually use it. "I, um, kind of ran over it, so I got *way* too close a look. The good news is, I think the turtle shell whacked it pretty good. It's *really* mad, though." The teenager shifted uneasily, absently tossing her knife from hand to hand.

"Damn it," Aspen muttered, shoving his bedraggled hat on his head. He flashed a look at Sumi, as if daring her to say anything about the mild imprecation. For once, she let it go. "None of us can handle a level 97 vamp, even if it's injured." His eyes shot around the house, landing on a small pile of firewood. He looked back at the girl, abruptly deciding to trust his instincts. It had worked out well with Sarave, after all. So far. "You're a Traveler, aren't you?"

"Oof, that obvious, huh? Yeah. Name's Rouge the Rogue. Uh, I just go by Rouge though." Rouge stuck out the hand that wasn't wielding her vicious-looking weapon, but when they all just stared at her, she took it back and wiped it on her leg nervously.

Aspen shook his head. "All right. Here's what we're going to do…"

Eight minutes later, Aspen stood outside the door of the small house. In one hand was a hastily-sharpened wooden stake, and in the other was a blazing torch. His lean jaw was set, but his eyes were wide and frightened.

A dry voice sank into the night like ancient blood flowing stickily across a dirt floor. A tall, stretched shape stepped into the flickering circle of light. Gray skin stretched taut as a canvas on an artist's canvas, peeling back from eyes and teeth so that it looked like a mummy stripped of its wrappings. "Those little toys won't hurt me, blood bag. Give up, and I will let you sleep as I feast on you. *I am hungry.*"

The last three words rang with power, pulling at the human in front of him, weaving a spell that told his prey to give in, and offer itself up because the vampire's need to feed was much greater than the life of any mere living organism.

Aspen's eyes went wide and blank, and he staggered forward a single pace. As he did, the vampire stepped forward to meet him. A sticky web, invisible in the brown grass, pulled tight as Sumi reeled it in from her place on the roof of the house. The vampire, starving and wounded, fell to one side, screeching in terrible fury. An instant later, a large bat, all skin and bones and huge, vicious fangs, hung in the air, free.

The moment it changed, Aspen's eyes sharpened, pale gold in the torchlight.

"Now!" he shouted.

A small figure landed on top of it, leaping from the blackness of the circle of trees. Her legs clamped tight on each wing, and a multi-bladed dagger flashed out to stab at the monster's brittle skull. It shrieked and gurgled, writhing in her grip, unable to change forms because the sharp wooden stake the group had loosely strapped to the blade was still lodged in its flesh, exactly as they had hoped.

The moment the cadaverous horror was trapped, every member of the party flung themselves toward it. They would have only moments before it overcame its surprise and shrugged them off. It was still far more powerful than they, even in its weakened state.

Aspen's stake sunk deep into its chest. Rouge's blade sawed at the neck. Sumi jumped across the intervening distance and sank her fangs and eight clawed feet into its belly. Khor crushed its wing beneath his cloven hooves and stamped on any part of its body that wasn't hidden by one of his companions.

A screech echoed through the clearing before the house. It was a sound no mortal throat could have made; the voice of a dying creature who was never meant to die. It thrashed viciously, cutting at Khor's side with its sharp talons. It tugged Sumi free of its decaying flesh, batting her away, and she vanished into the darkness. Aspen grunted as he twisted his arm to keep his crude wooden implement digging into its chest.

Finally, the bat sank to the ground, still fighting, but feebly now. With a squelch and a sucking sound, the head finally parted from its body. The abhorrent thing rolled limply away, landing on its side in the grass, black eyes staring and fanged mouth still snarling in death.

A moment passed. Two. Golden light sprang from four bodies, illuminating the darkness for one beautiful second of relief from the horror that had just passed.

Silus' piping little voice came out of the darkness. <Wow. What did I miss?>

🦇 🦇 🦇

The house was distinctly crowded with a human, an elf, a spider, most of Khor's head, two young mountain goats, an ostrich's head and shoulders, a bat, and very nearly two goblins. Rouge had taken Sarave's appearance in stride, which Aspen felt was commendable of the girl. She didn't seem to possess the prejudice against the 'Dark Races' that so many of the Travelers seemed to have, perhaps because she, herself, was a member of a race that was often ignored and derided.

The girl struggled more with Sumi, and still kept as far from the arachnid as possible in the tight space. Kayli was snuggled in the elven girl's lap, though, and her slim brown fingers ran through the little goat's silky fur. Kayti rested on the hearth near Aspen's feet. Silus sat in the crook of Aspen's neck and shoulder and listened with rapt attention as the rogue told her story.

"...so obviously we couldn't get down the mountain in one go. We had to keep climbing up, getting out the shell, and sliding down again. There were a few close calls, but the shell cracked when we fell off the first cliff, so I could see out a little bit. It was enough to lean side to side to move the shell around most of the obstacles."

Khor whuffled and shoved his muzzle into the girl's back, which was all he could reach. <Tell her to get on with it! How did the vampire come to be chasing her?>

Aspen scratched the side of his rather long nose and cleared his throat. "What about the vampire, then, lass?"

"Oh! He was lurking around the bottom of the pass, looking totally suspicious. He practically stepped right out in front of us. I didn't even have a chance to dodge! We popped up over a rock, and there he was. Next thing I knew, the shell made this strange hollow knock and just...fell apart. There he was, nasty black blood running down his head, and looking more pissed than my dad is going to be when he finds out I'm out here and there's no way through that pass until spring." She chewed worriedly on her lip.

"I wasn't even supposed to leave Bright without him, and now I'm stuck over here unless I die and respawn back in the city, but if I do that, I won't..." Her voice choked off, and she tugged hard at the curl wound around her forefinger. The little goat in her lap opened a big blue eye just enough to nuzzle the hand that was no longer petting her, and Rouge returned to stroking mechanically.

Aspen coughed, and got up to take the teapot off the fire. He bowed his head as he poured tea into three clumsily carved wooden cups. After handing one cup each to Sarave and Rouge, he sat down again and sighed. "So, you ran?" He flicked a glance at the ostrich, who was greedily eating from a bag of grain Rouge had pulled from a magical storage pouch. "Even on your bird, I doubt you could outpace a high-level vamp, especially enough to get ten minutes ahead." He tried to keep his voice neutral, but he could tell she knew he didn't believe she was telling the whole story.

Rouge sipped her tea, grimaced slightly, and set her cup down on the table in front of her. "Codswallop's really fast, and I gave him a cinnamon roll, so that doubled it."

Sarave's eyebrow quirked. "Cinn-a-mon roll?"

"Oh, yeah! They're great! Double your speed and stamina recovery for thirty minutes!" She looked crestfallen. "I only have one left now, though."

The little goblin woman held out a hand in an oddly imperious gesture. "I see." At the girl's hesitation, her fingers curled, and she softened her command with a smile. "I return it as is. Promise."

Rouge shrugged, and a flawless cinnamon roll appeared in her hand. The scent of warm, fluffy bread, luscious, creamy sugar, and the perfect amount of cinnamon filled the room. Four bellies instantly growled, and both Khor and Codswallop snapped at it, cracking their heads together sharply. Rouge cast a worried glance at them, and handed the roll to Sarave. The goblin examined it, her eyes widening.

"High grade food! Where you get? Who make?" In her excitement, Sarave's accent thickened, until her listeners could barely understand her.

Rouge held out her hand, and Sarave handed the pastry back without hesitation. It vanished back into wherever the elf's belongings went when she didn't need them. "It was a quest reward. I'm going to go back to the enpee... Um," she glanced around and flushed, her cheeks darkening visibly. "I mean, the person who made them, and see if I can buy more."

Silus tilted her head, soft fur brushing Aspen's jaw. <What's an enpee?>

Sumi murmured quietly, though no one else could hear her. <I've heard of this. An 'NPC' is what the Travelers call all those of us who were born in this world. It seems to be,> her tone turned wry, <rather derogatory, which is no doubt why she's embarrassed.>

The little bat snuggled deeper into Aspen's shirt collar. <What's dur..og...>

Shaking a pedipalp slightly in her version of a sigh, Sumi spoke affectionately but firmly. <I'll explain later, little one. Hush.>

Silus heaved her own sigh and settled down grumpily.

Aspen pretended not to have heard the exchange, and prompted the elf, who seemed to have a tendency to wander off topic. "The vampire?"

"Duh, sorry." Rouge rapped herself on the forehead with a knuckle and continued. "Yeah, I vaulted onto Wally and grabbed a cinnamon roll for him. He took off faster than I've ever seen him go, which is saying something. That vampire was right behind us, but we could hear him falling back little by little. He wasn't giving up, though, so when I saw the light coming from your house, we ran straight here. I figured if I turned in the old gnome's quest, I could at least get a level and maybe be able to help fight that bad guy."

"Old gnome?" Aspen frowned. "Gnomes retreated below ground centuries ago. No one has contacted them in at least a hundred years."

Rouge rolled her eyes. "Literal much? I mean the Head Librarian in Bright. He always reminds me of a dusty little garden gnome." She grimaced. "Well, he used to, anyway."

Aspen sat up, nearly dislodging Silus, who squeaked a protest. "The Head Librarian? He set you this quest?" He stood, pushing his chair back with a thump, and this time Silus did drop off his shoulder and fly up into the rafters, where she hung upside down, grooming the small silver tufts in front of her ears in visible irritation.

Aspen crossed to the small crate, which he had left on his bed. He tried to open it, but made no progress against the heavy lock that held it shut. "Damned old man," he muttered. "There's no key."

The rogue raised a hand as if to call attention to herself. "Let me try! I got [Lockpick] to level 12 just before I left Bright. That's a pretty basic lock. I bet I can open it." She flushed again. "Um, not that I looked at it. Or thought about it. At all."

Aspen tossed the hefty little crate back to the girl. She caught it easily, and he gave her a lopsided smile. "Give it a try, then. Check for traps first though, eh?"

"You sound like my dad," she muttered, as she set the box on the table and bent over it. A moment later she shook her head. "It's clean. The old man may not have wanted it to be easy to open, but he didn't want anyone to get hurt, either." A ring of small bent wires of various shapes and thicknesses appeared in her hand, and she leaned over to insert one into the lock.

A heavy silence fell, broken by a loud click as the lock sprang open. Rouge started to open it, then paused, visibly suppressing her curiosity. She shoved it toward Aspen, grinning ruefully. "There ya go."

Aspen smiled, liking the energetic little elf more and more. Thief she might be, but she clearly had some integrity. He picked the box up and opened it. "Ah."

Rouge was almost twitching. Silus's eyes gleamed brightly from above, and even Sarave rubbed her chelicerae together in agitation. It was Khor, though, who broke the silence with an impatient bleat. <What is it?!>

Aspen turned the box so they could all see. Inside, on a royal blue velvet lining, sat a book and a small leather bag. Rouge squinted at the contents of the box, and after a moment her eyes grew puzzled. "It just says *Book* and *Pouch* when I try to [Identify] them. Are they special?"

Aspen closed the box and set it down. "Well, I think we can all agree on the 'book' and 'pouch' identification." His eyes were twinkling mischievously, and the girl huffed in annoyance.

"Oh my gosh! Why are all middle-aged guys the same? Come on, just tell me what they are already!" Her tone was sheer exasperation.

Aspen chuckled. "I asked the Librarian to look for books on blacksmithing and anything else he thought would be useful to us in our new life here. He sent rather a lot of books with us, but obviously he found another one that he thought I'd need. I suspect the bag contains some seeds I asked for. We couldn't get them when I left, thanks to a rather, ah, tight timeline." He smiled and shook his head at Rouge. "Nothing worth you getting in trouble with your father over, I'm afraid."

Rouge opened her mouth to reply, and then glanced up and to the side again, much as someone did when they received a quest notice. She growled in frustration. "Ugh. Time's up. I'll be in trouble for sure if I stay any longer. Is there someplace I can stash my Zombie while I'm gone?"

Silus, Sumi, and Khor's mental <Zombie?> was nearly drowned out by Aspen and Sarave's simultaneous matching outburst.

Rouge stared at them for a moment, her hazel eyes puzzled at their strong response. Then she laughed and waved a hand dismissively. "Oh! No, not a real zombie. That's what we Travelers call it when we log off... Um, when we send our souls back to our world, and leave our body here. Have you ever seen one of us doing something, but not responding, or just standing around for a long time?"

Sumi waved a leg in comprehension, Khor grunted, and Aspen nodded. Silus just squeaked, <What?> but stopped when Sumi gently shook a pedipalp at her.

"Okay, good." Rouge said. "So, while I'm gone, my body can do some basic stuff, but *I* won't be there controlling it. We call it a Zombie, since the body is moving around, but nobody's home." She tapped her temple, then looked around to see if they understood.

Aspen's eyes narrowed. "You can do 'basic stuff'. What does that mean?"

She shrugged. "Take care of my mount, follow someone, walk someplace, go to sleep. I can't fight or recover health or anything, so if something attacks me, I'll die." The girl looked around. "I probably shouldn't have told you that. You could just kill me after I log out. But I have to stash my, um, body somewhere, and you guys just seem really... nice. So can I please rest here somewhere until my, er, soul gets back?"

Sumi's front two legs clicked on the table thoughtfully. <Are you thinking what I'm thinking, Aspen?>

Aspen grinned. "Yes, Rouge. I'm sure we can work something out. Now, this Zombie you're going to leave us, can it work in a field?"

Rouge's eyes widened, and then she nodded. "Um, I haven't ever tried it, but probably. I won't recover Stamina, and I can't use skills, but I could, like, hoe and weed and stuff. I think."

"How about chop wood and haul rocks? Or break up rocks?" Aspen asked gleefully.

"Yeeeeees? I think I could do that." Her expression went thoughtful and distant. "Yeah, I can," she made strange wiggling motions with the first two fingers on each hand, "'chop the closest tree into firewood' or 'carry the closest rock to designated location'."

"Hmm." It was Aspen's turn to be thoughtful. "I think we'd better not have you carry rocks yet, then. I've made a few piles, and I wouldn't want you to get confused about what goes where. The tree thing, though... Can you limit it to a certain number of trees in a certain area? There's a stand of fruit trees left over from an old orchard that need to stay, but otherwise we need to take out all the stumps and trees to the south and east of the house for oh, say, half a mile. We don't need them, it would clear the sight lines, and once we get a well, we'll want to put fields there."

Hazel eyes flicked up and to the side again, and she nodded. "I can do that.

I'll need someplace to rest, though, 'cause otherwise I'll be worn out when I come back. Plus, you guys need to take care of Codswallop." She got up and went to scratch the ostrich's head, and Aspen could swear the bird purred. "Got that, Wally? You listen to them, okay? I mean, within reason." She looked over her shoulder at Aspen. "I'll be back in about two days."

Aspen glanced outside at the lightening sky and nodded. "That would be good. We'll all be getting up about then, so you won't disturb anyone." He pointed at the pile of somewhat dry grass in the corner. "I can freshen that up, and you can sleep there. Will that work?"

Her fingers twitched, as if she were pushing and pulling at something. Then she nodded and held out her hand. An old axe appeared in it. "I knew this thing would come in handy someday. I've set my Away Instructions to chop all the trees in that area, and I'll come back and rest from dark until dawn. Just ignore me, 'cause I won't be able to respond, and I won't need any food or anything except rest. Just make sure the bed is super comfy so I can get the full Well-Rested buff, okay?"

Aspen nodded. "It's a deal. We'll watch over your… zombie… until you return, and in exchange you do some work around here."

She grinned. "Awesome! Now, I really have to go! Bye!"

Her eyes went distant, fingers gliding through several final movements, and then her face went neutral, and all life went out of her eyes. She turned and walked out of the house, pushing past Codswallop and Khor as if they weren't there. A minute later, they heard the rhythmic sound of chopping begin.

Silence fell over Aspen and his companions. Once again, it was Silus who spoke first. <That was really creepy.>

Everyone who could hear her nodded in unison.

The next day was taken up in settling in the new additions to the family, tending the field, and beginning work on an extension to the house. Not surprisingly, Sarave didn't know anything about farming, since she had spent her whole life either underground or in a city. She was a decent cook, though, and quite good at sewing, so it became her job to put together a few outfits for herself, and expand Aspen's pants, among other things. She also took over cooking, much to Sumi's relief. And Aspen's as well, though he knew better than to say so.

Rouge the Rogue's zombie worked constantly. It didn't pause for breaks, drink, or food, just as she had said, and while it wasn't fast, it was amazingly consistent. It cleared away any plant taller than four feet high, apparently considering that the definition of a 'tree'. They had a few close calls in the beginning, since it didn't care how the trees fell, and a couple of the nearest ones almost hit the house. She was soon far enough away that that didn't happen anymore, but Aspen made a mental note to be more specific in the future.

Codswallop followed her around dejectedly. He ate and drank as needed, but his eyes were fixed on the girl's zombie. The only time he moved except to follow Rouge from tree to tree or back to the wood pile was when he had to dodge out of the way of falling debris.

Silus slept in her cabinet during the day, so Aspen was quiet as he hauled out the old grass bed and replaced it with a fresh one. While he was at it, he took more soft bedding down to the cellar for Sarave, and gave her all but one of the down pillows he had found stuffed tight into a bag when he unpacked the wagon. He wasn't sure whose idea the pillows were, but he sensed the touch of Sumi's pedipalps. The spider was often bossy and sharp, but she was also a caretaker at heart.

In any case, he was glad to find the bag of pillows, and doubly glad when he saw Sarave's response to his gift. He had suspected that she might find it difficult to sleep in her condition, but the look of relief on her thin face was almost painful. When tears threatened to overflow, he departed hastily, granting her the privacy she obviously desired to allow her to gain control over her wayward emotions.

Sumi, freed from the responsibility of preparing food, was able to make more spider-silk cloth. The fabric was strong, but the weave wasn't tight enough for it to be used as everyday clothing. It couldn't be dyed, and, if cut, it would quickly unravel, so it had to be woven or sewn whole. She also produced silk thread, which she wound around a bobbin for Sarave to use. The goblin exclaimed over its strength and fineness, and happily began working with it.

The spider also began to refill the metal flasks of her milk. The fluid was only good for around a week, even in the opaque and airtight containers. In less durable or porous vessels, it could become useless within a day. Sarave was surprised to discover that the potion that had healed her at the cave was produced by an arachnid, but as a goblin, she had likely ingested things at least as disgusting, so she accepted it with surprising aplomb.

Khor was kept busy hauling rocks and stumps on a cart that was basically just the bottom part of the wagon they had used to travel here. Now that Aspen's initial week of boosted stat gains was done, he was allowed to ask for help, and Khor gave it, though grudgingly. The two of them rapidly produced several growing piles of stones that looked like they would be good for various projects.

Kayli and Kayti, now brushed until they gleamed nearly silver in the sunlight, trotted happily at Khor's heels or side wherever he went. Aspen kept expecting the Greater Goat to tire of them, and try to chase them off, but it seemed he had never-ending patience with their antics. Even when they played chase in between his great hooves, he only slowed and stepped with greater caution.

Aspen himself spent a little time with each of them. Mostly, when he wasn't piling stones or other debris into the cart for Khor to take away, he worked on digging out and then laying a foundation for another room and a small barn. He decided to attach the barn to the house, at least to begin with. The body heat of the animals would help warm the house, and the heat from the fireplace would help keep the animals warm. Once he was able to build a proper barn, the old space could be used as just another large room.

He and Khor went to the river to fill the cart with a slurry of clay, straw, and sand. When they brought back the cart, Aspen covered it so that it wouldn't dry out too quickly, and then he began to fill in the spaces between the rocks of the wall. They were using the best of the rocks pulled from the nearby area and the field, but they were still all shapes and sizes. He tried to keep similar sizes together, and quickly became proficient at finding a stone that would fit into the next space at least well enough that he could fill the gaps.

The hardest part was when they came to framing the doors and windows. Aspen had read all the books on building that the Head Librarian had sent, and they practiced by taking down the damaged supports in the old house. Aspen carefully examined the workmanship to see how they were put together. He used a clear glass tube filled with water and a little bit of air as a level, and first fixed the house, then set the frames for the new buildings.

After lunch - a nutritious meal consisting of dried muskrat meat cooked in a stew of wild roots and herbs until it was soft - they all set to work again, and by nightfall, the walls reached about the height of Aspen's waist. It wasn't much, yet, but it would provide a wall to help keep the little goats safe through the night, and they would work on it again tomorrow. It wouldn't be ready to roof, especially as the thick slurry that held it together was still drying, but it was getting there.

With at least one more vampire out there, they would need all the security they could get.

☙ ☙ ☙

Aspen was awakened early the next day by the whisper touch of one of Sumi's pedipalps on his arm. His eyes shot open in the darkness, and his hand fell to the staff beside the bed.

Sumi's mental whisper brushed just as softly at the edge of his consciousness. <No danger. I need to show you something before the others wake.>

He frowned slightly, but climbed down from his bed as quietly as possible. It was still dark, and the moons were just slivers of light in the sky, so he trailed his hand along the now-familiar walls of the house until he came to the front door. He felt a slight pressure as a thread of sticky webbing attached to his hand, and then tugged gently taut.

This was a trick he and Sumi used to use during the war. When your opponents were called the 'Dark Races', there was probably a good reason. Their enemies lurked in the darkness and beneath the ground, and it was often more than your life was worth to carry any source of illumination. Of course, Aspen eventually found other ways to see, but this was the one he and his team had used first, and Sumi was his oldest remaining companion.

Trusting the spider completely, he followed the gentle tug on his skin. She sent slight tremors through the strand, letting him know when to turn left or right, duck or step high. He quickly realized where they were headed, but he didn't have the terrain memorized yet, so he was grateful for her guidance.

By the time they stopped, the faintest edge of light was beginning to show on the horizon. In the very deep gray dimness, Aspen was just able to make out the faint smudges of the small plants that occupied the field.

"What's wrong?" he murmured, unsure why they were there. "I know I haven't been back out here since we planted, but I knew you were checking on it, and with the irrigation, it shouldn't need water." He crouched down and fingered one of the leaves near him. It was velvety soft and strong, and even in the faint light, he could see that it was a brilliant green.

<Aspen.> Sumi's voice was exasperated. He was missing something obvious. <How quickly do you think plants usually grow?>

He shrugged. "I... don't know? Birdie grew some flowers and herbs back home, but I didn't really pay attention. Not exactly my end of things, you know?"

Sumi waved her pedipalps in an expression of exasperation that came through in spite of the inhuman appendages. <You are not generally so blind, so I must assume you are being intentionally obtuse. Look closer, my friend. The sun is rising, so do so quickly.>

Aspen frowned, and knelt down in the damp earth, ignoring the wetness seeping into the knees of his trousers. He leaned closer to the burgeoning plant. "Is it… glowing?"

A spider leg gently pushed the glossy little leaves out of the way, and revealed the softly luminescing stem. He stared, then crawled quickly along, focusing on each little sprout and seedling. When he reached the end of the row, he stood, brushed off his pants, and hurried to look at the others as well. When he reached the far edge of the field, he turned and gazed at his friend blankly.

"What in At- Gina's name is going on?"

The arachnid was walking along the rows, tucking her sharp legs into the ground and flicking invasive weeds aside. The weeds were rare, spindly, and shallow-rooted. <In Gina's name indeed,> she muttered. <Something is causing these plants to grow far faster and stronger than usual. It also makes the weeds wilt, and these would die today or tomorrow even if I didn't uproot them.>

He scratched his head. "What do you think it is? The water? The location? Maybe someone cast a spell of abundance on the farm, and it's still going? Seems like a long time for a spell to still be active without any maintenance." Aspen was plucking at the little weeds and examining their withered stems.

<Aspen.> The tone was exasperated.

He looked up. "What am I missing? You sound like my mother when I went outside to play and got my good clothes dirty."

The arachnid abruptly changed the subject. <How did you heal Sarave?>

His brow furrowed. What did that have to do with plants? "I gave her one of your potions…"

<No. My milk is nutritious and has mild healing properties, but its greatest benefit lies in that it provides the body what it needs to repair itself quickly and well. It cannot cure poison, and certainly does not restore missing body parts. You *know* this.> She was calm now. Cajoling. She was leading him toward something.

He swallowed. He did know. Too well, in fact, since he had seen more than one former comrade die even after being given one of Sumi's potions. If he was honest, that knowledge had been niggling at him since the healing took place, but he had thrust it to the back of his mind, convincing himself he needed to deal with more urgent matters such as getting to safety and slaying vampires.

<Two miraculous things have happened since we arrived here. At *least* two. What is the common thread that ties them together?>

He looked down, avoiding the sharp gleam of her glittering black eyes. He ran through the events in his mind. Even if he only considered the plants and the healing, there was really only one thing they both had in common. He looked up and cleared his throat. "Me?"

The spider's posture relaxed slightly. <You.>

He waved his hand at the expanse of cheerfully growing plants. "I can't grow things. Honestly, I expected to struggle to grow enough food for the four of us, and you don't even eat plants. Birdie gave me a little plant that ate flies once, and I killed it within a week. I knew I wouldn't be a great success as a farmer, but you all insisted we leave. I just wanted to find someplace peaceful to…" The last word hung in the silence between them, unspoken. *Die.* He had come here to die. His friends, the ones who loved him best, had likely come expecting to bury him by spring, but determined that he would not die alone.

It seemed that something, or someone, had other plans.

"You think I'm still a mage." His voice was rough, the words dragging past his throat like broken glass.

<I do.>

"You think I have healing and life magic."

<I do,> she said gently.

"I *can't*! Sumi!" His voice tore itself apart, and his chest heaved as he struggled for breath. "Sumi," he choked out, "I am… I *was* a necromancer. My magic was all death and suffering. Birdie was the healer. She-" He stopped, tears coursing down his hollow cheeks. "You all *felt* my magic die. When the link snapped –"

<We felt something, certainly. Through Atae's grace, you gave us each a

part of your soul, binding us to you, servant to master. That bond was certainly broken. But we were still able to communicate. *Something* remains. Do I think what you are now is the same as what you were before? Certainly not.> A leg slashed sharply. <I think you blame yourself, and your magic for what happened to Birdie, and...>

"Yes!" The cry was wrenched from him, raw with grief laid bare. "*Yes*! I blame the thing I was, the thing made by dark magic, for what happened! How could I not?"

Sumi's voice was gentle. <You were made by your own choices, as are we all. Magic opened many of those choices to you, and the fact that you were gifted in the darkest magics opened still others, but magic in itself is not evil. *You* were never evil.>

"I was uncaring! I wanted power and more power. I forgot what was important, and I let her, *her* of all people, pay the price for it! If that's not evil, what is?" His pale topaz eyes were bleak and filled with self-loathing.

She clicked her chelicerae. <Uncaring, maybe. You were proud. You let yourself believe that your needs were more important than those of anyone else. In the end, though, you did the right thing. You were selfish and human, not evil.> The spider tapped his leg with her pedipalp as if she could take some of his pain with a touch.

His voice was a whisper, forcing its way past the bile filling his throat. "I just want to be a farmer. I want to succeed or fail with my own two hands. I want...to fade away, quietly..."

<That's not what Birdie wanted. That's not what she died for, and not why Gina and Atae gave you a second chance that no one else has ever gotten.> A many-jointed leg waved gracefully over the field. <You of all people know that nothing is free. *This* is the first hint of Gina's price for her aid, and perhaps also her gift. This and the ability to heal that goblin woman and save her baby. You are still a mage, Aspen.>

Aspen's legs felt suddenly weak, and he sank down on the dark, fertile soil and buried his face in his hands.

The darkness behind his eyes couldn't block Sumi's last, insistent words. <Long ago, in your ignorance and pride, you asked the universe for the power to change your life. You were fortunate that it was only Atae who answered. This time Gina calls you. It's time to listen.>

☙ ☙ ☙

By the time the two of them returned to the house, they could hear the sound of Rouge's Zombie chopping wood, and smell the scent of a warm, fruit and grain-filled breakfast wafting from the windows. Khor was lurking outside the house, posture tense. Sumi bobbed in acknowledgement when his eyes met hers, and his body relaxed. The huge goat nodded and nudged the two little kids ahead of him toward the field he and Aspen were clearing of stones.

Sarave looked up when they entered. Her yellow eyes took in the tear streaks on Aspen's face and the hollowness of his cheeks. She looked at Sumi, who waved reassuringly before retreating to her favorite spot near the fireplace. The little goblin woman attempted a smile, but it was nervous and half-hearted at best.

"You look," she hesitated, searching for the right words. Shaking her head in frustration, she finished with, "Hungry. Did you not sleep?" She handed Aspen one of the rough wooden bowls filled with a steaming mix of cooked grains and berries, with a fried egg on top.

He smiled tiredly at her. "I slept well enough, though Khor's snoring would be enough to keep a deaf turtle awake. I just had a bit of an early wake-up call today. I'll recover." He sat down with his food. The bowl wobbled as he set it on the table. "The meal looks delicious. Thank you."

Sarave's smile was more genuine this time, though it was still tinged with concern. "You are welcome. Thank you for provide ingredients." She sat down with her own bowl, and bowed her head toward Gina's statue as she always did before a meal. Her lips moved in silent prayer, and then she looked back up. "Is there anything I need do today? Should I just keep-?" She waved her hand around the much-tidier house, indicating all the work she'd done since her arrival.

Aspen shook his head. "Truly, what you have been doing is a huge help. I'm afraid none of us are particularly good house-keepers, and while we all like to eat, we haven't much enthusiasm for producing the meals." He patted his belly. "At this rate, I'll be very glad you're also a seamstress and working on letting out all my pants."

The goblin woman chuckled, her face almost pretty in the dim light of the kitchen. "My Jeremy say this too. I'm glad to help." Her vocabulary and grammar were improving daily, and he suspected she'd soon have nothing left of her initial struggles except the clicking, musical accent.

Aspen looked toward his bedroom. He had left the curtain that served as a door open when he left, worried that any small sound might be enough to wake the others, since they were all on high alert until the situation with the vampires was resolved. "I do have one thing to ask."

She looked at him attentively and nodded.

He hesitated, but forced himself to continue. "I need to read the book the Head Librarian sent today. It's a little more unusual than I led our little thief friend to believe. I didn't want to tempt her too much on such a short acquaintance. I'll need quiet and privacy. It's important that I not be interrupted." He looked a bit chagrined to be asking for quiet when he knew that the things she could do mostly required some level of noise.

Sarave laughed softly, covering her sharp teeth with her hand. "I will find something to do. Sewing needs much light. I see in dark, but thread is small, small. And, I think babe," she rested a tender hand on her swollen abdomen, which had visibly dropped in the last day, "likes warm sun. She sleeps when it warm."

Aspen looked away, his smile strained. "She, is it? Are you so certain it's a girl? No smelly, noisy boys for you?"

She shook her head, her smooth black braid waving softly against her back.

"Boy or girl, matters not. Jeremy, wished for girl. He wished for little me." A dark flush of embarrassment rose up beneath her skin, which was now a healthy shade of green. "He prefer that to 'great oaf' like him. I-," her voice cracked, "I would happy be to have such oaf again, but it is as Gina will."

Aspen smiled sadly, his own pain finding company and ease in recognizing itself in another. "Enjoy the sun with your little one, then. Keep close to Khor though, if you would. He'll watch your back while you work."

She nodded and stood, holding her hand out for his empty bowl. He handed it to her and stood, towering over her in the small space. He felt oddly awkward after their moment of shared sorrow. Clapping his hat onto his head, he turned to the door. "I'll go out and check on the new walls. I want to see how the slurry has set, and if it's ready for more stones or needs to dry longer. I was a little preoccupied when I went by earlier."

Sarave nodded, already dropping the dishes into the wash basin. "I wash up, then go sew. Grains delicious, but hard as wall when dry."

He laughed and stepped back out into the sunlight.

The wall looked strong and mostly straight. The warm, dry weather had set the slurry enough that he could probably continue working on it without risking what they already had, so Aspen knew what he'd be doing in the afternoon.

Now, though, it was time to face the Book. Sarave soon stepped outside, her glossy hair covered by a spider-silk kerchief and carrying a basket of mending. Aspen slipped into the house behind her, and sat in his small bedroom with the large book on his lap. He stroked the soft blue leather, and a scent, reminiscent of warm metal and the smell that hangs in the air after a thunderstorm, rose up from it.

He had been planning to ignore the book. When he left Bright, hidden in the back of a wagon, dying inch by inch, the Head Librarian had come to him. The little man had told Aspen that he would send books like this north with a reliable courier when he could. They were no longer safe in Bright.

Aspen tried to tell him they'd be no safer on a farm with a broken old soldier and a trio of creatures who were only there out of a misplaced sense of loyalty, but the other man would hear none of it.

"Sumi will get you up, like it or not, boyo," the bent old man had insisted. "You have years left to live, and I don't believe for a moment that you won't live them. Your heart and body are broken, but broken things can be repaired. You know, Birdie would want you to keep them safe." The Librarian knew exactly which buttons to push, and so Aspen had agreed.

So, here he was, with a Skill Book on his lap. An actual useful Skill Book, at that. When the Library was moved to the school, Duke Geral had confiscated all the Skill Books that had been stored there, 'for the good of the Kingdom!' After Akuji's defeat, the Head Librarian had asked for them to be returned, but Geral claimed they were on an estate outside Bright that had, conveniently, been utterly destroyed by the Lich lord's army. When the Head Librarian asked why the books had been kept there, instead of relatively safe somewhere in Bright, the Duke had kicked him out.

Skill Books were extraordinarily rare and valuable. Each one represented the sum total of all the knowledge of its author at the time of its writing. They required a piece of the writer's soul to create, much as Aspen had used some of his own soul to create his companions from the beasts they were born to be. Tearing a piece of your soul free was both agonizing and difficult, and the part lost would never grow back. As a result, most masters wrote only one such tome, usually toward the very end of their lives.

The authors also set strict limitations on who could use them, weaving those requirements into the book itself. This ensured that only a worthy heir would use the text, which became nothing more than paper and ink after the first reading. They rarely left the hands of the author's family, and were used by the most promising descendant of the person who wrote them. That descendent would then create his or her own book, and so continue the cycle.

As the Human Kingdoms fell, however, the precious books were lost, destroyed, sold to collectors who locked them away, or simply used by someone who then died before they could write a new one. In order to properly use a Skill Book, the reader had to fulfill the author's requirements and also be a mage of some kind. Whether or not the skill itself used mana, it took magic to absorb the knowledge inside, and more magic to create another text.

One Master. One life. One Book.

When read by a person with all the qualifications for a given book, that person could gain, over time, all the skills of the original Master. Some readers lacked the fortitude or magic to finish a book, and those books were lost, unusable by anyone but them, while they were unable to use it. These were often the ones that ended up in the hands of collectors.

The other type that ended up with collectors were the silly books. *The Book of Puns*, by Master Comedian Sat Ire. *One Man's Journey to Speed Walking. Miss Rose Learns to Boil Water!* Their authors were undoubtedly great at their Skill, but that didn't make that ability worthwhile to anyone else.

These were also the books that the Head Librarian occasionally came across as they re-catalogued the Great Library of Bright. The obviously important books on things like swordsmanship, leatherworking, spear throwing, horse-back riding had been carefully stored in the Library, awaiting someone qualified to read them. Geral had taken all of those, but the ones the nobility considered 'useless' - about things like styling hair into gravity-defying towers and training fleas to perform tricks - had been lost in the move.

Five such books were already in a specially-sealed box in the cellar below. However unimportant their contents might seem now, they were precious parts of someone's soul, and deserved to be saved until they could be used, as they had been intended to be. Now the Head Librarian had sent another, and this one...

If he could read it, this one could mean the difference between a small, nearly worthless plot of land and a farm that would make, well, the author of the book proud. The first step was simple. He had to determine if he could even read the book.

When he read the title, he had known that this book could help him. In fact, it could change everything. Of course, the chances that he would meet the requirements set down by the author were miniscule, but it hadn't really mattered. He had lacked the one thing required to read any Skill Book. He had no mana. It had been ripped from him, every point stripped away as if it were a piece of his skin, peeled away from his soul by a dull blade.

He knew Sumi had seen the book. He knew she saw him put it away, ready to hide it in the cellar with the others the next time Sarave left the house. Sumi would have known that he would never even try, no matter how useful it might be, even if, by some amazing (and likely Goddess-given) chance he met the demands set down by the author.

So, the wise old arachnid had shown him the field. She led him through his own insistent blindness to see what he needed to do. He had mana. He had to try.

Aspen took a breath and turned the first page of *Mage-Smithing Farm Implements* by Joanna Deene. A jagged spike of pain drove into his head, and a woman's face appeared before him. Her hair was more silver than gold, and her skin was leathery and seamed with age. She only had one good eye, which seemed to stare through him, judging and weighing. He hung in emptiness as his heartbeat pounded in his ears. Finally, she nodded.

Joanna stood, a little girl of five or six, watching her mother work. The heavy hammer rang out as it sparked against the red-hot metal of the shovel blade forming on the anvil. The smell of hot metal filled the area. The smithy was far from traditional, since the metal was heated with her mother's magic. No blazing forge filled the space. No bellows, charcoal, or heavy leather gloves would be needed.

Her mother looked up and saw Joanna standing there. She smiled, her sweat-drenched blonde hair pulled back out of her face, skin ruddy with effort. She released the tongs she was using to grip the hot metal so the hammer wouldn't strike her fingers, and crouched down.

"Do you feel it, Jonny? Hold out your hand. Don't touch it! Just get near enough to feel the heat, and close your eyes."

Joanna held out her little hand, dirty and tanned, until she could hardly bear the heat radiating from the object resting on the anvil. Her mother cradled her fingers in her much larger, rougher ones. Joanna closed her eyes.

At first, there was nothing but heat. It built until she thought she would have to pull away or be burned, but then a wash of cool, sharp, something *passed through her hand from her mother's. Her nose detected a sudden increase in the smell of hot metal, but it no longer seemed as though it could hurt her. The heat, in fact, faded to a gentle warmth, and she felt her mother pull at her hand.*

"Open your eyes," her mother whispered.

She opened her eyes to see her hand half-buried in liquid metal. It seeped between her fingers, no longer holding the shape of a shovel, but now simply a white-hot fluid. She looked at her mother, her mouth stretching in a brilliant smile.

"I did it, Mama!"

Her mother gently pulled her hand back, a matching smile on her own face. With a thought, the mage-smith cooled the metal. A normal smith would have ruined it, cooling it so fast, but not Joanna's mother. A perfect handprint was left behind in cool, gleaming iron.

Joanna reached out and picked up the metal slab, grunting slightly at the weight. "Don't you need it for your shovel, Mama?"

Strong arms gave Joanna a hug, and her mother's unique scent surrounded her. "I have more. You keep that. Practice with it, if you like. Remember how it felt to channel the magic. You'll be powerful one day, Jonny. But even those who are gifted need to practice to make the most of their gifts."

The little girl stared at the smooth, perfect image of her hand in the iron. Yes. She would be the BEST.

Aspen closed the book and laid back, gasping. His head was swimming, and for several lengthy minutes his own lanky body with all of its middle-aged aches felt utterly foreign to him. Nonetheless, a grin spread across his face, matching the expression he'd just seen on young Joanna's face.

He could do it! He was, indeed, still a mage of some kind. What kind, he didn't know. His original Class had been stripped from him by Akuji's terrible power. When his Goddess, Atae, repudiated him, and Gina took him up, everything had changed, and the repercussions of that change were still unfolding.

Usually, a child began an official apprenticeship, if you could find a Master willing to take them on, by the time they turned twelve. By fourteen, apprentice or no, they would pray to their God or Goddess and be granted a broad Class, such as Thief, Healer, Soldier, Cook, Farmer, Tailor, etcetera. When that base Class reached level 20, if they had fulfilled the other requirements, they could pray again, and be granted a Specialization.

In order to advance, you had to have the right skills and stats for the Class you wanted, but if you had been training in it for at least two years, it would usually be offered to you.However, each child was given a choice of three Classes for which they were suited, and occasionally one would choose a Class they wanted instead of the one for which they had been trained.

Aspen had done exactly that. He had grown up in southern Quarternell, near the town of Jumping Hollow, when the end of Humanity hadn't yet been so starkly visible. His father worked for a tailor in town, and his mother was the sole teacher in their little village. She had begun training him from the time he could read, but he had little interest in scholarly works, and less interest in teaching children who didn't want to learn.

When he was twelve, he entered the one small temple that stood in the center of Jumping Hollow. He was supposed to pray to Minetra, goddess of knowledge and craftsmen. Instead, he simply knelt in the center of the temple floor and prayed to any god who would give him a way to escape his monotonous life.

Atae accepted him, and set him on a path far different from the one his parents had envisioned for him.

That path was a long and hard one. It led him higher than he dreamed, and, in the end, it took him to depths deeper than his twelve-year-old self could possibly have imagined. He lost his stats, his Skills, even his Class and his goddess. Worst of all, he lost the only good thing he had made from a selfish and arrogant life. Only the heroism of his few remaining friends had brought him out alive, and for a while he cursed them for it.

He lived his life now for them. They could have, *should* have, left him behind. He had nothing left except to repay them, and he would do it.

Sumi. Khor. Little Silus, who had been barely more than a child when all this happened, and whose mother died while saving Aspen. Now there were Sarave, her babe, and those ridiculous miniature goats, with their soft, magical fur. They all depended on him, in one way or another, and he would do better this time around.

It all started with this book.

Chapter Nine

Rouge

Rouge's Zombie was already cutting trees when she entered *Veritas*. She felt the shock of a powerful impact through the worn wooden handle, and released her grip, leaving the axe blade half-buried in the trunk of the tree she had been chopping. Looking around, she could see that she was very nearly half a mile from the house, surrounded by neatly-piled logs and tree stumps.

Curious how her Zombie's little adventure had affected her character's growth, she pulled up her character sheet and Away logs.

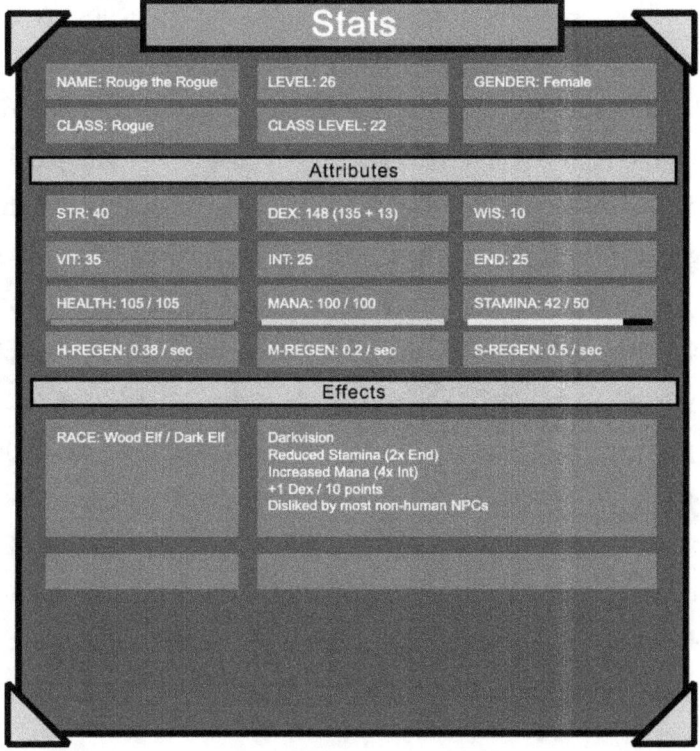

For chopping 500 trees, you have opened the Merry (Wo)Man sub-class. As these happy rogues live in the woods, they gain +2 [Stealth] when in wooded areas, an increased 10% chance of a successful [Backstab] when in wooded areas, and a +5% chance of receiving rarer items from enemies slain in wooded areas. They have a -2 [Stealth] in any non-wooded area. If you would like to accept this sub-class, please pray at any shrine to your chosen Deity.

Rouge sighed and swiped the message away. This was a slightly rarer sub-class than Assassin, Mugger, or Highwayman, but if she'd wanted her character to be restricted to the forest, she would have gone full wood elf, instead of choosing to be half dark elf and dealing with the animosity most NPCs instinctively felt for her. As far as she knew, this was a new way to get Highwayman, so she might post about it on the forums later, but she still wasn't interested.

She eyed the 'level 22' after her Class with dissatisfaction. A Class rose rapidly when you used the Skills specific to it, and slowly if you didn't. Once you reached level 20, however, experience gain in your base Class slowed to a crawl until you prayed and accepted a sub-Class. At that point, all the experience the game had held back would be awarded to you, minus some percentage depending on how rare your final Class was. If you ended up selecting something common, like Mugger, you could lose as much as 50% of your banked experience, so waiting too long could still handicap your character.

The system was designed to encourage players to select a sub-Class quickly, which kept the game from growing stale while you tried to do exactly what she was doing, and find something really rare or interesting. Rouge was going to out-stubborn the game, though. Until she found exactly the right sub-Class, she would remain a simple Rogue, even with her glacial leveling speed. She'd heard that if you managed to earn an Epic or rarer class, the game might even reward you with *bonus* experience for your effort, though that might just be an urban legend.

The good news was, with the experience points she'd gotten for helping kill the vampire, and completing the 'Follow the Red Brick Road' quest, she'd leveled *three* times, and was able to break the 100 point barrier in both Health and Mana, thanks to the boost in Mana she got for being half dark elf. That meant her recovery speeds in both those areas increased as well, which was amazing!

The girl closed the screen with a thought, then put the axe and all of the lumber around her into her inventory. She turned to walk back toward the small stone house, and jumped as she felt something hard tuck up beneath her arm. Acting on instinct, she started to whirl away, pulling out her Mambele, and found herself looking into Codswallop's wide brown eyes.

The large ostrich huffed a questioning warble, and Rouge relaxed, putting away her blade and throwing her arms around Codswallop's strong neck. "Oh, Wally! I'm sorry! Have you been following me this whole time? Did they take good care of you while I was gone?"

She flicked through her own status screen, and noted that she had the Well-Rested buff, which granted increased recovery speed and resistance to debuffs such as Sleep and Hypnosis. Once she'd skimmed through her own sheet, she pulled up Codswallop's.

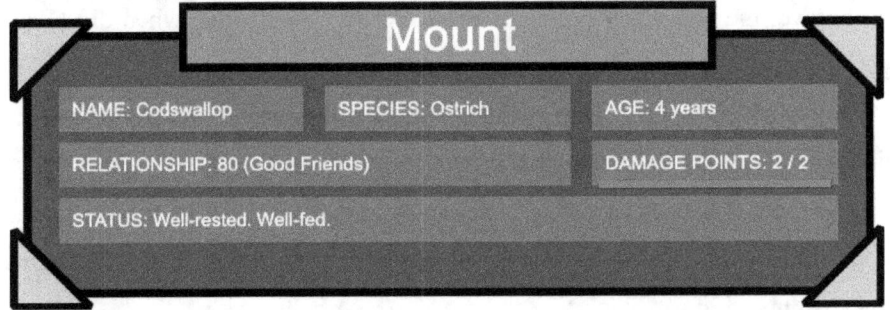

That was one worry taken care of. She couldn't do much except hope she read these NPCs right, and they would do as they promised. The almost comically oversized goat was a little rough around the edges, but everyone else seemed really nice, especially the little goats and the adorable little bat. She really hoped she could figure out how to increase her Reputation with the bat – Silus? She really wanted to scrootch those little ears and see if they were as soft as they looked.

Rouge and Codswallop reached the house, and Rouge looked around. There was a *huge* pile of logs to the side of the house, so she unloaded her inventory there, and started looking for the residents. As she rounded the side of the house, she saw that Aspen had been busy. There were new, incomplete walls sketching out a space as large as the house itself, and then another smaller area next to it. Both were attached to the existing house, and looked like they were pretty well-built, though the base of the walls were a little thick and uneven in places.

She heard a strange noise coming from the other side of the closest wall. It was a sort of muffled *phoomp*, followed by a yelp, and then soft giggling. "What the…?"

She popped her head around, and stared at the sight in front of her.

Aspen, all lanky six-foot-whatever of him, lay sprawled in the dust. Smoke spiraled lazily from the ends of his brown hair and the cuffs of his shirt. The skin of his hands looked pink and angry, but he looked more exasperated than pained.

Sarave, the extremely pregnant goblin woman (and since when did NPCs get pregnant?), crouched awkwardly next to him, wrapping his closest hand in a damp cloth. From the pile of wet cloths in a bowl nearby, this was not the first time she had done this. She looked much better than she had last time Rouge had seen her. She wore loose, simple pants and a tunic, and looked clean and tidy. She'd obviously taken a bath and washed her hair, which now hung in a thick, shiny braid.

It was Sarave who was giggling, though she'd seemed far too serious to be the type who would laugh at someone else's pain. Then Rouge caught sight of something in the dirt behind Aspen, and, once she parsed out what it was, she too began to laugh.

The two, accompanied by the giant spider, who wasn't *quite* as creepy out in the bright sunlight, turned to stare at Rouge, surprise wiping away all other expressions. Sarave, in fact, seemed to sink backwards, hiding behind the man who must be almost three feet taller than she was.

Rouge pointed at what she had at first thought was a very oddly-shaped metal bowl next to Aspen.

"How did you manage to make a bowl shaped like your butt?" She looked at it again, noting the heat waves rising from its surface even in the warm sunlight. "I assume it's yours, since nobody else around here is that big."

Aspen, bless him, flushed beet red and struggled to his feet. He started to brush down his pants, then grimaced and stopped. "Um, yes. I'm working on a new skill, and it's more difficult than I'd anticipated." He looked down at his raw, blistered fingers, which were already beginning to heal as his health recovery kicked in. "It's a bit frustrating, so we were having a moment of, ah, stress relief."

A small giggle came from behind him, and Sarave clapped a thin hand over her mouth, as though embarrassed at being caught having fun.

"Oh." Rouge grinned at them. "I totally understand." Then she pulled out her favorite seven words. "Is there anything I can help with?"

Nothing happened.

Aspen shrugged. "We really appreciate you using your... Zombie, to help out the last two days. You looked a bit worried when you left, and I was actually wondering if there's anything I can do to help you."

I, her gamer-brain noted. Not *we*. He wasn't volunteering his friends. Somehow she must have gotten a few more Relationship points with him than the others.

"Well," she shrugged, trying to look as young and innocent as possible, "I do actually have a couple of things I could use some help with."

He raised an eyebrow in inquiry. Could all middle-aged men do that? It made her feel like she'd done something wrong, and now he was waiting for her to 'fess up. She managed to catch her defensive glare before it could do more than narrow her eyes, but she had a feeling he'd caught it, and laughter creased the corners of his strange brownish gold eyes. Topaz. That's what that color was.

She coughed. "I was kind of curious about someone, and the Head Librarian suggested I come and ask you about it. The HL said the guy moved up north, so he sent me up with that box."

Aspen frowned, gingerly rubbing the back of his neck. "HL?"

"Head Librarian." She rolled her eyes. "If he's going to use that as his name, I'm going to shorten it, because that is too many syllables to have to say every time. I mean, what if there was a problem? Like one of those great big stacks of books falling on his head? Wouldn't it be faster to say 'HL, duck!' rather than 'Head Librarian'?"

The tall man shoved his rather ridiculous hat (Was that straw? Reeds?) back off his forehead and rubbed right above his eyebrows. Seriously, why did all adults do the same things? Finally he nodded. "I grant you the point, but-"

"Yeah, anyway, the HL said you might know where this Duke Penbrooke went, since you have the only human habitation up here." It took her a moment to notice that both Aspen and Sumi had frozen when she said the name. Nothing as obvious as the Head Librarian almost attacking her, but the man's expression locked down, and Sumi's pedipalps, which usually waved as she communicated with her pet-master, lifted into a vaguely aggressive raised posture.

Aspen's pale eyes were cold as he regarded her, and he must have sent out a message for the big goat, because she heard heavy hooves thudding toward them. "Where did you hear that name, and why are you so 'curious'?"

She nearly slapped herself in the forehead. How could she have forgotten how strongly the Head Librarian had reacted? Why should she have expected anything else from this group? It all tied into a Secret Quest, after all. Obviously it wasn't going to be as simple as asking. She should have farmed some Reputation with them before she even opened her mouth. Her only excuse was that she had to get back to Bright before her dad realized she was missing. That meant, basically, *right now.*

She backpedaled, holding up her empty hands. From their looks, they hadn't forgotten that items appeared directly in her hands from her inventory, and recognized it as a false reassurance. She squinted, and saw that though the tags over Sumi and Khor's heads had turned slightly yellow, Aspen's was still green. She had a chance, then. She quickly rolled out the explanation she had practiced while on her way north. Codswallop had found it very convincing.

"Look, I was in a temple when I overheard some people talking. I was praying, and I didn't look around until I was done, because *rude*, right? Anyway, I didn't see them, but they were talking about this Duke Penbrooke, and how he needed to come back to Bright and fix something. I'm kind of a lore buff." She quickly saw that she'd lost them with that bit of slang. "I mean, I like history a lot, and I've never heard of this Duke Penbrooke."

She took a deep breath, trying to slow down before she completely scrambled her words. Dying would be the fastest way to get back to Bright, but it wasn't exactly an optimal solution. Plus, being killed by a goat was just *embarrassing.* "So, I figured I'd go and ask the HL, because he's a good guy, and I did him some favors when I cleared out his rat problem. Plus, he knows *everything*, right? But when I asked, he got all scary and cryptic, and sent me up here with a timed quest, like he wanted to get rid of me or something..." Her voice trailed off and her eyes widened with realization.

"Oh. Em. Gee. He *did* want to get rid of me! He was worried I'd talk to the wrong person and get in trouble, or get someone after this Penbrooke guy! He gave me that quest just so I'd be stuck up here until spring! That sneaky little-!" Her voice was annoyed but admiring by the time she was done talking, and she peeked at the tags above the NPCs to see that they had all settled back into a solid green.

One side of Aspen's lips quirked up, and he tugged the brim of his stupid hat back down. She kind of felt like an Old West gunslinger had just tied the strap back down on his holster to show that he wasn't going to shoot the next idiot who opened their mouth.

"That does sound like something the Head Librarian would do. Especially if you're the young lady who killed the rodents eating his books. When I last spoke to him, it was after you'd cleared the final quest, and he was quite admiring. I got the feeling he'd taken you under his wing a bit, as well, so sending you here to get you out of the way makes sense." He tilted his head, considering her.

"He might actually be sending me some help, too. This first winter will likely be difficult, and there is a lot of preparation to do. In addition to that, we believe there are at least one, if not two more vampires on the loose in the area."

Quest: "Winter is Coming" available.

Help Aspen prepare the farm for the winter. Clear and plant three fields. You probably want to get some gardening gloves.

Success: +20 Reputation with Aspen. +10 Reputation with all other farm residents.

Failure: -20 Reputation with all farm residents.

Accept: Yes/No?

Bells went off in her head. Quests! In fact, that sounded like a whole *chain* of quests. Unfortunately…

"Ah, unless it's something I can help with pretty quickly, I'm going to have to wait and come back in the spring to help you." It was her turn to duck her head and look embarrassed.

Aspen frowned. "What do you mean? There's no way back through that pass until spring melt. It's a death sentence for you and your bird to even try."

She grimaced unhappily. Seeing them all getting ready to do her in a few minutes ago had reminded her of a possible solution she hadn't considered before. "Yeah. I'm going to need somebody to kill me."

Shock wiped all expression from the NPCs faces. Even Sarave poked her head out to stare at Rouge.

"What?" Aspen asked, deep voice blank with surprise.

"Yeah, so, here's the deal. You guys know I'm a Traveler, right?" They all nodded. Even Sumi waved an affirmative leg. "And you know Travelers respawn? Kind of like lesser beasts and unnamed monsters, right?" Again the silent chorus of agreement. "So, I'm, like, *way* out of bounds right now. My dad had to work last week, and he couldn't play with me." Confusion took over from understanding, and she waved a hand.

"I mean, in our other world, we have lives kind of like you do. We work as, um, seamstresses, and salespeople, and, uh, coach drivers. My dad is a teacher. It's the end of the year for his school, and he had to give his students all these really hard tests, to make sure they learned what he was trying to teach them, I guess." She was pretty sure they could tell from her voice that she wasn't actually sure what the value of Finals was, but they nodded anyway.

"So, he told me to be super careful, and stay in Bright, and blah blah blah, don't get in trouble." She could see comprehension dawning on Aspen's face, though Sarave still looked befuddled. "But he's going to be logging on any time now, and he'll expect me to be waiting for him in Bright, like a good girl." She wrinkled her nose, and those little creases of amusement showed up back at the corners of Aspen's eyes.

She waved a hand, indicating the small house and the vast expanse of sky. "If he finds out I'm up here, I'm going to be *so* grounded, and he won't let me play... Um, come back, for months. Probably not the rest of this school year at least. So, I need to get back to Bright. I *was* going to try to walk back, even though there's snow up there now, because I can respawn at my last save... Um, the temple in Bright. I figured even if I die, I could get back before he even knows I was gone."

Aspen opened his mouth, but she knew what he was going to ask, so she hurried on. "I just can't kill myself, because, uh, the Gods punish us for that. Anyway, since I don't have a time-sensitive quest anymore, I can wait and come back in the spring. Which I will! I'll make sure I don't talk about this Penbrooke guy to anyone until I get back, I swear!" She held up two fingers in what she hoped was the Scout salute.

Aspen actually did bury his face in his hand, rubbing at his temples. He drew in a long breath, lowering his hand, and shook his head before looking from Khor to Sumi. Sumi's whole body swayed indecisively, but Khor stamped his feet eagerly. The goat definitely seemed ready to take care of business.

The man looked back at Rouge and frowned. "So you want us to kill you to prevent your father from finding out you disobeyed him? Because it's, what, faster than heading up into the mountains and dying from exposure or animal attack? Then you'll come back in the spring why? Just to sate your curiosity about this person who may or may not exist, and may or may not be a Duke? It seems," he paused, looking up at the sky, "morally and logically shaky, at best."

Shockingly, it was Sarave who offered a suggestion. Her smooth, lilting voice was surprisingly rich coming from such a small body, and it captured their attention in spite of its hesitant tone. She stepped out from behind Aspen, hands over her enormous belly protectively.

"Morality is right and wrong, yes?" Her wide eyes, yellow from sclera to iris, were steady as she looked between the two humans. "You both worship Gina. Pray. Ask her to send sign. Gina will guide you." She set her small, pointed chin, as though she expected a rebuke from one or both of them, but Aspen just grinned and reached down to gently pat the small woman's shoulder.

"You're brilliant, Sarave! Gina won't talk to me for a while. Something about a quest I'm in the middle of, but maybe she'll come have a chat with our little Traveler here. The Goddess has certainly been poking her pretty little nose into *my* business enough, it's only fair to spread the love." He snorted a laugh and turned back to the house, waving at them to follow.

Rouge swallowed a giggle. When Aspen turned away, she could finally see that the hot metal he had been playing with when she arrived had burned holes in the seat of his pants. She could see flashes of pale cloth, the generic NPC undergarment, as he walked, and she was a little surprised he wasn't feeling a draft.

Looking over, she caught Sarave with her eyes on Aspen's rear, her hand over her mouth again. Rouge grinned at the little goblin, who giggled in return, and everyone followed Aspen into the house. Khor took up what seemed to be his usual place, with his hairy chin resting on a windowsill. Aspen and Sarave took seats by the table, and Sumi skittered with chilling speed up toward the roof. She heard small bleats from outside, and realized that the kids were back to playing around the massive goat's hooves.

On the table, resting in a place of honor where the best light from the fireplace would bathe it, sat the beautiful statue of a woman that Rouge had briefly seen before. Looking closer, she realized that it bore a striking similarity to the statues of Gina she had seen in temples before. Those usually had a distant, regal air to them, however, and this one definitely had a mischievous tilt to her lips and a crinkle of laughter at the corner of her eyes.

Sarave quickly folded her hands and bowed her head toward the statue. Her face was tranquil and happy when she raised it again, and for a moment the goblin was almost pretty. "For long and long, I was frightened to follow Gi-na. Now I can be no fear. I proud to worship Gi-na." She pressed one hand over her heart, and the other over her belly, then looked over at Rouge. She nodded encouragingly.

Rouge glanced over at Aspen. He was watching the goblin woman with a little smile, but when he caught Rouge's eyes on him, the expression smoothed . He sighed and folded his hands in front of him. "Your Holiness. Gina." He said, correcting himself. "I find myself with a bit of a moral dilemma, and while I hesitate to ask you about anything serious, you are a goddess, and you probably deal with situations like this," he glanced at Rouge, "*kind of* like this, anyway, all the time. If you'd show us a sign to help with the decision, that would be very helpful. Um, Yours, Aspen." He finished awkwardly, and looked back up. He quirked that eyebrow at Rouge again.

She gulped. She knew the Gods and Goddesses of *Veritas* were as 'real' as anything else in the game, and that sometimes they would actually respond to the prayers of both players and NPCs. She'd even had it happen herself recently. Still, when she went to a shrine or temple, she usually just interacted with it enough to set a save point or ask for a blessing. This felt way too much like actually, well, *praying*.

"Okay. Um. Well, Gina, it's like this…"

There was a flash of light, and the world spun away.

Rouge was surrounded by a formless gray mist. She reached out, but couldn't feel anything. There was no sound, no smell, not a hint of a breeze. She started to panic, reaching out to wave away the fog as if it were a physical thing. She thrashed, and realized that she couldn't see her hands in front of her. She had no body….

There was a small pop, and a beautiful meadow appeared around her. Rich emerald grass carpeted the ground. Birds sang, leaves blew and rang like windchimes in a soft spring breeze. Rouge fell to her knees, nauseated. If she could have vomited in the game, she would have. What just *happened?*

As she struggled to control her churning stomach, she heard the rustle of branches, the sound of silky fabric brushing grass, and the edge of a vibrant green gown appeared in her vision. A perfect, softly-glowing hand appeared before her, open and clearly offering her assistance in getting to her feet.

Rouge reached out, her own caramel skin suddenly seeming dull against the glow of the other. She pulled herself to her feet, then looked up. She met eyes that were impossibly rainbow-hued, and luscious red lips that smiled merrily.

Then, as those rainbow eyes took in Rouge, they widened in shock. The woman (goddess?) slashed out a hand, and everything... stopped. The birds didn't sing. The breeze didn't blow. The leaves froze in impossible positions.

A melodious and extremely agitated voice emerged from those red lips. "Emilieu! *Emily!* Where are you?"

Emily, the NPC who represented the user interface and helped guide players during character creation, appeared instantly beside the glimmering woman, who Rouge assumed was supposed to be Gina. The pseudo-AI generated by the most sophisticated automated learning program yet created was wearing a drapey white gown and had her usual bun softened into a feathery updo, but it was indisputably her. Rouge stared, open-mouthed.

"Yes, oh great goddess Gina?" The voice was the same uninflected feminine tone that had bothered Rouge when she was creating her avatar. *Veritas* made such realistic NPCs, but its user interface couldn't even sound interested? What was up with that?

"Cut that out," the goddess snapped. She pointed at Rouge. "Who is *this?*"

Emily's gaze didn't falter, but Rouge was sure she knew exactly where Gina was pointing.

"This is the player who received your quest, Gina."

Gina frowned, the expression sitting strangely on a face clearly made for smiling. Possibly literally. She looked back at Rouge, and her expression softened when she saw Rouge's concerned gaze shifting back and forth between the two women. The goddess waved her hand, and two plush, turquoise chairs appeared, one behind each of them. Gina plopped unceremoniously into hers, and gestured for Rouge to take the other. Rouge awkwardly complied, and Gina promptly started gnawing on a fingernail. She stared into space, her eyes flicking from side to side.

After a moment, she looked back at Rouge. "Okay. So, Zoey Williams. Birth date February 7, just turned fourteen a few months ago. Legal guardian Marcus Williams, 40, who logged on twelve and a half minutes ago. Let's get Mr-" Her eyes flickered again. "No, *Dr.* Williams here too. He's going to need to hear this."

A moment later Motte was standing beside them, hand raised as though he was about to pick something up. His face went blank for a moment, and then he saw Rouge, nearly lost amidst the deep cushions of the large chair. His face went through a kaleidoscope of expressions before settling on one she recognized as, 'You have a *lot* of explaining to do, young lady'.

Rouge sank even further into the chair, silently praying it might turn out to be a mimic and just swallow her whole.

Gina's expression was carefully neutral when she waved, making another chair appear next to Rouge's. Motte remained standing, face equally noncommittal. With a small sigh, Gina stood in one smooth movement, seemingly unhindered by the marshmallow mounds that made up the chair. She stretched out a graceful hand to Motte, and he shook it mechanically. She smiled.

"So pleased to meet you, Dr. Williams. I do wish it were under different circumstances, but I hope we can come to a satisfactory understanding once we clear up a few matters. I'm... one of the developers of *Veritas Online.*" As she finished talking, the glamor of the goddess Gina faded away, leaving a pretty but solemn woman in her early twenties. She had strawberry blonde hair pulled back into a loose chignon and deep blue eyes. Her flowing gown shifted to a simple but stylish blue business suit, and matching blue flats appeared on her previously bare feet.

She turned back to Rouge, looking apologetic. "I'm so sorry for being abrupt, Zoey. Or would you prefer Rouge?"

The girl stared, then choked out, "Rouge?"

The dev nodded. "My player nickname is Lady Fayre, but you can call me Fay. Now, Rouge probably has some idea why she's here, but," her blue eyes flashed to the apprehensive look Rouge was certain must be plastered all over her face, "given the circumstances, I suspect Dr. Williams is rather lost."

Motte's face was blank. That was his waiting face. The face that said he was going to see if the person he was speaking to was going to shove their foot down their throat, or somehow manage to save what seemed to be a Situation that had gotten Out of Control. "You can call me Motte." He didn't use Fay's name, and Rouge winced. This was not going well.

Fay nodded. "All right then, Motte." She looked down and took a deep breath. When she looked up, her expression was determined. "How much do you know about Veritas Corporation?" She looked between the two of them, including Rouge in her question. Rouge's estimation of her rose a little. Once another adult was present, grown-ups often forgot that 'children' were present and could use their own puny brains.

Motte answered first, deep voice sounding disconcerted. That was good. He was ready for something bad, not a history lesson, and he always liked to show his 'depth of knowledge'. "It's a gaming company that's been around for a fairly long time. Around sixty years, I believe. Started by the current CEO's grandfather, so it's a family business. Privately owned, though recently there have been suggestions that they may go public."

He hesitated, brown eyes assessing Fay's reaction. When she just kept watching him expectantly, he went on. "They've done well, but mostly localize and distribute games created by smaller or foriegn companies. When they do make their own games, they use third party game engines to create their own content. At least that's how it worked until *Veritas Online*."

Rouge thought fast. If she wanted to hold her own and be counted in this conversation, she needed to add something. She remembered an article she'd read online not long ago, "They hired some hot-shot engineers and programmers starting about a decade ago. Around five years ago, they made a breakthrough linking existing medical technology (that they don't like to talk about) and Automated Learning. They created the headsets, which let them create real VR, and here we are."

Fay smiled broadly at them both, clearly delighted. "You're completely right! There are a few more pieces of this, which aren't public knowledge, and I'd very much like to talk to you about them, because they could well affect you a great deal. Unfortunately, I had to sign an NDA, a Non-Disclosure Agreement, myself as part of my job. I've already pushed the bounds of that NDA, but…" She sighed, and the smile slipped away.

The dev's blue eyes were pleading as they went to Motte, clearly able to see the distrust written all over his face. "You see, I made a mistake. I set something in motion that will affect both the game and the company. I was…distracted, and left out something extremely basic." She turned back to Rouge. "I left out an age requirement in a quest line I created." She closed her eyes, suddenly looking overwhelmingly tired. "Such a simple, stupid mistake."

Her eyes opened again, and she smiled warmly at Rouge. "Not that I don't think you can handle it! I looked at your play record when you were selected for the quest. You meet every requirement perfectly. The mistake was entirely mine. In an effort to allow you privacy, I didn't look at your player profile, which compounded the issue. The quest is-," she hesitated, biting her lip. "I can start it over with another player, but no one else, not a single other player in the entire game, suits it as well as Rouge does. Moreover, if I have to start over, the odds that it will fail are…significantly increased."

She spread her hands helplessly and looked at Motte. "And here we are. This *secret* quest," She emphasized the word, and Motte's eyes widened as he realized what she meant. "will require following an extremely difficult story line, and there will be… choices that a child may struggle with, especially one with the strong moral compass Rouge has. That compass is a big part of why she was selected. Never, in months of playing, has she killed or injured an innocent person."

Fay smiled at Rouge affectionately. "In fact, she has spent more time talking to NPCs than players, and has logged more hours doing essentially pointless quests for NPCs than any other ten players in the same amount of time. Like retrieving a doll for a little girl who misses her daddy, in exchange for pennies and a common item." Rouge shifted, suddenly wondering just how much of the time she'd spent in the game this woman had observed in one form or another.

Fay looked back at Motte, who had visibly softened at this complimentary description of his daughter. He now looked more concerned than defensive. Fay continued speaking. "Again, I'm so *very* sorry, Motte. I would never have intentionally done anything to draw Rouge into this. I will do my best to keep her safe, and, in fact, I can even allow her to share her quest with you, though it is still a *secret* quest." There was that emphasis again. "You may not speak of the quest in the game, and once the first part of the quest is done, you'll have to trust her to do the rest, because those quests have been approved by a committee at Veritas Corp, and I can't touch their code."

Motte was looking mulish, and Rouge winced again. That was his 'I'm not going to change my mind' face. "Look, *Fay*," His baritone landed on the dev's name the same way she had verbally underscored 'secret', and Rouge saw Fay wince a little. "I'm sure this is all a big deal to you and your company. But the safety of my daughter is the biggest deal to me."

He gestured around at the too-silent garden. "This is a game. We play it for fun. Rouge gets to play *at all* because I trust her." He switched his flat gaze to Rouge, then back to the other woman. "I'll be honest. I'm not sure what I'm going to do, yet, but Rouge knows that there are reasons for every rule I make. She chose to break several of them, and there will be consequences."

Rouge sat up straight at this. "Dad!"

Ignoring Rouge's outburst, he looked at Fay and crossed his arms. He put on his non-committal 'teacher' face. "You have five minutes to convince me to care, and then my daughter and I are going to log off, and it'll be a long time before you see either of us in game again, if ever."

A muscle in Fay's jaw clenched, and she held out her hand. A piece of paper appeared in it. "This is an NDA. I've kept it simple. No legalese, no tricks. It says that you won't communicate what I'm about to tell you to anyone else, in any way, unless it's the only way to avoid legal trouble, in which case you will call Veritas Corp, and we will either pay your own lawyer or provide you with one. I give you my personal promise that no harm will come to you or your daughter."

Rouge struggled out of her cushy chair and stood stiffly in front of Motte. She knew how he felt about signing *anything*. She used her absolute best begging voice, and applied Puppy Eyes at full blast. Her words tumbled over each other.

"Please, Dad, please. I swear, it's nothing bad. I broke the rules, and I went out of Bright by myself, and I know I'm in big trouble, but *please*, Dad, *please* let her explain. I really, really want to do this! You know I want to work on games when I get older. I think this is going to be *amazing*. I can handle it, and I swear I won't ask for anything for my birthday or Christmas, and I'll... I'll get a job this summer like you told me I should. *Please?*"

Motte's mouth drew down in a frown, but he accepted and scanned the simple contract Fay handed to him. He shook his head, looking up. "I can't read this properly right now. I want a physical copy, and a video recording of you describing this to us. If it isn't exactly what you say it is, you can't hold us to it. No tricks saying we didn't understand something."

Fay's face lightened with hope. She snapped her fingers. "Done. I've sent copies to both the phone number and the digital contact you have listed in your player account. The hard copy will be overnighted to your home address and

ELIZABETH OSWALD

your work address."

Motte took a deep breath, glanced at Rouge, and signed.

Fay began to talk. Fast. Apparently, she was taking Motte's time limit seriously.

"You know that Veritas Corp is a family business. It's wholly and privately owned, and with its previous level of moderate success, that was never really an issue. The owners were comfortable, the employees were happy. Anyway, with the success of *Veritas Online* and the desire of the current CEO to retire, all that has changed. For the last two generations, one family member got the CEO position, and the others would get a cut of the profit while doing none of the work.

"Now, two factions have formed in the company. One wants to remain private. They're happy being able to do what they want, without input from outsiders. They - we - just want to make games" Her lips twisted into a wry half-smile. "This group sees that there are potential uses for the technology we've developed in everything from the medical field, to the military, to trans-continental business. We already have people who use *Veritas* to conduct face-to-face meetings in order to reduce travel."

She nodded at Motte. "As you know, because of the way *Veritas* interacts with the brain, we don't comprehend and retain the written word in the same way we would while logged out. That limits some of these options, at least for now. That said, we also want to create a better world, both for humanity, and our planet as a whole. We see so much possibility for the uses to which our technology could be put. We want to release the base tech to the world. Free. We'll hold back some proprietary information, and the results of our most recent innovations, but give scientists all over the world the same opportunity we had, to develop from the same original baseline we did."

She took a breath, stuttering to a halt, her cheeks flushed. "Then there's the other side. They want essentially the same thing, but they want to sell the information. The tech would still be out there, and people could use it to create all those things, but we, *they*, would make a huge profit. More money than even a thousand people could spend in their lifetimes. It also means that only those who are already astronomically wealthy would have a chance at buying the tech. Huge corporations. Governments. The tech would disappear down a rabbit hole until whoever bought it used it for their own purpose, or someone else discovered some variant of it."

Fay shook her head, glossy strawberry-blonde hair gleaming. "I'll tell you now, it was a freak accident that we figured it out. The chance that someone else would do it deliberately? Well, it's honestly miniscule. It happened once, and it can happen again, but I doubt that it will. Certainly not in time to prevent an unbreakable monopoly."

Motte's face was set in stone, and his voice was cold, giving nothing away. "What does that have to do with me and my daughter?"

A sad smile flickered over Fay's face. "An accident began this, Dr. Williams. Motte. An accident may end it. As you may have noticed, we like games. I proposed a new one. A game within a game, with everything on the line. Our CEO, Carl Landon, decided to tie it to the next World Event in *Veritas Online*."

Rouge's eyes widened. "*My* quest? It's leading to a World Event?"

Fay nodded, grinning at Rouge's ill-concealed excitement. "The quest was created by me. Mr. Landon and a committee of game designers and board members approved it. If I win, the tech flies free, and the real world and the world of *Veritas* will change. For the better, I think. If I lose, the tech will be sold to the highest bidder, and *Veritas*' changes will be…different. The large event will occur, but the direction it guides the game will shift significantly."

Rouge and Motte's eyes met. Rouge attempted a tentative smile, and her dad's left eyebrow shot up. The girl looked back at Fay.

"We like the idea of free tech. But now that we know, what's to stop us from just making everything go your way? I mean, isn't this," she motioned at the three of them, "cheating or something?"

The other woman sighed deeply. "There's another player involved. Well, a few, really, but one of them is on our side, and she still doesn't know anything about all of this. Have you ever heard of an influencer named Bree Stephenson?"

Beside Rouge, Motte's body tensed like a dog scenting a rabbit. Or, in Max's case, bacon. "Oh, yeah." Her dad sounded like a teenage boy talking about the girl he was crushing on. Rouge grinned to herself, because she knew that was basically what he was.

Bree was a social media star, and had been for over twenty years. She had started out with a channel on Twitch that was basically her, as a super-hot teenager, streaming game-play while wearing little more than a series of outfits that revealed more than concealed her personal assets. Once she started a Patreon, she would wear different costumes for people who paid her increasingly exorbitant rates. Throughout this process, she impressed fans with her gaming skills , her insightful and often amusing commentary about different features of each game, and the way she knew exactly how to pluck the heartstrings (and other things) of the hundreds of thousands of young men (and women) who watched her.

After about five years of this, she added a YouTube channel. On it, she would visit game companies, locations where games were set, and interview designers and players alike. A few wealthy Patrons even got to play against her, live. She was *good.* She had a combination of charisma, intelligence, humor, and jaw-dropping good looks that sent her to the top. At one point, she even had her own Netazon show where she did much the same things she did on her YouTube channel, but with even bigger celebrity guests.

Motte, meanwhile, was a geeky teenager. Just a few years younger than Bree, he grew up watching her from her days as little more than a warm body in a bikini to when she could make or break a new game with a simple review. Motte would still, to this day, vigorously defend her to anyone who claimed she was nothing more than a pretty face and a fabulous figure.

Fay grinned. "We asked Ms. Stephenson to join the game. She's currently in game, somewhere along the quest line, in disguise. She's actually testing some new tech for us, as well, and it'll be really exciting to see her review. But, as far as she knows, she's *just* here to rate the tech. She doesn't know anything about the game, and she can't know. If she finds out, or her identity is compromised, I automatically lose. Her presence was my idea, and the tech is my baby, so if she or it fails, it's game over."

She paused, thinking, then gestured a few times, pressing invisible air-buttons. "Here, this is a recording made by Ms. Stephenson's communication and retinal implants. She gave it to us to use for the promos we're creating to advertise our new feature." She glanced at Zoey's dad, and there was a sly twinkle in the bright blue eyes. She knew she had him. "I'm sorry, Dr. Williams. I know it'll probably put us over your time limit, but maybe it'll help if you take a look."

The garden and the chairs vanished, and Rouge suddenly found herself looking out through someone else's eyes. It was disorienting, to say the least. A camera sat in front of her, with a large clear window beyond. Several chairs and desks filled the outer area, and people bustled around or sat at desks. Everyone looked cheerful.

There was a sort of picture-in-picture in the top right of her vision, and several graphs and numbers hovered to her lower left. A female voice was speaking, and as it did, a graphed line charted sharp peaks and valleys. That was probably telling her something about the sound, but Rouge didn't know what. As she watched, a rolling number that looked like a countdown began to flash a gentle red. Thirty seconds remained of…what?

In the video feed on her upper right, Rouge saw Bree Stephenson smile into the camera, her lop-sided grin twinkling with shared amusement that reached out to every viewer of her popular show. Her husky contralto drew in everyone listening to the live stream. Bree was winding up an episode of her show where she reviewed a new game created by a small, independent company. Rouge remembered watching it with her dad, and thinking that the game looked seriously fun.

"Thanks for playing with me, everyone, and I hope to see you here again on Friday. Remember, if you enjoyed the show, don't forget to subscribe so you never miss an episode!"

The view faded to scrolling text and a brief surge of familiar music. The view shifted to take in a young woman. Her strong, square face was filled with equal parts admiration and determination. A pale, freckled hand stretched into Rouge's line of sight, and Rouge realized that this was the hand of the person through whose eyes she was seeing. *Bree Stephenson's* hand.

The young woman accepted her hand and they shook as they both came to their feet. Several of the graphs and charts, as well as the picture-in-picture, vanished from Rouge's view. Wow! Was that what having a retinal display was like? That was *so cool.*

"Thank you so much, Zihara! You did an amazing job, and I really appreciate you coming out to the studio, such as it is." She cast a glance around at the room in which they sat, which was a surprisingly small space mostly filled with two soft white chairs and several gaming systems set off to the sides. The rest of the area was taken up by lights, cameras, and several high-tech screens on stands, presumably ready to show whatever she needed.

Zihara tugged at one of the beaded pink and black braids that cascaded around her face and smiled nervously, flicking a look around. "Thank you. You have no idea how much it means for me to be here. Though," she flushed a little, her brown skin darkening, "if you don't mind my asking, why…?" She waved around at the room.

Bree stood, glancing down as the freckled hands brushed at the fitted but casual blue t-shirt she wore. Rouge could hear the smile in her voice when she replied. "Honestly, I've worked in shared maker spaces since I moved the show out of my second bedroom. I like it, and it's nice to talk to other creatives about their work and what they're interested in. I tried the whole 'studio with a crew' thing, and it just made me feel like I was alone. This way, I hire some of the other people in the space to do the things I can't, and sometimes I help them out with things, too."

The slightly shorter woman stood, too, tugging nervously at her own t-shirt. It was a rich, deep blue, with a graphic which read 'The Wayfarer's Song' on it, above a picture of a beautiful ship floating in troubled waters. "That's... really cool, Ms. Stephenson. I wish we'd had something like that while we were making *Wayfarer*. We felt pretty darn alone sometimes."

She smiled, an expression that shifted her bold, plain features to something striking. "You have no idea how much it meant to me when you endorsed my demo. And then to invite me on your show when the game released..." She shook her head, beaded braids clicking slightly as they swayed.

Bree looked over as someone knocked tentatively at the door. "Ah, that'll be Leonie. She's a vet, and does an adorable short about animals, and the crazy things they do. Watch out for the goat. She nibbles everything. Also, it's still Bree. I'm only Ms. Stephenson to doctors and people who get on my bad side."

She reached out her slim, freckled hand and pulled open the door, revealing another woman who also looked to be in her late thirties or early forties. She was wearing a curly blonde wig, elf ears, and a floaty purple dress. A miniature goat trotted in without hesitation and immediately began chewing on the corner of the desk.

The short woman waved. "Hey, Bree! Great show!" Her big blue eyes smiled at Zihara. "I'm going to have to check out your game. I love that your main character can turn into a bird, and I'm a sucker for any game with tons of character customization and variable story progression."

Zihara just nodded, brown eyes huge as they went from the elf to the goat and back again. Leonie just laughed and gently ushered the other two women out of the studio, hauling a wheeled cart with several covered cages on it back through the door and closing it firmly behind her.

Bree lowered her voice slightly, though there was no way Leonie could hear them inside the undoubtedly very sound-proof room. "She had a snake get away once because a guest freaked out, and now she's really strict about who's in the studio. You should have seen John. He hates snakes, and until Lee caught it, he refused to step foot in the building."

The two women continued to chat as they walked through the building, with Bree waving to various people as they passed them in the halls or in open workrooms. When they finally reached the front door, Bree stepped out into the sunshine and blinked, the vision flickering, then sneezed. "Sorry. Photosensitive." She waved her hand, brushing at her eyes.

"Anyway." She held out her hand again. The pale skin was bleached by the bright sunshine, and the freckles stood out against the gleam of the reflected sunlight. "It was so wonderful to meet you, Zihara. I love supporting indie artists, and when you start on your next game, I hope you'll give me a heads up. I'll gladly review it, though I warn you my reviews are always honest, so you'd better keep up the good work!" Her voice was teasing, but Rouge knew her millions of followers counted on exactly that honesty, and she had a solid reputation for not bowing to the whims of either friends or big corporations.

Zihara smiled, relaxing now that she'd completed her most difficult task to date, and met a personal hero to boot. "I will, Bree. Thank you again!" The two women waved, and Zihara walked off down the street toward the parking garage where she'd left her vehicle.

At the corner of Rouge's vision, she saw Bree's hand, with a bright red curl of hair wrapped around her forefinger. She wound it up and loosened it again as she muttered to herself. "Do I have time for a boba tea? Ugh, no, I really need to get to work on the script for-"

A notification popped up on the right side of her vision as she turned to head back into the building.

Incoming call from Veritas Corporation.

She hesitated, then stepped back out onto the sunbathed sidewalk. Subvocalizing, she murmured. "Accept call."

An image popped up, to the right and slightly overlapping the view of the street. A grim looking older man looked out of the camera. He didn't smile. "Ms. Stephenson."

Bree must have nodded, the view of the street moving up and down. "Mr. Landon," she said almost inaudibly. Rouge had heard that the mics embedded in the jawbone of people with implants were so sensitive they could pick up the slightest vibration and translate it into sound, so Bree probably didn't need to actually raise her voice above a low whisper at all.

Carl Landon's smile was perfunctory, and there was no warmth in his face or voice. "I'm sure you've heard from Miss Andrews. She said you've had a week to look over the Non-Disclosure Agreement and the other 'literature' our lawyers have generated for you."

There was a pause, and Bree sighed. "I have. I've shown it to a lawyer friend of mine, and he made a few edits that passed your legal experts yesterday. As I'm sure you know. I...." She paused for a longer moment and the view of the street went black. She must have closed her eyes.

"Yes." She said firmly, nodding and opening her eyes again. "I'll do it. I'll need to pre-record some episodes and arrange for a sabbatical, but I'll do it. But-"

He nodded sharply, cutting her off. "Good. I like a person who can make up their mind. I'll have Miss Andrews get in touch to arrange the details. Have a good day, Ms. Stephenson." The image faded before she could even complete a polite response.

Bree shook her head, and Rouge wondered if she was as annoyed by the old man as Rouge was. Maybe Bree knew him well enough not to mind? Or maybe she just didn't care. She was, after all, a super popular influencer, and hardly anyone even knew Carl Landon's name. Well, presumably other people in the gaming biz would know him, but Rouge was willing to bet that 'popular' wasn't a word any of *them* applied to him either.

The vision jumped, and Bree looked down. Big brown eyes looked back up at her. A little boy was holding onto the loose cloth of her soft gaucho pants with a death grip. His…young mother? Sister? stood nearby, half-heartedly trying to get him to release Bree. The two looked at her with matching expressions of mingled excitement and trepidation.

Bree crouched down so that her eyes were at the same level as the little boy's. "Hello. How may I help you?" Her voice was gentle and inviting.

"Um, um…" He stammered, and finally the girl with him jumped in.

"Are you Bree Stephenson? We watch your show all the time. He loves that you review games for kids, not just adult ones. He saw you and he just ran over. I'm really sorry!" The words tumbled out, and the girl flushed.

Bree reached up and stroked the little boy's soft hair back from his flushed little face. "It's okay. I'm glad you came to say hi. I love to know what parts of my show people like. Then I can do more of that. Did you like it when Viktor from CandyThunderHeart came to visit me?"

Both heads nodded vigorously, and Bree chuckled a little. "I was surprised how nice he was. I'm glad he didn't do his finishing move in my studio though. I'm not sure I could have eaten all that cake." The boy giggled.

Five minutes later, after a selfie to show their friends (it turned out Jess was Henry's much older sister), the two went on their ways with smiles and happy waves. Bree waved after them, then turned to go back into the building behind her, whistling her theme song cheerfully.

The vision ended abruptly. Rouge blinked and swayed, and saw that Motte also looked a little shaky. Had he gotten the Bree-treatment, too? If so, how weird was it to see the world from the viewpoint of the woman he'd had a crush on for decades?

Father and daughter looked over at Fay, who was grinning again. "That's amazing, isn't it? It's one of the things we're working on. Eventually, it'll be interfaced with *Veritas* to provide a full first-person experience, but I've had other things to deal with and haven't gotten around to it yet. Hold on, though. I have one more for you."

This time, it was only the world around them that changed. The garden vanished, and Bree Stephenson appeared, wearing a bodysuit that left nothing to the imagination. She was sitting quietly on a soft white chaise half concealed by a silver ovoid that looked vaguely like Rouge's *Veritas* gaming pod, but much sleeker and more futuristic. Her hair was completely hidden beneath a rubber cap covered in electrodes, and her face was bare of makeup. She was still gorgeous, but her freckles were much more obvious than usual.

People in lab coats adjusted and tested the multitude of electrodes attached to her body. The room was silent except for the quiet murmur of the workers and the soft humming of machinery. After a few moments, a gentle beeping joined the symphony.

A middle-aged Hispanic woman adjusted a final knob and turned to Bree, smiling brightly, though Rouge thought she saw the barest hint of concern behind the professional cheer. The badge ganhging around her neck read VERITAS CORPORATION, Dr. Mariana Perez. "There you are, Bree! You're ready to go. You know the drill by now, so just lie back and let the pod take care of the rest."

Now that she was outside Bree's head, Rouge could see the woman's trademark lop-sided grin. Rouge glanced over instinctively toward Motte, and was shocked to see that he was actually standing beside her, as was Dev Fay. "I do indeed, Doc." Bree said. "Once more for the win, eh?"

Dr. Mariana Perez just sighed, her professional smile slipping into a troubled frown. "I very much hope so, for everyone's sake. You know I'm a little worried-"

Bree raised a hand. "I know, Dr. Perez. I respect your opinion, but I told, ah, Miss Andrews I'd do this, and I will."

The doctor shook her head at her patient's stubbornness. "Well, no matter what, I want you to know that I'll be right here, twenty-four seven, monitoring your status for the next week." She pointed to a corner of the room, where a hospital bed stood ready. "After that I'll be able to be here within 15 minutes if anything of concern arises."

Bree nodded seriously, reaching out to touch Dr. Perez' arm reassuringly. "I know, and that's why I asked for *you* to be my team lead, rather than that pompous ass, Veralt." She gave a wry little smile. "Everything is going to be just fine, and I'll see you soon." She chuckled slightly, as if at a shared joke.

Reaching behind Bree, Dr. Perez pressed a series of buttons, and the bed Bree was sitting on slowly began to sink down and withdraw fully into the egg-shaped pod. As the lid closed over Bree's thinly clad form, the scene flickered to one Rouge was much more familiar with.

Character creation for *Veritas Online*.

Bree appeared in a burst of soft white light. She wore the pale blue tunic and loose pants that everyone wore during character creation, as far as Rouge knew. A blonde woman stood before her with a bland smile on her pretty but forgettable face. She spoke in an emotionless, professional tone.

"Welcome back to Veritas Online, Bree. Is it time to finalize your character?"

Bree nodded, flicking a little salute with two fingers. "Yep, it's finally time, Emily. Let's do it!"

Emily nodded, expression unchanged. "You will have to delete all of your previous game data, as only one character is allowed per user. Are you aware of this?"

Bree sighed and rolled her eyes. "I signed all the paperwork, Emily. I'm ready. Not like I'm losing that much anyway."

Emily nodded, then froze in place for a split second. "I have a message from GMBridge. Would you like to receive it?"

Laughing, Bree nodded. "I'm sure I know what it says, but let's hear it."

The carefully modulated feminine voice shifted to a firmer tone as Emily spoke. "Be careful. Remember, you can always change your mind."

Bree ran a hand through the long waves of vibrant red hair that fell around her digital shoulders. Her bright green eyes twinkled as she laughed. "Nope, nice try, 'Bridge'. No way I'm passing this up now that I'm here. I told almost thirty million people to watch reruns for six months and I'd have a huge show for them when I got back. They'd probably riot if I chickened out and came back early!"

"Is that your reply?" Emily asked.

Nodding, Bree said. "Yep. Just add 'I love you'." A hint of a shadow crossed her face before she set her shoulders firmly. "Do you have my character ready, Emily?"

"As you requested, Bree. The GMs have approved it, as well."

"Let's see it, then."

A form solidified in the air in front of the slim, lovely woman, but to Rouge's frustration, it was completely blurred out. She couldn't even tell if it was human. Rouge slid to the side, trying to see if she could get any clues if she looked at it from a different perspective, but the shifting shape only darkened further in response to her movement. Rouge glanced at Fay, and found that the woman was watching her, amusement sparkling in the blue eyes. Rouge resisted the urge to stick out her tongue and turned back to watch the scene play out.

Tiny smile lines deepened around Bree's twinkling emerald eyes as she circled her new avatar, much as Rouge had attempted to do. She chortled softly, in a way Rouge had never seen her do on any of her vids. "Oh, this is going to be grand. It's perfect! I haven't been able to review *Veritas Online* because of the requirement that the avatar be based on the player's actual appearance. Every time I tried, someone recognized me almost immediately. This time, though," she laughed gleefully, "no one is going to guess!"

Emily nodded, face as emotionless as ever. "Are you ready then, Bree?"

Full lips curving in an anticipatory grin, Bree Stephenson nodded. "Let's knock their socks off."

The garden reformed around Rouge, and as it did, it returned to life. Birds sang, bees hummed, and the rich scent of sweet honeysuckle and gardenia flooded her nose. Rouge felt like dancing.

Beside her, Motte held up a hand. His eyes were glittering, and his bass voice was as excited as Rouge had ever heard it. "You're saying if we play this quest through, I'll get to *play with Bree Stephenson?*"

The developer laughed. "Yes. I can guarantee that you will spend a significant amount of time with Ms. Stephenson. Just remember, if you even think you know what character she's playing, you *can't tell her.* Also," she looked back at Rouge, serious again, "the path that leads to a win for me may not be as obvious as you think,

"In spite of how it seems, I was *very* particular in the rules I set down to determine who the quest would go to. In fact, the code for it was rather daunting to write. Which is how I missed one of the most basic rules." She sighed. "If you follow your instincts, the heart and mind that made you the player I was looking for, we'll all win. This conversation is actually skewing the odds in favor of my opponent. You'll second guess every choice, now, wondering what I would do."

She locked eyes with Rouge, utterly serious. "So, *don't do what you think I would do.* Do what feels right to *you*, and don't hesitate."

Fay rocked back in her chair, closing her eyes and breathing out slowly. When she opened them, she looked at Motte with the same seriousness she had offered Rouge. "I'm afraid I've gone over my time, Motte. I appreciate your forbearance. Unfortunately, I can't give you much time to answer. My opponent and their lawyers will be going over every word of our conversation, and they'll be allowed to give an equivalent amount of information to their player. I'm certain they'll eke every dreg of an advantage they can out of what I've said. At most, I can give you a week, but then they'll be so far ahead of us we'll have no chance."

Motte shook his head. "No need. You say you're on the side that wants to release the tech?"

Fay nodded.

"And you *swear* no harm will come to my daughter?"

Another nod.

"And I'll- Um, *we'll* get to play with Bree Stephenson?"

There was definitely a suppressed grin there, but Fay nodded again, firmly.

"We're in, pending the contract being exactly what you claim it is. Now." He looked over at Rouge and frowned. "We're logging out..."

"Wait!" Rouge raised a hand like she was in school, and both adults looked startled. The girl turned to Fay. "So, I'm kind of, like, doing you a favor, right? So, maybe, you could do me-," Motte's expression was darkening dangerously as she spoke, and she coughed slightly. "*Us*, I mean, a couple of little favors too?"

Fay tilted her head slightly, expression wary but eyes sparkling with mirth. She looked more like Gina now that she was starting to relax, and Rouge could see how the Goddess' avatar was definitely based on the pretty game developer. "Possibly. If it's not something that would count as cheating. Remember that anything I do for you, my opponent can do for your opponent."

The elf girl stopped, then paused for a moment, staring up at the frozen blue sky. "Okay. Yeah. So one favor for each of us, if they're okay." She outlined what she wanted, and Fay thought about it for a moment, then smiled.

"Since you already own the item in question, and you are a minor, I think I can grant both of these requests without it being questioned overmuch, or granting too much assistance to our competitor." She looked at Motte. "Is this what you want, as well?"

Motte was looking relieved. "Yes. That would be very helpful, actually." He cut his eyes back to his daughter. "*Now*, we're logging out, and you and I are having a *very* long conversation."

She gulped.

Talk they did. Zoey told her dad everything. From that first quest, and realizing what it meant that it was Secret, to asking Aspen to kill her and then praying to Gina. He just sat there, listening, his face gave nothing away, even to her.

When she was done, he looked her straight in the eyes and asked, "That's everything?"

She swallowed hard and nodded.

"Because if I find out you left out anything - *any*thing - you're grounded for a month. No calls, no hanging out with Jace, nothing except school, homework, and books." His voice was steel.

She nodded so vigorously she could feel her curls loosen.

His eyes narrowed, and he sighed deeply. He ran his hand over his head, deep creases forming around his eyes and between his brows. He looked every day of his forty years. "Zoey, do you know how I felt when I got yanked in there and saw you in that great big chair like a little girl who got hauled down to the principal's office?"

Zoey's heart dropped into her feet. Her dad was all about making sure she was prepared for 'real life'. He would talk to her about almost anything, if she just asked. Their whole relationship was based on honesty, and she knew she'd messed that up. Even though she hadn't ever really been at risk, the fact that she'd intentionally lied to him - even by omission - was a pretty big deal to him.

"I'm sorry, Dad." She was nearly whispering, and she felt hot tears burn the rims of her eyes. "I didn't know…"

"*You never know!* That's what I've been trying to teach you! The world isn't always a safe place, and even though *Veritas* is just a game, the rules are in place to protect you. All I ask is that you talk to me if one of those rules seems too restrictive, instead of just breaking it. Now," his deep brown eyes narrowed on hers. "What do you think should be the consequences of your actions?"

She gritted her teeth. She *hated* when he used psychology on her! It was so much easier when *he* picked the punishment, and then she could just complain about it. "Um, I'll keep up my grades. No allowance or gifts until this is over, and I'll get a real job this summer."

He raised that eyebrow. "Who do you think is going to hire a fourteen-year-old?"

"I… don't know?" Honestly, she hadn't intended to get a job, even though she'd told him she'd think about it.

He smiled slightly, looking smug. "Retail. Fast food. Dog walker. Barista. Not much fun there."

She grimaced. Her dad was of the opinion that everyone should have a retail job at least once, so they could see how much it sucked, and learn to treat people in the service industry with respect. She was of the opinion that people sucked, and she'd already learned that lesson.

"Okay. I'll take whatever I can get." She chewed on her lip in frustration, but she already knew she wasn't going to win here.

"You're also grounded."

Her eyes shot up. "What? But…"

"Fay said we could have up to a week to decide. I won't compromise our chances by taking all of that time, but you need to think about the choices you made. You're lucky it was in a game, and you're right, the worst case was probably getting PKed and maybe harassed. Nonetheless, the choices you made tell me a lot about what choices you might make in the real world, and I'm not very happy with them."

He sighed again. Zoey took a moment to note that *a lot* of sighing had been occurring today. Seriously, were people not taking deep enough breaths? When you got mad, did you breathe faster and need to, like, catch up? She tuned back in a few words late.

"…go to school, come straight home, do your homework, eat, and write me a 20 page essay on what you could have done differently."

"*What?!*"

Her dad grinned. "Kidding. The rest of it is real, though. Zoe, I want you to think about something." He locked eyes with her. "You're not going to have a whole lot of people in your life who you know have your back, 100%, every single time. I know there are things that are hard to tell me because I'm your dad. That's okay. But when your safety - emotionally, physically, or, someday, financially - is at stake, you talk to me. No matter what anybody tells you about who you can tell, or how you think I may react. Even if it's a 'Secret Quest'." His voice was wry, and he hitched the eyebrow at her again. "Even if I'm angry, or disappointed, I'll always be there to back you up. You feel me?"

Zoey snorted and wiped tears from her eyes. He was so lame. "Yeah," she said, "I feel you."

Chapter Ten

Aspen

W hen Rouge's eyes went flat as soon as she started praying, everyone else around the table tensed. Then, when nothing else happened, they waited. And waited. And waited. Finally, they came to an unspoken consensus that the girl had – what did she call it? – logged out, and they returned to what they had been doing before she showed up with her rather dramatic request.

Aspen and Sarave stood in front of the house. Aspen held a heavy piece of metal that had once been a rusty shovel blade. He focused, closing his eyes and frowning as he tried to control the rising heat that flickered under his palms.

Calling the heat wasn't a problem. The problem was getting it under control, much less making it feel like the pleasant warmth Joanna had described. Sarave's job was to use the half-rotten handle of the old shovel to knock the metal away from Aspen's hand if things got out of control. Which they had. Repeatedly.

Aspen felt rather abashed when he thought of his childish attempt to see if he could conduct the magic through his buttocks. It was just that Sarave had been looking so concerned, and it seemed like it might make her laugh. And it worked. The small female was far too serious, and the lines of worry around her eyes refused to soften. He was sure there was still something she didn't trust him enough to share, and he was determined to show her that she could rely on him.

He sighed, then opened his eyes abruptly as he realized that the metal in his hands was soft and warm, not threatening to burn him to the bone as it usually did. He stared down at the metal pooled in his palms. It swirled placidly, almost as if it were happy to be used again. He prodded it gently with his magic, and it *hummed* back at him, content and warm. What the…?

Sarave was staring at the metal too, her face awed. "Even dwarves, can not do. They use magic, but," she smacked the old handle against her palm, and half of it broke away and fell to the ground. "They make metal do what they want. This-" Her large yellow-on-yellow eyes nearly glowed, even in the sunlight. "It *happy*. What did you do?"

Aspen grinned, suddenly figuring it out. "This Skill is emotion-driven. When I was trying to shove magic into it, it shoved back. When I got frustrated, it burned me. When I stopped, and thought about," he glanced at the little goblin woman, "ah, more positive things, it responded positively." He remembered the love and trust Joanna had felt when she touched the metal, her hands cupped in her mother's strong, callused fingers.

"What next?" Sarave's soft voice was almost wistful as she looked at the cheerfully-roiling incandescent metal.

"Ahhhh." Aspen would have rubbed his neck, but he didn't want to sear his flesh from his spine. "I don't know? I guess I ask it to… be something else?" He tilted his head as he contemplated the goop, then pictured the head of a sledgehammer as clearly as he could. The metal blooped in discontent, but slowly began to solidify. When it eventually hardened into a solid mass again, Aspen dropped it, arms shaking from the strain.

"Well." Aspen did rub his neck this time. He stared down at the solid block resting in the dust in front of him. "That didn't work."

Sarave squatted down awkwardly, staring at the misshapen chunk. "What you try to make?"

"A sledgehammer."

She tilted her head, and he guessed this was a new word to her. He mimed lifting a heavy hammer and bringing it down forcefully, and she nodded understanding. Her eyes twinkled, but her tone was conciliatory. "It better."

The goblin woman hauled herself up using the stump behind her that she had been sitting on most of the morning. Lines of weariness creased her face, and even her pointed ears drooped slightly. "You now done? I begin lunch."

He chuckled, but scooped up the hunk of metal. "Are you telling me to stop playing around and get to work?"

She looked up at him. Her lips were thin and pale, but her eyes twinkled. "Never say such."

He offered her a half smile and sketched a bow. "As you wish. I'll get back to my wall, and you can cook lunch."

Sarave braced her hands on her back, arching her back against the weight of the child in her belly. "That I do, then." She gave him a small smile, then waddled into the house.

He shook his head at her pride, watching her go.

<The babe will be born soon. It seems too large for her to birth easily. We must watch her carefully.> Sumi's voice was soft, and he glanced up at her where she was sitting in the shadow of the wall. Sarave likely hadn't even noticed the spider, though he had seen her skitter silently out to join them not long after he started practicing again.

He nodded in agreement. "Birth was never something I focused on overmuch, but I know the basics, and hopefully Gina will help as well. We can only wait and see."

Aspen gave a deep sigh and turned to the piles of rocks Khor continued hauling in from all over. The Greater Goat was having far too much fun digging with his huge hooves and kicking the stones onto the cart. The little goats had decided it was a fun game as well, and small pebbles littered the ground nearby. He tugged at his hat brim. "Guess I'd better get back to work. Keep an eye on her for me, would you?"

<Of course.> The spider's voice was amused. <I'm sure I have one to spare.>

🪰 🪰 🪰

Lunch was an awkward affair, with Aspen and Sarave sitting at the table beside Rouge's staring form. Aspen finally tried picking the girl up and moving her, but it was as if she and the chair were part of the floor. No matter what he did, she wouldn't budge. Finally, with a muttered apology, he threw a thin blanket over her. He didn't know if she needed to breathe when she was like that, but the blanket wasn't a dense weave, and the silent stare of someone who was usually so full of life was extremely unnerving.

The rest of the day passed as had the previous two, though without the constant sound of Rouge's Zombie chopping in the distance it seemed strangely quiet. Nonetheless, the new walls continued to rise, and he was able to use some of the long logs Rouge had cut to create window and door frames. He left the windows tall and narrow, too tight for anyone to climb in or out, but enough to let in a decent amount of light. The walls, which were close to three feet thick at the base, gradually narrowed as they rose, and by the time they stood eight feet tall they were only about a foot wide.

Aspen set down the wooden plate he was using to spread the heavy slurry over the stones of the walls. He wiped his brow with a filthy hand and stepped down from the barrel he had been standing on so he could see the top of the wall.

<Well. It's better than nothing.> Khor's voice was laconic, and his beard wagged as he chewed thoughtfully. <But how am I supposed to fit in there?>

The tall man shook his head. "We'll build a bigger one next year, when we have more time. Right now, we need someplace for the little goats, and maybe some other animals, when we get them. We'll have to go back south in the spring and buy some chickens, and maybe a few cows. Milk would be nice, and we certainly have plenty of room for them to graze." He motioned to the extra-wide space he had left for the doors. "In the meantime, you'll just have to back in and bend down. I can't make it taller than the original house. Just remember it's not forever."

Khor snorted. <*Back* in? Do you think I'm a boat reaching dock? Should I attach lamps to my saddle so you can see me at night?>

"Well-" Aspen said thoughtfully, and Khor snorted even louder, scratching his hoof in the dirt.

They were interrupted by Silus' piping little voice. <Sumi and Sarave say you need a bath, Aspen. Let's walk to the river! It's time for dinner, anyway, and I've been wanting to show you a patch of berries I found! They're really tasty!>

Aspen smiled as his smallest friend swooped in to land on his shoulder. "I'm sure I could use a bath at that. Let me grab some soap, and-"

A single thread of web shot out of the nearby window. A sliver of their precious soap was stuck firmly to the end. Aspen caught it without thinking, and Silus giggled. <Sumi said you'd say that, and you aren't allowed in the house until you're clean.>

He sighed the sigh of the put-upon male and followed the little bat.

🦇 🦇 🦇

That night, after everyone else had gone to sleep except Silus, who was patrolling the area, Aspen sat on his bed, staring at the book on his lap. He carefully wiped the rich red juice of Silus' 'tasty berries' from his fingers, and pushed the bowl of fruit aside. He lightly smacked his own cheeks, then nodded decisively. He opened the book.

Joanna stared, mesmerized, as the hammer rose and fell. Her mother gripped the piece of metal with her tongs, an expression of concentration on her face. The girl, now ten years old, could feel the magic flowing out of her mother and into the small ingot that was slowly being shaped into the long, thin head of a hoe meant for weeding in narrow spaces.

She moved closer, reaching into the pocket of the leather apron she now wore more often than not, and felt the piece of metal her mother had given her nearly five years before. It had been worked, over and over, sometimes forming into something that resembled what she imagined, but more often not. She had even borrowed a hammer from her father's smithy. It was utterly mundane, but it should have helped at least a little!

With a last, almost gentle, strike, her mother released the fully-formed hoe, her magic continuing to suffuse it as it cooled rapidly, preventing it from turning brittle and weak. The older woman looked over at Joanna and smiled as she wiped beads of sweat from her brow.

"What do you think, Jonny? Are you ready to show me what you can do?"

Joanna flinched back. "I- Mother, I-"

Her mother frowned slightly. "You seemed to be doing well last time we talked. What happened?"

Sighing, Joanna reached into her pocket and pulled out the warped piece of metal, setting it on the anvil in front of them. They both looked at it in silence for a moment.

"What were you trying to make, Joanna?"

She looked up, startled. Her mother rarely used her given name, and when she did, it was usually because she was in trouble. This sounded gentle, though, and Joanna swallowed down the lump in her throat.

"A trowel." She waved her hands, mimicking the rough shape of the tool. "Just a simple one. But no matter what I do, it just looks like this!" She poked at the metal, and felt a sharp twinge as the soft pad of her fingertip met a hidden point in the mass.

Her mother smiled, and walked over to a wall of tools. Row upon row of perfect, gleaming farming implements hung neatly, and the tall woman reached down to take one of the lowest. A trowel. She brought it back, and handed it to Joanna.

"Have you used a trowel, Jonny?"

"Of course I have! A thousand times! I've helped with the planting for years!" Her voice was a plaintive cry.

The tall woman smiled. "Close your eyes then. Here, take this." After Joanna closed her eyes, her mother pressed a tool into her hand. "What are you holding?"

"A trowel," Joanna muttered in frustration.

"Hmm," the other woman murmured. "Are you?"

Joanna felt her eyebrows pull together, and she clutched the object in both hands. She traced the warm wooden handle, round and new. No hands had yet worn it smooth. No sweat had polished it to a brown gleam. She traced over the ferrule connection, where the tang attached to the handle. Down to the blade, still sharp without years of hard soil to wear it down... Wait, that wasn't right. Her frown pulled tighter as she traced the shape of the blade.

"This is a potting scoop!"

A warm chuckle told her she was right. "You knew that because you thought about how the trowel should feel as you held it. You imagined it sliding into the earth, and felt it do its job. When you work the metal, you must know the object you're trying to create. Not only the technical aspect, as a smith like your father does, but the use, the life of the tool. Tell it what it needs to be with your heart and your soul. Then strike, and guide it into shape."

Joanna opened her eyes and looked down at the potting scoop her mother must have palmed with the other hand while picking up the trowel with the hand she could see. She felt an odd, warm affection for it as she stroked the blade gently. This scoop didn't need to be as sharp or strong as a trowel. Unlike a trowel, it didn't need to dig up stones, cut roots, or break apart clods of earth. No, this was meant to move soft, fertile earth in the greenhouse. Its deep belly and sides would prevent spilling, and move the moist soil as seeds were tenderly tucked into their warm, peaceful place of birth.

She felt the metal warm beneath her hand, and her mother chuckled as she took the scoop back and hung it on the wall. "This one is done, Jonny," she said in her husky voice, "but you should go and try making your own. Or a trowel, if you wish. Just remember to think about its purpose, as well as its shape. Feel the final tool in your hands, and imagine the joy of the person who wields such a fine implement."

Joanna looked up at her mother, tall and strong and wise. She nodded, feeling certainty rise in her once more. She could do this. She would make her mother proud.

೮ ೮ ೮

The following morning Aspen woke to the sound of Khor's harsh bray, and the goat's voice in his mind. <Intruder! Stranger! Wake up!>

Aspen rolled from bed, his hand on his staff, stumbling toward the doorway. "This is getting to be a very bad habit," he muttered as he swept the heavy web-cloth aside.

Sure enough, a large man stood in the road in front of the house. He held his hands wide, and though he wore heavy black armor, like a warrior, no weapon hung at his side. His face was strong, brown, and handsome, and his lighter brown eyes were direct as they met Aspen's. When he spoke, his voice was a rich basso cantante and Aspen had a momentary thought that his singing was probably excellent. Then the content of the words broke through his early morning haze.

"Good morning. I'm Motte Bailey. I'm Rouge the Rogue's father. I think she mentioned me."

Aspen stared. "You can't be."

Motte chuckled. "I am, I assure you. Rouge and I had a very interesting conversation with, um, Gina yesterday. She made me an offer I couldn't refuse, and as part of that offer, she transported me here from Bright. I can have Rouge come on for a moment if-"

Aspen stared, bemused. First it was a goblin, complete with burgeoning offspring. Then the young Traveler child showed up. Now, here was another Traveler, turning up unexpectedly on Aspen's doorstep. He and the others had gone north specifically because there *was no one else up here*. Casting a glance at the sky, he wondered what other surprises his new goddess might have in store for them.

Motte waved his hands to capture Aspen's attention and shrugged apologetically. "Ah, is there any chance I could put my hands down, and maybe come inside? I assume Rouge's Zombie is in there, since she doesn't seem to be out here anywhere. I'd like to make sure she's okay, if you'll convince your goat not to trample me to death."

Aspen groaned slightly and rubbed his eyes. "You might as well. I don't know how you're going to fit, but it seems someone put out a welcome sign for half of Quarternell, so we may as well get used to it."

The other man smiled sympathetically as he lowered his hands. His fingers twitched, and his massive armor vanished, instantly replaced with a simple cloth tunic and leather pants. Somehow, he looked even more intimidating than before, since you could now see how much of his height and breadth were just *him*, not his gear. "Is that better?"

Aspen just sighed. "Not really, but come on in." He stepped back inside and pulled the cloth hanging out of the way. He flicked a glance around and saw that Sumi was still on guard. Sarave was nowhere to be seen, so presumably she was still in the cellar, safely hidden until they were certain this man was what he claimed.

The big man walked forward with the careful grace of someone who knew he was larger than most buildings were made to handle, and that others found his sheer physical presence intimidating. He slid in through the door, brushing both sides of the doorframe with his broad shoulders, and ducked under the lintel. He paused just inside the house, while his eyes adjusted to the dimness.

After a moment, a frown formed on his face. "Where's Rouge?" A hint of threat brought his deep voice even deeper.

Aspen felt like smacking himself. He walked over to the table and cleared his throat slightly. "Ah, sorry. She's right here. The blank stare was a little, um, disconcerting." He pulled the cloth off the girl, who was still sitting at the table as if she were praying to the small statue across from her. Her lifeless hazel eyes were wide open.

Motte stared disbelievingly, and then a chuckle rose up from the depths of his chest, blowing the tension from the room. The man laughed so hard he doubled over, clutching at his sides and chuckling until tears squeezed from his eyes and he had to wipe them away.

"You... just... threw a cloth... over... her..." he finally managed to wheeze out. "Oh, I am never going to let her live that down." He swiped at his face, still smiling. The laughter wiped years from his visage, until Aspen would have been more inclined to think him the little elf girl's much older brother.

When he could finally breathe normally again, Motte walked the two steps across the room to Rouge's side and scooped her easily into his arms. Aspen stared. "How did you do that? I tried to move her yesterday, and it was like trying to move a mountain!"

The other man shrugged. "It's because I'm her father. Zombies aren't supposed to be movable unless they're following instructions. Keeps them from being captured or abducted. They can be killed, but not moved. But, since she's a child, and I'm her parent, I can move her if I need to. Now," he looked around, "where can I put her so she's out of the way? She's grounded for a few days, so she won't be back soon."

Aspen motioned to the pile of grass covered with a large, soft fur that they had made for Rouge's Zombie to sleep on. "Over there is fine. Can you, ah, close her eyes, by any chance?"

Motte chuckled again, though he shook his head in denial. He carefully stepped over to the makeshift bed and laid down his surprisingly small burden. He rolled her on her side so she was looking away from them, and then tugged the fur over the slim form. When he tucked it tenderly beneath her chin and stroked the curls back from her face, Aspen felt the last of the tension leave his body. There was no doubt that this was a loving parent, not someone here to hurt the girl, or, by extension, anyone else.

The big man straightened and smiled apologetically. "I can move her, but I can't really change much else. Stand her up, sit her down, or put her someplace else. That's about it. At least this way you won't feel like she's staring at you, and you'll get a spot back at the table." He glanced around. "Is this everyone? She mentioned a bat, a pregnant goblin, some mini-goats, and an ostrich mount."

Aspen sat down at the table and nodded. "Silus, the bat, is asleep now. She trades watches with Khor at sunrise. Codswallop, the ostrich, is in the barn with the little goats. Well, what will be the barn, out front. You'd probably have seen him, but Khor blocks the door pretty thoroughly." He raised his voice. "Sarave! You can come up now! It's safe!"

He waited a long moment, then another. Motte was looking around expectantly, but Sarave didn't push the cellar hatch open. Aspen frowned and stood back up. Crossing to the opening concealed behind some small barrels in the corner, he knocked. "Sarave?"

Nothing.

Finally, hesitant to intrude upon the goblin's privacy, but becoming increasingly concerned, he pulled open the hatch and motioned to Sumi. The spider skittered down, but returned rapidly. <She's gone. The pack she made for herself is gone as well. She must have snuck out when Silus' patrol took her away from the house.>

"Damn it!" Aspen crossed to his bedroom and grabbed his hat, slapping it on his head. He sat on the bed to pull on his boots, the only other item of clothing he had removed before losing to the exhaustion that reading the book always seemed to bring.

Motte stood too, expression turning serious. His eyes flickered as he looked for whatever had caused their alarm. "What's going on?"

Aspen crossed the house and pulled aside the cloth covering the outer door. "Sarave is gone. She's been acting…oddly, since the babe dropped. I should have had Silus keep watch on her last night. I think she's gone to have the child alone. I don't know why, but I suppose we can ask her when we find her." He shook his head grimly. "We can't just leave her. The child is too large to be born easily. Both of their lives are in danger every moment she is without aid."

The others followed him out into the bright sunlight, blinking against the sudden glare. Aspen looked around. "Damn it! I wish we at least knew how long she's been gone. We'd have a better idea where to look."

Khor whuffled at the ground nearby, his long beard wagging in the dust. <A few hours at most. I can still catch traces of her scent here. It's not strong, but if it was left from yesterday, I wouldn't be able to smell it at all.>

Aspen looked at the Greater Goat. "Can you tell which way she went?"

Khor snuffled some more, then walked around the house toward the river. When he got a few paces into the longer grass there, he suddenly reared back, sneezing violently. <Pepper! The goblin dropped pepper down in her path!>

Aspen relayed the information as Khor continued sneezing convulsively. Motte frowned. "She's smart. What's over in that direction?"

"The river. It seems too obvious though, especially since she didn't lay down the pepper until we were already heading this direction." Aspen's topaz eyes were concerned as he looked around, desperately hoping for a clue.

The click of Sumi's legs drew his attention to the spider. <I can find her.> She sounded self-satisfied.

He looked over at her, brows raised. "How?"

She delicately reached into the grass and lifted a single shining filament into the sunlight. <After our talk yesterday, I decided to take some precautions. I hoped it wouldn't be necessary, but,> she lifted her front legs in her equivalent of a shrug, the rest of the thought obvious. <I covered her in tiny, short strands of thread. She'll never even notice them, but they'll drop off when she brushes

against something. We can track her as long as they don't run out.>

Aspen nodded, thinking fast. He looked back at the goat. "Khor, you stay here. Protect Silus, Rouge, and the kids." To the spider, "Sumi, you're in the lead. Go as quickly as you can, but don't lose the trail."

A large hand fell on his shoulder, and Motte's bass voice rumbled from behind him. "I'd like to help too, if I can. I'm faster than I look, and if you meet any mobs, I can help, at least as long as Rouge is safe here." He made another of those small gestures, and his dark armor reappeared, this time including a heavy helmet that covered his entire head and face except for his brown eyes, which showed through narrow slits.

Aspen hesitating, but nodded agreement. "Come on then. Khor will keep all of our little ones safe, while we help make sure the newest member of the tribe arrives safe and sound."

A notice, the first in a while, appeared in front of Aspen's eyes.

Quest: "It's Somebody's Birthday" begun.

Sarave has run away. Find her, and help her however you can.

Success: Variable.

Failure: Sarave and the baby die.

Sumi scuttled off through the grass, following silver glints only she could see, with the two men following close behind.

It didn't take Aspen long to determine that Sarave's path was headed back toward the foothills to the east. The closer they got, the more nervous he became.

"Why? Why would she go back? Doesn't she remember there's probably still at least one vampire out here? She's no fool, so why?" Aspen muttered to himself as they jogged along through the grass, trying to make up as much time as possible. They needed to find the goblin woman and bring her home before dark, or they risked being near the vamp's lair with no cover.

Motte, who had been filled in on the situation as they traveled, glanced back at the other man. "You found her in a cave, right?"

Aspen nodded.

The big man shrugged. "Where did she come from? Was there a passage in the back of the cave? Or did she come from somewhere nearby? Maybe there's a hidden tunnel that she was afraid someone else might follow her through? Goblins love to dig tunnels, and it wouldn't surprise me if she knows of one or more bolt-holes she thinks would be safe for a while. Mothers feel the need to create a safe space to give birth, where they have everything they might need. We call it 'nesting'. Maybe she has a nest somewhere."

Aspen huffed in frustration. "Perhaps. She said she stayed in the mine because the smell of the vamps kept other predators away. I suppose that doesn't mean it was her only hideaway, just the one she felt was safest. Sarave is smart, and having a backup location to run to is definitely smart. You're probably right. Now," he focused on Sumi's rapidly-moving form ahead of them, and his voice became grim, "we just have to hope she made it there safely, and that we catch up soon."

They traveled in silence for a few more miles. Both men had decent stamina, though Motte's was clearly higher. The man covered the ground without a shred of effort showing on his face, and Aspen felt he could have moved even faster if he hadn't had to stay behind Sumi.

Shortly after they entered the thicker woods in the foothills, Sumi veered sharply south, picking up speed. <I think,> she sent to Aspen, worry clear in her voice, <we have a problem.> The spider stopped by a tree, one leg touching another delicate strand of web. She prodded something dark and sticky nearby, holding up a clawed foot that gleamed black in the light that filtered through the trees. <Blood,> she said simply.

"Damn it!" Aspen couldn't contain the outburst, causing Motte to look over at him, brows raised. Aspen shook his head. "She says it's blood." He looked back at the arachnid. "Is it Sarave's?"

Sumi waggled the leg. <Not my department. Not vampire blood. Not spider blood. Some kind of humanoid. It's all the same red, and it looks and smells the

same. At a guess, the child is coming, and something is wrong.>

Aspen looked at Motte. "It's likely Sarave's, which isn't a good sign. We need to hurry."

Sumi bobbed up and down in agreement, and took off, moving even faster than before. Aspen knew this was taking a toll on his friend. She had good endurance, but the unusual wear-and-tear on her joints over this long distance had to be painful. He cursed mentally, and picked up his own speed, ignoring the subtle shimmer of a stat increase as he did so.

The path jogged back and forth in no apparent pattern, and more blood began to appear. Even Motte and Aspen could see it without Sumi's help now. Finally, they came to an area where the grass was beaten down, and several nearby twigs were broken or bent. They were all tense and silent as Sumi investigated. The two men kept a wary eye out, and their hands rested on the hilts of their weapons.

Sumi came to a stop with a leg on a small rock half-hidden by a broken branch. It was smeared with a thick, dark substance. The spider touched it with a pedipalp, then drew back and hissed. <Vampire blood. I think the goblin hit it with this rock while trying to fight it off. She must have sensed it following her some time ago, and that's why she laid such an erratic trail. It likely carried her off to its lair.>

Aspen growled at the unfairness of it. Sarave had escaped persecution, left behind a murdered husband and all the family she had ever known, and nearly died in an abandoned mine. She had survived it all, only to run right back into the very creatures whose shadow she had used as protection, and all for what? For some secret she hadn't trusted him enough to share? Why did he continually fail those he wanted to protect?

Motte's calm voice pulled Aspen back from his momentary lapse into self-contempt. "Do we know where the lair is? Or can we track them?"

Sumi waved affirmation. <It's likely to be back at or near the mine. Vampires are territorial, and they wouldn't have left their coffins in such an

exposed place if they had any alternative. Unless the cave is completely collapsed, its home will probably still be there.>

Aspen growled. "She says it's likely to be at the mine where Silus and I first met Sarave, and she's right. It's pointless to go there, though. The first one was level ninety-seven. This one has survived longer on less, and is likely to be stronger. It's almost certainly smarter than a vamp half-dead and mad from hunger. All we'll achieve by following is our own wasted deaths."

Motte shook his head. "You forget, I'm a Traveler. Death is only an inconvenience to us. Plus, I'm almost level ninety-six myself. You can't be too far behind, the way you've kept up on this run. Either that or you've packed a lot of points into Endurance, which I guess might make sense for a farmer. If you can fight at all, I should be able to hold it long enough for you to take it down. Rouge said she couldn't see much in the last fight, but you refused to give up, and your creatures bit and clawed for all they were worth. If I tank it, Sumi can bind and bite it, and you can stake it. I think our odds are better than fifty-fifty." The confidence in that deep voice was unshakeable, and brought Aspen back to the moment.

He drew in a deep breath. "All right then. They're weakest in their bat shape, since they lose their ability to mesmerize and use their claws. They can only bite and fly. If we can get it to transform, then get some wood into it so it can't change back, Sumi can bind it while we take its head or heart. They're ungodly strong, so it will break her web, but if she can keep it in place, we'll stand a chance, especially if she can bite it. Her poison does little good against them, since their blood moves too sluggishly to move the poison around much, but the area immediately around her bite will start to rot or become paralyzed."

Aspen's topaz eyes flicked to the side, where the name of his quest hovered. "I have a quest, and it's still active, so she's not dead yet. If we have any chance at all, I want to try."

The other man grinned. "That's what I like to hear. I got a quest, too, and it's a pretty good one, so if we can clear it, that'll be a nice bonus." His large, armored hand waved around. "Lead on."

Nodding, Aspen turned his back to Sumi. The spider, recognizing the invitation, leapt up and crouched on his broad shoulders. Motte shuddered slightly at the sight, but to his credit said nothing. Aspen looked around, orienting himself, and then plunged into the underbrush, heading straight toward the mine.

Once they were no longer restricted to the speed Sumi could travel while following the web threads, the two men were able to run much more quickly. Soon, Aspen's heart was pounding in his ears, and his breath came fast and hard. He didn't slow, but pushed through, and the flicker of a stat increase popped every few minutes to reward his efforts.

A quarter mile from the mine entrance, at the beginning of the widened path, Aspen slowed, then leaned forward, heaving in deep breaths. His throat burned, his side ached, and he suppressed a racking cough. Beside him, even Motte breathed a little heavier, doubtless weighed down by the heavy armor he wore.

Sumi leapt down from Aspen's back, and though she wasn't exactly heavy, he suddenly felt a hundred pounds lighter. The spider skittered ahead, vanishing into the darkness. <I'll scout ahead. I'm out of practice since Silus does most of the reconnaissance these days, but I had plenty of practice before.> Aspen tapped his staff twice in acknowledgement, and Sumi vanished into the darkness.

The two men crept slowly forward until they could just make out the mine entrance. When Aspen and Sarave had left, large rocks had mostly blocked the opening. Those rocks were nearly all gone, and there was no sign of them. Instead, one of those strange, round passageways was bored into the stone. Whatever created those, it was obviously still around, and likely helping the vampires.

Aspen shook his head. Vampires had one kind of magic: mind magic. They could cast Confuse, Frighten, Terrify, and Mesmerize. Once a vamp had control of your mind, it would feast on you at its leisure. If you were lucky, you would die. If it wanted to create a new vampire, it would wait until you were all but dead, then open its own veins and have you drink some of the tarry fluid, leaving you a soulless, blood-sucking, undead slave.

So, how were the creatures creating these strange passages? It had to be magic, and it wasn't one he recognized. That meant there was a variable. Something he had no knowledge of, which could easily turn the tide of the battle. They were committed, however. He wouldn't leave Sarave and her child in the hands of the monster in this mine any longer than he already had.

Sumi came scuttling back out of the opening, silent except for a whisper of eight clawed feet on stone. Motte twitched violently at her sudden appearance, but controlled himself without making a sound. Behind the visor of his helm, his eyes were narrow and determined.

<Sarave and one vampire are at the end of the second branch on the left. After that, rocks block nearly everything, so I think there's nothing else hiding deeper in the mine.> Sumi paused, considering. <At least, not anything that is immediately concerning. Sarave is mesmerized, and the vamp seems to have decided to play with her for a while instead of draining her dry immediately. I don't know why, but at least it gives us a chance.>

Aspen quietly passed this information to Motte, along with a warning to avoid looking in the vampire's eyes no matter what. The big tank nodded, and the two men rose and began to make their way down the passage. Motte led, after removing his gauntlet so it didn't make any noise scraping over the stone.

The first side tunnel came up far sooner than Aspen expected. His concern for Sarave drove him forward faster than was probably wise, and he was also able to move much more quickly than he had last time he came here, thanks to his increased strength and endurance. The two men noted the passage, and Sumi quickly checked it, just to make sure nothing had appeared in it since she had passed a short while before. She gave Aspen the all clear, and he tapped Motte to let him know they were ready to go ahead.

Motte found the second opening by nearly falling into it. They turned a curve, and the wall under his hand was simply gone, leaving him off balance. He fell backwards into Aspen, nearly knocking both of them down, but the lean farmer's strength had increased enough that he was able to help the tank regain his footing. Once they were both stable again, they froze, listening.

From the passage came a tinkling, scratchy laugh. A sweet and measured voice echoed down to them.

"Eight-legged spider and noble men,

Have come to play with me again.

I rested long enough, I think

To earn a sip of this darling drink.

But if you should seek those lost to life,

Then I'll gladly act as your midwife.

I'll thank you for helping my empire

 Grow, by making you my new vampires!"

The two men stood still for a moment, staring into the darkness as if they could make it give way through sheer force of will. Motte swore softly under his breath. "Guess we've lost the element of surprise. Should I pop a light?"

It took Aspen a moment to parse the Traveler's meaning, but then he grunted an affirmative, closing his eyes as he did. A flare of light made the blackness behind his lids turn red for a long moment, and then he blinked his eyes open. Motte held a small thieves' lantern, with smoked glass panels muffling the light of the glowstone inside. Only one panel was open a sliver, but it was enough to cast a soft light that seemed very bright after the total darkness in which they had traveled.

Above the opening of the tunnel, Sumi was flattened to the wall, her legs trembling slightly. <Some warning would be nice,> she said sharply.

Aspen grimaced guiltily. "Sorry," he murmured, as quietly as he could.

The creepy, discordant voice came from the dark opening beside them again.

"If you're going to take all day,

Before you come on in to play,

I'm going to take a little nip,

And help myself to another sip."

A wet sound echoed down the passage, followed by a pained cry. Sarave must have been released from the [Mesmerize], since a vampire's victims usually felt no pain unless the evil creature desired it. No doubt the vampire hoped hearing their friend suffering would convince them to move before they were ready. It nearly worked, too, as Aspen had to grit his teeth hard against the urge to rush in. Instead, he forced himself to wait, and looked at Motte, who had replaced his left gauntlet and stood with his axe and shield in hand.

"Ready?" Motte asked.

Aspen nodded, and the larger man held his shield in front of him like a battering ram, and rushed down the hall. Aspen hurried on his heels, and was in time to see the other man careen to a halt as he saw their enemy.

The creature was nearly as emaciated as the first vampire had been. She had recovered some substance from drinking Sarave's blood, but the goblin was small, and the vamp hadn't fully drained her yet. Aspen suspected that the vampire had sensed someone following them, and hoped that leaving her first victim alive would allow her to lure in juicier morsels.

Stringy black hair was braided into a crown on top of the monster's head. The strands were dry and brittle, and pulled against the taut, stretched flesh on her skull. Her eyes were banked red embers, and her long yellow fangs were bared by her dry, thin lips. Her body was covered by the decayed remains of a rich gown of an archaic style, and the fabric hung loosely around what must once have been an attractive figure, given the cut of the cloth.

In clawed hands, so thin and yellow it was hard to tell they weren't just dry bones, hung Sarave. Her green skin was as gray and sickly as it had been when Aspen first met her. Her clothes were stained with blood, and her long braid was loose and tangled. Worst of all, her throat glistened in the light like raw meat. Dim yellow eyes were barely open, and when she saw Aspen, her hand lifted slightly, then fell back to her side. A single tear ran from her eye and slid down her filthy face.

The vampire held Sarave's body as a living shield. Motte had obviously hoped to rush her, crushing her between his shield and the wall. Unfortunately, that would crush Sarave as well, and the goblin would never survive. Motte had managed to halt his rush, but at the cost of being off balance.

The vampire grinned, a grisly baring of bloody fangs, and sang out, "There you are. I knew you weren't far!" She glided forward, flinging Sarave to the side. The goblin woman hit the wall hard and slid down in a limp heap.

The vamp moved fast. Motte managed to raise his shield to block her first blow, a clawing reach of her taloned hand. Then she was, impossibly, perched atop his shield like a dreadful crow, well inside the reach of his axe. Worst of all, she was staring directly into his eyes.

The warrior stood for a long moment, locked in the dreadful gaze, until she reached out and turned his head slowly to look back at Aspen. "There, that way. You see your prey," she cooed. Motte's glazed eyes peered out through the slit of his helmet, and he nodded.

She shrieked with insane laughter, launching herself away from the large man, flipping backward in the air to land on the huge stone sarcophagus that filled a third of the room. Motte took one step, then another. He rushed toward Aspen.

Fortunately, there wasn't enough room for the warrior to achieve a full [Battering Ram], and Aspen was able to dodge. The big man rammed into the wall, his shield crunching as it hit with full force, and chunks of stone sprayed out. Aspen grimaced. That would have really, really hurt.

Looking around quickly while Motte prepared for another charge, Aspen saw that Silus' original evaluation of the space was correct. Besides the now cracked sarcophagus, which could easily have been mistaken for a stone table when it was closed, the room was empty except for a few chunks of stone, Sarave, and the three combatants.

No! There were four!

Aspen glanced up at the ceiling in time to see Sumi spray a broad, sticky stream of webbing at Motte's feet, entangling them. Motte grunted as he tripped and fell, then began to hack at the web, which only served to trap his axe as well.

The vampire's eyes snapped up to the spider, and she hissed angrily. "These are my little flies. There's no need for you here, spider spy!" She leapt up, stretching out her bony arm toward the arachnid, who had had to come closer in order to trap Motte. Her grip caught one of Sumi's legs, snapping one of its fragile joints like tinder. The pop was loud in the small space. Sumi's agonized mental cry brought Aspen back to himself, and he threw himself into motion.

Planting the butt of his staff on the floor, he used it to vault over Motte's struggling form, landing agilely near the bottom of the stone coffin. He dropped a metal vial of Sumi's potion near Sarave's limp hand, praying that she had enough strength to use it. Her body was so still and silent that he could only be certain she wasn't dead because his quest hadn't failed.

He lifted the staff, staring up at the vampire, locking his eyes on the end of her nose. In her skeletal face, the sunken nose was more prominent than it would otherwise have been, and he found it a little easier to avoid looking into those gleaming red eyes. To her, however, it should seem that he was looking right at her.

He growled internally. Once, she would have had to fear looking into *his* eyes. As a master Necromancer, he could have controlled even this powerful undead creature, forcing her into obedience. This never even would have been a battle. He'd lost all that, though, and now it was time to see if that would be his doom, or if his knowledge of the soulless monsters he had once commanded would still allow him to win.

He gripped his staff in both hands, knuckles white, as she released Sumi's leg and dropped down to land on the lid of the sarcophagus again. A high-pitched, broken giggle escaped her narrow lips. "You came to me, tasty morsel, and though your stance looks very martial, I know you want to bow and scrape, so I can pop you like a grape!"

Aspen let his knees begin to bend, bracing himself with the staff in his hands as the vampire drifted closer. Her nostrils flared as she neared, and he focused on that. Anything so he wouldn't actually look in her eyes! He knew this would never work with a vamp that was at full strength and in possession of all its faculties, but if this one was insane enough, and hungry enough...

The vamp came a step closer, and her ragged, blood-stained yellow claws reached out for him, opening and closing in greedy grasping motions. With a practiced twist, blessing Sumi for forcing him to practice with Khor for hours until this became second nature, he pulled the two halves of his homemade staff apart, revealing the fire-burnished wooden spike that had been hidden inside. He lunged forward, stabbing for her shriveled heart.

She shrieked, turning at the last moment so that the spike entered her side instead of her abdomen. Still, it was in her, and wood in a vamp meant...

Behind him, Motte drew in a gasping breath, then released an angry roar. He struggled against the webbing that held him. Seeing that the vampire was staked, and her mental powers broken for the moment, Sumi dropped down beside the large man. She released him from the webs, then collapsed with a stagger, blue ichor running from her broken joint.

Motte lunged to his feet, face twisted and teeth bared. His axe was still tangled, but his shield lay on the ground beside him. He picked it up, and ran across the small room to where Aspen was still struggling with the vampire.

Aspen's skin was shredded from the vamp's claws, and her teeth snapped perilously close to his throat. He had one forearm beneath her chin, pushing her jaw away. The other hand held the stake in her side, leaving him with no defense against her powerful strikes. He could feel his blood draining out through the accumulating wounds, and it was all he could do to hold on.

With a massive thud, Motte's shield came down on the monstrous creature. He pressed her against the coffin, and they could hear her bones creak under the pressure. This time, Motte kept his eyes down behind the shield, simply using his impressive strength to keep her pressed flat like a grotesque flower. The tank looked over at Aspen, who was sitting on the floor, staring at the broken staff in his hand. The spike had snapped when Motte hit, popping off the piece that was now buried inside the vampire's putrid flesh.

Aspen looked up. "She's still staked! She can't transform! We just need to cut off her head or destroy her heart!"

Motte glanced over, gritting out, "Whatever you're going to do, do it fast. She's stronger... than... she... looks!"

Aspen nodded and looked around. With Motte's axe tangled, and Sumi unable to free it, he had no sharp weapon. His staff was cracked, and the spike broken. The only thing in the room was rock!

He felt a tug at his ankle, and looked down. Yellow eyes gleamed up at him from a gray face. Sarave had dragged herself to him, leaving a trail of blood on the ground behind her. He could see the potion bottle on the ground where she had started. The discarded cap lay beside it. The goblin woman's voice was weak but clear as she held a piece of glittering white ore up to him.

"Melt... her... heart."

His eyes flew open, and he grabbed the ore. On second glance, it was more like a crystal, cracked on the bottom where it had broken from a larger piece, then rising into a sharp point. His hand closed comfortably around the bottom, and he looked over toward the two struggling against the sarcophagus.

The vampire had scored several deep gashes into Motte's shield, and while he was still holding her off, he was visibly weakening, while the vampire was as vicious as ever. The expression on her face said that she knew she could outlast him, the look of insane glee twisting her face into a horrific mask.

Aspen took a breath, then ran full force toward them. The undead female was so focused on Motte that she didn't even see Aspen coming. The crystal stake drove up under her ribs and into her useless heart with shocking ease, and thick, black blood began to ooze out over his fingers. A banshee howl tore from her throat, and she redoubled her efforts. Motte's feet began to slip.

Aspen closed his eyes. He focused every fiber of his being on the ore in his hand. He *pushed* with his body and his mind at once. He felt his hatred, terror, and disgust fill the shard. He added his need to protect, his worry for Sarave and Sumi, and his own fear of letting down someone who was counting on him. He felt the fragment warm under his hand, blazing hotter and hotter until he could feel the inferno through the vampire's skeletal form.

The shard melted, and where it touched black blood, the liquid exploded, the concussive force blowing the monster apart and throwing Aspen and Motte back. Motte, protected by his shield and armor, quickly sat back up. Aspen, on the other hand, felt his head crack against the stone floor, and everything went dark.

🍎 🍎 🍎

The first thing he saw upon opening his eyes was Motte's concerned face. The man was no longer wearing his helmet, and he was holding a metal vial in his hand. Motte must have just administered one of Sumi's potions, and the boost to Aspen's health was enough to bring him to consciousness.

"I had… a hell of a nightmare," Aspen muttered, raising a shaky hand to gingerly touch his head. He was rewarded with an echoing thump inside his skull, and decided that perhaps that was not his wisest decision today. Admittedly, given his recent actions, it seemed that his Wisdom stat still needed significant boosting.

Motte's face was a study in relief and exasperation. "Damned right you did. What made you think blowing up a vampire while you had your hand in her guts was a good idea?"

Ah, another decision to add to the list. There were getting to be too many to fit on the trophy. Aspen shakily pressed his arms against the ground, levering himself up. His head threatened to explode, and Motte quickly placed a strong arm behind his shoulders.

"Idiot! You need to lie down!" The deep voice was definitely edging more into irritation than relief.

<He's right. You're in no condition to move, yet. You need to rest there for at least another hour, and preferably overnight. You most certainly have a Concussion debuff, and likely a Fractured Skull as well.> Sumi sounded like she was landing in the annoyance camp as well.

Aspen felt his eyes well with relieved tears. He'd been so afraid the spider had been injured beyond recovery in the battle or the final explosion. Now, there was only one person left to worry about. "Sarave?" His voice was raw and painful, and he had to force himself to look around.

Motte shook his head, expression doubtful. "She's alive, but I don't know how. We gave her two more of those weird potions, and the spider patched her up as well as she could, but… There's a lot of blood, Aspen. I think the baby is stuck, and the goblin is too weak to push. She wants to talk to you."

Aspen nodded, and starbursts bloomed in his vision. Okay. No more nodding. He raised his hand and felt Motte's larger one grasp it. The big man all-but lifted Aspen to his feet, and half-carried him over to the limp form of the small woman, now resting on a blanket presumably donated by Motte.

Aspen felt his legs wobble beneath him again, and Motte carefully lowered him back to the ground. This brought Aspen's face next to Sarave's small, frightened, tear- and blood-stained face. The goblin had her eyes closed, and was murmuring something in her own language, invoking Gi-na often and with reverence. When she felt Aspen drop down beside her, she opened her eyes.

The wavering smile she attempted broke his heart, and caused a split in her lip to open again so a dribble of fresh blood oozed down her chin. "Aspen. Friend. So… sorry."

He reached up and clasped her hand carefully. "No, it's my fault. I'm sorry I didn't talk to you about whatever was bothering you. I should have, but I was afraid you'd hate me for pressing too soon. I should have-"

She rolled her head in denial. "My fault. Should trust. I…" Her hand pressed to her belly, and she grunted as a pain wracked her small frame. When it was done, she had to force her clenched teeth apart with a hiss. She reached out to grasp his hand with her last desperate strength. "Cut babe out. Not too late. Save her. Please!"

Aspen drew back, horrified, shaking his head.

Motte murmured quietly from behind him. "She's asked that several times. We told her no, but, honestly, if we don't do something soon, they're both going to die."

Aspen wildly cast about for any other solution. "Do we have any more potions?"

<None. I cannot make more right now, either. My body is using everything it has in its own healing.> Sumi's voice was quiet and grim.

Motte shook his head as well. "I used the last of mine a few days ago. I was getting ready to replenish my supply when Gina grabbed me and sent me here. I've got nothing."

"No. No. This is not going to happen this way." Aspen's teeth gritted, and he used the pain that brought to force the fog from his mind. Something... Something was prodding at him. A thought, a memory, a suggestion. An image of a field of growing plants, at least a week further along than they should be...

Aspen leaned over Sarave. His hands covered hers on her abdomen, feeling the muscles ripple with another contraction. Sarave screamed with pain, and Aspen prayed.

Gina! Gina, I know you can hear me! I don't know what you did to me when you accepted me a year ago, but you gave me magic. I know I'm not a very good devotee. I know I make fun of you, a little, sometimes. But please, if anything in what you gave me will let me heal, even a little, let me do it now. She deserves better than the life she's lived, and her child deserves better than an early death. You healed them once. Do it again! Please!

For a hundred pounding heartbeats, as one contraction ended and rolled right into another, leaving the goblin gasping and weak but still writhing in pain, nothing happened. Then a warmth spread beneath Aspen's hands. It was different from the heat of the forge, and far different from the bitter cold of the grave that had been the touch of his magic for most of his life. This was birth, growth, creation, and a strange kind of unfolding. Something deep inside of him opened up like a flower turning toward the sun.

Liquid incandescence spread out around them, flowing and eddying like the waves of the sea on the sand. The warm breeze of a gentle spring day spread over the chamber, replacing the stench of copper and rot with the scent of crushed pine needles. They drew in simultaneous breaths, and Aspen felt instantly better, refreshed in heart and body.

Beneath his hands, Sarave convulsed once more, then twice. Motte swore, then reached down, scooping something from the ground. Sarave spasmed again, and her eyes fluttered closed. A weak cry came from Motte's direction, followed by a hiccuping little breath, and a much stronger cry, protesting the light and sound that suddenly surrounded the new life that had entered the world.

Aspen thought he felt a slim, comforting hand settle over his where it rested on Sarave's belly, and then it, and the warmth and light, were gone. He slumped forward over the goblin he had come to consider his friend, exhausted and refreshed at once. His headache was gone, as were the scratches and bruises that had covered him. Thin scars, as from long-healed wounds, marked the deepest of the injuries, but that and his filthy, torn clothing were the only sign he had been in a battle at all.

Sarave's chest rose and fell in a reassuring rhythm beneath him, and he scrambled back off of her. Her wounds were gone as well, though far more scars covered her than had been there before. Her throat, especially, was riddled with raised, silvery marks. Nonetheless, she seemed to be merely resting, and as if in confirmation, a notification flashed in front of his eyes.

Quest: "It's Somebody's Birthday" complete.

You have saved Sarave and her baby. Sure, you had to ask for help, but everybody needs help sometimes.

Success: Sarave and her daughter are alive. You learned a new skill

[Pray], and a new spell [Healing]. Don't expect it to work so well next time. You got a boost for asking nicely. +1000 experience points. Maximum reputation with Sarave achieved.

A new golden glow suffused him, but this time, he knew exactly what it was. He was leveling up. He closed his eyes, basking in the light, then shook it off and turned around.

Motte stood behind him, gently holding a mewling baby in his arms. The infant was smaller than a human baby, but definitely larger than Aspen imagined goblin infants usually were. Its skin held a healthy pink glow under a faint hint of lime green, and its ear tips were slightly rounded, instead of reaching sharp points like its mother's.

Motte looked up, rocking the babe in a way that said he'd spent many hours with an infant in his arms. His face had the slightly goofy grin that most people got when they saw a newborn. "It's a girl," he almost whispered. "Her tag says she's half-goblin, half-human. I didn't even know that was possible!"

A hundred clues clicked into place in Aspen's mind, and he could have slapped himself for being so stupid. Looking back, the clues were all there. If he hadn't been so blinded by his own assumptions, he might have seen this coming. *This* was why the goblins had killed Sarave's husband and poisoned her. *This* was why the baby had always seemed so huge. *This* was why Sarave had run away.

"It's illegal," he said softly. "Humans are looked down on if we have children outside our own race, but the other races take it even more seriously. Nearly any of them will kill any half-breed they find. With the war over, though, this was bound to happen. Theoretically, a goblin *could* marry a human, and with all the races now mingling in Bright..." He waved at the fussing newborn with an expressive gesture. "I just hadn't even considered the possibility that the child might not be pure goblin."

Motte stroked the wisp of fine hair on top of the baby's head. His expression was tender as he stepped past Aspen to gently place the newborn on her mother's chest. The baby instantly began to squirm against Sarave's chest, eyes still closed as it instinctively sought sustenance. Sarave's eyes flickered open. The expression on her face, the love and wonder, choked the voices in the throats of both men, and they looked away to give her privacy as she pulled her child close.

Finally, Aspen cleared his throat, raising his voice just a bit so that there was no way Sarave could avoid hearing. "They'll be safe on the farm. No one will injure a mother and child while I and my friends have anything to say about it. No one here cares what race they are."

A little sob came from behind them, and the two men smiled at each other in shared understanding.

At that moment, a small, polite cough came from the sarcophagus beside them. It was followed by a small, polite voice. "Ah, excuse me, please. In light of that comment, I do hope I can ask for your assistance, and that you'll give me a moment to speak before you judge me by *my* race."

Aspen and Motte whirled around, looking for the source of the voice. There, sitting so that his head just poked up through the crack in the lid of the great stone coffin, was another vampire.

Motte swore, and his great axe appeared instantly in his hand. Sumi reared back, raising her chelicerae menacingly. Aspen reached for a staff that wasn't there, since it was lying across the room, shattered into splinters.

The vampire, an elderly man with pale skin and thin, white, neatly-combed hair, raised his hands up through the wide crack. His nails - and they were nails , not the thick, ragged yellow claws of his brethren - were neat, though dirty. Silver shackles hung around both wrists, and raw, ulcerated skin glistened unhealthily from beneath the tarnished metal.

He grimaced, revealing two small, sharp canines in his top row of teeth. They were far from the two-inch fangs on top and bottom that most vampires sported. Add the teeth, the nails, the shackles, and the apologetic tone of his voice together, and you got something Aspen had never come across before.

Aspen raised a hand, halting Sumi and Motte, while at the same time moving so that his own body was between the vampire and Sarave. "Who... What are you?"

The vampire lowered his hands back down, hissing slightly as the cuffs slid over his abused flesh. "Well, that is rather a long story," he said. A heavy accent weighted his vowels. "I believe you now have plenty of time to listen, but I suspect I may not have enough time to speak. I do apologize, but Jezerey chained me just before you arrived. I'm afraid I must ask you to release me before my hands burn off."

Aspen's eyes narrowed. "That wouldn't be enough to kill you."

The elderly vampire coughed slightly. "I hate to correct you on such a short acquaintance, but it would quite likely be enough to, well, not kill, since I'm no longer alive, but eradicate my existence. I am, thankfully, somewhat different from the vampires you have met before." A grimace of distaste passed across his face. "But that difference does come with a few drawbacks. All in all, I believe I got the better end of the bargain, but at the moment it's difficult to say."

Motte shook his head. "I don't know what to make of it. I was just offered a quest to free him, but I don't know if I should take it or not."

Glancing over at Motte, Aspen hesitated, filing away the information that Travelers could *choose* their quests, instead of having them assigned by the gods. "Take it," Aspen decided, ignoring Sumi's hiss of disagreement. "But we'll take Sarave and the babe out of here before we let him go. He'll have to wait that long."

The vampire grimaced, but nodded his understanding. Motte twitched a finger, as the Travelers often did when performing their special magic. Sumi clicked her chelicerae disapprovingly. Aspen turned back to Sarave, who was sitting up on the blanket. The drying pool of blood and a faint tracery of pale scars were the only signs of her ordeal, though she still looked tired. In her arms, she clutched her sleeping infant protectively.

Reaching down, he gently helped the goblin woman to her feet. Once she was standing, swaying slightly, Aspen knelt, holding out his arms. "May I carry you? I brought you out of this place in my arms once before. It seems most fitting that I do so again. I hope that if there's a next time, however, you'll make your own way out."

She smiled a little at his feeble attempt at humor, but nodded. "Soon good, please."

He scooped her up and began to jog out of the room, though he hesitated when he reached the edge of the light cast by the glowstone. He turned around and looked at Motte sheepishly. "Do you have another one of those stones?"

❦ ❦ ❦

Sarave was quickly settled behind the same ore cart that Aspen had used to hide his backpack the first time he'd come to the mine. After a few moments of debate, Sumi agreed to stay to watch over the goblin and her daughter, and Aspen returned to the room at the end of the round passage.

Once Aspen and Motte were alone with the vampire, Aspen took a small piece of wood left over from his broken staff, and unceremoniously stabbed it into the back of the creature's shoulder, where it would be very difficult to remove, but cause no serious injury. The vampire winced and hissed, but made no protest. Motte struck off the cuffs and chains with two swift strokes of his axe.

Immediately, the golden coruscation of a level up surrounded Motte, and he grinned, saluting Aspen with his weapon. "Quest complete, and it took me to level ninety-six! Not bad for an old man."

Aspen snorted. "Old man, my-" he glanced around, half-expecting Sumi to interrupt him, but sighed and changed what he was going to say anyway, "hand. I'm older than you, and I'd be surprised if I'm level 20 yet."

Motte's brows lifted in amazement. "Twenty! That's…"

A polite cough interrupted them. They turned back to the monster in their midst, who sat quietly rubbing his wrists, which were now healing since the silver cuffs weren't constantly burning him any longer. The vampire smiled apologetically. "Ah, I'm very sorry, gentlemen, and I wouldn't bother you, but this sliver of wood in my shoulder is, um, quite uncomfortable. I'd be very grateful if you would decide if I'm to be destroyed or set free."

Aspen's face hardened. He exchanged a glance with Motte, who shrugged. Aspen scowled and addressed the vampire. "Fine then. I'll warn you though; the slightest hint that you're considering attacking us or running and we'll put you down like we did your friend."

The elderly vampire's face was a study in distaste. "No friend of mine, I assure you. Once, she was a powerful Queen, though she was sadly fallen even before the, ah, madness took her, and she was never a person who inspired particularly positive emotions in others. Thus the fact that she was forced to keep me in shackles in order to, ah, compel my obedience. Unfortunately, she was both stronger and faster than I, so my attempts to escape only ended in ignominy."

"How did you come to be here, if you weren't companions, then?" Aspen asked, eyeing the marks which were now all but gone from the other's wrists, leaving only sickly yellowish bands of shiny skin behind.

"Ah, that is the long story. I shall tell it willingly, and let you judge me as you will, but first, what do you know of how vampires are made?"

Motte looked back and forth between the other two. "Where I come from, they say vampires are made when a vamp drinks all the blood of a human, and then right before they die, forces the human to drink from the vampire. Then the human appears to die, and is 'reborn' three days later as a new vamp. Is that right?"

Aspen and the vampire nodded at the same time, then gave each other wary glances. The vamp continued, "That is indeed how we, er, proliferate. Do you know, however, how vampires were created in the beginning?"

The two men exchanged blank looks. "I assumed you were created by the Gods, just like the other races," Aspen said.

The vamp's laugh was tinged with bitter self-mockery. "The Gods. Indeed, no. Humanity has much to answer for, and vampires are simply another notch on the tally sheet." He leaned back against the coffin, and began his story. His halting speech grew more confident as he went on.

"My name is William. Some five hundred years ago, give or take, I was an earth mage. I was no particular genius, but I was powerful and competent, and the owners of several large mines often hired me to create tunnels for them. I was well paid for my time, and lived comfortably. I had no grand aspirations to be more than I was, and after my wife died of a pox, I settled into a solitary but satisfactory existence.

"My wife and I were never blessed with children, and I was semi-retired. I needed no more money for my simple life. I lived alone, and only went to town a few times a year, so no one would miss me. This made me a perfect target for a cult who wished to attempt an… experiment. I was abducted in broad daylight, from my own home, never to walk as a free man again.

"That night I was taken to the palace of the queen of my land, Jezerey, the very vampire you so recently slew. She was a foreign princess who had married our King and produced an heir and a spare, but it was a political match, no more. As she grew older, and her children grew apart from her, she was left, nearly forgotten and relegated to an estate on the outskirts of the city. She was, as I have mentioned, something less than an appealing soul.

"Jezerey wished, as so many do, to live forever. She had used the one thing she did have in abundance, money, and hired sorcerers to find a way for her to do so. When the sorcerers failed, she turned to darker and darker sources, until she became enthralled by a death cult.

"The cult was able to provide what she sought, in the form of three drops of the blood of a god. Atae, the ruler of the Chaos Pool, deity of darkness and death, had once walked this earth in mortal form, as did the other gods. What their motivations were, I dare not guess, but they sometimes left behind scraps of themselves, and these mementos became powerful relics.

"Atae herself had nothing to do with the atrocities the cult committed. However, Lamashtu, a former servant of Atae, brought the blood to the cult. What she received in return, I do not know. Lamashtu conducted a spell for Jezerey, which, when combined with the blood of one of Atae's chosen creatures, would grant eternal life to one person for each drop of the goddess' blood.

"By the time I was dragged from my home and thrust upon the ground before the Queen, Jezerey had already learned the true cost of her greed. First, she had tested the spell on her elder son, who would be King after his father's death. When all seemed well, she cast the spell on herself. Thus, she found herself a vampire.

"Forced to hide from the sun and drink the blood of mortals in order to continue her unclean existence, she began to create a series of tunnels to connect every part of the city. Her husband was among the first to fall victim to her hunger, and her son was crowned. He had no wish to be ruled by his mother, however, and attempted rebellion. Without remorse, she had him forced into the sun until he turned into a tower of flame.

"She had discovered, by now, that anyone she turned herself was forced to become her servant, utterly unable to defy her. So, she turned her younger son, Kalif, who you slew a few days ago, and ruled him as a puppet-king. Then she attempted to raise an army of undead. She found that, in addition to the weaknesses of which you know, any mage she turned lost all but the mind magics that are a vampire's natural gift."

"What?" Aspen exclaimed, "That's not true! Liches are undead mages! I've fought them myself, and I know very well that they can cast spells other than those purely of the mind."

William nodded. "That's true. But liches, while undead, are not vampires. They have found some other method of achieving undeath, but they do not drink blood."

Aspen cast through his memories for any instance when he had seen a lich feed on anything but life force. He was forced to admit that the old vampire might well be correct, and nodded for the other to continue.

"No army in that time stood a chance without a large cadre of mage-soldiers. Not even one that consisted of horrific monsters with speed and strength far beyond that of any mortal warrior. Jezerey knew she could hire or conscript such a force, but she was never certain of her power over them, not as she was of her vampiric offspring. She wanted a mage who was utterly loyal to her.

"So, she found me. I was a capable earth mage, well known for my skill in creating stable tunnels quickly and reliably. Not strong enough in power or personality to challenge her, but providing exactly the magic that she needed most. I was brought before her, and this part I remember as if it were yesterday." He paused, glancing over at the scorch marks that were all that remained of his former captor.

"Her madness was already well begun by the time I met her, but she was as vibrant and beautiful as she must have been in her youth. You could see how she had convinced a king to wed her. I knelt on the cold stone tiles, knees burning from the force with which I had been pushed down, and could barely speak through my fear and awe.

"'Little mage,' she asked, 'do you know who I am?'

"I nodded, as the guards, horrific cold creatures who smelled of death, had already told me that I was to be brought to their queen.

"She smiled, utterly joyless, and stood from her throne. Her dress was so heavy with brocade that it should have scratched the floor, but she seemed to hover above it, blood-red eyes blazing in her snow-white face.

"'Then you know that you are the most fortunate of all mortals. I have brought you here to give you a gift, that you may become my greatest servant.'

"I am not ashamed to admit that I trembled in fear. I didn't know what she was, but I knew she was no mortal, and that my death was staring me in the face. It was all I could do to nod again, and I think my teeth were chattering.

"She reached out, and one of the vampire minions set a dagger in her hand.

Its tip was glass, and in that glass was a single drop of something so red it was black except when a flicker of light caught it just so. Another cold courtier handed her a cage, with a small, terrified creature cowering inside.

"She opened the cage and took out the animal, which appeared to be some kind of bat, though it had much larger hind feet and smaller fangs than any I had seen before. I was fairly well acquainted with the beasts, having worked in caves my entire adult life, but this was definitely a type I didn't recognize.

"Without further ado, she handed both to a woman who had been standing behind me, unnoticed. Indeed, all I could see even then were two dark-skinned arms covered in a voluminous satin robe, and a shadowed face in a deep hood. The woman began to chant, rhyming in a strange language. Two guards stepped up and grasped my arms, pulling me up to stand before her. She pressed the momentarily quiescent bat against my chest, over my heart, and with a single stroke, pierced us both. I felt the moment the tip of the knife broke off in my heart, releasing that fluid drop, and then I died.

"Three days later I woke in darkness. Jezerey sat beside me, silent as I thrashed and cried, feeling for the first time the frigid stillness of my flesh. When I calmed, she spoke.

"'Cast a spell, William. Any spell, so long as you do not attempt to bring harm to me. Cast a spell, for I wish to see.'

"I cast the first spell my master taught me, decades before. It was an apprentice's spell, to gather up the dirt and dust nearby into a pile. I used that spell so many times it was second nature to me. My magic was slow, as sluggish as my body felt. But it did respond, and a weak puff of dust rose from the floor, then sank back again.

"She laughed. It was utterly insane, and I tried to run from her, stumbling from the room. A guard caught me before I took two steps into the hall, and brought me back. There, I found that Jezerey was not alone, as I had thought. She had a boy with her. Not too young. Perhaps seventeen. He was covered in bites, and his blood streaked his skin and stained the shreds of his clothes. His eyes were exhausted and terrified.

"Jezerey thrust him at me. 'Drink, vampire. Empty him entire.'

"I blanched. The poor boy was drained already, and you could see that he knew he could not survive another bite. He looked, in fact, a bit like my nephew Roger, who was not terribly bright, but could always be counted on to enjoy the company of his old uncle for at least a little while. I caught the lad in my arms, and lowered him gently to the ground, staring at the madwoman in incomprehension.

"'Drink? Does he have wine?' I asked, rather inanely, I fear. In my defense, I had just died and woken again, and I wasn't at my best.

"She scowled, revealing long fangs, still red from her own meal. 'His blood, you fool. Do you not feel its pull?'

"I reached up and lifted my own lip, feeling that my canines were slightly longer and sharper than they had been before, though nothing compared to hers. Perhaps they would grow? All I knew was that the only feelings the boy roused in me were pity and revulsion.

"Jezerey reached out and lifted the lad's arm, cutting it open with a sharp fingernail. Blood oozed sluggishly, and I vomited all over her gown.

"The Queen sent for Lamashtu, but the sorceress was nowhere to be found. Bargain complete, she had taken her prize and vanished. While Jezerey screamed and railed in fury, my own hunger grew, but nothing and no one she brought before me tempted me.

"At last, Jezerey brought me to a slave pen, filled with terrified and oppressed humanity. She told me to find someone to eat. I was terribly weak by then, and if those poor creatures had tried, they probably could have killed me. But they were so defeated that they simply stood there as I walked by.

"I caught a whiff of a delectable smell. The most wonderful, delicious scent I had ever encountered. In a trance, I followed it to a slop bucket nearby. There, on top of the filth, was a half-rotten apple core. I snatched it up, bit into it, and pulled its rancid juice into my mouth.

"You see, Jezerey had, of course, used the largest Greater Vampire Bats she could find for the spell she had used on her first son and herself. For me, since she wanted a meek mage who worked with earth, she found a rare tunneling fruit bat. A fruit bat!" The vampire broke into slightly hysterical laughter.

William finally managed to control himself, shaking his head at the foolishness of his former mistress. "I had no interest in blood, but I could drain a pineapple dry in moments. There was no chance I could create an army of mages for her, as she had hoped, because the moment any blood touched my lips I was sent into convulsions of regurgitation. She tried draining mages herself, and then feeding them my blood, but that had the same result as when she gave them her own.

"Meanwhile, I was not nearly as affected by sunlight as she and her vampires. I could travel outside, covered in a cloak, and only burn a little. I flatter myself that I also retained far more of my original intelligence and personality. Unfortunately, that personality was never a strong one. So long as she fed me, and no atrocities were committed before my eyes, I could pretend that I was simply doing a job, much as I had done all my life, creating passages from one place to another.

"She continued in this manner for hundreds of years, becoming more mad and power hungry with every passing year. But as monstrous as Jezerey was, there is always a greater horror. Eventually she went too far. She overstepped the bounds of human evil, and encroached on the territory of one more powerful than herself. Lich Lord Akuji noticed us. He is master of all undead, and easily broke the link between Jezerey and her progeny, transforming Jezerey's countless minions into his own. Only we three were able to escape, and even we felt his call.

"We found our way here, far from Akuji's domain, in human lands where the last mortal resistance stood. Jezerey and Kalif were weak, nearly starving as we had found no humans on which they could feed in several days. It was summer, and fruits were abundant, so I had no problems, but when we came to this mine and found signs that it had recently been abandoned, they could go no further.

"I had tried to escape several times, both in the preceding centuries and in the past few days, and so Jezerey, who was powerful enough to bear the touch of the metal for short periods, began to keep a silver chain on me, preventing me from moving more than a few feet from her. When she found that she was too weak to continue on, she had me create these tunnels and sarcophagi. She lined mine with silver, then had me get in and lie on a cloak. If I so much as moved, I began to burn. Once she was certain I was trapped and helpless, she and Kalif laid down as well and went to sleep.

"An explosion woke us. My coffin was cracked, and I was able to escape into the woods. Jezerey followed me, and sent Kalif to see if there were any humans nearby from which to feed. I suspect you know the rest of the story."

Aspen and Motte looked at each other, and then Motte held out his hand. A single apple appeared there, shining and perfect. Motte threw it. "Here, catch."

The vampire snatched the fruit from the air in a motion almost too quick to see. His eyes shone with hunger, and he instantly sank his fangs into the fruit. A slurping sound filled the room as the two men watched, astonished. The apple sank in on itself, becoming a pale, shriveled remnant of its former self.

William dropped the husk, wiping a drop of apple juice from the corner of his mouth with an air of embarrassment. His chin sank to his chest, and his entire posture was tired and hopeless.

As one, Aspen and Motte looked at each other, and stepped away from the old vampire.

"No," said Aspen.

"Yes," said Motte.

Aspen growled. "He's a vampire. I know them! They're incapable of being anything but evil."

Motte raised one eyebrow. "You're the one with a fugitive goblin and her half-human baby living in your cellar."

"That's different! Sarave is – "

"*How* is it different, exactly? They're each themselves, not their species. Honestly, I've never met a goblin who wasn't a rotten, thieving little monster before. But I'll tell you one thing. This ga… world has taught me to expect the unexpected." Motte grimaced a bit. "Actually, being a parent taught me that. Rouge is very good at finding the unexpected."

Aspen barked a laugh, running his hand through his hair so it stood up in a sweaty, bloody mess. "Yes, I've noticed that as well. And, if I'm being truthful, I never would have expected to like a goblin as much as I like Sarave, either. I gave her a chance because she was pregnant, and she invoked the name of my goddess, and I don't regret it." He glanced at Motte, then sighed, "I would not have expected to like a Traveler, either. I've heard and seen terrible things. You lot seem to think that murder and theft is an acceptable answer to nearly any problem. But you and Rouge are making me question that as well."

Motte quirked a smile. "Fair enough. Most, um, Travelers would gladly kill you and your whole family if they got a quest to do it. Hell, I might have, myself, before Rouge joined the game. She's different, though, and I learned to be different by being with her. Maybe this sad bastard is different too."

Looking down, Aspen stubbed the toe of his worn leather boots in the ground, and quietly grumbled, "Damn it."

The two men turned back to the vampire, who was still sitting there, shoulders slumped, the picture of dejection.

Aspen cleared his throat, and William looked up slowly. "Fine," Aspen said, "You go free. But on one condition."

William stared, pale reddish eyes large in his bone-white face. "Anything!"

"You have to stay nearby. Check in with me periodically. If I'm going to let you go, I need to know that I'm not condemning anyone else by my mistake. There's no one else around except us, so as long as you're here, I know you can't hurt anyone. Unless the whole darned country comes trooping up here." He muttered this last under his breath, but Motte heard and chuckled softly.

The old man shook his head. "I would gladly stay here. I've always been a solitary man, except for a few close friends and family, but winter is coming. I feel the snow in the air, and the nearby mountain pass is already closed. I'll have to travel to find food, or else sink back into slumber again, and I doubt I'm strong enough to wake up on my own without something like the explosion happening again."

Quest: "Idle Hands are Apofis' Workshop" begun.

William needs food. You have a farm. Find something for him to do and help him survive the winter.

Success: Variable. William lives until Spring. You gain an ally.

Failure: William is forced to flee OR William starves.

"Why are all the quest rewards variable?" Aspen threw his hands up in the air, and Motte gave him a sympathetic look. "Fine! I have a farm. That means I grow things, at least in theory. Harvest will be who knows when, thanks to… reasons… but it looks like we'll have enough to share." His eyes narrowed. "You said you made tunnels, right?"

William nodded vigorously.

"How about this, then. I'd like to work this mine, and I have a very small house, a lot of land, and more people keep showing up all the time. You work on creating tunnels so that I can access the mine, and build rooms and passages under my house so everyone has somewhere to live, and maybe some storage. I'll pay you in fruits and vegetables all winter. Deal?"

The vampire smiled so broadly that his small, sharp fangs were on full display. "That sounds wonderful! I, um, can't thank you enough for this opportunity, and I promise you won't regret it! Ah, one thing, though, if I may?"

"What?"

"Would it be too much trouble to remove this rather irksome splinter from my shoulder?"

William wanted to stay and begin work on excavating the mine. He felt confident since there were still plenty of edible plants nearby, so he didn't believe he needed anything from Aspen just yet. Aspen and Sumi were less than certain leaving the vampire unattended was a good idea, but Motte was on the old man's side. After much discussion, they compromised, and agreed that they would send Khor up to check on the vampire every other night. This would doubtless annoy the goat, which Aspen silently considered to be an added bonus, though Sumi was less reticent in sharing her satisfaction. Thus it was that the small group left the vampire behind, though Aspen cast more than a few glances behind him, hoping he wasn't making a terrible mistake.

Sumi perched on Aspen's shoulders, while Motte exchanged his armor for something more comfortable and carried Sarave and her baby easily. Sarave was wan and exhausted. The worst of her physical injuries may have been healed, but clearly she was far from hale and hearty. In spite of this, she refused to let anyone else hold her daughter, and used some cloth Motte pulled from his storage as both a wrap dress and a sling to hold the newborn. When she fell asleep in Motte's arms with her child on her breast, both men sank into tired contemplation as they concentrated on walking quietly through the woods.

Aspen finally broke the silence, though he spoke softly. "Should I expect Rouge's mother to turn up on my doorstep next?"

Motte grunted softly, as though struck. "No. She isn't very involved in Rouge's life anymore. We got a divorce years ago, and she remarried. She moved away a few years ago, and I got full custody. She was never a, ah, 'Traveler' anyway. She prefers her own world to anyone else's." Bitterness tainted his last words, though he had begun with a carefully-neutral tone.

The sound of their steady footfalls filled the awkward silence. Aspen cleared his throat. "I'm sorry. I didn't mean to bring up bad memories. If it helps, I do understand, a bit. When I was very young, I fancied myself in love. We ran off together and wed, against her family's wishes. By the time they found us and convinced her to divorce her pathetic, base-born lover, we had already spawned a baby. She left me and our daughter the day the babe appeared." He looked up into the starry sky, blinking moisture from his eyes. "That child was the only good thing I ever did."

Motte shook his head, looking uncomfortable but sympathetic. "I'm sorry. Though I'm sure you're too hard on yourself. You seem like a good man. I wouldn't be trusting you around my daughter if I thought otherwise."

<Listen to him, Aspen.> Sumi's soft voice echoed in his mind.

Aspen's fists clenched against his sides, then slowly relaxed. "I appreciate that you feel that way. I'm doing my best to make up for my past mistakes. I'll never be able to redeem myself entirely, but I do try." He cast a glance at the sleeping goblins in Motte's arms, and smiled. "I think I may have canceled a bit of my debt today."

Motte's deep chuckle made Sarave stir slightly, and then she settled again against his warmth, her breaths coming slow and even. "Unless you were a mass murderer, you're probably all right."

Aspen walked on in silence.

🦇 🦇 🦇

It was nearly the deepest part of the night by the time they saw the house in front of them. Motte was using another glowstone, taken from his inventory, to light their path, and they were nearly upon the small stone building before their light-addled eyes could make it out. Sarave was sleeping again, though she had woken twice to feed the infant. Sumi had jumped down from Aspen's shoulders an hour or so before, and ran ahead into the darkness. He assumed she had gone for her own meal, and wished her well of it. She knew that watching her eat was disturbing to most people, so she usually did it away from the others.

Silus was the first to notice them. <Aspen! You're back! Did you find Sarave? Is she all right? Is this the Traveler man? Did Sarave have her baby? I'm so sorry I didn't see her go! She must have been very sneaky!> The little bat glided down to land on Aspen's shoulder, nuzzling up under his chin.

Aspen chuckled. "Yes, mostly, yes, yes, and it's all right, little one. Sarave planned her departure very well. We'll have to see about staggering your scouting pattern in the future, but that's a problem for another day. Did anything happen while we were gone?"

<Khor was *very* cranky because you left him behind. The ostrich wouldn't eat anything. He just sticks his head in through the window and kind of sings to Rouge. Kayli and Kayti chewed Khor's beard off while he was napping, and he looks so funny!>

Aspen chuckled and relayed this information to Motte and Sarave, who had woken when they stopped moving. Motte placed the goblin woman on her feet, bracing her carefully until he was sure she could walk on her own.

The warrior shook his head, looking at the large bird, who was still standing with his head thrustin through the window of the house. "I'll have to try to feed Codswallop. Rouge has probably been giving him some kind of special feed, and now he won't graze on his own. Or whatever ostriches do."

Sarave looked much better after her hours-long rest. She cradled the baby to her chest, but walked with surprising confidence as she headed for the front door.

<What's the baby's name?> Silus asked, and Aspen stopped dead.

"I don't know. I didn't think to ask."

<You didn't *ask*?> Silus sounded scandalized.

Aspen shook his head and began walking again, now slightly behind the others, though his long legs quickly made up the short distance. "No one else asked either. We were a bit busy with two vampires."

<Two! You killed two vampires?> Silus sounded duly impressed. She had never actually seen one of these powerful undead, though she loved Khor's tales of how he heroically slew hundreds of them by himself.

"Only one, and I had a lot of help. We left the other one behind digging tunnels."

<Whaaaaaat?!> Silus' golden eyes seemed ready to pop out, and her ears were twitching madly.

Aspen leaned his cheek against the bat's soft head and smiled. "It's a long story. We'll tell everyone in a bit. Right now, we need a meal and a bed."

<And a bath.> Sumi's acerbic voice joined the conversation as the three-foot arachnid dropped down from the sod roof of the house.

"I'm not walking to the river right now, I'm sorry, Sumi." Aspen plucked at the dried vampire on his shirt fruitlessly. "I'll take off my clothes, but I'm too tired for anything more."

<That's why I hurried to get here before you. I told that great useless lump of a goat to go down to the river with the wagon. We put a waxed tarp in the back, and he filled it and brought it back. Had to drag the whole wagon into the river to do it, so now the house smells like wet wool, but at least you can wash.> Sumi's voice was smug.

The man sighed in resignation. "Fine. Where is it?"

<Still in the back of the wagon. We couldn't get it out without dumping the water. It'll make it easy to take away the filth once you're done, at least.> The spider pointed beyond the house with a leg.

Aspen raised his voice to speak to Sarave and Motte, who were listening to his side of the conversation while pretending they weren't. "Sumi and Khor brought water from the river so we can wash up. It's in the wagon behind the house. Sarave, would you care to go first?"

The goblin's face softened into the first genuine smile Aspen had seen since her rescue. "Yes, friend Aspen," she said simply. "Thank you."

He smiled back, feeling flakes of dried gore crisp off his cheek as he did. "You're very welcome. Ah," he hesitated as Sarave turned toward the direction Sumi had indicated. "What's your daughter's name, if I may ask?"

Sarave turned back, her face lit by the combined glow of the moons, the stars, and Motte's glowstone. She smiled again, looking at the tall farmer. "Juniper. J for her father, Jeremy. And a tree for the man who saved her life, twice. It means 'evergreen'."

Aspen looked down at the adorable little green face that was all that was visible of the baby in its wrappings, and laughed.

Chapter Eleven

Rouge

Zoey sat beside Jace, staring at her lunch. Her friend was munching on his own sandwich silently. She sighed loudly, and Jace looked up, grinning. "That sounded like a request for conversation, if I ever heard one."

She wrinkled her nose at him, but shrugged. "Yeah. I'm grounded."

Jace's blue eyes widened behind his glasses. "You? What did you do?" His astonishment was reasonable.

Zoey had realized a long time ago that the best way to get her dad to leave her alone was to go along with his weird urge to talk about her life. It's not like she usually did anything that needed hiding, and if she did, well, a little selective omission generally solved that problem. Her grades were good, she didn't get into fights (no thanks to Mirna), she didn't date, and she even did her homework on time. She was practically perfect! Her dad was being *so* unfair!

"My dad is being *so* unfair!" She clapped her hand over her mouth when she realized that it had come out exactly as whiny as it had sounded in her head.

Her friend pushed his glasses up his nose, eyes dancing. "What happened?"

Zoey growled, frustrated. "You know that, uh, *thing* I can't talk about?"

Jace nodded.

"I didn't talk about it with him, either, because *duh*. So, I did a few things he told me not to, and I didn't tell him those things either, and there was a timed quest, and so I couldn't wait for him even if I could tell him, and he was busy anyway, so it's practically *his fault*." She stuffed the last of her salmon sushi flavored potato chips into her mouth and chewed angrily.

Jace's head tilted to the side, as it did when he was pondering something seriously. "So, your dad trusted you to do what you were supposed to do, and you didn't, and now you're in trouble? Huh."

She stared at him. "Whose side are you on?"

He grinned. "Yours, of course. Welcome to being a totally normal, rebellious teenager, Zoe." He mimed an explosion above his head. "Ding! Level up!"

Zoey stared, but finally laughed and relaxed a little. "Yeah. I guess it's not that big a deal, right? Happens to other people all the time. At least I'm just grounded from the game for a day, and grounded at home for the rest of the school year. Not like I go anywhere anyway," she muttered.

Jace grimaced at this news. "Well, we *were* going to go to the opening day of the new indie superhero movie next week, but yeah, it's not like we can't stream it later."

She clicked her tongue. "Shoot! I forgot about that. Sorry, Jace."

He shrugged, though she could see that he really was disappointed. "No big deal."

Zoey brightened. "I'll be back in Bright in just a few game months. I'm sure I'll have some cool quests to share. We'll do them together! Though," her face dropped again, "I also have to get a job this summer."

Jace's jaw dropped. "You? A job? You said you'd rather have bamboo sticks poked under your nails than get a job!"

She sighed again, poking desultorily at the crust of her almond butter and honey sandwich. "Apparently the bamboo sticks weren't available. Dad was thinking about canceling our accounts and selling the equipment. Drastic steps had to be taken." She hoped she sounded sufficiently dramatic with that last sentence.

He laughed, shaking off his disappointment. "Yeah, okay. If things got that serious, then clearly a few weeks of being grounded aren't that big a deal."

Zoey grinned back, and was about to respond when an ear-achingly familiar voice came from behind her.

"Oh, is this where you losers eat now?" Mirna emerged from beyond the mostly unused dumpster the two friends had been using as their 'no one wants to go there' shelter this week. She smirked at the two of them as she flipped her brown ponytail (today's 'signature' braided extension was a virulent green).

Two of her cronies appeared behind her. Their faces showed badly-faked surprise, and Zoey hoped neither of them was planning to go into show biz. Or, on second thought, maybe they should. The thought of their ignominious failure brought a smirk to her lips, and Mirna's eyes narrowed.

"This is the perfect place for you. Obviously even trash knows where it belongs." The taller girl sneered as Zoey and Jace silently stood and began to gather their lunches. Mirna's brown eyes flicked toward the dumpster. "Why are you here, little dirt munchers? You worried you're going to *contaminate* normal people with your grossness?"

One of the other girls, Annie something, twittered. "Maybe they don't want us to see that all they have to eat is dirt."

Zoey gritted her teeth, but just finished putting away her half-eaten sandwich in her *Kimi ni Todoke* retro lunchbox. Jace was already packed, but stood by waiting for Zoey, resolutely looking anywhere except at the bully.

Mirna's face twisted as she looked at the scratched and worn metal lunchbox. "What is that thing? Who even uses a lunchbox anymore? And what's with the ugly cartoon chick on the front?"

Zoey clutched her lunchbox to her chest defensively. "It's anime. My mom gave it to me."

Mirna mimed vomiting. "Oh, your precious mama? I hear even she doesn't like you enough to-"

Zoey launched herself at the tall girl, fingers stretched to scratch at her smug face. Jace caught her at the last second, pulling her back. "Come on, come on, Zoe. She's not worth it. Let's go!" Holding her hand tightly, he pulled her away. Mirna and her friends laughed, though Zoey thought Mirna looked a little shaken at the close call.

Zoey sat on the bottom stair near the main office. It was against the rules to block the stairs, but all that would happen if someone decided to complain was that they'd get chased off. Anyway, this was one place Mirna wouldn't dare harass them, since she might actually get caught playing her favorite vicious game.

Jace had his arm around her shoulders, which was also technically against the rules (no touching in public spaces except hand holding), but they didn't care at the moment. "It's okay, Zoe. She's just a beezie. Just let it go. Don't give her the satisfaction."

She sniffed, wiping at her eyes and nose with the back of her arm. "It just makes me so *mad*! What did I ever do to her except be born? Why can't she just leave us alone?"

Her friend shrugged. "Figure that out, and I'll give you a million bucks. My mom says people like that are just so unhappy they take their misery out on other people. I think that's BS. That girl is just messed up. At least school will be out in two weeks, and we'll have eleven whole weeks without seeing her face. Who knows, maybe she'll be run over by a bus by then."

Zoey choked out a giggle, wiping at her eyes one last time. "I'll settle for her just moving away."

Jace grinned. "That works, too." He carefully examined her face as the first bell rang to let them know it was time to head to fourth period. "You cool?"

She took a deep breath, nodded, and stood. "Yeah, I'm cool."

As she was about to wave goodbye and head for Bio, her screen buzzed in her pocket. She frowned and pulled it out. During class time, screens technically shouldn't be able to receive calls or messages except from within the school intranet. That did not, however, include anyone in the office, and apparently this was close enough that she still had reception. She filed that away for future reference and glanced at the screen. It showed one missed call and a voice mail.

Jace looked surprised. "Your dad?" He knew she wasn't allowed to give out her number without permission, so the only people who had it were family members and Jace himself.

She shook her head. "Unknown number." She lifted the screen to her ear, pulling up her voicemail app. She listened, her face becoming progressively more shocked. When the message was over, she played it again.

Jace watched, ignoring the bell that told them they were now late for class. "What's wrong, Zoe?"

Zoey looked at him, hazel eyes huge. A grin spread over her face. "It was a job offer. From the local headquarters of Veritas Corp. They offered me a summer internship."

Jace's mouth hung open. "Holy crap, Zoe! That's amazing! Why didn't you tell me you applied there? Do they have any other openings?"

She shook her head, puzzlement beginning to bleed through her excitement. "That's just it, Jace. I didn't apply. I haven't applied *anywhere*."

🌱 🌱 🌱

That night, Zoey sat tensely watching her dad's face as he listened to the voicemail play from the speaker on her screen.

"Miss Zoey Williams. Thank you for your application for a summer internship at Veritas Corp. Thanks to your excellent resume and the recommendation of Ms. Andrews, we would like to offer you an intern position in our Design Department, working with Ms. Andrews. If you are interested in this position, please let us know as soon as possible. As I am sure you're aware, these positions are highly sought after, and if we have not heard back from you within 48 hours, the position will be offered to the next candidate. You can contact me at-"

Her dad's finger tapped the button to hang up, and he looked at Zoey. "Well, this explains the rather cryptic e-mail I got today. It was from a Ms. Bridget Andrews at Veritas Corp, and the NDA we agreed to was attached. It also mentioned helping with your job 'problem', and asked if it was okay if she mentioned you were looking for a position to a friend. 'Fay'," he applied ironic finger quotes to the name, "must have remembered that you said you'd get a job this summer. She's probably worried that a real job will interfere with the time you have to spend on the quest. And I suppose you think I should let you take the job." He fixed her with stern brown eyes.

Zoey's fists clenched in her lap, and it was all she could do not to yell an affirmative. Instead, she cleared her throat and started on the list of excellent reasons for accepting that she'd come up with during the last five hours. She'd even forced herself to wait to tell her dad about the offer until after dinner, since she'd once read that judges sentenced fewer prisoners to death after lunch than before.

"Well, Dad, you *did* say that I need a job. You didn't specify what kind of job, and this would be working in game development, which is *actually* the field I want to go into after college. It'll look amazing on my college application, and when will I get another chance like this? I can apply for jobs and do something in retail next summer! I mean, I still have three more years to be miserable all summer working for minimum wage, right? I've heard of these internships on the boards, too, and it sounds like they actually involve a lot of hard work, so it's not like it'll be *fun*-" She cut off the spill of words when her dad raised his hand.

A little smile twitched the corner of his mouth, and she felt herself relax a little. He wouldn't be smiling if he was really going to make her get a job bagging groceries. Right? *Right?*

He sighed and rubbed a hand over his hair. "Okay, kid. Yeah. This is a pretty great opportunity, and I'm not going to take it away from you just for the principle of the thing." He frowned seriously. "I *do* expect you to get a basic part-time job next summer where you can really suffer properly, though."

She squealed and threw her arms around him, bouncing in glee. "Thank you, Dad! Thank you, thank you, thank you! I'll call them back tomorrow on lunch. Oh my *gosh*, Jace is going to *puke* when he hears…"

That warning hand went up again. "Hold on, Zoe. You're going to have to ask them exactly what your responsibilities will be, and how many hours you'll be expected to work. When do you start? What are you expected to accomplish while you're there? What kind of training are you going to get? Is it even a paid internship? Where are you going to work? You're assuming it'll be at the big office building downtown, but Veritas Corp is huge, and they have smaller offices all over the place. How are you going to get to and from work? What's the dress code, and do you have clothes that will work, or are you going to have to *borrow* money from your dear old dad to upgrade your wardrobe?"

"Oh, man, daaaaad! Why do you have to make everything so complicated?"

Her father smiled wryly. "Life is complicated, Zoe. You know that better than a lot of kids your age, but there are some aspects you haven't had to deal with yet. This is one of them. You get answers to those questions, and then make your decision. You're the one who has to deal with the consequences, so get all the information before you decide. You don't get to quit just because it's hard, right? No excuses."

"Yeah, okay." She bit her lip. "Can I tell Jace now, though?"

Her dad ruffled her curls. "Yeah, kiddo, you can tell Jace."

She grinned, gave him a quick hug, and bounced up the stairs.

Chapter Twelve

Aspen

The next morning, Motte's Zombie had taken the place of Rouge's, at least in that it was hard at work at dawn. The older man had been able to set his Zombie to work on pulling stumps, breaking up boulders, bringing good-sized rocks back to be used, and even gathering herbs from the wooded area near the river. The sound of a pickaxe woke Aspen far earlier than he wanted, but that seemed to be the way of it when Travelers were around.

Sarave and Juniper were safely ensconced in the cellar, curled up together in warm furs. Motte had balked at this at first, claiming that newborns in his world should never be covered in loose blankets. Aspen and Sarave both had assured him that this was safe and common practice in Quarternell, and he had finally given in, though not without a few dubious glances at the fur pile.

Upon waking, Aspen cooked some of their few remaining eggs, mushrooms, and meat, and took a plate down to the goblins. Sarave ate voraciously, fed the baby, and then fell quickly back to sleep. Fortunately, the sounds of banging from above were nearly inaudible through the ceiling.

Aspen finished his own breakfast at a remarkably-rapid pace, then rinsed the dishes and set them in a bucket to be taken down to the river for washing. He wondered if William could drill down to create a well. This was definitely something worth asking about when they next saw the vampire.

He snorted at himself. Already he was making plans which depended on an undead. He dearly hoped that he wouldn't regret the decision he had made the night before.

Shaking his head, he stood up. "Well, nothing to do but wait and see. For now, though, I'd best see what I can do about earning my title of 'Farmer'. So far, I'm more of a field hand."

<It's about time.> Sumi's exasperated voice echoed in his mind, and she dropped down from her favorite place in the shadows of the sod roof. <I thought you were going to pretend you had nothing to do but play with Travelers and goblins forever.>

Aspen shrugged. "It's more fun than the alternative, I suppose."

<If you don't want to farm, why did you choose farming out of all the options we gave you?> Sumi's irritation was increasingly clear as the spider followed Aspen out into the bright morning sunlight and the chilly morning air.

Aspen's feet turned almost of their own accord toward the field they'd laid out what seemed months ago. "You know why, old friend. Birdie would have loved being here. Well, except for the fact that there aren't any other people. There weren't *supposed* to be any other people, anyway. Besides, it's not like we had anywhere else to go where no one would be trying to kill us. At least up here when something tries to kill us, it's nothing personal."

Sumi bobbed in her version of a laugh. <True enough. You have always had quite a talent for engendering strong emotions in others. It is rather nice to deal with such relatively simple and clear situations. I certainly don't miss all the politics involved in being a war necromancer.>

The tall man stopped as they reached the broad field, green leaves now shining brightly in long rows. Aspen stared. "Are those flowers?"

<They are. The bees have been very happy the last day or so.>

"Well." Aspen cast his eyes upward and lightly pressed a hand to the Goddess' Seed, still attached to his chest, though he was so used to it now that he often forgot it was there. "Thank you, Gina. I'm not sure what you're up to, but I'm certainly glad of it." *For once,* he thought, but kept that part to himself.

He turned toward Sumi. "Ah, do you, by any chance, remember which rows were which plants? I thought I would be able to tell by the way they looked, but…" He waved a hand toward the array of leaves, dark to light green, broad to narrow, lobed and smooth. "I have no idea."

Sumi laughed at him again. <Come with me.>

🐝 🐝 🐝

By the time lunchtime rolled around, they had labeled all the rows, fixed a few leaks in his hasty irrigation system, and pulled weeds. It was a good thing Sumi had been watching the field every day, because Aspen would have been hard pressed to guess which plants were weeds and which were vegetables, except that the weeds were universally small and withered.

As he went, Aspen made sure to murmur prayers to Gina for the continued growth of the field. He wasn't sure what the goddess had done to him, exactly, and whether the spell that made the crops grow was his or hers, so he tried to cover all the possibilities.

Aspen and Sumi returned to the house, to discover that Sarave was already up and preparing the meal. Her babe, already visibly larger, and examining her surroundings with inquisitive eyes, was strapped to the small goblin woman's back with the cloth Motte had given her the day before.

Sarave smiled as they entered, and waved a wooden spoon at them. "Sit. I made dish given to goblin mothers. Motte brought herbs, and some very healthy. I be glad when Juniper walk in one week. She heavy now than inside."

From the door, Motte's deep voice exclaimed, "A *week?*"

Aspen and Sarave looked around, surprised. Rouge had said that time traveled twice as quickly in their world as it did in her own, so Aspen hadn't expected to see either of the Travelers until that evening at the earliest.

Sarave was the first to recover from her startlement, and she nodded. "Probably? I no see babe not spawned before, but goblin infant take seven days to walk. Juniper probably same." She grimaced slightly, and kissed the top of Juniper's soft head. "I hope."

Motte closed his mouth. "I knew I'd never seen a pregnant N… Uh, Native, before. I take it this is fairly uncommon?"

Aspen nodded, this time. "Most children simply spawn, and while they are usually infants at the time, they are sometimes older. When a woman becomes gravid, it's because the babe is part of some god's greater plan. I'm hoping Juniper is Gina's gift, but we'll see as the child grows."

The larger man shook his head and entered the house, ducking his head under the lintel and making his way over to sit at the table. "I know a lot of women who would love your world. In mine, they carry every baby for nine months, then it takes around a year before it starts to walk, and another year before it begins saying more than a few words. At around five years, we send them to school, if we can, and after eighteen years or so, they move out."

It was Aspen and Sarave's turns to stare with their mouths agape.

"Nine months?" Sarave's voice was choked. "I thought one month was long time! Your females strong!"

Motte laughed and shrugged. "Well, that's not wrong, but while some women love it, others hate it. I think they're all ready to be done by the time it's over, though. Rouge's mother hated every moment of being pregnant. That's why we only had one kid." He glanced at the lump of furs that was his daughter and smiled slightly. "I would have had at least one more, if not two. Children should have siblings."

Aspen shook his head. "How old is Rouge, then?"

"Fourteen. You're only allowed to play- Ah, that is, become a Traveler, after you turn fourteen, and then only if a parent or guardian is with you. This world, how real it is, it can be scary for kids." The big man's expression was serious and a little concerned as he watched his daughter.

Aspen's chuckle was bitter. "Yes. This world is hard on children. I'm glad ours grow faster than yours. It sounds like it's similar after they reach the age of five, but little Juniper will be walking in a week, talking a month after that, and she'll be nearly ready to begin learning by spring." He glanced at Sarave. "Do you know how to read and write?"

The goblin woman shook her head, expression somber. "Jeremy teach me words. A little read, too. He die before- "

Aspen cleared his throat, wishing he knew how to comfort the small woman. Given how quickly she was learning, he wondered how long she and her human husband had actually been together. Sarave was quick-witted, and It seemed that if she'd had more than a few weeks to learn, she would have been fairly fluent.

"Would you like me to teach Juniper, when she's ready? And you as well?" Aspen asked, carefully. Some people had no interest in reading, and he didn't want to force her into anything.

Sarave's face lit up. "I love love! I wish to learn more, but *goblin'te* only use symbol for count and mark tunnels. All else is lots many song."

Aspen nodded, and opened his mouth to say that he would love to hear some of her songs someday, but thankfully he was interrupted before he could embarrass himself or her when a small goat hurtled through the door. It was Kayti, her black-streaked fur nearly covering her eyes as she used her teeth to pull at Aspen's pant leg. Right behind her came her sister, who latched onto the other side and began to pull with equal insistence. Both little goats were making the odd little bleat-whinnys that they had settled into over the last few days. They were also visibly larger, though they still stood no taller than Aspen's knee.

Aspen and Motte both stood quickly. Sumi spoke up from where she had been eating her own lunch out of sight in the shadows above. <I'll stay here

with Sarave and Silus. Go see what they need. They went to the river with Khor to eat the sweet grass there. The old goat is no doubt causing trouble again.>

Aspen nodded, and the two men ran.

ಀ ಀ ಀ

At the river, they were greeted with an astonishing sight. Khor was, indeed, in trouble, but it seemed not to be his fault this time. The huge goat was surrounded by irate ducks. The huge mother Greater Duck dwarfed her offspring, who were already several times larger than a normal Lesser Duck. The mother and two ducklings were quacking angrily, while Khor tried desperately not to step on a third duckling, smaller than the others, which was attacking his hooves with its blunt yellow beak.

It looked, to Aspen's amusement, rather as if the goat was trying to dance with the littlest duck, while the family of waterfowl urged them on. At that moment, Kayti and Kayli rushed into the fray, attempting to shove the duckling away with their furry heads, and soon it was impossible to say where one creature ended and another began.

Aspen put his fingers in his mouth and blew a piercing whistle. Instantly, every head turned to look at him. Khor's expression was beleaguered. <Make them stop!> the Greater Goat begged.

It was all Aspen could do to keep the amusement from his tone. "What's going on here?"

The mother duck pointed one wing at Khor and the other at her littlest duckling. Then she opened her beak and explained with a resounding "Quaaaaack! Quack quack quackquackquack!"

Aspen nodded as if he understood. "Khor, did you step on the duckling?"

<No! I was just eating lunch with the little ones when these birdbrains appeared out of nowhere! She shoved the little beast under my feet, and just started to leave! Of course I shoved it back at her, and then this began.> The goat's usually mildly grumpy voice had an edge of hysteria.

Motte was frowning, axe in hand. "What's going on? Are the ducks attacking? Why isn't he defending himself?"

Aspen reached over and gently pressed on the other man's forearm, and Motte lowered his weapon reluctantly. "We helped this duck a while back. We destroyed an old dam upstream, and the water washed her nest away. We helped her retrieve some of her eggs. We've been wary but friendly neighbors ever since. I don't know what's going on now, though."

"What?" Motte was aghast. "You destroyed a beaver dam? Don't you know how important those are to the local ecology? They're incredibly helpful in managing water systems. You were lucky to have one nearby!"

Aspen waved his hands defensively. "The dam was abandoned. It had gathered a lot of debris, probably from years of spring floods, and it definitely wasn't working as intended any more. Plus, a family of muskrats had moved in. They weren't bothersome yet, but with such a good environment, it wouldn't be long before one evolved into a Greater beast and became truly dangerous."

Aspen shook his head. "I don't think your muskrats and our muskrats are the same. Do yours-"

Khor's acidic voice interrupted the conversation. <If you wouldn't mind, Aspen, I could use some assistance here. *Now*.>

Aspen turned back to his old friend and barely choked back a laugh. The goat was covered in young creatures. The two larger ducklings were sitting on his horns, pecking at the fur on his ears. The littlest duckling was still going after the fur around his ankles, and Kayti and Kayli, having lost interest in the battle, were chasing each other in and around his legs. Khor looked as if he would just as soon step on them all and be done with it.

The mother duck, apparently coming to a similar conclusion as to the goat's feelings on the matter, quacked loudly at her offspring. All three stopped what they were doing, and the two on the goat's horns flew down somewhat shamefacedly, if a duck could be so. The little duckling continued attacking for a moment before his mother gave a more insistent quack, and he finally stopped, though he was clearly disgruntled.

As the duckling waddled away from Khor, his body became more clearly visible to Aspen, and the man suddenly had an inkling what this was all about. One of the duckling's wings was smaller than the other, and beneath his feathers the shape was somewhat twisted. This, then, was probably the duckling whose shell had been damaged.

Aspen looked up toward the mother duck, who was looking at her offspring and back up to the sky. She fluffed her feathers slightly, and hopped in place. "He can't fly, can he?" Aspen asked the Greater Duck softly.

She tilted her head and quacked sadly. Leaning down, she put her beak under the little one's fluffy bottom and pushed him away. He quacked, suddenly looking lost.

"Do you want us to take care of him for you? You're already late flying south. If he can't fly, then you'll have to stay or leave him behind." Aspen's voice was kind.

The mother duck pushed her duckling harder, so he tumbled beak over rump, and she began running and flapping her great wings. Her two larger offspring followed swiftly, and soon all three were in the air, flying south without another look back at the duckling they'd left behind.

The duckling, who weighed no more than twelve or fifteen pounds, and was much smaller than the rest of his family, settled on the ground suddenly. He tucked his head beneath his good wing, and disconsolate quacking could be heard from within his feathers.

Aspen approached slowly. "Motte? Do you have some kind of creature feed in your storage?"

The other man, now weaponless, moved quietly behind Aspen. He passed an ear of corn into Aspen's hand. It was still warm, and Aspen shook his head again at the convenience of the Traveler's stockpiles.

Aspen knelt down in the grass next to the young Lesser Duck. He placed the corn on the ground by the animal, and waited. Kayti and Kayli, nostrils flaring, began to edge toward the treat. The duckling, as if he could see them, darted his neck out and snatched up the cob, taking it away a few steps so he could gobble the soft, sweet kernels. Motte pulled a few more perfectly cooked ears out of wherever they came from and gave them to the little goats, who began to eat them enthusiastically.

Aspen reached out and held out his hand. He'd never spent much time around birds, so he wasn't really sure what to do. Did you let them sniff you, like a puppy? The duckling pecked at his finger, pinching it hard enough to hurt.

"Ouch! All right, little fellow. I understand. It's just that your mother left you with us, and I don't think I want to know what she'll do if she comes back next spring and you're not here. Won't you come back with us? We have a nice barn going up that you can live in."

The duckling turned a beady black eye on Aspen, then twisted his head to examine the others suspiciously as he finished the last bit of his corn. Seemingly making up his mind, he stood, then jumped up onto Aspen's bent knee, leapt to his shoulder, his head, and then launched himself toward Khor, who had come closer to investigate his erstwhile attacker. With a few pitiful flaps of his wings, and using his beak to pull himself into Khor's long fur, the duckling found himself atop the Greater Goat. He raced up and settled in the shaggy wool between his horns. "Quack," he said, firmly.

Khor sighed. <I think I'll call him Nuisance.>

This time, Aspen did laugh.

Chapter Thirteen

Rouge

When Zoey got home from school the day after receiving the internship offer, she was nearly ready to explode. She had called Veritas Corp back, gotten all the random factoids her dad wanted, and accepted the job without hesitation. She told Jace, who just wanted her to 'put in a good word' for him, even though she could tell he was about to burst from envy. She sent her dad a message letting him know. Then she had to wait.

Wait until classes were over. Wait for the bus ride home. Wait through dinner, homework, and School Talk. Finally, she had had enough.

"Dad! You said I could play *Veritas* today. Right? Can I go now?" She was all but bouncing in her chair, and her dad grinned.

"I wondered how long I could drag this out before you exploded. Yeah, kiddo, you can go." She was out of her seat and racing for the stairs before he could finish speaking, so he had to yell after her. "Make sure to read the game announcements when you log in!" Pfft. As if. She had better things to do than read about how the devs changed the spawn rate of Rock Trolls or nerfed [Fireball].

Zoey was out of her clothes and suited up in record time, and she whacked her head on the pod door as she climbed in. "Oww!" she groaned, rubbing her ear. Staring up, she blinked her watering eyes. "Fine, I'll slow down!" She finished getting ready more carefully, laid down, tugged her helmet down over her face, and said, "Emily, start *Veritas*."

She fell.

🍎 🍎 🍎

Rouge 'woke' nestled in a pile of furs in the corner of the main room of the house. She immediately noticed that some things were different. One window had been enlarged to a door leading off to a room that hadn't been there before. There were now real doors in the house, and the old, rotted frames of the windows and doors had been repaired or replaced. She shook her head, wondering what else her dad hadn't told her.

Oh! The announcements! She sighed and pulled them up. The very first one jumped out at her.

> **Hear ye, hear ye! Thanks to the unprecedented period of peace between the races of *Veritas*, a new time of fecundity has arrived! NPCs will now be able to get pregnant, though their pregnancies will be shorter and the children will grow faster than those of Travelers.**
>
> **HALF-BREEDS are now available as both NPCs and playable races. Half-elves have long been known, due to that long-lived but infertile race's desperation for offspring. However, all known sapient races will now be able to reproduce with humans. Be aware, however, that half-breeds are deemed undesirable by any parent race except humans and elves. If you choose to create a new character and play as a half-breed, you will automatically be assigned a Relationship with any member of your non-human parent race in a range from Neutral to Loathing.**

NPCs may rarely attempt to kill you on sight. Humans will be slightly more accepting, ranging from Interested to Distaste.

"Whoa," she murmured. When she had created her character, she didn't want to be a human like her dad, because while they were decent all-round characters, they weren't particularly good at anything. Plus, she was already a human, and she wanted to try something else, and the only other option was Dwarf, and she had zero interest in being even *shorter*.

At first, she thought she'd be one of the three elven races, because elves were cool. Unfortunately, each of them had their own drawbacks. They all spawned in their own kingdoms, to start. The Dark elves were the most interesting, but they lived underground, and were pretty much universally hated by everyone else, so that was out. She wanted to play with her dad and Jace, and it would take ages to finish the tutorial and figure out how to even get to the human country of Quarternell.

Next, she'd started looking at half-elves. You couldn't be half Dark elf, because they saw everyone except other elves as animals, not people. Half High elf was a super common choice, but the darkest skin tone you could get was a light tan, since they were supposed to be the total opposite of the charcoal-skinned Dark elves. Half Wood elf had some perks when they were actually in the trees, but took a pretty significant agility debuff when they went into populated areas.

Veritas provided a Barbie doll-sized version of the potential avatars during character creation. She had been playing with the adorable little manikins when she (totally accidentally) dragged the little Dark elf on top of the mini Wood elf, and realized that she could actually combine two types of *elves*, not just elf and human. Thus, Rouge was born.

Widening the racial options was a real game changer. Literally. When *Veritas* launched, you could only be a human, thanks to the initial story of having to defend humanity from the oncoming undead horde. Once the war ended, a player could choose to be human, dwarf, or any of the elves. Elves were physically weaker, but agile and magically adept, so if you wanted to be a crafter or mage, that was the way you went. Dwarves went the other way, with crazy endurance and strength, but not much magic. Humans, of course, were squarely in the middle.

Now, the developers were opening up way more races. Even with the reduced Relationship for half-breeds, if a player chose to spawn in Quarternell, it wouldn't matter too much. Rouge herself had proved that, because she'd started out with a low negative Reputation with practically everybody, thanks to being half Dark elf, and she'd gotten into all those weird quests because they raised her Relationship out of the sewer. *And* it definitely said all known sapient races! Did that mean Dark elves were included now, too?

Plus, NPCs could get pregnant! That explained why she'd never seen one before Sarave! The goblin must have been the very first one, tied to the Secret Quest that was supposed to change the world. These, then, were the first changes, and Rouge was there to see it happen!

She heard a baby start crying, and her head jerked up, eyes focusing on her surroundings again. She leapt to her feet, running toward the sound. "Oh my gosh! Dad! I missed it!?"

She stumbled out into the sunlight, stopping as she saw Sarave standing there, a baby strapped to her thin body, hanging clean clothes from a line made of Sumi's silk. Sarave and the baby both turned to look at Rouge, and she squeaked in excitement. The baby was *so* cute!

"Oh my gosh, Sarave! You had the baby! *When* did you have the baby? Can I hold it? Is it a boy or a girl? Did you name it? It's adorable!" It was. Its huge eyes were a hazy blue-green-yellow, and a dandelion puff of soft brown curls framed its face. Small, slightly pointed ears poked out, and its little bow-shaped mouth burbled and smiled as it reached out toward the elven girl.

Sarave was clearly surprised, but recovered quickly, smiling tiredly as she began to unwrap the baby. The child was *huge* for a newborn, especially one from such a diminutive race. The goblin spoke carefully, putting together full sentences for the first time since Rouge met her. "Her name is Juniper. She was born two days ago. You may hold her, but you must sit. She is begin to crawl, and can be full of wiggles."

Rouge blinked, remembering that 'children would grow faster than those of Travelers'. That was certainly true, if this two-day-old baby was trying to crawl! She sat, then held out her arms, accepting the warm weight of the small child. She nuzzled her cheek into the downy hair, and smiled as she felt little fingers latch onto her ear. The smile dropped away a moment later, as the pudgy digits pulled surprisingly hard. "Ouch!" She clapped her hand to the tender appendage. Juniper giggled and reached for it again.

Rouge held the baby out at arm's length and made a face at her. "Phew. It's a good thing you're cute. You don't smell as bad as I expected, either."

Sarave looked somewhat insulted, and reached out as if she would take the child back, but Rouge snuggled Juniper close again and smiled apologetically. Sarave softened slightly, but asked, "Why would the baby smell bad?"

"I dunno." Rouge sat the little goblin down in her lap and tickled her, laughing at the burbling giggles the baby produced. "Because of the diapers, I guess."

Sarave cocked her head to one side. "What are 'diapers'?"

"You know, what babies poop in." The elf girl stuck her thumbs in her ears and waggled her fingers at Juniper, who suddenly looked less certain of this new person in her life.

"What is 'poop'?" Sarave asked, returning to her laundry, though she kept a close eye on her child.

"Poop is… You know, feces. Like what animals. You eat, the food goes through, and the poop comes out. I know poop is a thing. My horse once- " Rouge froze, fingers in mid-tickle. "Holy cow, you guys don't poop, do you? I mean, people. *People* don't poop in this world." She had a sudden realization that she had never seen a bathroom in Veritas, and never seen or heard an NPC discuss their own waste. Maybe it was part of the whole thing where no one was ever really naked. The game automatically covered 'private parts' with basic underwear. Hard to do if you had to go to the bathroom a couple times a day.

Sarave was shaking her head even as her deft fingers continued to move. "I think I know this word. Animals poop. Trackers follow it, and it is used to create-" She pointed to a flower nearby and mimed it getting larger. "Thing that make plants grow. Only animals do this."

"That is just... weird. I mean, it makes sense, because poop is *gross*, but it's still weird." Rouge continued to tickle the chubby little baby belly in front of her, grinning at the chortles thus produced.

A huge hoof appeared suddenly in her peripheral vision, and she looked up. And up. That goat was just ridiculously large. "Um, Khor? What happened to your beard thingy? And why is there a duck on your head?" She suppressed a giggle, because really the giant ruminant kind of made her nervous. He just looked crabby all the time.

The goat huffed, tossing his head in annoyance. The brown and tan duck flapped his iridescent green wings slightly, and Rouge squinted at the bird more closely. There was something wrong with one of them, wasn't there? The fowl used his beak to hang on like a rodeo cowboy on a bucking bronco. She nearly chewed off her lip, choking back her laughter, even as she wiped away the green slime that got on her when Khor snorted.

"Oh! Rouge! You're back!" It was Aspen, looking healthier than when she'd seen him last. His chest and face had definitely filled out, and his nose didn't look *so* big in comparison to the rest of his face anymore. He was almost good-looking for a guy even more ancient than her dad.

She smiled up at him and waved, keeping Juniper snuggled against her with the other arm, even as the baby wiggled in an attempt to roll away. "Hey, Aspen! Did you miss me? Sorry I left like that. It looks like a lot happened while I was gone!"

Juniper was beginning to whimper, waving her arms in the air and looking around. Aspen reached down and took the baby, holding her with a practiced ease that said he'd done this before. He bounced on his toes slightly, and the baby quieted. Sarave smiled, her yellow eyes warm as she gazed at the pair. Aspen smiled down at the baby, missing the goblin's expression entirely. "Oh, a few things. Did your father tell you about William?"

Rouge shook her head as she got to her feet and dusted off her butt. "He refused to tell me *anything*. He said it was part of my punishment. Who's William? Did someone else turn up, or is that the duck's name?"

Aspen chuckled, handing Juniper back to Sarave. Mother and child snuggled for a moment before the goblin woman began wrapping the baby back up. Aspen watched, and this time it was the goblin who missed the look on his face Aspen forced his attention back to Rouge, and tilted his head toward the bird who was now settled comfortably between Khor's broad horns. "The duck's name is Nuisance. William is a vampire, but he only eats fruits and vegetables."

Rouge gaped. "What? Like, a vegetarian vamp? A... A fructipire? Veggipire? What even is that?"

Aspen shook his head. "Gina only knows. Strange things have been happening ever since we got here, and it seems they plan to continue to do so. In any case, I talked to Motte about what you should do when you returned, and he suggested you help me with the fields."

The girl nearly groaned. Her dad was *still* punishing her. She rolled her eyes and resignedly said, "Okay. How can I help?"

Quest: "Training Montage" available.

Aspen needs help with his field. Assist him in whatever way he needs until the first crops are harvested. Not a single plant should die from lack of care.

Success: +10 Reputation with all members of Aspen's household. A new spell.

Failure: Nothing.

Accept: Yes/No?

Ooo! A new spell! What kind of new spell? Who knew? Who cared! This was awesome! She immediately clicked the Accept button, even as she heard Aspen saying something about hoeing and weeding.

The game wasn't kidding when it said 'training montage'. She just wished she could skip forward the way the old vids always did. But no, she had to suffer through every minute of it. For *two weeks* of game time. As a result of all her hard work, she gained the skills [Hoe], [Dig], [Mulch], and [Fertilize]. That one was gross, because yeah, animals definitely pooped, and there were a lot of them on the farm now. Fortunately, the adults knew to do their business in a small area set aside for that purpose, but the duck and the kids were still little, and they hadn't 100% figured it out yet. Motte, especially, seemed to take far too much joy in making her find these little accidents and clean them up. She was definitely going to bring this up when he tried to tell her next summer that she hadn't suffered enough in her job *this* summer.

The same two weeks that Rouge was doing her Training Montage, Zoey spent one boring real-life week studying for and then having finals. She was limited to one hour of daily play time during test week. Usually, it wouldn't have been any at all, but they still hadn't figured out what she needed to do to move her quest along. For once, the limitation was okay, because honestly, she'd rather study than dig one more trench under the sweltering heat of the late summer sun.

Now, finals complete, and a summer of Extreme Awesomeness ahead of her, Rouge stood in the mid-day sun, leaning on a hoe as she and Aspen critically examined their work. They were refreshing the irrigation troughs after a hard rain the day before, and it was hard, muddy work. All around, plants stood as tall or taller than her, with nearly ripe fruits and vegetables glistening in the light.

Aspen, who looked much healthier than he had a month before, pushed his tattered, sweaty hat off his forehead. The sun glinted off his gold-streaked brown hair, and his skin looked smooth and healthy. She knew he hadn't had time to go adventuring, so how he kept looking like he was gaining levels, she didn't know. Probably some NPC thing they hadn't figured out yet.

"Looks good, kid." Aspen reached over and ruffled her hair the way Motte liked to do. Over the last few weeks of enforced togetherness, they'd come to have a shared camaraderie, especially when they were working.

Rouge wrinkled her nose, but grinned at him. "Your part too, old man."

He grinned back at her, and they stood for a while, admiring the (almost) fruits of their labor.

Out of the corner of her eye, Rouge caught a flicker of movement. She turned her head and saw the two little goats, alone and chasing a butterfly into the stand of fruit trees nearby. They were usually near Khor or under his hooves, so seeing them without the huge ruminant immediately caught her attention. Those trees had been carefully pruned, fertilized, and the area around them cleared, but it was still difficult to tell exactly where the little creatures were going.

She glanced over at Aspen, and saw that he was also watching the kids. She tilted her head toward them in invitation, and he grinned, gently placing his hoe on the soggy ground next to the field. It looked like they were going on an adventure!

Quest: "Going on a Bare Hunt" available.

Those little kids are practically naked without their protector. Find out what they're up to and make sure they're safe.

Success: Information. +5 Reputation with Aspen, Khor, Kayli, and Kayti. +200 Experience Points.

Failure: Variable.

Accept: Yes/No?

Having already decided she was going after them, this was an easy yes. Bonus!

The young goats, who were now closer to adolescents than babies, were bouncing along, oblivious to anything except the brightly-colored insect they trailed. Occasionally, one of them would leap on top of a rock or stump, using the height to jump toward the insect, which always seemed to dance just out of their reach.

Rouge and Aspen followed in a truncated parade, trying hard not to disturb the adorable scene unfolding in front of them. Rouge triggered [Sneak] as soon as they moved into the shadow of the trees, figuring she might as well earn some skill experience while she was at it.

The two little goats frolicked through tall grass and over hillocks. They bounced from rocks, fallen branches, and once, memorably, Kayli bounced from her sister's head, which elicited a braying complaint that nearly made Rouge giggle and break her [Stealth].

At long last, Kayti jumped from a particularly tall rock on top of a small hill, and caught the butterfly in her mouth. Instantly, a deep golden glow suffused her, and she grew visibly larger. Her wool grew silkier and more lustrous, and a small bump on her forehead bulged up, beginning to push the fur of her forelock aside. The soft wool, which had been streaked with deep black, smoothed and lightened, seeming nearly pearlescent.

Rouge stopped in shock. The goat had leveled! Leveled from catching a butterfly! No combat, no death, just an adorable kid catching an insect and then promptly spitting it back out so her sister could catch it too. Which she did. At which point Kayli also glowed and grew. Her fur remained white, but that white was so bright now that it seemed to shine.

The elf girl looked over at Aspen, who was crouching behind a berry bush nearby. He was smiling, but seemed completely unsurprised. This was it! This was the explanation for how he continued to improve his stats. NPCs, humanoid and otherwise, must get quests just like players! *Veritas Online* just kept being more and more awesome.

The two goats nuzzled each other, seeming pleased with their advancement. They began to trot back toward the farmhouse and their favorite Greater Goat. Aspen and Rouge followed quietly, sharing a smile about the entertaining moment in the life of their little friends that they had been privileged to witness.

Then Kayti stopped. Her nostrils, barely visible as shadows in the waterfall of fur, quivered, and her mouth opened so she could sniff the air. She veered sharply to the left, and her sister followed close behind. Rouge frowned slightly, wondering what could have triggered this response in the usually-timid kids.

Creeping after them, she watched as Kayti, then Kayli, began to sniff the ground. They walked in a widening circle until Kayli seemed to catch the scent again and headed down a narrow trail toward some bushes. Kayti was right behind her for a moment, and then the larger sister pushed ahead, head down and pace determined.

They walked quite a distance, eventually passing out of the grove and back into the bright sunlight. Rouge's [Stealth] and [Sneak], which depended on having at least some shadow to blend into, immediately failed, but the goats were too focused to notice her sudden appearance. Rouge and Aspen both continued to hang back and made as little noise as possible.

The kids were absolutely fixated on whatever they were tracking, and Rouge could hear the sounds of the river growing louder. Whatever the goats were after, they were getting worryingly far from the house. If there were any predators nearby, it was likely they'd be living close to water. None of the humans or animals had seen anything, as far as she knew, but even a beast that would be frightened of something human-sized might take a chance on going after two small creatures as small and defenseless as the kids.

Rouge was about ready to hurry forward and gather up the little animals when they stopped near an overhang with a dark area beneath it. Aspen, who was close behind, touched her shoulder softly and murmured, "That's where we fought the snake and rescued the duck eggs. It's not a safe place. We should gather them up and head home."

Rouge nodded and picked up the pace. Too slowly, as it turned out. Kayli, inquisitive as ever, had edged into the darkness of the overhang. Then there was a rustle, a bleat, and the little goat was gone. Kayti instantly charged after her sister, with Aspen and Rouge close on the goat's heels.

As soon as Rouge entered the shadow of the surrounding trees, she triggered [Stealth] again. Her racial [Darkvision] from being half Dark elf kicked in as well, and she could see dainty hooves vanishing down a narrow passage ahead. Aspen swore, staring blindly into the opening.

"I can see them," she whispered. "They went down a passage that's probably too small for you. I'll have to go ahead."

Aspen's face was frustrated, but he nodded decisively. "The hole above the cavern where the snake lived is still there. I'll check and see if I can get in that way. If I can't, I'll come back here and wait for you. Go!"

She huffed affirmatively, then slid into the darkness as quickly as possible, heading after the goats. They were too far ahead for her ten-foot radius of vision, but fortunately the tunnel didn't branch until it came to a deep pit. She peered down into the hole, but it was too deep to see the bottom, and she could hear running water below anyway. If the goats had fallen into the pit, they must have died instantly, because otherwise they would be bleating madly.

Her heart sank until she looked around again. There was a narrow ledge to the right of the pit, and she saw several little hoofprints in the fresh mud. The tiny, agile goats could definitely have passed that way. Swallowing hard, she grasped the bare roots covering the wall beside her, and crept along the rocky ledge. Rouge was glad she had the [Acrobatics] skill to help her at times like this. As she moved, she could see that a narrow crevice split the darkness ahead. She was about to duck into it when she heard a scuffle from the other way, further down the root path, and then the little braying neigh sound that the kids made when they were frustrated or scared.

She passed the crevice, putting one foot in it to give herself a good solid step so that she could nearly throw herself forward into the darkness. She took three running steps, lightly dancing from one root to the next, until she touched down on solid ground, and her hands fell on something wet and slimy.

She shoved the thing away, choking back a disgusted cry. The lump bleated pathetically, and she saw that what she'd touched was a thoroughly muddy goat.

She couldn't tell which of them it was, through the muck, but from the size she thought it was Kayti. Usually, all forms of dirt slid right off the kid's magical wool, but this one was so doused in it that whatever ability repelled filth had been overwhelmed.

Rouge reached out, forcing herself to ignore the muck so she could comfort the shivering little creature, making shushing sounds as quietly as she possibly could. Slowly, the quivering eased, and the goat began to use her nose to push her human friend toward the end of the tunnel. With a final pat, Rouge stepped forward again.

A patch of something lighter in front of her became clearer as she neared. She knelt down, touching another muddy kid, and relief rushed through her. Then she realized that the goat wasn't moving. Only the faintest movement of her ribs showed that she was still alive. Plus, what *was* the sticky stuff covering her lower half?

Only Rouge's recent acquaintance with Sumi allowed her to both recognize the web for what it was and not freeze with horror at what it implied. Instead, hearing a soft, familiar skittering sound above her, she rolled instantly to the side. Looking up, she saw her attacker as it dropped down, fangs bared and glistening. She squinted a little and used [Identify] to see what she was up against. The label above the five-foot monstrosity read: *Crab Spider – Level 25*.

"Darn it! Why is it a spider? I mean, I hate snakes more, but spiders are right up there!" Rouge's Mambele appeared in her hand, and she slashed out. The blade skipped over the creature's hard carapace, barely missing the eight glittering black eyes. The spider hissed and pulled back, throwing out a line of web and attempting to vanish back into the darkness.

Rouge had seen Sumi use that trick, though, and threw her Mambele, slicing through the web before the mob could rise more than a few inches. Using [Return], she summoned the weapon back to her hand, just in time. The arachnid raced forward to attempt another bite now that its withdrawal had been foiled.

Sumi's constant (creepy) presence had inured Rouge to spiders after a lifetime of fearing them. It had also given her a much better understanding of arachnid anatomy. Rouge rolled to the side, then used her momentum to push off from the wall of the tunnel. She vaulted over the bulbous abdomen, thrusting her knife down into the area where the two hardened areas of exoskeleton were joined by a flexible thinner material. The blade sank deep into the spider, releasing viscous fluid and causing the arachnid to rear up, raising its front legs and attempting to scrape its attacker off on the wall of stone and hard-packed earth.

You have dealt 85 points of damage to the *Crab Spider*. The *Crab Spider* is Bleeding.

Rouge clung tenaciously, well aware that she didn't want to be in front of those large, vicious fangs, or at the mercy of the powerful legs. She felt her breath explode out of her as she was slammed against the wall, but she dug in with her blade, slashing it from side to side, attempting to sever the two halves of the creature's body. Notifications flooded her vision as she dealt damage, until she dismissed them with a thought.

The spider was significantly damaged when its wild thrashing managed to catch a root in Rouge's belt and pull her from the beast's back. She found herself dangling from the wall, helpless, as the monster spun, flinging ichor from its wound. The great fangs stabbed down, burying themselves in her thigh. She shrieked, though it was more in disgust than pain. As a minor, her pain settings were automatically set to the minimum of 20%. A new kind of notification rose into her view.

The *Crab Spider* bites you for 37 points. You are Poisoned.

Thrusting out her hand, she summoned her weapon from where it was still buried in the spider's body, tearing the injury wider. The spider staggered, and she stabbed down at its eyes, which were exposed by its position with its fangs in her flesh. With quick movements, hampered by the new tremble in her hands as the poison began to work through her body, she stabbed and cut at the eyes, blinding the beast. It pulled back, fangs yanked from her leg, and reared up, then collapsed over onto its back. The legs flailed in the air once, twice, then curled in and the arachnid lay still.

You have defeated *Crab Spider*.

You have gained one level in [Thrown Weapons].

You have gained one level in [Knife Wielding].

You are now level 26.

You are Poisoned. You have lost 10 points.

Rouge slashed her belt, severing it so she could drop down onto the floor. Her wounded leg collapsed beneath her, and she rolled over onto her back, frustrated and powerless. There was no way around it. She didn't have any items or potions to combat poison, so the debuff would almost certainly kill her. She'd be locked out of the game for two hours, which was more time than she had left in her game session for the day.

You are Poisoned. You have lost 10 points.

Worst of all, Kayli was injured, probably bitten, and there was nothing she could do. The little creature would die, and it was all Rouge's fault! She closed her eyes, waiting for the final notification and auto-logout.

You are Poisoned. You have lost 10 points.

She felt something hard pressing against her leg, right where the spider had bitten her. It seemed to sink into the wound slightly, and a soft silver light filled the dank space. She looked down, and saw Kayti, clean of mud and glowing softly, her head pressed against Rouge's thigh. Beside the first kid stood her sister, wobbly but upright, equally clean and also leaning down to press her forehead into Rouge's body.

You have been healed of Poison by the *Lesser Unicorn*.

You have been healed of Poison by the *Lesser Unicorn*.

Rouge stared down at the two animals she'd thought merely adorable and amusing young goats. *Unicorns*? How had they missed that? All of them? She squinted slightly, pulling up the tags above the animals. Motte and Rouge preferred to treat the game as if it was reality, and the tags were immersion-breaking, so they kept them off by default. Aspen had told them the small animals were goats, and Rouge had simply never bothered to check. Above Kayti it said *Lesser Unicorn – Level 9*. Over Kayli's head floated *Lesser Unicorn – Level 8*.

Rouge laid her head back on the muddy ground and laughed until tears ran down her face.

Chapter Fourteen

Aspen

A spen stood in the entrance to the cave, barely able to keep from trying to force himself through the narrow passage ahead. Not only was he blind, but he was also much broader than he had been during the attack on the serpent. He'd almost been too large to make it down through the hole into the snake's cavern the last time he'd seen it. He was certain neither Rouge nor the kids were there, anyway.

"Damn it!" He beat his fist against the earthen wall, furious and frustrated.

<What happened?> Khor's deep voice was uncharacteristically worried, and Aspen heard the large goat's hooves breaking through the foliage behind him. <I thought the little ones were napping by the house, but when I went to check on them, they were gone. I tracked them here, but smelled you and the elf trailing them as well, so I thought you must have them. Where are they?> By the time he was done, the goat's tone was nearly frantic, and his eyes jumped between Aspen and the dark cave mouth.

Aspen nearly growled. "They're in there. I don't know what happened. It looked like they smelled something, and they tracked it here. Kayli was taken into the cave by *something*, and Rouge followed. That was nearly an hour ago, and I'm too big to fit in there anymore!"

Khor reared back, hooves flashing. He brought them down against the dirt and roots that formed the roof of the tunnel, calling out, <Kayli! Kayti!> over and over.

Aspen grabbed at the long fur on Khor's side. "I *know*, Khor, but we can't help them if you bring the cave down around their ears! We need Sumi and Silus. They can get in there and help, or at least tell us," he swallowed hard, "what happened."

Khor danced in place, eyes white-rimmed and wild, but at least he stopped beating at the opening. <You don't understand. Gina entrusted them to us. We have to->

A small, exhausted voice called out from deep in the tunnel, cutting the goat off mid-rant. "Has he stopped now? We'd like to come out, but we can't if he's going on like that. Kayli and I are hurt, and I don't think we're up to dodging falling rocks at the moment."

Aspen shouted in relief. "Yes! Yes, he's stopped! Come out, Rouge!"

The young girl limped out, blinking in the sunlight. In her arms was a sleeping kid, gleaming a white so pure he had to squint against the glare. Aspen took the little goat quickly, gently running his hands over her to check for injuries. There were two raised round marks on her shoulder that could be wounds, but they were healed and pink beneath the silky fur.

When he brushed the fur away from her face to check her eyes, he felt a small protrusion in the center of her forehead that he was certain hadn't been there before. Was something tangled in her fur? Had she cracked her skull? He gently moved aside the fur, and found something like a tiny, swirled lump of bone there. It didn't look red or swollen like a wound, though.

He looked up, confused, and saw Rouge grinning at him through the mud caked all over her face. She was clearly tired, but also very much enjoying his reaction. "Yeah," she said, "there was a big nasty spider in there. It bit Kayli and me. I killed it, but we were poisoned. Kayti healed Kayli, and then they both healed me. Saved my life, because that debuff was going to kill me, no doubt."

Aspen's mind whirled. Healed her? How in Gina's name had they done that? Unless…

He cast his mind back to when he first met the kids. He remembered how they seemed able to sense the magic in the Goddess' Seed he wore. How vague the Definitely Goats quest had been, and how snarky the quests had been in general since Gina decided to take a personal interest in him. How very odd Khor's reaction to the little creatures had been.

He looked up at the Greater Goat, who was worriedly checking Kayti over in much the same way Aspen had checked Kayli. "Khor," Aspen said, his tone carefully neutral. "Are these goats actually unicorns?"

Rouge burst out laughing, and Khor looked up. <Took you long enough,> the overgrown ruminant replied derisively.

🐐 🐐 🐐

Several hours later, Aspen stood looking over the main field. Rouge and Motte had logged out, and their Zombies were currently resting in the beds they'd made to go in the new room off the house. Khor, complete with Nuisance hat, was back at the house with Kayli and Kayti, who really were resting after their frightening ordeal. Sumi and Sarave were making dinner and caring for all the young creatures in the house, including a half-goblin, a small bat, and two now-adolescent unicorns.

He shook his head. He couldn't believe he'd been so blind. He'd known the 'goats' weren't just normal creatures simply from the way they stayed so clean, but honestly he'd thought they were just a wool-bearing species that Gina might have sent his way as a little apology for putting him through hell at Sumi's pedipalps during the beginning of the Goddess' Boon quest.

He should have known better.

Aspen looked out over the field, and thought about everything that had happened since they'd left – fled really – the capital. He'd truly thought the only thing left for him was a quiet death. He'd join his Birdie in the Chaos Pool, and his friends would be left feeling that they had tried everything to save him, so they didn't suffer through the self-loathing that filled him for so long.

That self-loathing was fading, though, somehow. How it was that he had to leave a city of tens of thousands for a land where no one should be in order to find a new family, he didn't know. He closed his eyes and remembered those he had lost. The first had been Orion, Sumi's brother, who had perished years ago in a battle that didn't change anything except to those who died or left loved ones behind. Miya, Silus' mother, who had been his scout and friend for years until she had Silus and asked if she could retire. He had thought she, at least, was safe, but she had insisted upon going out one more time to save him, and hadn't come home.

Birdie. His precious Lark. The only light in what had become a life filled with death and loss. She had been a priestess of Gina, a healer, and the only reason he had survived what Akuji had done to him. She had refused to give up when everyone else had declared him lost, and given her own life so that he could live. It was a sacrifice for he could never atone.

And yet. Somehow he no longer felt that he needed to die for his failures. His new family, his new life, brought him a peace he never would have believed he could achieve on this side of the Chaos Pool. Sumi, with her sharp mind and generous soul, kept him grounded. Khor, with his arrogance and utter loyalty, kept Aspen going even when he most wished to give up, if only so he could prove the annoying goat wrong once again. Silus, who was always ready for snuggles and jokes, reminded Aspen what it was to give and receive unwavering love.

Even Sarave, though he knew she might well leave as soon as she could safely do so, was a reason to live, and a reason to hate himself a little less. She and Juniper, who was already showing herself to be a happy and mischievous child, wouldn't even be alive if he hadn't been there to save them. The goblin woman and her energetic child were already helping to fill a space in his heart he had believed would be empty for whatever remained of his life.

His mouth quirked as he thought of Rouge and Motte Bailey. Rouge was too free-spirited to truly remind him of Lark, but the two had one thing in common. While others paid lip service to their own ideals, Lark and Rouge were both more than willing to do whatever it took to follow through. Rouge had described to him some of the quests she had done in Bright, thinking she was just telling him amusing stories, but he could see how much she cared for the residents of this world. Cared in a way that most Travelers and even his own people didn't.

Motte was harder to figure out. Clearly, Rouge was his first priority, but the way he had stood up for William… Aspen thought that Motte was more of an idealist than he would like to admit, and he respected the other man for the strength to keep believing in something better even while the world tried to break him of such romantic dreams.

Finally… Aspen drew in a deep breath, practically hearing his ribcage creak as it expanded. His eyes closed, and he sank into his other senses. He heard the flick of wings, the crunch of dry leaves as a small animal passed through the orchard nearby. He felt the brush of the wind, and the chill of a crisp evening. The scent of fresh turned earth, green grass, pine resin from recently cut trees, and the slight musk of decaying leaves all mingled together in his nostrils.

He opened his eyes again, and looked out over the field of growing things. Plants hung heavy with vegetables. Broad spinach leaves, far larger than they had any right to be. Beautiful feathery carrot leaves, growing up higher than his knees. Vines loaded with so many pea-pods they had to be held up with solid log trellises, not just propped up with sticks. Cabbages the size of Khor's head, and broccoli florets that could serve as bouquets in a royal wedding.

This food would keep his family and friends strong and healthy all winter. With the Travelers here, he wouldn't even have to worry about storage. They could keep everything fresh in their inventories until it was needed. They had even been able to salvage quite a few apples and persimmons from the orchard. William definitely wouldn't need to worry about running out of fruits and vegetables this year, and Aspen had plans for the old vamp's tunnels that would make sure they never needed to worry about running out of space again, even if half the city of Bright descended on them.

Aspen smiled and pulled his hat from his head. Pressing it against his chest, he bowed his head. *Thank you, Gina. I'm glad I'm a farmer. I'll make you proud, I swear.* Then he opened his eyes, reached out his hand, and plucked a single pea-pod from the vine.

ẽ ẽ ẽ

"It's about time!" Gina exclaimed, and he blinked as he realized that she had once again swept him into her magical garden. "I thought you'd never harvest anything! The fruit didn't count, since you didn't plant it, and Virac wouldn't let me talk to you until you picked something you grew yourself, and it took you forever!"

Soft arms circled his chest, and he looked down to see that the beautiful Goddess was hugging him as tightly as she had the first time she'd summoned him.

He coughed uncomfortably. "I'm sorry, Your Goddessliness. A lot has been happening, and I wanted to wait until I was alone."

She stepped back and looked at him, her eyes swirling with annoyance. "Gee-Nah! That's what you call me in your prayers. Why can't you say it to my face?"

Aspen looked down. "It just doesn't seem right to call you by your name when you're standing right there." He twisted his hat in his hands awkwardly.

"Get over it!" She bopped him lightly on his head, though she had to stand on her tip-toes to do so.

He chuckled, and the goddess grinned at him cheekily, eyes whirling green and violet. "I'll do my best, Gina. Ah," he rubbed his nape, "thank you for everything you've done for me... for us. But, do you mind terribly if I ask you a question?"

She tilted her head, sparkling lights drifting from her strawberry blonde curls like celestial glitter. "Of course not. I may not answer, but you can always ask. I'm not like Atae. I won't punish you for *asking*."

He opened his mouth to defend his former goddess, then sighed, remembering one of the few really useful pieces of advice his father had given him: never get in between feuding women. "Well, then." He looked up and met her bottomless gaze. "What in the world did you do to me?"

He held out a hand, palm up, and examined it as if it could give him the answers he sought. "I'm still a mage? And I can heal? I was surprised enough that I could still talk to Sumi, Khor, and Silus, after our soul bond was broken. I thought you must have just set me back to no class, like a child. I was going to ask you to make me a Farmer, once I was sure I was going to stay here, though that was something I certainly never aspired to before. But now," he shook his head, "I don't know what to think."

She grinned and set a delicate finger on her lips in a shushing motion. Then she leaned in, lowering her voice conspiratorially. "I made a new class just for you. You are Gina's Champion, and my Champion is a Druid."

Aspen frowned. Being a Champion sounded very little like being a farmer. "What does a Druid do, exactly?"

Gina grinned. "Well, I don't know that I want to tell you *exactly*, but I can give you a *general* idea. There are some priest-type bits, some animal-related bits, some healing, some magical growth and plant bits, and some things you haven't figured out yet." She made a cute little moue of uncertainty. "I've been stretching it a little to let you do the magical smithing, since it has to do with farming implements, but don't let it wander too far, or I can't be sure how well it will work."

"That's... a lot."

Gina nodded. "That's why you're the only one, so far. A test case, sort of. So don't do anything to make Virac mad at me, all right?" She smiled that teasing smile again, and he got the distinct feeling that this was a case of 'do as I do, not as I say.'

"Of course, Your Divinity." He grinned back and half bowed.

She laughed, startled. "Are you *teasing* me? Aspen! I'm shocked! I wasn't sure you had it in you!"

He scratched his chin. "Did I not do it right? I didn't think I was that boring."

Her smile softened, and she laid a gentle hand on his chest, near where the Goddess' Seed was attached. "Not boring, exactly, just…" She tilted her head. "Maybe a little tightly-wound? You've been through a lot."

He rested his hand over her smaller one and smiled. "Perhaps. But thanks to you, and the gifts you've given all of us, I think things are getting better."

Gina tilted her head and rested her forehead on his chest. Her voice was a little muffled. "I hope so. I hate seeing you so sad. I know even I can't do anything about it, but-"

He patted her shining hair awkwardly. Soft sparkles, like falling stars, drifted from her curls. "Sorry, my Goddess. I'll try to make better choices from here on out."

She poked him in the belly, and he huffed a surprised breath. Then she stepped away and smiled brightly again. "You'd better! Don't make me regret accepting your request!"

He paled a little. "Ah, no. I don't want to do that."

She patted him on the arm. "We understand each other, then. Now." A deep, cozy white chair appeared behind her. It had no legs, but instead floated like a soft cloud in the air. She plunked down into it. "Do you have any more questions for me?"

He frowned, thinking. "Can you help with my quests at all? Lately they've been a little," he looked up, searching for a polite way to say it, "irreverent."

Gina giggled and tucked her legs up underneath her. "Nope. That's part of the Gina experience. Just relax and enjoy it. I know you're used to Atae's boring quests, but I like to have fun with it."

Aspen sighed. "As you wish. Well, then…" He hesitated, and gave the reclining goddess a sharp look. "It seems like I'm gathering a large group of beings in a place where no one is supposed to be. Any ideas why?"

The goddess looked up and whistled silently. "Um, well… You know, there are god things that I can't really talk about…"

"Like why a Traveler child got a quest to come out here and find Duke Penbrooke, who everyone is supposed to believe is dead?" Aspen's gaze was level as Gina stuck her fingers in her ears.

"Caaaaan't heeeear yooooou!" she sing-songed.

He raised his voice. "Like why the first half-breed goblin that anyone knows of turned up in my mine?"

She hummed.

"Like why three – *three* – vampires, who are supposed to be extinct, suddenly showed up in that same mine?"

No response except that she began braiding her hair into a soft mass as she stared into the impossibly clear sky above.

He sighed in resignation. "Are you five? Fine," he grumped. "Then maybe you can tell me what I'm supposed to do with a bunch of sentients who can't even communicate? I'm getting very tired of being the only translator, and my friends aren't that good at charades."

She popped up straight, releasing her hair. "Yes! That I can help with!" She kissed her palm, then flattened her hand and blew over it toward him. He felt a soft bump on his forehead.

Quest: "Get This Party Started" begun.

You need everyone to be able to talk to each other. Maybe try having a party? Everyone just needs to get together and communicate. They say good times plus crazy friends equals amazing memories. You definitely have some crazy friends, so why not go all in?

Success: Communication will become easier.

Failure: You get to keep on keeping on. Have fun with that.

Aspen groaned. Why could it never be easy? "A party? Really?"

Gina nodded enthusiastically. "A good party can solve anything!" She hopped up, raised her arms, and began to gyrate her hips. Sparkles flew in every direction as music came from everywhere. She began to fade, and winked at him with rainbow eyes just before she popped out of existence.

Aspen closed his mouth. Then he opened it again. "I had more questions!" he yelled up at the sky.

He heard a laugh, and then he was back by the field, a single juicy pea-pod resting in his hand, which glowed softly with the light of a skill increase. "Definitely not Wisdom this time," he muttered, then popped the sweet pea into his mouth. His eyes closed involuntarily, and he moaned. "Oh my goddess. That's amazing."

ế ế ế

The twilight had sunk into full darkness by the time he made it back to the house. The bottom of his shirt was filled with all kinds of vegetables, and he walked with a bit of a waddle as he tried to juggle the cloth over his extremely full belly.

He walked past Khor, standing in the door of the stable, snoring loudly, a spit bubble on his mouth expanding and contracting as he breathed. The two kids – foals? – rested by his hooves, exhausted but none the worse for wear. Aspen opened the door quietly. One of the goat's large eyelids flicked open just enough to make certain the intruder was a friend, though Aspen's scent and the sound of his footsteps had doubtless announced his arrival from quite a distance.

Inside, the fire was banked. The door to the back room, which held the Traveler's sleeping Zombies (that description, however accurate, still sent chills down his spine), was closed, and no sound came from within. He could just hear Juniper fussing in the cellar, so Sarave was undoubtedly getting ready to feed the little one. Soon the babe would start on solid foods and sleep through the night, and they would all be glad of that.

Silus and Sumi watched him from the rafters. The spider's two largest eyes

324

glittered in the firelight, and the six smaller ones occasionally shone as well, making her look like her head was twinkling slightly. Silus released her hold on the roof as Aspen entered and glided down to land on his shoulder, where she burrowed into his neck.

<You always have all the adventures while I'm sleeping,> the little bat groused. <I'm glad you're all right, but next time, wake me up! I could have helped a lot in that tunnel!>

Aspen set his burden down on the table. The vegetables nearly overflowed its small surface, and he scooped them together into a mound, then thought better of it and pushed a selection of the biggest ones over in front of Gina's statue before he sat down.

He stroked the soft silver fluff in front of Silus' ears. She looked a bit bigger again, and the silver was more pronounced. She must have gotten another level at some point recently. Soon, she would be almost as large as her mother had been when she died.

"You need your sleep, little one. You're up all night on guard. Just because the vampires are gone doesn't mean we can lower our defenses. Plus, we were just supposed to be working in the field. We had no idea anything more would happen."

The little bat mumbled some more, then relaxed against him. <At least you finally figured out about the unicorns. It was really hard not to tell you.>

Aspen snapped upright. He cast a narrow look up at Sumi, who was suddenly occupied with weaving a dense piece of webbing. "What? You knew? You *both* knew? Why didn't you tell me?"

Silus giggled. <It was funny! You even convinced the Travelers that they were goats too! We thought about telling you when they showed up, but we didn't know them that well, and some people hunt unicorns, you know. Why would they do that? Everyone knows unicorns are one of Gina's favorite creatures, and if her order finds out you killed one, you'll get in big trouble. Plus, they're really, really nice.> The little bat's voice was suddenly very young and a little lost.

Aspen sat back again, though he cast one more pointed look up at Sumi, letting her know he'd be talking to her again about this in the future. For now, he had a child to reassure. "Unfortunately, unicorn parts are rare and sell for a lot of gold. Kayli and Kayti, though, are under our protection now. Do we let anyone hurt our friends?"

<No!>

He nodded firmly. "That's right. I don't believe Rouge and Motte are likely to try anything, either. Rouge had the perfect opportunity today. She could have killed them while she was in that tunnel and claimed the spider did it, and we'd never have been the wiser. Instead, she carried Kayli out, even though she herself was grievously wounded. That Traveler girl is good people, and her father won't do anything that would hurt his girl, body or soul. We'll keep an eye on them, of course, but I think the kids will be safe."

He paused, then glanced up at Sumi. "Do you know what a young unicorn is called? It feels a little odd to keep calling them kids, as if we still believed them to be goats."

The spider stopped pretending deep concentration on the work she was doing, which looked to be a new blanket for Juniper, since the baby was outgrowing the old one. <Greater Unicorns are vanishingly rare, and are often thought to spring full-formed from Gina's magic. A young one has never been proven to exist before. Given that, I don't know that any particular name is correct. They obviously look like goats when they're young, so 'kid' seems as appropriate as anything else.>

"Not helpful, Sumi," he mock-growled. Silus giggled.

Sumi shrugged with her pedipalps and front four legs. <Perhaps a foal, since once they become Greater Unicorns they'll look more like fuzzy horses? If you wanted to be more fanciful, you could always make something up.>

<A shimmer? They're very shiny.> Silus' voice was hopeful.

It was Aspen's turn to shrug. "As good as anything, I guess."

Sumi's tone was slightly regretful when she spoke again. <A shimmer does, indeed, seem like a good name for them. I suggest, however, that we continue with 'kid'. Calling them goats protected them from scrutiny when Rouge and Motte came. If others come, which seems likely, if they're searching for Duke Penbrooke, perhaps a little misdirection would be wise. Once their horns grow in fully, of course, there will be no hiding what they are, and we can reassess then.>

Aspen and Silus sighed simultaneously.

<All right,> the bat said reluctantly. She moved to the edge of Aspen's shoulder, preparing to fly off so she could go out on her rounds. <Before I go, is there anything *else* I missed?>

Aspen started to shake his head, then paused. "Well," he said, rubbing his jaw where Silus' soft fur had tickled him, "I did talk to Gina again."

<You what?> Both females spoke at the same time.

"Hmm, yep. She told me she couldn't talk to me again until I harvested my first crops. Whatever magic is hastening the growth of the plants finished this afternoon." He waved his hand at the table heaped with produce. "As you see. Silus, you should try some."

She wrinkled her nose even more than it was naturally wrinkled. <Yuck. Vegetables. I prefer fruit.>

He grinned, eyes twinkling. "I think you'll like these." He picked up a pea pod and shelled the peas. Then he set a single pea on his shoulder next to her. She edged away as if it contained a contagious illness. He nudged it closer with his fingertip, and she nearly fell off. "Try it!"

Slowly, eyes closed, she leaned in, sniffing. She poked out her tongue and licked it. Her golden eyes flashed open, and she leaned forward, practically inhaling the green orb. Her cheeks bulged as she chewed. <More!>

Laughing, Aspen began to shuck the peas, eating the shells himself until he was firmly told to 'just give me the whole thing!' After that, the greedy little creature was far too busy to talk.

Sumi, however, remembered the topic at hand. <What did Gina say?>

Aspen shook his head. "Not much we couldn't have guessed, really." He stopped, mouth quirking slightly. "Well, not *me*, maybe. You lot probably have it all figured out, though."

Sumi whipped out a line of webbing, snagged a small fur from the pile by the door, and with a tug, flung it in his face. <It was all in good fun, Aspen. You've been too serious for…a long time.>

"Well, good news." Aspen grinned wryly, removing the fur. The bat on his shoulder hadn't even paused in devouring everything he set near her. "Gina agrees with you. She said we need to have a party."

Chapter Fifteen

Rouge

Z oey's alarm clock went off at 6:30 AM. Her eyes cracked open, and after a moment of disorientation, she shot up, swinging her legs out of bed almost before she was fully upright. It was the first day of summer vacation. The first day of her new job at Veritas Corp!

She and her dad had gone thrift store shopping, and she'd used her saved allowance, which he'd matched, to get a good work wardrobe made up of five blouses, four pairs of slacks, and two skirts that could all be mixed and matched. Then they'd headed to a shoe store and picked out the most comfortable pair of shoes they could find that would go with her new wardrobe.

Now, she pulled on her nicest blouse and one of the skirts, together with the comfy shoes. She wiggled her toes in the square toebox, wishing again that any of the cute shoes had also been comfortable. Oh well. She definitely wasn't one to suffer for fashion, so she just gathered up her curls into a puff on top of her head, applied some hair gel, washed her face, and headed downstairs.

Her dad was already up, making celebratory pancakes. After a quick good morning hug, she snagged the butter and syrup out of the fridge and set the table. As she poured them each a glass of orange juice, Max whined at her feet. She flopped his silky doggy ears, silently promising to slip him some eggs next time her dad made any.

A few minutes later, a large stack of pancakes was placed triumphantly in the center of the table, and she looked up to see her dad's grin. "Didn't burn a single one this time. Help yourself, kiddo."

He sat down and speared two pancakes with the forks she had set out. After applying excessive amounts of syrup, he began to eat. She grimaced, grabbed her own double stack, and poured syrup into a small bowl. She dipped each bite as she cut it, so she'd get the perfect amount of sweetness without the pancakes going all soggy and nasty.

They ate in companionable silence, until they reached the last pancake. Zoey looked at it. Her dad looked at it.

"Rock, paper, scissors?" He held out his fist.

Zoey sighed and shoved back her chair, picking up her plate. "It's all yours, Dad. I don't want to fall asleep at my desk or something." She grinned at him cheekily, silently reminding him of a story he once told her about falling asleep at work until a friend blew in his ear, making him shriek and fall out of his chair. He had been trying to warn her of the dangers of staying up too late at night, but she'd never let him live it down.

He groaned as he moved the last breakfast bread to his plate. "I never should have told you that story."

She laughed as she rinsed her dishes and put them in the dishwasher. "Nope. Never give your kids blackmail material." She tilted her head thoughtfully. "Never give *anyone* blackmail material."

"Good advice. For example, if someone knew that when you were in preschool, you found out boys go potty standing up, and when you tried it, you..." Her dad surreptitiously slid the last half of the pancake off the plate and onto the linoleum floor, where slurping noises immediately began. She was far too busy attempting to spray him with water to call him on it.

He ducked, laughing, and brought over his own plate. He took her place at the sink, and she picked up her lunchbox from the counter. She'd been told there was a good cafeteria on the Veritas campus, but her dad had made her do the math on how much it would cost to eat out five times a week, and no *way* was she doing that. Good thing she liked peanut butter sandwiches and apples!

"All right, Zoe." He glanced around. "Anything else you need before we go? You have your bus pass, ID, screen, and a little cash?"

"Yeeeessssss! Dad, come *on!* You've only gone over this a hundred times!" She held up the slim packet that held her cards and cash. One thing she'd insisted on in all her clothes was actual, *usable* pockets. What did clothing designers think, that all women carried massive purses? Some of the pants she'd liked had 'pockets' that were actually *decorative*, and were sewed shut! What. The. Heck?!

He rubbed his hand over his nearly bald head. He'd gone in for his bi-annual haircut, and now there was only a light shadow of stubble on the sides, and a slightly longer layer of hair on top. She'd come by the whole 'not worrying too much about how she looked' thing pretty honestly.

"I know, Zoe. I promise, after today you're on your own. The whole point of this is to help you see what being a grown-up is really like. Nobody's going to tell you to get up on time or charge your screen when you go to college. Still, it's not like I just stopped being your dad."

He looked a little sad, and she gave him a hug. "Yeah, okay, Dad. I'm only fourteen. You get to boss me around for another three years, at least."

He snorted. "At least. This is why people have kids, you know. Just so we have somebody to boss around."

Zoey rolled her eyes and muttered, "I believe it." She patted Max on the head and opened the door. "Come on, or we'll be late!"

The college campus was about five miles from the Veritas campus (why were they both called 'campus' anyway?), and there was a bus route that went straight from the school to Veritas. Her dad started work at 8, and she was supposed to start at nine, so he could take her most of the way, and she'd catch the bus at 8:15, which should get her to work around 8:45. Perfect, right?

Completely autonomous cars hadn't appeared yet, though the car manufacturers had been promising them since before her dad was born. It was partially due to fears of having someone hack such an integral system, and partially due to the fact that even though the systems were nearly perfect by now, inevitably there would be something that failed, causing an accident, and the politicians would tighten regulations, *again*, achieving nothing.

Nobody quite trusted the system, and definitely nobody actually wanted to entirely give up the independence of driving themselves. Her dad said it was because too many idiots still thought they could drive better than a computer, but all she cared about was that she still had to take the bus or have someone take her places instead of being able to get in a self-driving car and tell it to "take me to work", which would just be *so cool*.

The drive to college was filled with news radio and their usual banter about recent world events. She wasn't even really paying attention, but yet another part of her dad's effort to raise 'an intelligent, educated, and useful member of society' was making sure she knew who was doing what where, so she could pretty well wing it.

By the time they got there, she was itching to go. Somewhat literally, because she was wearing pantyhose for the first time since her dad stopped forcing her to go to church, and they really, really sucked. She was pretty sure the crotch of them was dropping slowly, and soon people would be able to see it below the hem of her skirt. So as soon as he stopped his car by the curb near her stop, she jumped out, almost twisting her ankle on the curb. What she wouldn't do for Rouge's dexterity!

"Bye, Dad! Love you! Have a good day!" She waved as she dashed away, leaving him with a blank expression and arms held out for a hug.

"Hey!" she heard him yell after her, "call me on lunch!"

"Yeah, okay!" She threw him a double thumbs up without even looking, and dived into the small crowd of people waiting for the bus. She looked around curiously, wondering if any of these people might be her new co-workers. She tried to covertly hike up her pantyhose while she examined them.

By the time the bus came, she'd decided that only two of them were possibilities. The two girlies with their sparkly devices and two-inch long fingernails were definitely not headed to work. They were giggling about how cute the barista was at their favorite coffee shop. Three guys and another girl were all dressed too casually for office work. Probably summer quarter students who didn't have an early class. The last two were a man and a woman, both dressed in business casual, with briefcases and everything.

She rolled her eyes. Who still carried a briefcase? What were they, secret agents? Then she glanced down at her *Kimi ni Todoke* lunchbox and felt her cheeks warm. Maybe she shouldn't go throwing stones. Maybe they just *liked* briefcases, or maybe that was how they carried their lunch.

In any case, when they all filed onto the bus, she found the closest seat she could to keep an eye on them. The man was a short, tan, brown-haired guy, probably not too long out of college. The lady was a little older, blonde, brown-eyed, with pinched lips and a too-tight bun. Zoey decided that she was not interested in getting to know her, so she focused on the guy.

As soon as he sat down, he opened his briefcase. She tried to see inside without being obvious about it, but only caught a glimpse of a few pieces of paper and... a box? Ha! It probably was his lunchbox! He pulled out two wireless earbuds and set them in his ears. Then he unrolled a super fancy screen, one of the new ones with the screen that could stretch! He touched the screen a few times, then rolled it up again and leaned back in his seat, closing his eyes.

She sighed. So much for that form of entertainment. She looked around, clutching her lunchbox and kicking her feet nervously. She'd had to buy a bus pass, because she hadn't used public transportation enough to make it worthwhile before. This was only the third time she'd ever ridden alone. There were definitely a wide range of people to watch.

The bus pulled up outside the Veritas campus at 8:47, by which time the majority of riders were dressed in business casual like the two who had gotten on at the college. Zoey had relaxed and started to enjoy the feeling of anonymity that came from being just another face in an ever-changing crowd. She never even had to take out her screen, because there was always something to see. The lady who meowed like a cat. The houseless man that no one would sit next to, which made her sad. The pretty lady who sat in the outside seat and refused to move for any of the three different guys who tried to sit next to her. If this was in-game, she was sure she could have gotten a quest out of all of them.

Most of the bus riders got off at the same time she did, including the man and woman who had gotten on with her. She stepped to the side as everyone else flowed around her, clearly knowing exactly where they were going. She just stood, staring up at the glistening glass and stone façade of the building.

It was flat in the front, but the sides were shaped like a step pyramid. The base was broad, and each floor became narrower as it rose, so the top, the twelfth floor, was much smaller than the first level, with a flat roof. There was supposedly a fancy private garden and entertainment area on top, but the company had asked map-makers like Gloogel to blur the building in satellite views for privacy reasons, and drones and aircraft weren't allowed downtown, so the only photos were blurry and could have been taken anywhere.

The front was mostly mirrored glass, but a huge V made of glittering stone started at the top of the massive double doors and rose up to embrace the exclusive top floor. One of her chores at home was cleaning the windows, and she felt really sorry for whoever had to clean this monstrosity.

As the last of her fellow bus riders trickled away, she realized that she needed to hurry, or she would be late for her first day. She scurried after the crowd. It was time to find out what 'being a grown up' was really like. Yay, but ugh.

Zoey squared her shoulders, feeling the unfamiliar slide of her polyester blouse against her skin, and walked through the huge doors. They were automatic, and with the flow of people entering, they hadn't actually closed since the bus arrived. Inside was an echoing entry, with live plants, soft music, and a few areas with soft loveseats available for guests while they waited for some official person to come lead them wherever they were supposed to go.

A security desk stood in front of her. Two people sat behind it, eyes scanning the crowd and periodically dropping to look at a row of monitors in front of them. Behind them were a series of walk-through body scanners leading to a bunch of turnstiles. People were flowing through like water, and she had to fight not be jostled along by the flow.

She took a calming breath, though, and when she stepped up to the desk, her face held its usual bright grin. The tall man on the left barely glanced at her, too busy looking back and forth between the crowd and the screens. The person on the right, though, smiled genially. "Good morning. Are you looking for someone?" Their face was round, and the voice confident but neither low nor high. Zoey honestly wasn't sure if it was a man or a woman, especially in the carefully tailored uniform, which seemed designed to reduce any individual characteristics.

Zoey shrugged. "I'm Zoey Williams. I'm an Intern. I'm supposed to go to HR and see Ms. McKeene." She gestured at the couches nearby. "Am I supposed to wait or something?"

The guard smiled again and made a few gestures over the monitor. "Ah ha, there you are!" They turned the screen toward her, and showed her the headshot she'd sent in a week ago. Turning the screen away again, they reached under the desk and pulled out a locked metal box. They opened it with a thumbprint, and pulled out a plastic card. Zoey felt her eyebrows go up. These guys really took security seriously!

Handing her the card, the guard gestured behind them to a large machine. It looked like the luggage scanner with a conveyor belt she'd seen when she'd last gone to visit her mother. "Step right up. All personal items on the belt or in a bin to go through. Shoes need to go through as well. Then you can step through the scanner."

Nervously, Zoey did as she was told, placing her lunchbox and slim packet of personal items in a bin with her shoes and sending it through as the guard went to stand between the two devices. Once they scanned the items, they nodded, and Zoey stepped through, gulping a little even though she had nothing to hide. The light stayed green. The guard held up Zoey's metal lunchbox.

"Would you open this, please, Ms. Williams?" Zoey did so, mentally kicking herself for not realizing that a metal container might not be the best choice to bring to a real company, who clearly took security very seriously. The guard had her turn over her sandwich and apple, ran a wand over both of them, and handed Zoey back the bin containing her shoes and other items.

"Thank you, Ms. Williams. Now, if you'll step through that door," they pointed to a smoked glass door somewhat hidden in an alcove framed by large plants. The fancy white letters painted onto the glass said 'Human Resources'. "Ms. McKeene will be with you as soon as possible. I believe she's already with another intern, so it may take a minute. Hang in there." They winked a bright blue eye. "Welcome to Veritas Corp!"

She grinned back and gave them a salute. "Thanks! Do you always work this shift?"

The guard looked surprised. "Most of the time. Why?"

She looked around at the extremely ostentatious décor and the robotic passage of the human horde. "It'll be nice to see a friendly face. Thanks."

They grinned. "No problem. If you need anything else, let me know. I'm Sam."

"And I'm Zoey. Thank you, Sam!" They smiled at each other before Sam returned to their post, and she opened the door to Human Resources. No matter how much she wanted this job, if anyone tried to harvest her or came near her with a pickaxe, she'd show them what kind of a 'resource' she was!

Giggling a little at her own silliness, she stepped into a spacious but spartan room. Three chairs were spaced out along the wall to her right, and a desk sat to her left. A broad hallway lined with doors led away. The middle-aged woman behind the desk looked harried already, and it wasn't even nine yet. She glanced up as Zoey entered.

"Zoey Williams?" Her voice was sharp, but not unkind.

Zoey nodded, realizing that Sam must have given them some kind of heads-up that she was there.

"Take a seat. Ms. McKeene is with another employee, but she'll be available soon. She's very efficient. Just so you're aware, each employee may consult with any member of HR at any time, but each employee also has an assigned HR person, who will know them personally. You are assigned to Ms. McKeene, so in future, if you have any concerns, you will bring them to her if possible and appropriate." The woman issued a short, tight smile, and then returned to typing rapidly on her keyboard.

Zoey sat. She clutched her lunchbox. She kicked her feet in their comfortable shoes. She tried to pull up her extremely *un*comfortable hose without attracting the attention of the lady behind the desk. She was determined not to pull out her screen, because her dad told her that using a personal device would probably be a big no-no. There were no clocks on the wall, she didn't own a watch, and time seemed to crawl.

Just when she thought she'd go absolutely crazy, and her fingers were twitching without her screen, a door down the hall opened, and as it did, she could see the placard on it read 'Georgia McKeene'. The shuffling of feet sounded from behind the door, and the door closed and two people appeared. Zoey nearly groaned.

One of them was a stranger, a girl a bit older than herself, with brown hair in a French braid and brown eyes. Her neat khaki slacks and soft green button-down blouse were a similar style to much of Zoey's new wardrobe. Simple, tidy, and interchangeable.

The older woman was also a stranger, technically, but her face was familiar nonetheless. It was, because why would it not be, the blonde lady from the bus. Even from here, Zoey could see the creases already forming between her brows and bracketing her mouth from frowning so much. This was awesome.

Zoey mustered a smile as the two finished speaking and turned back toward the waiting room. The girl looked pale and nervous, but she managed a faint smile. The blonde woman sent Zoey a dismissive glance and turned to the woman behind the desk.

"Ellen," Zoey winced at the high-pitched whine of her voice, "send for a runner for Miss Francis. She needs the tour, and then she'll be working in Production with Mr. Guerry. Tell the runner they might as well come back when they're done. Miss Williams will be ready soon as well." With a dismissive nod of her head, she turned to Zoey.

"Follow me, Miss Williams. We just have to set up your badge and complete some paperwork." Without checking to be sure Zoey was coming, Ms. McKeene turned and walked back toward her office. Zoey followed, intentionally scuffing her feet as she went. Type-As like this woman *hated* that.

When they reached the office, McKeene entered first, heading straight to the desk. Zoey closed the door behind them, just a *little* harder than necessary, so it didn't quite slam. She allowed herself a small grin before straightening her face and turning around.

Georgia McKeene was staring at her, and even from the door, Zoey could tell from the flex of her jaw muscles that she was clenching her teeth. Zoey gave a slightly vapid smile, as if she had no idea that she might have done something to irritate the older woman, and went to sit down in the only available chair in the office.

The desk was smoked glass, sparkling clean, and incredibly tidy. Zoey didn't have a problem with tidy, but who had a glass desk without a *single* smudge or fingerprint on it? The chair was hard, too, and the legs seemed slightly shorter than usual. Zoey's feet actually sat flat on the floor, instead of only her toes reaching or her feet swinging free as they often did. She was sure it was a deliberate attempt to make the person sitting in it feel small, but Zoey was used to being small, and it didn't bother her.

Ms. McKeene summoned up a smile, showing no teeth behind her tight lips. She picked up a stylus lying beside her monitor and touched the screen, which looked like a VaLPAC (Variable Light Phase Angle Controlled) monitor.

The monitors were expensive, but linked to the unique implant or special glasses of an individual user. This user was the only one who could decipher the encrypted image, though it could easily be set to share or even display 'in the clear' as well. For screens that were generally private but might need to be viewed by more than one person, VaLPAC monitors were the best choice.

The older woman sat for several minutes in silence, paging through what Zoey assumed was her file. At this point, Zoey figured that most kids her age would be getting pretty worried, since the adult who was *supposed* to be assisting her was instead blatantly ignoring her. Zoey, however, was made of sterner stuff, and kept her hands relaxed in her lap as she looked around the room.

It wasn't particularly large or small, and there were no windows. A bookshelf stood against the wall to her left, and all of the titles were things like *Human Resources Management Applications 25th Edition* and *Human Resources Policies and Procedures Manual.* Given that most people used digital resources for things like that now, the books were pure showmanship.

She thought about what her dad would say about this woman, and finally settled on one of his favorite Shakespeare quotes. 'Who knows himself a braggart, let him fear this, for it will come to pass that every braggart shall be found an ass.'

When Georgia McKeene finally decided to remember Zoey was there, Zoey had discovered that there were six outlets in the walls, twenty-five ceiling tiles, and there was something that looked distinctly like a cigarette burn on the carpet, though it was mostly hidden under a corner of the bookshelf.

Ms. McKeene cleared her throat. "I see here that you're only fourteen. Our high school interns are usually sixteen to eighteen. I must ask, Miss Williams, are you quite certain you're ready to work a full forty-hour week? Veritas Corporation is a *real* business, and no matter who recommended you," here the woman's mouth pinched down even further, "you must fulfill your duties. A poor recommendation from us," *me* was the silent implication, "could derail your college plans, unless you're only aiming for community college."

Zoey grinned and shrugged, shaking off the venom while thinking of little unicorns. "Why not? I already work at least 30 hours a week, and take home another ten hours of work most of the time." She kept her voice cheerful and even, as if she had no idea that she was in a closed room with a snake.

McKeene looked startled, then frowned. "You mean school? School isn't a *job*, Miss Williams. You clearly don't understand *real life*. Nonetheless, what's done is done. I'll have your exit paperwork ready. Any time you decide this is too hard, just let me know, and I'll take care of it. You can go home and spend your summer swimming and going to parties."

She sneered slightly, though Zoey thought she might have been trying for a condescending smile, then tapped her screen with the stylus. A second passed, and a small sound came from the desk. McKeene reached down and Zoey heard the whir of an electronic lock opening. The woman reached down a little further and came up with an ID card with Zoey's headshot printed on it. She pushed a small pad attached to her computer with a wire toward Zoey.

"Please put your right thumb on the pad." Zoey did, and a second later, Ms. McKeene nodded. "That's enough." She pulled a single-use cleansing wipe out and carefully wiped down the scanner. It was all Zoey could do not to roll her eyes. She honestly thought her eyeball muscles would seize up from the effort.

The blonde woman tapped the screen again. "This is Georgia McKeene, employee number Golf Mike 77666. I am now recording the final verbal employment agreement between Veritas Corporation and Miss Zoey Williams. Miss Williams," cold brown eyes met Zoey's hazel ones, "you and your guardian have read and signed the non-disclosure agreements required by all employees of Veritas Corporation. Do you understand that if you disclose any proprietary information about the company or personal information about its employees to anyone outside of the company, you may be prosecuted to the fullest extent of the law?"

Zoey gulped, and for the first time felt a chill go down her back. This woman was a snake, and a beezie (as Jace would say), but she did actually have the power to do more than just try to intimidate Zoey with her stupid mind games. It was obvious that she was trying to scare Zoey off, but why? What did she have against a kid she just met?

Shaking herself like Max after the time Zoey tripped and spilled ice water all over him, Zoey sat up straight, planting her sensible shoes firmly on the floor. She'd learned a long time ago that the best way to deal with people who didn't like you was to pretend like you didn't even notice. So she mentally reached way down inside past her boring tan sports bra and grabbed onto her big girl panties.

"Yes," she said. "I understand."

Once Ms. McKeene finally got started, she was as efficient as the secretary had said. They finished going over the contract (which basically boiled down to: you do whatever we tell you – within reason – for forty hours a week. Don't be late. Don't talk about Fight Club.) Zoey was already exhausted. She had no idea how long she'd been trapped in that windowless room with that horrible woman, but it seemed like an eternity, and she desperately wished for her [Poof!] spell and Rouge's Mambele. With Dwarven Kombucha.

At last, though, a tentative tap came at the door, and the head of a girl in her late teens or early twenties popped in. Her eyes were wary, and she pushed her heavy tortoiseshell glasses up her nose with her middle finger. Zoey wondered if it was a deliberate gesture, or a habitual one.

"Sorry, Ms. McKeene. It's just that Ellen said you'd be done soon, and soon was about fifteen minutes ago, and they're looking for me..." Her soft voice held an accent Zoey couldn't quite place, but it was really pretty. Zoey loved accents.

Georgia McKeene glared from the young woman to Zoey, then huffed a beleaguered sigh. "Yes, well. I suppose we're done here." She smiled a saccharine smile at Zoey, hiding her teeth behind thin lips. "Do remember, Miss Williams, if you decide that things here are too difficult, just come to me. It's certainly no embarrassment for someone so young to change their mind."

Zoey nearly knocked her chair over getting to her feet, then awkwardly caught herself as she stumbled. Her left foot had fallen asleep! She picked it up and shook it as she smiled at Ms. McKeene with equal insincerity. "Thanks ever so much, Ms. McKeene. It's great to know that I have someone on my side." *I don't know who it is yet, but definitely someone else, because you wouldn't spit on me if I were on fire.*

Taking two steps back, wobbling on her now-prickly ankle, Zoey dove toward the doorway, practically pushing the newcomer out of the way in her haste. She waggled her fingers in a 'toodle-oo' goodbye, and then shut the door slightly too hard again. Quickly, she grabbed the other girl's wrist and all but dragged her down the hall.

"This way to get out, right? I'm super excited for this tour thing. Let's get started!" She grinned manically, and the girl's eyes widened. Zoey ignored it, pulling the other girl along as they passed through the waiting room and past Ellen, who got another finger waggle.

Zoey closed the door behind her and stepped around the corner of the little alcove so they'd be out of sight through the glass panels. Then she leaned back against the wall, pulled her left leg up to rest her foot on the opposite knee (cursing her pencil skirt as it tried to prevent that much movement) and began rubbing her ankle vigorously.

"Holy cow! Sorry about that, but I'm just *so* ready to start work, and my foot fell asleep while we were doing paperwork. Just a sec and I'll be ready to go." She threw a genuine smile at her companion, who seemed to relax a little, pushing up her glasses again. With her forefinger this time, Zoey noted, amused.

"It's sweet as, eh. No one's really looking for me. I just got tired of waiting. Plus, I know Ms. McKeene can be... difficult. She's my HR rep, too." She rolled her eyes, then stuck out a hand. "I'm Nina. Nice to meet you!"

Zoey grinned and shook. "Zoey Williams. Yeah, she was, um, challenging. But hey, maybe she's having a rough day or something."

"Nah, she's a real munter. Nobody likes her except some of the managers. You need somebody fired, she's your girl. They say she enjoys it." Nina wrinkled her nose.

Tentatively putting her foot on the ground and smiling when it wasn't painful, Zoey stood up straight. "I believe it. Um, if you don't mind me asking..."

"Where'm I from? Yeah, nah, everybody asks. My mum's American, and my dad's a Kiwi. New Zealander, you'd say. We spent most summers there when I was a kid, since my folks both work from home, and I picked up some of the accent." She shrugged, shoving the glasses up her nose again, though this time she used her forefinger.

"Nice!" Zoey said. "That must have been awesome! I've never even been out of the country."

"It was, but I had to keep track of two sets of friends. Never got to see my American friends during the summer, and missed my Kiwi friends the rest of the time. I love *Veritas Online* 'cause I can see everybody at once, and as a Veritas Corp employee, I get a free account." Nina flashed a thumbs up and a broad smile. "Anyway, where are you headed? The HR personnel usually tell me, but you kind of hustled us out of there."

Zoey bit her lip. "Uh, good question. Sorry. I just had to get out while I could. All I really know is that I'm in Design, supposed to be working with 'Ms. Andrews'. Pretty common last name, so I hope you know who she is."

Nina's eyes grew huge, and the glasses went up again. "Ms. Andrews? Really? Any chance that's *Bridget* Andrews?"

"Oh! Yeah, I think that's what my dad said." Zoey grinned.

"Keen! They assigned you to the boss! Does your dad work for Veritas and pull some strings for you or something? I've never heard of her having an intern before." Nina started walking toward the turnstiles, which now stood vacant and silent after the mad rush of the morning. "Here, you slide your badge in this side. It'll actually take it from you, and it won't give it back until it makes sure your thumbprint matches."

The older girl laid her badge on a green arrow in a card-sized groove in the top of the machine, face down, then pushed it forward slightly until the top entered a slot. The card vanished, sucked inside, and Nina pressed her right thumb to the matte black scanner next to the card input. A green circle appeared above it, and the turnstile clicked slightly, barely audible against the soft background music.

"One person per card, obviously. Regular employees have a few fingers on file, but interns only get the right thumb, so take good care of yours, eh? Knew a bloke once who smashed his thumb with a hammer over the weekend, and it took a while to get that sorted on Monday." She stepped through, and the turnstile gave way, then clicked softly again behind her. Her card appeared in a small groove next to her, and she picked it up, immediately putting it back in its badge holder on the lanyard around her neck. "Your turn."

Zoey carefully placed her new card face down on the machine, pushed it forward, and was slightly surprised at the force with which it was pulled from her grasp. She pressed her thumb on the black square, and heard the click. Walking through, she felt a fresh wave of excitement push out the uneasiness that Georgia McKeene had instilled in her.

Yeah, this was going to be awesome.

The tour didn't take long. Nina showed her how to get to the main bank of elevators, gave her an idea of who was where, and described the various other buildings on campus. It turned out there were a series of sky bridges spreading out from the main building, so you could either walk outside or travel through the glass tunnels on days with bad weather.

The other buildings held the cafeteria, a clinic, a gym (with a swimming pool!), the warehouse (where all items from office supplies to the mail arrived before they were checked through security and sent to their final destinations), and something like an old-time internet café, but with pods and disposable, single-use bodysuits.

Finally, Nina delivered Zoey to the seventh floor, which was where the Design Department made its home. From the hall, the floor was fairly bland, though images from *Veritas Online* and some of Veritas Corp's other, non-VR, games were scattered around. Nina stepped inside, where a pretty Black woman smiled at her from behind a desk. "Nina! Good morning! I heard we had a new intern coming in. Is this her?"

Nina smiled. "G'day, Jazmin! This is Zoey. She says she's supposed to work with Ms. Andrews?"

Jazmin tilted her head, her big gold hoop earrings swaying. "Oh. I knew someone was coming, but Bridget doesn't take interns herself. Let me call back and check." She touched a spot just in front of her right ear, activating her implant, and murmured quietly while the two girls shifted uncomfortably. After a moment, Jazmin's eyebrows shot up, and she spoke a little more before lifting her finger.

She smiled at them, warm brown eyes assessing Zoey curiously. "I guess you were right, Zoey. You won't be working directly with her, of course, but she's your supervisor. She wants me to take you back now." She stood, revealing that she was nearly six feet tall in her towering high heels. Zoey instantly felt like a Lilliputian discovering Gulliver washed up on the beach. Between her height, her immaculate dress, and her lovely face, Zoey was fairly certain Jazmin missed her calling as a model.

"Thank you, Nina. See you next time!" Jazmin waved gold and silver-tipped fingers at the younger girl, but Zoey didn't miss that the perfect manicure was on fingernails that extended only slightly past her fingertips. Useful, not just decorative.

Nina waved back, pushing her glasses up one last time as she exited. Before the door closed completely, Zoey could hear the girl start to whistle.

"All right then, Zoey!" Jazmin stood, half turned to face the hall behind her desk. "Follow me to meet the Wizard of Veritas!"

Zoey's eyes widened, but she followed the woman down the broad, well-lit hallway. They passed offices on the right, each marked with a nameplate. On the left were meeting rooms of all types and sizes. They were all glass-walled on this side, so she could see in and tell that they had all kinds of table and chair setups, and varying amounts of available technology. One was even furnished entirely in bean bag chairs!

Jazmin caught her look of surprise at that one and laughed a little. "That's for Harris's team. He's only thirty or so, but he's into retro everything. I guess tech companies in the 1990s supposedly had whole rooms of those things, so that's what he asked for." She stopped in front of another door, no different from the rest except that the nameplate was covered with yellow post-it notes that said 'Wizard of Veritas – Do Not Disturb'.

The tall woman laughed. "It started out as a way of teasing her, and she would rip it down. But someone always put it back up, so she finally gave in to the inevitable."

"What does it mean?"

"You've heard of the Wizard of Oz, right?" Jazmin gave her the kind of look people usually reserved for cute but not very bright puppies.

Zoey started to glare, and then sucked it back in and smiled instead. "Yeah, of course. I mean, why is she called that?"

Jazmin gave her that look again. "Didn't you look her up before you took the job?"

Zoey coughed and looked down, realizing that maybe she deserved the look a little bit. "Well, no. I was just excited to get the internship at all. I figured there was no way I'd be working with anybody important, so I didn't even think of it." Her voice trailed off at the end, and she felt her cheeks heat.

The other woman shook her head. "Bridget invented VR. At least, she invented the immersive VR that we use for *Veritas Online*. She literally *is* the woman behind the curtain. She made all the magic happen." With a wink of one long-lashed eye, she pushed open the door.

The woman sitting behind the desk wasn't anything unusual. She was pretty enough, a strawberry-blonde with blue eyes and a smattering of freckles across the bridge of her small nose. She wore a dainty pair of wire-rimmed glasses, no jewelry, and a pale blue button-down blouse that complemented her eyes.

She smiled and stood when they entered, and a short, curvy figure came into view. Some people would probably say she was a little overweight, but Zoey had always been jealous of girls with figures like that. Zaftig, her dad would probably say, if he talked about lady's figures in front of Zoey. She sighed a little, taking a moment to mourn her own boyish build before smiling in response.

"Thanks, Jazmin. I've got it from here. Expect Ms. Williams – Zoey?" with a glance at Zoey, who nodded, "Zoey, then, back out in ten or fifteen minutes. Hold my eleven o'clock appointment until we're done, please."

Jazmin nodded briskly, nudged Zoey slightly forward and gave her an encouraging smile, then gently closed the door behind her as she left. It didn't even click.

Zoey took a few steps further into the room, glancing around curiously. Like the woman, the office wasn't anything particularly out of the ordinary except for two things. First, she had *five* screens arrayed around her desk, all with the distinctive ValPAC logo and sleek design, so their contents were completely hidden from anyone but herself. Second, the entire left-hand wall was *covered* in video game action figures. They were arranged in scenes straight out of the games. Zoey was sure some of them had never been sold publicly, because if her dad had seen a figma for Lila of *Dragon Lila* in the kimono she wore while infiltrating the Han Castle, Zoey knew he would have bought it. Heck, he would have leased the house to raise funds, and thought it was a good deal.

Bridget Andrews saw where Zoey's eyes had stopped, and grinned, a little blush stealing over her pale cheeks. "I had a chance to meet Inzo Yamamoto a year ago. I gushed all over him about how much I loved *Dragon Lila*. It was embarrassing, actually, but I just couldn't stop myself. A few weeks later, she showed up in the mail. She's a hand-made piece, and I tried to return her, but he said his grandson loves *Veritas Online*, and wouldn't take her. Said he has a whole series of them."

She shook her head and grinned a wry half-grin that gave Zoey a sudden feeling of déjà vu. Where had she seen that smile before? Zoey shook off the feeling as Ms. Andrews continued speaking.

"Come on in and sit down, Zoey. We have a lot to go over, and not very much time. Oh, and please, call me Bridget. We're not much for formality around here. In this department, anyway." The woman sat down in one of the two chairs sitting in front of her desk. If she'd sat behind the desk, most of her would have vanished behind the array of screens, though her chair must be crazy tall to make her even as visible as she had been when they entered.

Zoey carefully sat across from her in a comfortable pale gray chair. She tugged at the bottom of her skirt and squeezed her legs together so that Bridget wouldn't be able to see just how far down her pantyhose had crept. She was pretty sure they were just going to puddle at her ankles any minute now, even though she'd found a bathroom during Nina's tour and pulled them up.

Bridget pulled off her glasses and set them on the desk, opening her mouth to speak. As soon as the small frames left her face, Zoey's déjà vu became full blown recognition.

"Holy cats, you're Lady Fayre! I mean, Gina!" Zoey just about came out of her chair, pantyhose forgotten.

Bridget flushed red as a tomato and waved her hands frantically, looking around as if to make sure no one was lurking in the closed office with them.

"Shh! Shh! Yes, but I can't talk about that! Seriously! I'm pushing it as it is, and the only way I got them to offer you the job was by making you into a guinea pig. If there's even a suggestion that I'm giving you information, we're all in deep...," she looked into Zoey's excited hazel eyes and gulped back whatever she was going to say, "in big trouble," she finished weakly.

Zoey nodded vigorously. "Yeah, okay, I get that. I really appreciate that you got me in, even if..." Her eyes narrowed. "*Heeeyyyy*, what do you mean, 'guinea pig'?" She had a nasty feeling her dad was about to get some payback for her not telling him about the quest.

The woman's eyes widened, and she suddenly looked very young. "You mean, Dr. Williams didn't tell you? I sent him all the documents last week, and he signed the medical release forms. I thought he would explain it!"

Zoey flounced back in her chair huffily, then sprang back upright as she felt an insidious creep from beneath her skirt. "No, he didn't tell me. That... that... *Dad*! And he wonders how I got to be so sneaky! What am I supposed to know?"

Bridget massaged the bridge of her nose, sighing softly and muttering something uncomplimentary about parents. Then she looked back up and gave that wry grin again.

"So, here's the deal. First thing in the morning, you're going to be the Design team intern. You report to Jazmin. She's the glue that holds us all together, and she'll give you your assignments for the day. We'll try to get you some experience with every team, so you can see how we work, but a lot of it will probably be fetching beverages, office supplies, and taking notes. You know how to type, right?"

Zoey pinched her lips a little, but nodded. She supposed it was a reasonable question. There were probably some Amish people who still couldn't type. Maybe.

Rolling her eyes at Zoey's too-obvious disdain, Bridget laughed a little. "Okay, okay, but seriously, you'd be surprised." She flipped a hand dismissively. "That's your morning. At one, you get a half hour for lunch. At one thirty, you need to be at Dr. Shaman- Um, Dr. *Sherman's* office in the Clinic building."

Zoey giggled. "Dr. Shaman?"

Groaning, Bridget covered her face with her hands. "Joe's going to *kill* me. I've already corrupted you."

Zoey just laughed harder.

Bridget peeked over her fingers, this time showing a full grin complete with devilish twinkle in the blue eyes. "I slipped *one* time because of his last name, and everyone just ran with it. Poor guy can't escape, now. Just don't call him that to his face, please? I'll never hear the end of it."

Grinning cheekily, Zoey nodded, crossing her fingers where she'd slid them down beside her legs so that she could surreptitiously grip the damned hose through her skirt. "Absolutely. But what am I supposed to do there?"

Eyeing Zoey suspiciously, Bridget continued. "Like I said, you're his new guinea pig. He has some tech that has passed adult human trials. It's ready to try out on teenagers. Nothing dangerous, obviously, but it is proprietary, so we need details to stay very quiet. Teenagers aren't well known for their ability to keep secrets, I'm afraid, and we've had trouble with leaks in the past, even when we used kids whose parents worked here and everyone signed NDAs."

As much as Zoey wanted to protest this broad generalization about her age bracket, she had to admit it was accurate, so she just nodded.

Bridget went on. "He's going to start off taking some baselines. Have you wear some sensors and a bodysuit, then do some activities. No big deal. Once he has an idea how your body responds to different input, he'll get you set with the equipment. Obviously, this is the top-secret part. You can talk about it with your dad when you're at home, because we know that keeping secrets from Dr. Williams is *not* okay, right?"

It was Zoey's turn to roll her eyes. "Yeah, right."

The crooked grin showed itself, and then the other woman finished up. "So, can you handle all that?"

"Uh, yeah," Zoey said, "except for one thing." She saw the concern cover Bridget's face and let it linger before she went on. "Do I have to wear pantyhose with a skirt at Veritas Corp? 'Cause if so, I'm out." She gave in and just tugged at the stupid undergarment.

Bridget looked away so Zoey could keep some fragment of her dignity intact, but that didn't stop her from laughing so hard her buttons almost popped.

Of course, there was paperwork. Bridget was way easier to work with than Georgia McKeene (then again, Zoey was pretty sure a drunk monkey would be easier to work with than Ms. McKeene) but it was still tedious. Zoey was already questioning her long-desired career path just because of how much documentation there was. How did anyone ever actually get anything done?

Fortunately, or unfortunately, Jazmin was ready to make up for it. For the next two hours, she ran Zoey off her feet, carrying everything from folders, to paperclips, to a *hamster*. (What did Harris's team need with a hamster? She was seriously afraid to ask, especially after she met the man and noted his own rather marked similarity to a member of the rodent family.)

Twice she was even sent out into The Void (as the Design Department called every other part of Veritas Corp, apparently because their brilliant ideas and creations tended to fall into the darkness, never to be heard of again) to take thumb drives to various people. Thumb drives were a technology almost as dead as optical disc storage, but it seemed that its very anachronism made it a favorite among people who didn't want anyone else to see what they were passing around, and didn't want it traveling through the company intranet.

One thing was very clear: people at Veritas Corp were secretive and paranoid. She wondered what or who they thought was out to get them, and if all of this was normal for a big company, or if it was as strange as it seemed to her.

Jazmin's last task for her was to take a list and run down to the cafeteria (so called because of how it functioned, rather than as any proper indication of the kind and quality of the food it served) and gather food for everyone who ordered something for lunch. She was pretty sure this was a hazing ritual, because who really orders a sub sandwich with exactly twenty-two pickles perfectly spaced, with eleven in each half, slathered in mustard, with nothing else on it?

By the time she gathered twenty-three drinks, seven sandwiches, two bowls of soup, four plates of pasta, and eighteen slices of pizza, she was exhausted. Fortunately, there were carts ready to hold and carry her booty back. She even saw several other harried young people doing the same thing, so she knew to scan her badge to 'check out' the cart so the wheels would unlock.

When she opened the Design Department door with her back, tugging the cart after her, she could practically feel all of that morning's excited optimism draining out of her. She'd stopped in the bathroom to finally tear off her hose, stuffing them down into the trash bin with a "Good riddance" filled with more venom than she'd have guessed she could feel for a hapless piece of hosiery. Now her bare, sweaty heels were rubbing uncomfortably in her sensible shoes, and she could really use a nap.

Jazmin took one look at her and tapped her screen with a stylus, which seemed to send out a department-wide chow call, if the sudden flood of people emerging from offices was any indication. "Sit down over there, Zoey." The tall woman pointed at one of the chairs in the small waiting area. "I was going to have you take everything back to these lazy ne'er-do-wells, but they can come get their own food today." Not a single one of the descending horde seemed to take offense at this description, and one man even tipped an imaginary hat as he grabbed his food from the pile.

Zoey dropped gracelessly into the chair, her feet giving a painful thump of gratitude as she did. Jazmin clucked in sympathy as she tugged a beverage and a bowl of pasta from the cart. "Guess I may have run you a little too hard this morning, hmm? I'm just so excited to have an intern to run all these little errands, I forgot you're only fourteen. You did a great job, though!

"Here," she said, digging through her desk, pulling out a plastic card with a small microchip in it. "It's lunchtime for you, too. We keep these cards for guests, so they can get food at the cafeteria without paying for it. It's good for up to twenty dollars. Don't tell anyone I gave you one, okay?" She winked at Zoey, her long false lashes exaggerating the gesture.

Zoey sighed. Another secret, albeit a little one, this time. She stood, grimacing as she put pressure on her feet, then brought out a real smile for the woman. "Thanks, Jazmin. I really appreciate it. I did bring a sandwich though. I don't want you to get in any trouble."

Jazmin's smile relaxed into something more genuine. "I appreciate that, Zoey. Not many worry about what might hurt someone else around here." For a moment, a flicker of something crossed her face, but then it was gone, and her smile was friendly and easy again. "It'll be all right, though. The only person that tracks them is Bridget, and she wouldn't mind. It's more that some of these moochers would insist that everyone should get one if I'm handing them out to employees."

She rolled her eyes, then shrugged. "This department is the best one in the company, in my opinion, but there are always a few bad apples in every barrel." Her gaze seemed filled with meaning, and Zoey gulped, reaching out to accept the card.

"Yeah, seems like that's just how it is," she said, even as she wondered exactly which of the 'apples' she now found herself surrounded by were the rotten ones. She had a feeling she was going to find out, one way or another.

☙ ☙ ☙

When Zoey sat down at a table in the cafeteria, tray laden with treats (including a cinnamon roll, because she just couldn't resist, even though none she tried was as good as Millie's) she was *hungry*. Like, 'just spent gym class running laps after forgetting to eat breakfast' hungry. She scarfed down her food in short order, leaving her with about ten minutes left of her lunch period to call her dad.

He picked up after just one ring.

"Hey, Zoe-"

"*Dad!*" Her voice was filled with all of the outrage of a teenager whose parent had managed to put one over on her.

He laughed, deep voice echoing out of the screen and causing heads to turn at nearby tables. She flushed and slouched down in her chair. "Dad," she hissed into the screen, "I can't believe you didn't tell me I'd be some kind of test subject, *and* that I would be working with Bridget Andrews, who is, like, the coolest chick ever!"

His confused voice filled her ear. "I knew you'd be working with Ms. Andrews, but why is she so cool?"

She started to laugh, feeling relief tickle her over-full belly. "Ha! You didn't look her up either!"

She could hear typing through the screen, and then a long pause as he read, finally muttering, "Holy crap."

She covered her mouth with her hand, giggling madly.

"Yeah, okay, I should have checked. I just figured she was a middle manager who was in charge of dealing with troublesome teenagers."

"Me too!" she managed to choke out, and his laughter joined hers.

When they both managed to stop laughing, though Zoey was left with a terrible case of the hiccups, he continued. "How has everything been going, though? Other than my little surprise?"

She glanced around, noting that most people were filtering out of the cafeteria, but some were lingering, including a few who had looked over after hearing her dad's rumbling bass. Zoey was used to that reaction from anyone who heard his voice, though, and she flashed an insincere smile at them. She quickly gathered up her trash, dumping it in a nearby bin. There was a campus map conveniently placed near the entrance, so she scurried over, and saw that the clinic building was the next one down out of the right-hand exit.

Before her dad could say anything else, she was out the door and glancing around for somewhere private. An empty bench under a tree halfway between the two buildings glowed in the sunlight, and she headed straight for it. Settling down, she heard her dad say her name again, slightly worried this time.

"Zoey?"

"Sorry, Dad," she muttered, looking around for anyone near enough to overhear her. "This place is weird. They have security everywhere, and the HR lady was a total witch."

"*Zoey!*"

She rolled her eyes. "Yeah, okay. She was sneaky mean, then. Like, she'd smile, but you knew she didn't mean it, and she kept telling me how people would understand if I quit. Then Bridget told me she couldn't actually talk to me because someone might think we were passing secrets…"

"What? Why?" He sounded as confused as she had been.

"Because," she looked around again, lowering her voice to a hiss, "*she is Lady Fayre!*" She let him choke on that, and she could practically hear the hamsters in his brain wheel overheating.

He groaned. "Of course she is. How did I miss that? I seriously thought Fay just passed all this off to a flunky. She didn't, though, huh? This is serious stuff if someone like Bridget Andrews is tied up in it. I mean, I got that from what she could tell us, but this is serious *to her.*"

Zoey nodded and stood. It was time to wrap this up and get to Dr. Shaman's office. Sherman. Whatever. "Anyway, I gotta go. Lunch is almost over, and I have to go be poked and prodded now."

His voice sharpened a little. "Nothing invasive, Zoe. No blood draws, and you shouldn't have to take your clothes off except to change in the privacy of a dressing room. That's in the paperwork. If anything happens that you feel uncomfortable with, you walk out and come home. Okay?"

"*Okay*, Dad." Her voice was sarcastic, but she was really glad he'd told her.

"I love you, kiddo."

"Love you too, Dad."

Zoey showed up at the office at 1:35, out of breath and definitely regretting the tuna fish salad sandwich she'd had for lunch. Her hiccups just wouldn't stop, the tuna was backing up a little, and it was just *gross*. So she was late, she was tired, her diaphragm felt like it was going to cramp up, and her mouth tasted like bile and tuna. It was fair to say she was a little out of sorts.

When she walked in without knocking, expecting another waiting area and another receptionist, or secretary, or whatever you called the people who actually knew what was going on, a medium height, medium brown, medium round guy sat behind a desk in a dark room. He looked up from his screen and grinned, revealing a slightly crooked lower front tooth.

If this guy was Dr. Sherman, he was way younger than Zoey expected. Like, thirty, tops. He was a slightly pudgy brunette guy with cheerful blue eyes and an effortless charm that had Zoey liking him immediately."You must be Zoey!" He twinkled, and that was that.

She grinned back. "Must be. Are you, um," she looked around the small room, "Dr. Shaman?" She clapped her hand over her mouth, trying to look as if she hadn't intended to use the nickname.

He laughed merrily. "Already heard that one, huh? Yep, that's me. You can call me Joe, though. Everyone does." He hitched a thumb at a door to his right, nearly invisible in the dimness. "Head on in there. I'll be in in a minute. I just need to finish up these notes. Sara's waiting for you, and she'll get you hooked up."

She nodded uncertainly, and crossed to open the door. Inside was the room she'd expected. An Asian Indian woman sat at a desk, typing madly. When Zoey entered, she looked up and smiled. "Oh! Zoey?" She had no Indian accent, which disappointed Zoey a little, but her voice was pretty nonetheless.

Zoey nodded, and the woman stood, holding out a slim hand with several gold bracelets jingling around her wrist. "I'm Sara. I'm Dr. Sherman's assistant, and I'll be working with you this summer. Let me show you to the changing room."

Zoey hiccuped.

Sara stopped, startled, then laughed musically. "Oh, dear. Would you like a bottle of water?"

Zoey nodded in relief. "So much!"

Sara led her to a small table beside a counter with a microwave and a minifridge. Opening the minifridge, she took out a bottle of water and handed it to Zoey. "Help yourself whenever you're here. Theoretically it's for samples, but we're not that kind of lab, so we just keep beverages in it. The water is for everyone."

Zoey guzzled water, washing the taste of tuna out of her mouth. She wiped her mouth with the back of her hand and looked around. "Do you, um, recycle?"

The other woman laughed. "A girl after my own heart. Recycling is in the cabinet. If you want to bring a reusable bottle, that's fine, too. No one will touch it."

Zoey tossed her a thumbs up, happy to notice that the water seemed to have soothed her hiccups.

Sara gestured for Zoey to follow, and they walked to a curtained room that looked a lot like a changing room at a doctor's office. She slid the curtain aside and pointed at the white cabinet. "Disposable bodysuits are in there. We'll make a special one for you once we have your specifications. When you arrive, you'll head in here and put it on. If you need to use the restroom first, it's down the main hall a few more doors. You can't miss it.

"Just fold up your clothes and personal items, and put them in the cabinet. They're safe, though if you have something you want me to lock up, just let me know." She smiled reassuringly and continued. "I'll apply some sensors once you're dressed. You don't need shoes, and leave off any undergarments with underwire or metal closures or strap adjusters. No jewelry, either, please."

Her dark eyes assessed Zoey, and, seemingly deciding that the younger girl was unlikely to have any of the offending items, she smiled again and finished speaking as she slid the curtain closed, giving Zoey privacy. "Let me know if you need anything!"

Somewhat uncomfortable, Zoey began peeling off her clothes. She was glad she only needed a lightweight sports bra (and, honestly, probably could have done without that, but it was the principle of the thing) so she could keep her undergarments on. She found a bodysuit marked 'Small' in the cabinet, and tugged it on, then put her clothes and her unused lunch box in and closed the door.

Stepping out, she struggled not to cover herself with her hands. *Why* did the bodysuits have to be so tight? She felt heat flush her cheekbones and ears, but Sara just smiled and motioned her over to a small examination table.

"Sit down, Zoey. We'll get these hooked up, and I'll let Joe know you're ready." With brisk efficiency, she opened several packets containing sensors of various shapes and sizes. With practiced ease, she attached them at about a hundred places on Zoey's body. Wrists, ankles, neck, temples, then several areas on the bodysuit that Zoey hadn't even noticed in her hurry. These spots were slightly thicker than the rest of the fabric, and had small metal protrusions for the sensors to clamp onto. By the time she was done, Zoey felt like a game of Stick the Tail on the Donkey that had been used by an entire preschool.

At last, Sara lifted a slender, semicircular device from a bag marked 'STERILE – Do Not Touch'. This she carefully rested so that it circled the back of Zoey's head, hooked up just over her ears, and ended with the tips of its arms attached to the sensors at her temples. Sara adjusted this until it was firmly in place, and then stepped back.

"Perfect! I'll be right back!"

☙ ☙ ☙

Dr. Shaman should have been called Dr. Sadist. For the next three hours, he ran her ragged, with only one fifteen-minute break to catch her breath and chug some more water. Zoey jogged on a treadmill literally until she couldn't keep up and almost rolled right off the end. She did sit-ups. She climbed a wall in the gym. They put her in a centrifuge like they were going to shoot her into space. Fun fact, tuna and cinnamon roll vomit was super nasty. They even suspended her upside down until she was seeing spots.

During all of this, Dr. Sherman and Sara had matching grim expressions. They looked at various displays and readouts. They barely spoke to each other, much less Zoey, except to tell her what her next task was. When they sat her down and started tapping various nerve clusters to check her response, she snapped.

"Okay, what is the big deal? Bridget- Um, Ms. Andrews said you were going to get some base values, but this is crazy! I like you guys and everything, but enough is enough!" Zoey reached up as if she were going to tear off a sensor on her neck.

Dr. Sherman huffed an amused breath, and Sara broke into a smile. The doctor held up a hand, eyes twinkling again. "Okay, Zoey. I'm sorry. The truth is, we were getting a little psychological profile, too. I'm not going to get into it too much, but we had to know that you'd speak up if you were pushed too far. Not that we intend to push you quite like this in the future, but knowing where your boundaries are as a subject will help us quantify some data later."

He put down his little rubber mallet (aka his instrument of severe annoyance) and gestured for her to hop down off the table and follow him. Warily, she did so, and Sara followed them, a little grin lingering on her lips. They walked over to yet another door, this one marked 'AUTHORIZED PERSONNEL ONLY'. An obvious security camera covered the door, and it was locked with a keypad, a thumbprint reader, *and* a card reader.

Dr. Sherman covered the pad with his hand and typed in a code that was clearly far longer than 1234. When that was complete, a green light flickered on in the center of the door. He inserted his ID in the card reader and pressed his thumb to the pad. Two more green lights joined the first, but it was still at least five more seconds before the door clicked, then hissed open. Joe stepped aside, gesturing for her to go first.

Zoey stepped through the door, and the lights came up as they detected motion. Inside, occupying all but a small area of the floor, sat the largest VR pod she'd ever seen. It had several panels standing open, revealing several more panels of displays and switches than her simple unit at home, and the seal was far thicker than the rubber gasket she was used to.

"Whoa. What's that?" She could feel her heart racing, and she saw Sara glance at her data pad and then laugh a little.

"That, Zoey, is the wave of the future." Joe was grinning broadly, eyes lit with pride. "A fully-immersive, long-term VR pod."

"Holy *cow*," Zoey exclaimed. "I *knew* it!"

Chapter Sixteen

Aspen

After Gina gave Aspen the party quest, it took a few days before both Travelers were available at the same time. Apparently, Rouge had a new job, and the hours were both long and exhausting. Aspen and his friends put the time to good use.

First, they harvested all the crops in the fields. Heaping mounds of carrots, sweet peas, beans, cabbage, and broccoli piled up before Motte's zombie scooped it up and placed it into his inventory. They would need to find a better way to store their produce, since the Travelers wouldn't always be there to help. Fresh items would last for one month after harvest, then become Decayed Produce, which would break down into Fertile Soil after another month.

Unfortunately, winter was three months long, so just leaving the vegetables out wouldn't work out in the long run. He knew most farmers hired a local magic user of some sort to cast a [Food Preservation] spell, if they didn't have a skill that did something similar, which allowed the items to remain good until used.

They hadn't expected there to be magic users here, so their original plan had been to wait twenty-nine days after harvest, and sprinkle salt on the vegetables, allowing them to become the most basic of all Cooked Recipes: Salad. That would have given them another twenty-nine days before they had to Cook them into something else, like soup. It wasn't a great plan, but it would have gotten them through the winter.

Now, though, things were different. He wasn't sure if he would be able to cast some form of [Food Preservation], but he was certainly going to try. Even if he was successful, though, they still didn't have a place to put all the produce. Frankly, the size and amount of the vegetables produced by whatever Gina was up to was staggering. The cellar would have been packed full to overflowing, so Aspen could only hope that William the vampire could really create enough tunnels and storage spaces to hold everything.

Sarave and Sumi prepared food for the party. They used the last of their eggs and flour to make a cake, as well as figuring out how to ferment some berry juice using honey from a hive of bees they found while clearing the orchard. Juniper, who was crawling well and starting to pull up on furniture, babbled gleefully as she picked up anything she found on the floor and shoved it in her mouth.

Khor kept a *very* close eye on the little unicorns, who had each leveled again from somehow climbing into the top of a large bush behind the house, and jumping from there onto the roof. Their horns were more distinct now, and Kayti's forelock and the slightly longer fur down her spine were fading to lighter shades of gray rather than solid black, while Kayli's fur seemed to sparkle. Both of them had developed what Rouge had dubbed 'butt tufts' when she dropped in briefly. They assumed the butt tufts would eventually grow into a Greater Unicorn's long tail.

Codswallop remained glued to Rouge, whether she was herself or a Zombie. The poor ostrich had little time for anyone other than his mistress, though he would grudgingly accept food from Motte or Aspen. When Aspen realized that he needed to return to the mine to talk to William, he carefully tried mounting the ostrich, who promptly sat down and buried his head in the dust, and wouldn't move until the human gave up.

So it was that Aspen and Silus, who refused to be left behind this time, returned to the mine. Silus slept snuggled up to Aspen's neck, hiding in the shadow cast by his hat. Aspen's Endurance and Strength were high enough now that he could jog the whole way, only stopping for a brief water break. He arrived around noon, and found that things were very different from when he left.

The broad entry of the mine system was open, and the walls were smooth and square. Even the tracks of the mining carts had been cleared, though they were broken or bent in a few places. All of the round tunnels were now closed, leaving only the last one, furthest down the main tunnel. It was mostly sealed, with tall earthen pillars blocking it, leaving just enough room for, say, a largish fruit bat to slip inside. Silus promptly did so, and returned a few moments later to report that William was there, sleeping so deeply that she was unable to wake him.

"Thank you, little one. Shall we go on and see what else our vampire has done?" Aspen gently scrootched the little bat's soft ears.

<Don't you mean fructipire? That's what Rouge says, and she's funnier than you.> Silus' sweet little voice echoed in his mind as she dropped from his shoulder and glided away out of the range of the light cast by his glowstone.

Aspen snorted. "Fructipire. Just a way of trying to make something horrifying into something cute." He raised his voice slightly. "Who says she's funnier than me, anyway?"

Silus' voice was faded and distant, but he could still hear the laughter in it. <Everybody.>

The tall man kicked a rock and sighed. "Fine," he muttered to himself as he began to walk. "I see how it is. 'You're too serious, Aspen.' 'You're not funny, Aspen.'" He mimicked Sumi and Silus' voices, and then sighed again. "They're likely correct, anyway. Even my Goddess thinks I need to throw a party."

He picked up his pace and soon found himself in the large area where he and Silus had first met Sumi. "I never did ask her how she made that skeleton," he murmured. His head shot up in realization. "The quest!"

<What quest?> Silus asked as she landed on his shoulder again. <Nothing new to report. It looks like it did the first time we came. A little cleaner, with smoother walls, and no skeleton.>

Aspen would have kicked himself if he was flexible enough. He pulled up his list of active quests, a long-time habit he'd fallen out of since nearly dying. Something about losing everything he cared about and wishing he could follow knocked the drive to advance out of him. It was time to start paying attention again.

Quest: "What Happened Here?" begun.

This mine was marked on the map found in the Great Library. No information was appended, and the mine is marked with a skull. This is unlikely to mean good things for you. Why was this mine abandoned? What was mined here? Find the answers to these questions.

Success: Experience. Unknown ore.

Failure: Variable. Loss of the opportunity to mine in this area.

So, why was this quest not complete? Only one thing sprang to mind. Aspen *still* didn't know what the miners had produced here. He was certain Sarave knew, but he wondered if he could figure it out for himself.

"Have you seen any loose ore, Silus? It might be white, or crystalline looking." The spike of crystal ore Sarave had given him to stab Jezerey could have been something the goblin carried with her for any number of reasons, but it seemed more likely she had picked it up from amongst the loose chunks in the room.

<I don't think so. The fructipire cleaned it up pretty well. I don't think there are as many loose chunks around as there were in the first place. The ore carts are even cleaned out. Do you want me to check again?>

Aspen rubbed the bridge of his nose. It seemed that 'fructipire' was going to stick, whether he liked it or not. "If you wouldn't mind. I know you were looking for enemies or other unpleasant surprises, not rocks."

By way of reply, Silus stepped off his shoulder and glided away into the darkness, The soft rustle of her wings was the only sound in the still cave, except for an occasional drip of distant water on stone.

Aspen looked around. Their first expedition had been cut off rather abruptly, and he'd only gotten a hint of how large this space was. Now, he walked the perimeter, realizing it was easily a mile in circumference, with broken tracks circling the outside, occasionally branching off down a short tunnel. It was clear that someone had hoped to expand the mine significantly, because the tracks just ended a few yards down each tunnel.

Signs of William's work were everywhere. Many of the walls in the main cavern and the short tunnels were rough hewn and crude. Nearly as many, though, were polished unnaturally smooth. The floors, too, had just enough texture so that no one would slip or trip while walking on them. Even the carts had been carefully returned to their tracks, though they were rather worse for having a cave explode around them.

Aspen came to the tunnel that seemed to be the source of the dripping sound. He nearly leapt out of his skin when something came flying out of it and circled him before landing on his back.

<Nothing,> Silus said, giggling.

He puffed out a breath. "I'm old, little one. One of these days you'll do that, and I'll just keel over, and you won't be able to laugh at me anymore."

<Oh, I'm sure we can still laugh at you. Sumi told me this story the other day about the first time you met Khor, and how he bucked you off so you landed in that lady's pie, and then she...>

Aspen hastily cut her off. "Yes, yes, I'm sure you all have a hundred amusing anecdotes about the good old days, but right now I'd like to finish this quest." He patted her head and pretended not to hear her snicker.

He walked down the passage, aware of Silus' warm body pressed to his throat, and held out his glowstone to reveal the walls as they narrowed around them. By the time he'd gone a dozen yards down, the tunnel was barely wide enough to pass a minecart through, and the ceiling was just above his head.

After another dozen yards, which made this by far the longest passage he'd found so far, and he came upon the source of the water. A thin stream ran from the wall, trickling over the stone so quietly that only the occasional droplet flung from the opening made enough noise to travel further than a few feet, even in the near silence of the cave. The water flowed into a small pool, and then into another narrow channel cut into the stone by erosion and the passage of time.

Aspen knelt by the stream and dipped his hand into the shallow water. It looked clean and clear, so he cupped a small amount and lifted it to his mouth. He sipped, and instantly spat it out.

"Ugh! Salt! Why is the water salty?" He wiped his mouth with his sleeve, making a face.

"Likely because this is a salt mine," came a voice from behind him, and he nearly fell into the water.

Quest: "What Happened Here?" complete.

Finally. You do like to take your time, don't you?

Success: 1000 Experience Points. Salt Ore. Unknown ore samples. Look in your pouch.

"Atae's cold behind, William!" Aspen clutched his chest, staring at the vampire who had appeared silently in the tunnel nearby.

William looked sorrowful. "I am terribly sorry, Lord Aspen. I would never have, ah, wished to frighten you. I am afraid I still tend to forget how easy it is to, um, startle the living."

Standing up, Aspen began brushing himself down, trying to recover his dignity. "William, you're over five hundred years old. I would think you'd be pretty good at this by now. Also, you don't need to 'Lord' me. I'm just a retired soldier."

The vampire didn't respond to the last part of Aspen's statement, but replied to the first, looking embarrassed. "Alas, I spent much of that time either, ah, *confined*, or in the sole company of vampires. They, I can assure you, are not easily, er, spooked." His pale eyes looked at Silus, who was trying to hide behind Aspen's neck. "Your charming companion disturbed my rest some time ago, but I do not wake, ah, easily during the day, so it took a bit to achieve full consciousness and come to find you."

The old man, who now looked merely ancient and sickly rather than undead, smiled with his lips closed to conceal his fangs. "I had thought you were going to, ah, wait until I joined you at your homestead come winter. Has something happened to change that?"

Aspen sighed. "I'm afraid so. I came to invite you to a party."

Aspen hadn't been sure how long it would take to find William, or how long they would need to explore the newly-reopened mines, but it was still fairly early when they were ready to return. The sun was still up, and though William could travel in sunlight if he was well-covered, there was no need for haste.

Motte had told Aspen that he and Zoey would both be available tomorrow afternoon, so that was when the party was scheduled. Meanwhile, the others had the preparations, such as they were, well in hand, and Aspen could take his time returning. Besides, Silus was snoozing comfortably in the warm shadow near his pack, which sat in the sun. The little bat wasn't used to being awake at this time, and she needed some rest.

Aspen sat in the shadows of the mine entrance as William stood somewhat awkwardly nearby. You could see from his twisting hands that he was nervous, though about what exactly, Aspen wasn't sure. Finally, Aspen pulled the chunks of ore from his pouch and began to juggle them. It had been a while since he'd practiced this Skill, so he was a bit rusty at first, but he quickly fell into a smooth rhythm.

It took nearly five minutes of this, but finally William brought himself to speak. "Ah, Lord Aspen, may I ask… What are you doing?"

Aspen grinned, internally giving himself a point in the silent contest of wills. "First, I'm no one's Lord, so Aspen really will do, thank you. Second, I'm juggling."

Another long moment passed as the vampire took that in. "And, ahem, *why* are you juggling?"

Aspen shrugged, catching each piece of ore handily and placing it in front of him until he had a small stack of stones. He gestured to them. "I got them as a quest reward. Apparently, these ores are what can be mined here." He scratched his jaw thoughtfully. "Though I admit that my knowledge of mining is essentially limited to which end of a pickaxe I should aim at the rock. Do you," he looked up innocently at the vamp, "have any idea what these are?"

William's face lit up, and he smiled, for once forgetting to cover his fangs. Aspen forced himself not to wince. The ancient man sat down on the ground across from the farmer, kneeling with surprising ease.

"This one," the fructipire said, "is salt, of course. A fairly pure variant, from the color and clarity." He touched the white crystalline structure. Then he picked up the next piece of slightly sparkly white stone, and examined it closely, finally grunting in satisfaction. "This one is gypsum. Used primarily in fertilizers, though I believe some also use it in building plasters."

Aspen sighed. That would have been good to know *before* they built the barn and the second bedroom. Honestly, though, it didn't do them much good unless they had some idea how to grind it, mix it, and with what. He nodded for the other man to continue.

"This one," William held up a crystal that looked just like the salt except for a slightly orange cast, "is sylvite. Also used in fertilizers. It is technically edible, but I would not recommend using it to season your soup, as it tastes quite bitter, and can be poisonous in larger amounts."

A thin finger pointed to the last three pieces, the ones that looked more like actual stones. William touched the first one, which was a chalky white. "This is limestone. Also used in building, though that is all I know about it. I spoke to many mine foremen, who loved to tell of how their contributions to the world were greater than any other, and the limestone foremen were quite proud."

The second one was a black and white flecked piece with a subtle shimmer. "This is dolomite. I believe it is simply ornamental, though I could certainly be wrong. I've seen it only rarely, myself. It was not common in my country."

Finally, the third, an oddly-layered piece of stone. "Shale. Also used for building, and often found and shipped together with limestone. It can be used to make arrowheads as well, though not very good ones, due to the difficulty of working with it."

Aspen scooped up the pieces, returning them to his pouch. "Thank you, William! Just knowing what they are is helpful. It seems that I'll have to head back to Bright in the spring to get supplies and gather information about these as well."

He stood, glancing up at the sky as he brushed off the seat of his much-mended pants. "I think we'll be under cover of the trees until the sun sets if we leave now. Will that work?"

William looked up as well, using his bony white fingers to gauge the distance of the sun from the horizon. He nodded. "With my cloak covering me, I should be well enough, though, ahem, if we reach the grassland before dusk, it would be better to wait until, ah, proper darkness falls."

Aspen nodded and tipped his hat back on his head, then hitched his pack up onto his back, revealing a sleepy bat who muttered grumpily. The tall man smiled and scooped her up gently, placing her on his shoulder. She burrowed down, and the trio headed for home.

🦇 🦇 🦇

The moons were almost full, and the stars bright and clear, and the men made good speed. Silus woke when it got dark, and flew ahead to catch insects for dinner, as well as keep an eye out for any aggressive mobs.

The two spoke awkwardly at first, simply commenting on their surroundings, and passed the occasional warning about rough terrain. Finally, Aspen remembered that the vampire could, in fact, turn into a bat, and asked him why he didn't do so.

William's response was a rusty chuckle. "I am a rather large and, er, unwieldy bat. The Lesser Burrowing Fruitbat which was used to create my, ah, current existence was more of a glider than a flier. It digs well, and climbs well, but flying any distance is, ahem, not one of its strengths. Add to that my age and inexperience, as Jezerey kept me, ah, chained and unable to fly for most of my immortal life, and you might imagine that my [Flying] Skill is insufficient unto the task before us."

Aspen was realizing that the man walking beside him was as much a victim of the vampires as any mortal they had drained of their lifeblood. He nodded his understanding, and the two continued on, the atmosphere between them nearly friendly.

Sumi and Khor were still awake when they arrived at the house. Sumi was on the roof, keeping watch, and Khor stood guard in the door of the barn, his broad chest and horns all but blocking the entry. The unicorns were sleeping between his hooves, and Nuisance was on the goat's head. Codswallop was on the other side of the house, with his head stuck in through the window of Rouge's room, trying to get as close to her as he could.

William paused at the door, wary under Khor's hostile glare. The massive Greater Goat pushed the kids further into the barn none too gently, and scraped his hooves in the dirt in unsubtle warning. In spite of the fact that Khor had met William a few times now, when he went to the mine to make sure the vampire was still there and doing as he'd claimed he would, the goat was still suspicious and unfriendly toward the vampire.

"Ah." The old vampire cleared his throat. "Perhaps it would be best if I find someplace else to spend my days. It seems that your home is," he glanced at the huffing beast nearby, "perhaps, *full?*"

Aspen took off his hat and ran his hand through his hair. "Damn it. You're right. I hadn't even thought of that. It just made sense to bring you back now. I want to talk to you about making some tunnels under the house, and perhaps a well, too. But you need somewhere to stay where you feel safe." He glared at the goat, topaz eyes glinting golden in warning.

<Perhaps I might offer a suggestion?> Sumi's voice broke in, and the arachnid dropped down from the roof.

Aspen jumped and turned his glare onto her. She serenely ignored him, though he would swear he heard Khor snort a laugh. Sumi continued. <The cave where we fought the snake, and Rouge battled the Crab Spider, seems to attract unwelcome neighbors when left unattended. It might be well to have someone stay there. Few creatures will dare enter the den of a vampire. This one smells different from the usual rancid blood and death, but his aura is still powerful.>

Aspen turned a thoughtful gaze on William. "Would a nearby cave be acceptable? You'd have the rest of the night to ready it before you have to go to sleep. It has at least one good-sized cavern. There's currently a skylight, but I'm certain you could fix it easily. It's near the river, and there's an old orchard and some berry patches nearby. We've picked them over fairly well, but there are still a few pieces of fruit available, especially high in the trees."

William smiled slightly. "That would be, ah, excellent. I can easily construct a, hmm, safe room in which to sleep, given only a few hours. Thank you for your understanding."

Aspen started to turn toward the river, but Sumi raised a pedipalp to halt him. <You have something to do here. I can lead the vampire to the cave.>

Aspen knew an order when he heard one. Sighing, he motioned to the three-foot spider. "Sumi says she'll guide you. I have one more task to do tonight, and I should be about it. If you need anything, just tell Sumi, and she'll let me know. She understands you, she just can't speak to you. The party starts tomorrow, late afternoon. Will you be able to come then, or will you have to wait until dark?"

The vampire nodded, stepping eagerly away from the looming ruminant. "I shall find a way, I am certain. I thank you, and you, Lady Sumi," he said, following the spider, who was already heading for the cave.

Aspen watched until the two were out of sight, then patted Khor on the shoulder and went into the house. He walked quietly to his room and entered, seeing that Sumi had already laid *Mage-Smithing Farm Implements* on his bed.

He kicked off his worn boots and sat down, sighing. Every chapter of the book took more out of him. He knew it was time to continue reading, but didn't look forward to the exhaustion that would plague him tomorrow as a result. Nonetheless, he opened the book.

Joanna threw the cracked sickle blade on the ground in frustration. Her little brother, Viktor, sitting nearby, smirked. "You should just marry Rodger, Jonny. Dad and I will carry on the smithy. Even Mother doesn't think you're good enough to be a real Mage Smith."

She whirled and glared at him, barely able to keep from throwing her hammer in his direction. It was true that her mother hadn't taught her anything in months, but it wasn't because she didn't think Joanna could do it. It wasn't!

"I'll be the most famous Mage Smith ever, Vik, you wait! You and Da will still be here breathing in smoke while I'm in the capital making tools for the Queen!" She pulled the leather thong from her hair, letting it fall loose around her shoulders, and stomped out of the smithy. It was time to talk to her mother.

She found Helena by the lake, staring out over the water, in the same place she usually was since little Annika, the youngest of her children, had drowned there last summer. Helena held Annika's little corncob doll and hummed softly to herself as her calloused hands stroked its yarn hair.

Joanna walked up quietly behind the older woman, swallowing convulsively as she looked at how thin she'd gotten. She missed her strong and gentle mother, and often wondered if it had been her instead of golden-haired and joyful Annie who had died, if her mother would be so broken now.

"Mother." She spoke softly, and the other woman turned a distant gaze toward her, smiling slightly.

"Jonny. What are you doing here? Aren't you supposed to be training?"

Joanna ground her teeth. "Mother, I can't. I've tried a thousand times, but when I try to temper the metal, it always fails. I don't know what I'm doing wrong, and I need your help!" The last comes out like the wail of a lost child, even though Joanna is nearly sixteen now.

Helena's eyes drift back to the lake. Her voice is absent. "Your father knows how to temper. He'll show you. I'm busy, just now. Perhaps I can help you later."

Something inside Joanna snapped like the failed blade she'd thrown aside earlier. She reached out and grasped her mother's arm, distantly shocked to realize that her fingers could now reach almost all the way around the once-powerful bicep. She pulled, and spun Helena back to face her.

"No! You say that every time! Mother, I need *you! I need you, right now. Annie isn't here! She's not going to run up here, looking for you. She's dead, Mother! But I'm* not!*" Joanna fell to her knees, hands clutching her mother's skirts as she sobbed.*

A tentative hand came to rest on her hair. "Joanna?" Helena's voice was confused, as if she'd just now realized that Joanna was there, in spite of having spoken to her just a moment before. Then she was kneeling, too, and her arms went around her daughter's shaking shoulders. A warm cheek pressed against Joanna's hair.

"My poor girl. I'm so sorry. I pray you never know a mother's loss. I'm sorry I let it blind me to the children who need me now. Hush, hush." Tender hands stroked her daughter's head and back.

Joanna's sobs finally eased, and she looked up into her mother's face. Helena's eyes were clear and focused for the first time in a long time. Helena pointed out toward the water. "What do you see, Jonny?"

Pain wracked Joanna's heart. Still the lake! She looked out over the water. "Nothing," she rasped out. "Just water."

"Is the water all the same?" Helena asked.

The girl frowned, looking again. "No. Some is cleaner. Some is clearer. Some is shallow, and some is deep."

"How do you know?"

"It's obvious! You just have to look at it!" Joanna stabbed a finger at the closest part of the lake. "This is brown and dirty because the water birds stir it up. The middle is dark and deep. The rapids where the water from the river pours into the lake are clear and shallow." She pointed to each area.

"So you use cues given by the appearance of the water to determine all kinds of things about it. Show me your iron."

Joanna stood and reached into the pockets of her leather apron, pulling out the warped piece of iron her mother had given her a decade before. She handed it to Helena, who curled her fingers around it. The metal began to glow hot and steady from between the older woman's fingers. Helena pointed.

"Here and here, look." Helena used her bare hands to pull the metal like taffy, drawing it out into a thick strand. "See how the edge looks like ripe wheat? The center is like a perfect summer plum. But down here," she moved the clump at the end, "this is a dull red, like your brother's face when I tell him he can't have any cookies until he eats his vegetables."

Joanna nodded, staring at the colors. Her father had told her to quench it 'when it was ready', and she had tried so hard to figure out what he meant. Annealing and hardening were generally easy enough; but when she tried to temper it, it always went wrong.

"The metal will tell you when it's ready. This wheat color will produce a sharp axe blade. A blue color can make a perfect spring, but will never hold an edge. Watch the color to make sure that it's even and perfect. Touch it." Her mother held out the glowing strand of metal.

Joanna reached out and ran a finger along the metal. Where it was golden, it seemed to hum with confidence and strength. The blue areas filled her with tension, tight and almost overflowing with energy. She realized that the feeling was familiar. This was what all her work felt like right before it failed.

"Forcing your will into the metal will bring it to blue quickly, but you need to coax it instead. Only a few things we make need to be blue. Let the warmth fill you, then hold the image in your mind. Feel it, whole and ready for use. Watch the color, let it tell you about itself, until you know it's ready. Then..." Helena flattened her hands, and Joanna could feel the chill as it enveloped the metal. Every hint of heat was removed, leaving a hard, shining bar behind. A drift of sparkling stardust rose from it, indicating that its quality was Good or better.

"What did you do?" Joanna whispered, running her finger over the smooth metal.

"It knew what it was meant to be, Jonny. I just let it go."

🥀 🥀 🥀

As the winter sun dropped low in the afternoon sky, Aspen surveyed the party arrangements. They had put together a large round table, with enough room for everyone. There were rough clay dishes for all the humanoids, including Juniper, who was now toddling and eating solid food. A custom-made chair lifted each of them to the right height to eat comfortably. Since the house was so small, much of the furniture and decor had had to be constructed and stored in the barn, but now that they were outside in the fading evening sun, it all looked quite fine, even if he did say so himself.

Each of the beasts even had their own place. Even the non-sapient creatures would have a place and a special meal, because why not? Codswallop, Silus, and Khor each had a bowl, while Sumi's plate was symbolic only, since her eating habits would make it difficult for anyone else to enjoy their meal. Kayti, Kayli, and Nuisance had bowls on the ground, but they were given space at the table nonetheless.

Sumi had woven a tablecloth, and Sarave had sewn simple decorative embroidery around the edges. Silus and Khor had fetched bunches of late fall flowers and colorful foliage, which Aspen had woven into garlands.

They had laid a massive bonfire with the twigs, bark, and branches left from making door and window frames, tables, chairs, and everything else that had occupied them since they came here. Aspen eyed the height of it with great satisfaction. It symbolized a massive amount of work, both individually and as a group.

Right on time, the attendees began to appear. Silus, Sumi, and Khor were first, with the lesser creatures nearby. The fading light of the sun caught sparkles in Kayli's fur, and Kayti seemed to leave a trail of refracted light behind her as she jumped and played.

From inside the house, a shriek of surprise echoed, and Aspen ran toward the sound. Sarave was half in and half out of the hatch to the cellar, clutching Juniper to her chest and looking more angry than frightened. "Aspen!" she cried, "that fructipire make tunnel into my home!"

Aspen reached down and gently pulled her up onto her feet, then crouched down so he could see below. "William?" he asked.

The vampire's reddish-blue eyes gleamed up from the darkness. "I do apologize, er, Aspen. I didn't realize anyone lived down here. I thought to, ah, start the tunnel system you told me of while we walked yesterday by creating a passage from the, er, cave to your home. It would provide an excellent escape route, in case of, hmm, trouble, and an easier path to walk to get water when the weather is poor."

Aspen heard Sarave huff slightly behind him, and then sigh, and didn't need to look to know that she had already forgiven the old vamp. He reached down a hand to help William up as well, though he was fairly certain the man didn't need it, no matter how decrepit he appeared. William hesitated, but clasped Aspen's warm hand with his cold, dry one.

"All is well, William." Aspen said. "You remember Sarave. She and Juniper live in the cellar, and one of your first tasks will be to make a more comfortable area for her to live. Ah, one thing though," he tilted his head, "are you sure nothing will use your tunnel to *enter* the house?"

William smiled as he stepped into the main room of the house. "Quite. I have, ah, sealed it behind me for now. We'll have to figure out security measures you and your, hmm, friends can handle on their own, but for now, nothing will be able to break through five feet of solid stone."

Aspen smiled, relaxing. "Thank you, then. That sounds good. Though I'm amazed you had time to tunnel all this way since you arrived."

The vampire ducked his head in what seemed to be embarrassment. "I only made it large enough for one man, for now. It's also, er, round, which is easier for me to make, and is self-supporting. Ladies Sumi, Silus, and Sarave will find it, ah, easy enough, but it will take more work before it's ready for you or Master Motte. Even Lady Rouge might, hmm, struggle at first."

Aspen clapped the old man on the back. "It's a good start, thank you. Though next time, please warn us first."

William bowed his head. "As you wish. I am sorry to have startled, ah, Mistress Sarave."

At that moment, Aspen heard voices outside, and he offered the vampire a small smile. William wouldn't easily be able to join them outside for a while yet, thanks to the lingering sunlight. Aspen motioned to a chair at the small kitchen table, with a carved wooden cup containing fresh fruit juice waiting for the fructipire. Once the vampire - fructipire - was settled, Aspen headed back outside.

Rouge and her father were returning from a distant part of the future fields, where their Zombies had been tasked with breaking up and gathering rocks. They waved hello, and continued their conversation as they walked to the rock piles to dump the gathered stones from their inventories.

"Dad, I'm telling you, it would be easier to break into Fort Knox! I know they're the only people who know how VR works, but I think they're as paranoid about each other as they are about outsiders!" Rouge's voice carried easily in the quiet air, as did Motte's reply.

"It seems to me that the factions she mentioned are both as strong IRL as they are in the game. I'm just glad you met some people you like. Work is much more bearable when you have friends there." Motte grunted slightly as he transferred a pile of stone onto the ground.

"That's the truth. I wanted to walk out after talking to Snake Lady. If I hadn't known she'd love it, I might have. What a witch!" At that moment, Codswallop realized that his mistress was back, and let out a loud warbling honk that they all recognized by now, cutting off the fascinating conversation. The bird had been lingering near the barn in hopes of being given something tastier than his usual kibble, and had actually let the Traveler girl out of his sight.

Rouge spun, arms reaching out to circle the large bird's powerful neck as he raced up to her, screeching to a halt with his head buried in her hair. He chirped softly, and Rouge hugged him. "Wally! I missed you, buddy! Work has been keeping me super busy! Good news, though! I'll actually be able to log on from work for a few hours every day from now on! They're studying my brain or something, so I get to come visit you."

Codswallop took his head out of her hair and burbled questioningly. Rouge laughed and patted the tuft of feathers on top of his head. "I know, Wally, that doesn't make a lot of sense to you. Just trust me. I'll get to see you more often!"

Codswallop hopped in place and fluffed his feathers, sending dust and downy tufts everywhere. Rouge groaned and swiped at her eyes. "Thanks, bud. Now come on! I hear there's a party!"

Aspen laughed and stepped forward, holding out his hand for Motte and Rouge to clasp. "Welcome back, Travelers. I'm glad you could come. With you here, I think we're ready to get started!"

He led everyone to the table, pointing out where they were all supposed to sit. William, thoroughly bundled into a heavy cloak, with leather gloves protecting his hands, sat on the side which was shadowed by the house. Next to him sat Aspen, then Sarave and Juniper, followed by Motte, Rouge, Codswallop, Khor, the kids, the duck, and Silus, leaving Sumi to William's right. In the middle of the table was the beautiful wooden statue of Gina, with a garland draped around her, and a plate piled high with the bounty of the season at her feet.

Motte, who had been working with Sumi and Sarave over the last few days, began to pass around trays of food pulled from his storage. There were, of course, samples of all the fruits and vegetables they had harvested. Various smoked meats, including rabbit and deer. Fallen nuts had been rendered into a heavy, dense flour which made a tough but tasty bread.

Finally, the finale, a two-tier cake made with the last of their eggs, some of their precious sugar, and far too much of the fine white flour they'd brought from Bright. This was followed by more of the fresh fruit juice, and a few bottles of fermented juice that Aspen had used some of Gina's divine magic to hurry along.

Once everyone had been served, Aspen raised his mug. "To all of us here, an unexpectedly fine harvest, and future friendships." Everyone who could raised their mugs, and happy gulping could be heard.

After that, it went downhill predictably quickly. Nuisance, once his belly was full, was determined to return to his now-usual place atop Khor's head. He accomplished this by leaping, fluttering, and beaking his way from Kayti's back, up the tablecloth, onto Khor's shoulder, and then finally up between the Greater Goat's horns.

Khor reacted to this with admirable stolidity. He had learned over the last several days that trying to dethrone the duck only led to the bird performing greater and greater feats of avian acrobatics in order to achieve his goal.

Kayti and Kayli lost interest as soon as their food was gone as well. Kayli, especially, always the more adventurous of the two, discovered that underneath the table was the *best* place to be. Once Juniper joined them down there, much to her mother's dismay, no one knew when they would be tickled, nuzzled, or prodded. The adults began to make a game of trying to catch whichever little miscreant had disturbed them, which led to shrieks of laughter and whinnys of indignation alike.

William, though he tried his best, had to retreat into the house after fifteen minutes or so. The sun had touched him a few times, raising red patches of burned skin, though he claimed it was unlikely to blister. He murmured apologies as he retreated, taking a great plateful of broccoli and gigantic carrots with him.

Sumi, who had eaten before everyone else, was uncharacteristically quiet. Silus had quickly migrated from her place at the table to Aspen's shoulder, where she ordered him to feed her peas as quickly as she could chew them. Khor, with a beleaguered sigh, settled down in the dirt so that he could watch the young ones beneath the table. Codswallop, sated, buried his head in Rouge's hair and refused to move.

Aspen sat with his head in his hands, not sure whether to laugh or cry. Sarave was trying to coax Juniper out from under the huge table, much to the toddler's glee. Motte was watching everything with a little smile at the edge of his mouth, and Rouge was patting Codswallop while laughing every time a unicorn or a half-goblin got close enough for her to tickle.

Aspen gulped his fermented beverage.

An hour or so later, nearly everyone had vanished. Rouge was playing with Codswallop, the kids, and Juniper, and their laughter could probably be heard for miles around. Sarave was cleaning up. Sumi was walking rounds, because Silus was passed out on a garland. She lay on her back, wings sprawled wide, distended belly facing the sky. Khor was, of course, watching over the unicorns, and by necessity the other children as well.

Aspen was… inebriated. He had had several cups of the insidious fruit beverage, which was apparently far more fermented than he'd given it credit for. He sat, slumped in his chair, staring toward the sound of laughter, while he nursed the last of his drink. Motte sat beside him, quietly contemplative.

Motte finally broke the silence. "Reminds me of when Zoe… Um, Rouge was young. Her mother left when she was five, and we shared custody. I rented an apartment, since I was just an assistant professor then. Rouge had three or four little friends in the building, and they'd turn up at all hours, laughing and playing until the neighbors complained." He shook his head, just a suggestion of movement in the dimness of dusk. "Never thought I'd miss it."

Aspen's mouth twisted into a wry smile. When he spoke, it was slow but clear. "Birdie was always quiet. I think she only had one close friend. When she was little, she'd come and read in my office with me, just a little mouse by the fire. I was busy training, and spent far more time trying to raise my status in the army than being a father. She was always there, somewhere, watching me, though."

He looked up at the sky, the last lingering light reflecting from his suspiciously moist eyes. "She didn't want any of the things I worked to create. Prestige and power didn't matter to her. Money was only a means to an end. The house, the grounds, the servants... they were just a place to live, and the only family she knew."

Motte's voice was quiet, as if he was afraid to say the wrong thing and stop this outpouring from a man who was usually restrained to the point of being mysterious. "It sounds like she loved you very much."

A silver trail trickled down Aspen's cheek. "Too much," he choked. "Between the war and my ambitions, I barely saw her while she was growing up. Then we realized that we were going to lose. Humanity was doomed, and everything I'd done was useless. I gave up, but she didn't. She was sworn to Gina's church by then. As much as she didn't want power, they seemed determined to throw it at her. She started a hospital that accepted anyone, regardless of whether they could pay, and cured wounds and diseases no one else could. They raised her up to train under the High Priestess, who was getting ready to retire. Then..."

He shook his head. "I was a fool. I just wanted to find a way out. Bright was under siege. We were all going to die, and I couldn't bear it. I didn't care about myself anymore, but I'd finally realized what a precious gift Gina had given me. I went to Lich Lord Akuji himself. I was the best necromancer humanity had ever produced, and when I faced one of his generals, he told me Akuji would take me in if I turned on my own people. Of course I laughed at him before I reduced him to dust, but soon enough I found myself on my knees before Akuji, begging him to let Lark go.

"He laughed. He said he would have me in a few days, perhaps weeks, no matter what. The worshippers of Gina are particularly delicious to the undead, and he wanted Birdie. He threw me into a cell. For days, he kept me there, leaving me to the pleasures of his servants, only coming to steal my skills and stats away bit by bit. It was excruciating.

"But Lark came for me. She, and Sumi, and Khor, and Silus's mother, Miya. It was a trap, of course. Akuji let them in, put up a token resistance, and then turned up himself. He killed Miya, leaving her newborn baby, left behind in the city with Lark's friend, without a family. Khor and Sumi were terribly injured. Both of them lost levels and skills. Akuji told Birdie he would let me live if she would swear herself to him."

The farmer bowed forward, resting his head in his hands. "She was stronger than I had ever been. She used the ultimate skill of the High Priestess of Gina. It's a single use skill that turns the life force of the user into enough power to revive anyone who is still alive. Akuji had forgotten me, lying there without the power to raise my head, so when I stood and used his own sword to run him through, he was taken utterly by surprise. He struck back at me even as I killed him, and took every point I had left. I should have died. Lark burned up her soul as an offering to Gina to keep me alive. Gina agreed, but only if I vowed myself to her, and turned away from Atae. Atae was loath to release me, but agreed at last.

"Thus," Aspen set his mug on the table with a hollow wooden thunk, "Lark died so I, worthless father, former necromancer - most reviled of classes, traitor to my kingdom, could become a hero. A hero!" His laugh was as empty as his cup. "I left as soon as I could. In the end, I had only a few true friends, and most of them came with me, ready to bear witness to my death."

He ran his hand through his hair, sighing. Motte sat, wordless and horrified. "Yet here we are. Listening to the joyful laughter of children. Gorged on the bounty of the earth and the Goddess I serve, though I am a poor replacement for my daughter. Having a *party*." He leaned forward and pointed at Gina's statue accusingly.

"It didn't do a damned thing, Gina! Yet another one of your quests that leave me feeling like even more of a fool, which is difficult, given my starting point. 'Get this party started' indeed. Well, here it is. Where is your communication, eh?" Aspen's voice was a little angry, but mostly lost and sad, more like a wail than a yell.

Motte sat up straight, looking intently at Aspen. He made a few motions with his hands, finally flicking a wrist as if throwing something at the other man. In front of Aspen's eyes, a notification appeared.

Player *Motte Bailey* has invited you to join a party. Accept: Yes/No?

Aspen stared, mouth open, before reaching out slowly to select 'Yes'.

"Yes!" Motte shouted. "They must have implemented another rolling patch! Partying with NPCs- I mean, Natives of this world. Look, for Travelers, a party isn't just a group of people who agree to work or quest together. It's, um, like magic, I guess. We can see each other's status, and," he grinned, and then his voice popped into Aspen's head, just like when his companions spoke to him.

::We have party chat.::

Thank you for joining
Aspen and Zoey in their adventures!

Continue reading in Book Two of Legendary
Farmer: Harrowing, available August 2022!

www.ingramcontent.com/pod-product-compliance
Lightning Source LLC
Chambersburg PA
CBHW070620260626

47161CB00007B/2508

* 9 7 8 1 7 3 7 6 5 1 0 0 0 *